DANCING IN THE RAIN

KELLY JAMIESON

To Olivia –
Kelly Jamieson

CHAPTER 1

Drew turned disbelieving eyes on the man who'd just spoken so crudely to the woman seated next to him at the bar. Did he really just ask her if she'd ever fucked a real man?

"Uh . . ." She glanced nervously at Drew.

"Does that line really work for you, asshole?" Drew asked him. "Pretty sure a 'real man' wouldn't use it."

"Fuck off, asshole," the guy said. "She's talking to me." "No, she's not. She's with me."

She wasn't, but this jerkwad didn't need to know that.

"Come on, bitch. I'll show you a real man. Not a pansy-ass hockey player with a bum knee."

Greeeaat. The fucker knew who he was. "Okay." Drew stood, drawing himself up to his full six-foot-three height. "You can fuck right off. Now."

The dude shot him a dirty look but moved away.

The woman gave an uncomfortable laugh. "Whoa. Thanks."

He hadn't really been talking to her, just sitting beside her at the bar. "What a dickhead." Drew followed the guy's movements with narrowed eyes, watching him stop next to another woman.

"Are you really a hockey player?"

1

"No." He picked up his beer and drained it, then signaled the bartender for another one. He'd lost count of how many he'd had tonight. "I'm Savannah." She held out a hand.

Drew took in her blond hair, spidery eyelashes, and high-maintenance manicure with her nails painted red and black in what looked like butterfly wings. She reminded him of his ex-wife.

"Drew," he said, shaking her hand.

"It's so nice to meet a gentleman." Her shiny pink lips curved up. "I'm not really a gentleman." He attempted a smile.

"Well, you rescued me, so I think you are."

Drew watched as Dickwad returned, this time with another guy. Their eyes focused on Savannah with undisguised lechery. Oh, for fuck's sake.

Annoyance burned in his chest. Along with the alcohol he'd consumed, the driving rhythm of the music in the bar, and the frustration he'd kept pent up for months, a wild, reckless feeling buzzed through him.

He was already pissed at the world. Apparently it didn't take much to make him bloodthirsty. And hell, a woman should be able to tell a guy to get lost without being harassed. He didn't even know her, yet he somehow felt responsible. So when Dickwad slid a hand around Savannah's upper arm and said, "Let's dance," Drew was on his feet in an instant.

"Seriously, dude?" he said to the guy. "Are you fucking hammered? Let go of her." "We're going to dance."

Savannah was trying to pull her arm out of his grip. "No, you're fucking not." And Drew lunged at him.

Savannah squealed as Drew landed a right cross on the guy's jaw. With a roar, the other man fought back.

Rage rose inside Drew in a burst of heat. He threw a flurry of punches, felt a crunch of bone, and had the asshole over the bar and helpless in minutes.

Bouncers pounced on Drew and dragged him off the guy. Blood dripped from

Drew's eyebrow and he swiped it away with the back of his hand, his chest heaving. "Get the hell out of here before we call the cops," one of the big bouncers said to him in a low voice, giving him a shove.

"Gotta pay for my drinks," he mumbled, reaching for his wallet. "Forget it. On the house."

Drew stumbled out of Jimmy's Kitchen and Bar, one of his favorite local watering holes, onto Southport Avenue. What. The. Fuck. Drunk, bleeding, and now he was fucking laughing. Damn, that had felt good. He shook out his throbbing hand as he walked unsteadily down the sidewalk to his Porsche. He had his hand in his pocket looking for his keys when he paused.

He closed his eyes. Okay, he was drunk and he'd been doing a lot of stupid, risky things lately . . . It was only a few blocks to his place. Driving was so much easier than trying to track down a cab, but . . . aw, fuck. Even he knew better than to drive drunk. With a sigh, he walked past his car and kept going toward Wrightwood.

Drew flashed the cute barista a smile the next morning as he accepted his large Americano and turned to leave the coffee shop. At nearly eleven in the morning, the café was almost empty. He'd slept in after a late night, but what difference did it make what time he got up when he had nothing else to do?

His temples pulsed with a faint headache, the result of those Fireball shots and too many beers last night, not to mention the small bar brawl. He was about to slide his sunglasses back onto his nose and step outside into the bright September sunlight when a woman stopped in front of him.

"Drew?"

The blond hair first made him think of Savannah from last

night. But no. He eyed her. Not one of the women he'd partied with lately either, so probably just a hockey fan who recognized him. He summoned a smile despite the small hockey sticks tapping inside his skull. "Yes?"

"Drew Sellers?"

"That's me." He studied the woman, taking in her thin frame and pale face, stylish short blond hair and dark blue eyes. Something about her tweaked his memory, but he couldn't place her.

She was studying him, too, those blue eyes big and hesitant as her gaze swept over him, lingering on the cut above his eyebrow. "You don't remember me, do you?" she asked quietly, not in an accusing or even disappointed tone, as he'd heard a couple of times when he'd run into women he didn't recall meeting before. "That's okay."

"I'm sorry . . . we've met?"

"Yes." Her teeth sank into her bottom lip and her fingers twisted the strap of her purse around and around. "A long time ago, though."

This was getting awkward and he wasn't sure how to extricate himself. Damn, he needed some Advil. "I'm sorry," he said again, lifting his eyebrows.

"Sara Watt." She shook her head. "I don't think you ever knew my last name. We met one night at Notre Dame."

"University of Notre Dame?" He frowned. "Yes."

Jesus, that was going way back. He'd played two years of hockey at Boston University, and they'd played against the Fighting Irish a couple of times a season.

"I didn't know your last name, either," she continued quickly. "Until a few weeks ago."

"Uh . . . okay."

Her smile stretched her lips but it held no humor. "We, uh, hooked up one night." Drew nodded. Yep, awkward. Not remembering that was insulting, but even if he did remember, it would still be awkward twelve or thirteen years later. He rubbed the

4

stubble on his jaw. "Forgive me," he said, trying not to be an asshole.

She licked her lips quickly. "It's okay," she said. "It was one night. It's not like you broke my heart." That tense smile appeared briefly again. "Look, um, I know this is weird. But I need to talk to you."

Drew's body went cold and still. Because those words were always enough to strike frozen fear into the heart of any man. Fuck, no . . . it was too ridiculous. This woman he didn't even recognize appearing out of the blue was not about to tell him he had a child he'd never known about. Why was he even thinking that?

He wouldn't be the first guy this had ever happened to, but it was pretty fucking bizarre if it happened now, when his career was over, his wife had dumped his ass, and his life was basically a goddamn wasteland of broken hopes and dreams. Sure, there were women who tried to claim a pro athlete had knocked them up. Didn't this chick know he had nothing to offer? It wasn't like he'd just signed a five-year, thirty-million- dollar deal with the Blackhawks. He was *done*. Done like lobster in butter sauce.

So that couldn't be what was happening here.

He held up a hand. "Look, honey, I don't know who you are, but you've got the wrong guy. And maybe you haven't heard, but I'm a washed-up, retired winger. There's no point in even trying this."

Her mouth dropped open. Those big blue eyes stared at him, and then cobalt sparks flashed in them. She snapped her mouth closed and her lips thinned. "I think you should hear me out."

Something about the expression on her face made him pause. She wasn't disappointed, and she was holding his gaze in a way that made him think she wasn't bullshitting him, whatever this was about.

He tugged the sleeve of his long-sleeved T-shirt to glance at his watch. "I have five minutes."

A lie. He had nowhere to go other than his house for Advil and an afternoon spent playing video games.

"Fine."

He gestured at a small table nearby. They moved over to it and sat. She had no coffee and he didn't offer to buy her one. The coffee he sipped slid into his gut and lodged there like a burning rock.

"I know you don't remember me," she said quietly, her purse on her lap. "I barely remember *you*. We got drunk at a party one night and slept together. I knew your name was Drew and that was about it." No. No fucking way. No. Drew closed his eyes.

"I'll just get right to the point," she continued in a low, steady voice. "I got pregnant."

"Knew that was coming," he said dryly. Her forehead creased. "What? You did?"

"Honey." He leaned over the table. "You're not the first chick to think she can make bank by claiming a pro athlete knocked her up. Why do you think so many guys carry their own condoms and nondisclosure agreements around with them?"

Her lips parted and she gaped at him again. "That's what you think this is?" She swiped a hand over her face then focused on him again. "Of course you think that's what this is. I don't blame you. Let me just set your mind at ease—I don't want anything from you."

"Then what the hell is this about?" Anger edged his tone, and he fought to keep from snarling the words.

"If you'd let me finish, I'll enlighten you," she said calmly. She sucked in a deep breath. "Yes, you have a nearly twelve-year-old daughter. Her name is Chloe and she's awesome. She doesn't know about you or that you're her father. I didn't know myself until a few weeks ago."

"I'm supposed to believe I'm the father if *you* didn't even know it yourself? If you slept with a bunch of guys, what makes you think *I'm* the father? Jesus." He pressed his fingers to his temples, now throbbing even more. "This doesn't make sense." This really couldn't be happening.

"I didn't sleep with a bunch of guys." Surprisingly, she didn't seem offended by his comment. "I slept with you. One guy. One time. We used a condom, because I was drunk but I wasn't stupid. However, shit happens."

"Fuck."

"I've had over twelve years to accept it," she said wryly. "Sorry, this is new for you. Anyway, I didn't even know that you didn't go to Notre Dame. I tried to track you down, but I couldn't find you. Nobody else knew you. One of my friends said maybe you'd just been visiting someone that weekend."

"I went to Boston University," he said slowly. "Played hockey there."

"I didn't know you were a hockey player." She met his eyes again. "I did know we were both freshmen."

He remembered now, vaguely. He was pretty sure the team had only traveled to Notre Dame once that year. He'd gone to a party after the Saturday night game with a couple of teammates . . .

"I'm really sorry. Believe me, I've had many years to curse myself for doing something so stupid. This is a lot for you to handle in five minutes." She gave a pointed glance at her watch.

"How did you find me?"

"It was a complete fluke, actually. I saw a picture of you in a *Sports Illustrated* magazine while I was waiting at the . . . doctor's. Once I knew your last name and that you were a hockey player, it was pretty easy to track you down." She paused. "I might not have done it, except . . . " She closed her eyes briefly.

Drew once more noticed how pale she was, blue veins visible at her temples, tendons in her neck standing out.

"I have stage four metastatic melanoma." Drew blinked, his body stiff.

"Like I said, I don't want anything from you. Chloe and I have done fine. But . . . well." Once more she met his eyes and this time they shone. Her chin lifted and her voice was steady as she said, "I'm dying. And since I have the chance I never thought I would, I thought I should do something about it before I'm gone. If you don't want to know Chloe, that's fine. It's your prerogative. She doesn't know about you, and if that's what you choose, I won't tell her."

Dying. Drew's chest felt flash-frozen. Breathing strained his lungs. He didn't even know this woman. He didn't even know if she was telling him the truth. But courage glowed in those blue eyes along with unshed tears and her terrible words felt real. "How long?" he asked, his voice sounding like a hairbrush was scraping over his vocal cords.

"Maybe a few months." She drew in a long breath. "I'll give you my name and contact information. I know this is a lot to take in. If I don't hear from you, I'll understand. But if you're interested in meeting Chloe, I feel I owe it to her to give her that. If *she* wants to meet *you*."

"You don't even know me." The words grated out. "I could be an asshole."

She gave a small smile. "I did some research on you, but yes, you could be an asshole."

"What kind of research?"

"Come on, you're an NHL player. There's all kinds of information about you."

"Was." He cleared his throat. "I *was* an NHL player."

"Right. I read that you had to retire because of a knee injury."

"Yeah." He hated to use the word "retire," but he had to face the reality that his career was over.

"Also, I checked the sex offender database for this state and had a PI do a bit of digging."

His eyes widened. "Jesus."

She reached into her purse and pulled out a business card and a photograph. She slid them both across the table to him. His gaze dropped to the small photo, a standard school photo with a blue background. A young girl's face beamed up at him.

She wasn't blond like her mother. Her hair was dark, like his. That didn't mean anything.

He studied the picture and couldn't really say he saw any likeness between him and the girl. Nor did she look like her mother, although she did have the same eyes.

Sara rose to her feet. "Sorry, I've taken more than five minutes." She nodded at the card and photograph. "Thank you for listening, Drew, and again, I apologize. Both for dumping this on you now, and for not being able to tell you when it happened."

"We were eighteen years old.".

She nodded. "I know. We were young. Hormonal. Maybe a little drunk." One corner of her mouth lifted. "But Chloe is the best thing in my life." Her voice choked a little. She could talk about her own death, but apparently speaking of her daughter made her emotional. "I'll never regret what happened for that reason." Her chin wobbled but she smiled. "I think you'd like her, Drew. But it's your choice, and I'll understand whatever that is."

She turned and left the coffee shop.

Drew watched her walk out, following her with his gaze as she passed the window. He turned back and his eyes fell on the picture again. He slowly reached out to pick it up.

His daughter. Really?

Jesus fucking Christ.

He did remember that night. And he did vaguely remember Sara, now. He remembered a cute, curvy blonde with a bright smile. So different from how she looked now, yet it was the same person. They'd flirted a little, drank a lot, and somehow ended upstairs in a bedroom at the house party. They hadn't talked a lot and they'd both been clear it was just a hookup. He'd left the next day to go back to Boston, and hadn't thought more about her.

Had he really left her knocked up? Not knowing who the

father of her baby was? Hell, there was no maybe about it . . . he *was* an asshole.

He rubbed his face.

Wait, wait. Hold the fuck up. He'd had no clue he was a father.

And honestly . . . he still didn't know for sure. Sara may say she didn't want anything, but he wasn't born yesterday or even two days ago. It was entirely possible this was some kind of scam.

He set down the picture, shoved his chair back, and stood. He grabbed his coffee. And paused.

Was she really dying?

He picked up the photograph and card and shoved them into the pocket of his jeans.

He strode out of the café and down the sidewalk toward his Lincoln Park home. The one he'd bought less than a year ago, when he was still married to Christy. Stupidly thinking his career would go on forever, stupidly thinking they might want to start a family, he'd shelled out big bucks for the five thousand square foot Frank Lloyd Wright- inspired house.

Now he lived there alone, rattling around like a marble in a crate. Ah well, at least it was an investment.

At home he went straight to the big U-shaped kitchen and opened the cabinet where he kept a good stock of painkillers. His knee was much better now, and he tried not to take pills more than he had to. It was a lot easier now that he wasn't playing. With his fucked-up knee, he couldn't play without painkillers. These days it was more often a hangover that had him reaching for drugs.

He popped an Advil and washed it down with a glass of water from the sink in the island. The sink that was full of dishes.

Ugh.

With his glass of water, he rounded the island and walked across the family room to the French doors that opened onto a deck and the yard, a big green space of lawn and shrubs. He turned and crossed to the huge gray sectional and sat on it.

A strange restlessness filled him. His muscles twitched and sitting still was impossible. He set the glass on the coffee table and rose again. Fuck. This was crazy.

That woman had just walked into the coffee shop and dropped a fucking firebomb on him. What the hell?

He pulled his cell phone out and quickly entered the password to unlock it then found Dougie's phone number.

"Hey, man," he said when his buddy answered. "What's up?" "Who is this?"

"Shut the fuck up." Drew rolled his eyes as he paced across the room. "As if you don't know. Listen, I've got a huge goddamn problem."

CHAPTER 2

Peyton peered at the call display on her office phone. Her sister's name appeared there and she grabbed the receiver. "Sara?"

"No, it's me, Chloe."

Peyton blinked, her stomach dropping. "Chloe. Hi. How are you?"

"I'm okay." Her niece's voice wobbled. "But Mom's not doing so good." "Oh, no." Peyton straightened. "What's happening?"

"She's just so weak . . . she's trying hard not to show it, but I'm scared." Peyton's heart contracted. "Do you want me to come?"

"Yes," Chloe nearly whispered. "Could you?"

"Of course." Never mind that she had client meetings, internal team meetings, training and onboarding sessions to conduct. And never mind that Sara and Chloe were in Chicago and she was in New York. This was her sister and her niece; pretty much the only family she had left. She'd anticipated this day would come, knowing there was no more treatment that would help Sara's cancer.

Shit, shit, shit. She closed her eyes briefly at the fear that swept over her in a cold wave. Sara was dying.

They knew this. That didn't make it easier.

"I'm going to check flights, pack a suitcase, and I'll be there tomorrow," she told Chloe. "Okay, sweetie?"

"Thank you, Auntie P. I didn't know what else to do." Chloe had called her Auntie P since she'd started talking.

"You did the right thing to call me. Your mom is very stubborn and independent."

"She says that about you."

Peyton laughed softly. "Yeah, well, she's right. We both are. Are you okay right now? Want to talk?"

"I'm okay. I just got home from school, and Mom's still in bed. I don't think she got out of bed all day."

Peyton bit her lip. "Can you make her something for dinner?"

"She says she'll do it. But I can tell it's hard for her. Plus, she doesn't eat." Chloe's voice skipped. "She tries to make me think she is, but she's not."

"She doesn't know you're calling me?"

"No. I thought if you just show up she won't be able to do anything about it."

"Good thinking, kiddo." Sara had been telling her for weeks that she was doing fine but she'd call if she needed her. She probably never would. Well, until she was worried about Chloe, because Chloe was her world. No way would Sara do anything to put Chloe at risk, even if it meant humbling herself to ask for help.

Peyton and Sara had argued more than once about how much help a single mom needed to raise a child. From the time Sara had accidentally gotten pregnant in college, Peyton had sworn to her sister she would be there for her, because despite her big sister's bravado, she'd seen the fear in Sara's eyes. Peyton had been in the delivery room when Chloe was born. She'd babysat Chloe while she and Sara both went to college, and after Sara had graduated and started her career. Peyton had been there to help comfort Chloe when her beloved grandparents had died, even though she herself was grieving, too. Sara hated relying on others but accepted help because it was best for her daughter.

After hanging up the phone, Peyton hurried out of her office to speak to her assistant. "Aaron, I need to go to Chicago as soon as possible. Can you check flights and see what there is? And we'll need to reschedule my meetings for tomorrow."

"When do you want to come back?" Aaron was already reaching for his computer mouse. "Your entire week is booked solid."

"I don't know when I'll be back." A sick feeling settled in her stomach. "Book a one-way ticket. We'll probably need to move things for the rest of the week. But I'll be in touch once I'm there."

"Gord is going to freak out," Aaron said, clicking away and staring at his monitor. "I'll deal with him."

Her boss was super-stressed about a new client they were working with, a huge pharmaceutical corporation, which had just reached a two-million-dollar settlement with the State of New York because the company had been inflating the cost of the intravenous drugs sold to Medicaid. Their reputation and, consequently, stock prices, had taken a hard hit, and their leadership team was challenging to deal with. Because of the stress, Gord had been even more demanding than usual lately, but surely even he would understand that her sister was dying.

She went to let her staff know that she was going to be out of the office for at least the rest of the week and to make sure they had what they needed and knew they could call her for anything. Many of them knew about Sara and were sympathetic, stepping up to offer help, which touched her. She had a great gang working for her.

She returned to her office to finish the spreadsheet she'd been working on when Chloe'd called. It was only a few minutes before Aaron appeared in her office door. "There's a flight tonight at seven. Too soon?"

Peyton scrunched her face up. "Yeah. I have to go home and pack. That might be tight."

"There are lots of flights in the morning. Eight-thirty okay?"

"Perfect."

"You'll be there around eleven."

And easily at Sara's home by noon.

She'd better go talk to Gord. Smoothing her pencil skirt down over her thighs, she strode down the hall to his office and knocked on the open door. "Hi. Got a minute?" She'd learned over the years the best approach with Gord was to be brief, be clear, and get the hell out. While some people liked to make small talk to open a conversation, Gord didn't even bother with pleasantries such as "how are you?" or "how's your day going?"

"My sister isn't doing well," Peyton stated. She'd already informed him that Sara's illness had become terminal about a month ago. "I need to fly to Chicago to be with her."

"When?"

"I've got a flight first thing in the morning." She also knew it was better to present a plan to him rather than to ask for permission. "Aaron and I will work on rescheduling things for the rest of the week. I'll be able to do some work remotely, though."

"You have an important meeting with RLM tomorrow." Clearly he was unhappy with this.

Peyton pushed back her own irritation. "I know." She wasn't going to apologize for this. "I'll talk to Paul and we'll set up another time."

"Shit." He frowned. "We've had enough delays in putting together the plan for them."

"I know." She paused. "Would you like to meet with them instead?"

He actually considered it for about two seconds, but she knew he wasn't as up to speed as he'd need to be to talk to them tomorrow. "No. Let me know what you work out."

"I will. I'll be in touch. Thanks, Gord."

She gave him a brief smile as she walked out. Nope, not even an expression of concern for Sara, like, "hope your sister's okay" or "take care." But she knew better than to expect that from him.

That was okay. Gord was an intelligent man with many good skills, but people skills weren't part of his makeup. Peyton had learned a lot from him, but she'd also learned about the kind of leader *not* to be. Unfortunately, dealing with him was taking up more and more of her energy when she should be focusing that energy on her job, the one she'd moved here to New York to take, the one that was going to grow her career in reputation management.

She paused at Aaron's desk. "Thank you for everything," she said to him. "You're amazing. I know I can rely on you to keep things afloat this week." Aaron's hard work and loyalty were invaluable.

He beamed at her words of appreciation. "Thank you. Whatever I can do, I'm here."

She stayed late at the office to try to wrap up and reschedule as many things as she could. Her neck was aching as she finally shut down her laptop and slid it into its bag then walked through the quiet offices toward the elevator of the Park Avenue high- rise.

Outside, traffic had eased somewhat on the Manhattan streets in the fall evening. Eschewing the subway tonight, she hailed a taxi to take her to her Chelsea apartment. She stared out the window as they drove, thinking about Chloe's call and about her sister.

Life was so fucking unfair sometimes. Fucking cancer.

Since learning about Sara's diagnosis, she'd had that thought more than once. She'd already been through a range of emotions that she recognized as grief, even though Sara was still alive. At first she'd been in shock, denying that it was possible her sister could die. It couldn't happen. It just couldn't. It was unthinkable. There'd been the ups and downs of Sara's treatment, times when Peyton was sure that Sara would be okay, then times when they got more bad news. Then she'd been angry. She'd questioned her decision to move to New York for her career, leaving Sara and Chloe in Chicago, and wondered if she moved back if that would make a difference. There'd been times she'd been so sad and down, she wasn't sure she could go on. Things were okay right now, but she wasn't sure she would say she'd accepted things yet.

In her apartment, she stood for a moment, overwhelmed with it all. She had no idea how long she'd be gone. Was this going to be a short trip to make sure Sara was okay? Or . . .

Her head dropped. She swallowed through a tight throat. What if this was the end?

As someone who liked to plan and be in control of things, she wanted to scream and cry and pound her fists against a wall at this uncertainty, this being at the mercy of a fucking brutal disease.

She straightened her shoulders and sucked in a long breath, heading toward her bedroom. She had to pack. It didn't matter what she took. If she ended up overpacking, whatever. If she ended up staying longer and needing more things, she'd go buy them. None of that was important in the face of Sara's suffering. And Chloe's.

She took off her suit and hung it in the closet, changing into a pair of yoga pants and a T-shirt. She threw a bunch of stuff into a big suitcase. Her toiletry bag was mostly already packed, stocked with travel-size containers of her favorite products for the frequent trips she'd recently had home to Chicago.

When her stomach gave a rumble of hunger, she paused in her packing to make a grilled cheese sandwich, watching the news as she ate. She'd have to be up early to get to JFK so she should go to bed, but she knew sleeping was going to be a problem as she worried about Sara and Chloe.

Somehow she managed to get a few hours' sleep, get herself out of bed, out the door, and to the airport. It was close to noon when she arrived at her sister's Chicago home, which was the house they'd both grown up in.

She had a key and let herself in. She heard faint voices coming from upstairs and she left her suitcase in the foyer and climbed the stairs, the voices becoming more audible. Laughter from an audience told her the television was on. She paused outside the master bedroom and gave a slow knock on the door before walking in.

Sara lay on the bed, dressed in pajama pants and a T-shirt, on top of the covers, smiling at the TV. Her head, wrapped in a colorful scarf, turned and her eyes widened. "Peyton!"

Peyton smiled and crossed toward the bed, watching Sara try to scramble off it. It was clearly an effort for her. "Stay where you are, you goof." She bent and hugged her sister. God. She was so thin, Peyton felt only knobs and bumps.

"What are you doing here?"

Peyton sighed. "Scoot over."

Sara shifted and Peyton climbed onto the bed beside her. She toed off her ballet flats and let them drop to the floor then stretched her legs out in front of her and adjusted a big pillow behind her back. "Chloe called me yesterday."

"Oh no, she didn't."

"She did. Don't be mad. She's worried about you." Sara gave a huff. "Hell."

"She's eleven, Sara. She's scared."

Sara dropped her chin to her chest. "I know," she whispered. "So am I."

Peyton's throat clogged up. She had to be strong. "I'm here, hon." She slid an arm behind Sara's shoulders. "And know what? I'm scared, too." *I'm fucking terrified.*

Terrified that she was losing her sister, the only family she had left. Other than Chloe, of course. Terrified that even though she was there, she wouldn't be strong enough. Wouldn't be able to handle what was coming; wouldn't be able to take care of Sara the way she needed. "So we're in this together." Sara closed her eyes. "I'm so sorry."

Peyton's heart wrenched. "Don't you apologize," she said, trying to keep her voice steady. "Do *not* apologize. This is not your fault."

"I know, I know. I just hate that I've disrupted your life so much."

"Oh, my God, that doesn't even matter." She hugged Sara's shoulders. "Was Gordo angry that you're taking more time off?"

"Yeah, I think he was." Peyton grinned. "Oh, man."

"Don't worry about it. I don't ask him, I just tell him. That probably pisses him off, too. I kind of enjoy it." She paused. "So what's happening, sis?"

Sara had been diagnosed less than two years ago. The cancer had spread to her lymph nodes and lungs. She'd had surgeries, radiation treatment, chemotherapy, treatment with a new type of monoclonal antibody that for a while actually seemed to be working . . . but then wasn't. The doctors were out of options now.

"I'm just so tired," Sara said quietly. "I can't believe how fast things changed. It's even getting harder to breathe."

"Chloe says you're not eating."

"That little tattletale." A smile drifted over Sara's face. "Yeah, I don't have much appetite."

This was not good.

"What are you watching?" Peyton nodded at the TV where a commercial now played.

"Ellen DeGeneres. She makes me laugh."

"Yeah. Laughing is good. I'll watch with you, then you'll tell me what needs to be done around here."

Peyton picked up the remote and fast-forwarded through the commercial to resume the show. She smiled and laughed along with Sara, but worry distracted her. This huge house was too much for Sara. Sara had lived there with her parents, who'd helped care for Sara. When their parents had died, technically half the house became Peyton's but since property values in Lincoln Park had skyrocketed, there was no way Sara could afford to buy out her half of the house despite her well-paying job as a corporate attorney in the legal department of First Insurance. It might have been smarter to sell, but they both loved the house and the neighborhood, and there were good schools nearby for Chloe. And Peyton had her apartment in New York, so it wasn't like she needed the money.

"Okay," Peyton said as the show ended, pushing to sit up. "What would you like? Something to drink? Tea? Junk food?"

Sara smiled. "You know what I'd love? McDonald's French fries."

"You got it."

"I was kidding. You don't have to go out and get me that."

"I'm here to get you whatever you want." Peyton grinned. "Back in a few." She'd haul her suitcase up to the guest room later. She'd also investigate the contents of the fridge and cupboards later and figure out what she could cook for dinner. Luckily, she knew the whereabouts of the nearest McDonald's and was quickly back with a bag of fast food.

She held it up as she entered the bedroom. "Here you go. Of course, I couldn't resist a Big Mac and some fries of my own. Also I brought you a chocolate shake."

"You're crazy."

"Maybe so. Let's eat."

She watched her sister eat, disappointed when Sara stopped after only a few fries. "Really?" she asked. "That's all you can eat?"

"Yeah." Sara lay back on the bed. "I'm sorry. I do appreciate you getting them."

Worry tightened Peyton's stomach again, and her own appetite disappeared. She smiled, though, as she removed the uneaten food. "Have some more of that milkshake. I'll let you rest a bit while I bring my stuff up."

"How long are you staying?"

"I'm not sure." Peyton kept her voice cheerful. "As long as I need to."

"Oh, Peyton." Sara rolled her head on the pillow. "I love you."

"Love you, too. I'll check in on you in a while."

Peyton fought back tears as she settled her things into the guest room. It would do no good to break down now. That wouldn't help anyone. She tried to distract herself from fearful thoughts about Sara by tidying up the house and making a shopping list. She could put together a quick pasta dish with things in the cupboard tonight but tomorrow she'd go out and pick up a few groceries.

The phone rang and she automatically reached for the cordless handset in the kitchen. "Hello."

"Sara?"

"No, this is her sister. Just a moment, I'll go see if she's awake. Can I ask who's calling?"

Silence met this request as she walked out of the kitchen toward the stairs. Then the man said, "Uh, it's Drew Sellers."

The name meant nothing to her. Maybe a friend of Sara's? Or someone from work? "Okay, just a moment."

She ran lightly up the stairs and poked her head into Sara's room, holding the phone away from her. "Hey, hon, you awake? There's a phone call for you."

"Mmm, yeah, I'm awake." Sara pushed up. "Who is it?"

"Drew Sellers."

Sara shot bolt upright, staring at her bug-eyed. "Really?"

"Um, yeah, that's what he said."

Sara motioned her over with an urgent wave of her hand and reached for the phone. "Drew?"

Peyton turned to leave to give Sara privacy, although curiosity fizzed in her chest. But Sara waved at her to stay.

"You did?" Sara said. Then, "Well, of course it did." Sara listened again. "What do you want to do now?"

Peyton watched emotions flicker across Sara's face as she listened again then nodded. "Okay. No. Not tomorrow. That's too fast. You and I need to meet again and talk about a few things first."

Peyton frowned. Who? What was going on?

"I'm not sure," Sara said. "I'll call you back." After listening again, she ended the call. She pressed the button on the phone and lowered it to the bed. She turned and met Peyton's eyes.

"What's going on, Sara?"

"Well." Sara took a deep breath, her chest lifting and falling. "I have a long story to tell you."

CHAPTER 3

Drew read the document once more, the one that stated Drew Sellers was not excluded as the father of Chloe Watt. The one that said there was a 99.99% probability that he was her father.

Christ.

He'd let that knowledge sink in for a couple of days, not sure what to do about it. But really, he *had* known what to do about it. And he'd picked up the phone and called Sara Watt.

There was no way he could spend the rest of his life pretending he didn't have a daughter. Ignoring her. He knew that would haunt him forever.

Sara wanted to meet with him before telling Chloe about him. That made him impatient.

Waiting made him crazy. He'd never been good at waiting. Maybe he'd been called foolhardy a few times. Impetuous. Impulsive. But right now he had no choice.

He had so many questions. Since that morning Sara had walked into his crappy world and dropped the knowledge about his daughter on him, he'd had a hard time not thinking about it. There was so much he didn't know.

Sara was dying. Was she married? It was entirely possible there was a husband, maybe even other kids in the picture. There was no way she'd want him to take Chloe, if that were the case. He imagined Chloe part of a big happy family. Only not so happy because the mom was dying.

That fucking sucked.

Maybe it would be better for Chloe *not* to know about him. If there was another man she thought of as her father, did it make sense to rock that boat? Maybe it was a mistake wanting to meet her. On top of impulsive, he'd also been called selfish a time or two (mostly by Christy, his ex-wife). Maybe he was only thinking of himself and what he wanted, and not what was best for Chloe. Which meant he sucked as a parent because parenting was all about putting your kids' needs before your own.

But Sara wouldn't have offered this if she thought it would be bad for Chloe . . . would she?

He had no idea if Sara was a good mother. But yet, he thought she was. The love and devotion for her daughter had brightened her face. Sara was well-spoken, obviously educated, and had been dressed in clothes that were good quality. She clearly was able to provide for her daughter.

Drew paced around his living room as still more questions formed in his head. Was Sara a stay-at-home mom? Or did she work? What did she do? They'd been freshmen and hadn't shared their hopes and dreams for the future during their one drunken hookup.

Nice. They were going to have to come clean to Chloe about how she'd been conceived. Maybe Sara had already told her that part of the story, though.

And what about *his* family? He and Christy had no kids, but he had two brothers and a sister, with six children between them. And his parents. And a crusty grandma. What the hell was he going to tell *them* about this?

He rubbed the stubble on his jaw as he contemplated that. Chloe not only had a dad she didn't know, she also had six cousins and a bunch of aunts and uncles. But again, maybe she already had that.

Fuck, he knew nothing about Sara Watt, other than she had a sister. The sister who'd answered the phone when he called the other day.

Inspiration struck and he moved from the living room to the den, which was a sort of office for him. Not that he did any kind of work there. But his computer was there and he was soon doing a Google search.

Sara Watt's LinkedIn profile came up. There was a small photo of her. Yep, that was her. Corporate attorney at First Insurance. He read her experience, skills and education, including, yes, a law degree from Notre Dame.

Huh. A lawyer.

He found a few other brief mentions of her, but not much else. Only more questions. Having a baby at age eighteen, or maybe nineteen by the time Chloe had been born, hadn't held Sara back from getting an education or apparently having a successful career.

He glanced at the time on the computer. He was supposed to meet some guys for dinner, some of his buddies who were arriving back in town for training camp. He was still wearing the sweatpants and T-shirt he'd pulled on when he rolled out of bed at the crack of noon that day. He'd better make an effort to clean himself up and look like he had his shit together.

His insides twisted up, cramping painfully. These guys were his friends, but he was fucking dreading seeing them.

He should be at training camp. He should be lacing on his skates, taping his stick, enjoying the feel of the puck on his blade. He should be shooting at the net, feeling that sweet satisfaction of seeing the twine bulge. Laughing on the ice with the guys, sweating through drills, harassing the rookies who were all nervous and trying to make a good impression.

Seeing these guys was just going to remind him how fucked he was.

He considered blowing them off. But Sam was picking him up, and he had to face him. And he still had a speck of pride left because the last thing he wanted was people feeling sorry for him.

He clenched his jaw as he jogged upstairs to the big master suite, which was nearly empty. Christy had taken the bedroom furniture, and all he'd bothered to replace it with was a king-size bed that didn't even have a headboard, and a long, low dresser. Thank fuck they'd had a prenup or she'd have taken him for a lot more.

Already the bitterness that rose up his throat when he thought about Christy and their divorce had faded to nearly nothing. Guess he wasn't that heartbroken after all.

He stripped off his clothes as he walked, dropping them on the dark hardwood. He stepped into the bathroom. He loved this bathroom. Spacious and bright, it wasn't fancy, just plain white walls with white wooden blinds on the window, dark wood cabinets, and white towels. There was a huge white soaker tub at one end, but he rarely used that because the shower was his favorite thing.

He paused in front of the big mirror above the double-sink vanity and rubbed a hand over the stubble on his jaw. Shave? Nah.

He opened the glass door and stepped into what was nearly a small room, tiled with beige stone. He was a big guy and he liked to have elbow room when he was shampooing his hair. Plus, there were like, ten different jets of spray including one that rained down on top of his head, and a corner bench where he could sit.

Too bad he couldn't live in this shower.

He was ready when Sam rang his doorbell, shoving his wallet into the pocket of a pair of black dress pants. He turned back the cuffs of his shirtsleeves as he walked to the door to let Sam in.

"Dude!" Sam grabbed his hand and slung his other arm around his shoulders in a bro hug. "Good to see you!"

"Hell, yeah. You, too." Drew stepped back. "How was your summer? I saw all those Instagram pics you posted from Europe."

"Yeah." Sam grinned. "We had a great trip. How are you doing?"

Ugh.

"Great." He grabbed his keys. "Let's head out."

Sam had lots to talk about after a busy off-season, thankfully, and Drew just had to keep a smile tightly in place as they drove to Fabian just off North Michigan. They walked into the dimly lit, expensive steakhouse with leather booths and lots of dark wood.

The other guys were already there, Chase and Gersh and Johnny. Gersh was a veteran on the team, and Chase and Johnny had been acquired in trades about five years ago. Along with Dougie, they were his best buddies.

But now Dougie'd retired and had a corporate job that Drew didn't understand. And Drew was retired not because he wanted to be but because his fucked-up knee betrayed him, while his other friends continued to play. Chase, Gersh, and Johnny were all happily married family guys and now he wasn't. He felt different. He wasn't one of them anymore. He felt like he didn't fit in anywhere now. Just adrift on an endless ocean of crap, no map, compass, no directions . . . hell, no destination. No identity. He was nobody now.

While they all chirped at each other and shared tales about their summer and their kids, he laughed and tossed back Rusty Nails until the room was pleasantly blurry and the ache in his chest had faded. The guys went crazy ordering appetizers—shrimp cocktails, crab cakes, and the foie gras that Sam insisted on ordering because he'd had it in France.

Talk turned to the upcoming season, speculation about the prospects, including the newest draft picks, and how they'd do. Drew ordered another Rusty Nail. Nobody seemed to notice he wasn't saying much, and that was fine.

He probably shouldn't hang around with these guys much

now. It was just too goddamn painful. He slumped in his chair and contemplated his beverage.

"Hey, Selly."

Drew lifted slightly unfocused eyes to look at Sam. "Yeah?"

"What's up with you? What are your plans now?"

Drew grimaced. "Got no plans right now."

"What're you going to do?" Johnny asked. "Now you're retired."

Drew shrugged. "I dunno. Step told me I can come work as an adviser again this season." Step was Ivan Stepanov, general manager of the Hawks. Technically, Drew was still under contract with the team for one more season, but he'd be spending this season on long-term injured reserve. For the remainder of last season, he'd hung out as an alleged "adviser" but he knew better than anyone that he didn't really have a role. He was just there, cheering on the guys. He didn't think he could handle that again this year. "But I don't know," he continued, swirling his drink in the glass. "Maybe I need some time off to just enjoy life." He almost threw up a little in his mouth when he said that.

Sam snorted. "No offense, dude, but you don't look like you're enjoying much." He studied Drew. "And you need a haircut."

Drew laughed and cuffed the back of Sam's head, with its nearly shoulder-length blond hair; the dude was voted player with the best flow in the league. "Fuck off."

"No, seriously."

Drew frowned and raked a hand through his hair. "Whatever," he muttered.

"Got any ideas what you want to do?" Gersh asked.

"Nah. Had lunch with Dougie the other day. I do know I couldn't stand working in an office every day like he does now."

Gersh shuddered. "Yeah, same."

"You went to college," Sam reminded him. "What'd you take?"

"Buncha bullshit courses," Drew said. "Easiest ones I could. I never finished my degree after I got drafted."

Because he was Drew Sellers, first-round draft pick, young and invincible, who was going to make millions of dollars and play hockey forever. Who needed a plan B? Not him!

Dumb fucker.

His cell phone vibrated. Frowning, he fumbled it out and peered at the illuminated screen in the dark restaurant. Sara.

He quickly answered the call. "Hey. Drew here." "Hi, Drew. It's Sara."

"I know. I added you to my contacts."

"Oh. Okay. I'm just calling back to set up a time for us to meet."

His gut seized up. He caught the curious glances of the other guys. "Hey, can you hang on a sec?"

"Sure."

He lowered the phone and motioned to Gersh sitting next to him in the booth. "Sorry, guys, I need to take this call. Can I get out?"

Gersh slid out and Drew followed. He walked across the restaurant between tables, the phone back at his ear.

"Sorry about that. I'm just having dinner with some friends."

"Sorry to interrupt. We could talk later . . . or tomorrow."

"No, no, it's fine." He swallowed, his mouth suddenly dry, alcohol churning in his gut.

They arranged to meet the following week.

"I don't know what your schedule is like. Would you be able to meet Tuesday night?"

"Anytime. My days are wide open."

"Oh. Well, then maybe in the afternoon. That would be better —Chloe's at school."

"Sure. Where?"

She paused. "Could you come here?"

"Of course. Just give me your address."

She told him and he recognized the street name. It wasn't far from his place if he was remembering correctly. They agreed on a time and ended the call.

Before he went back into the restaurant he stood on the sidewalk next to big pots of flowers and greenery. People walked by enjoying the fall evening, while traffic passed along the one-way street toward North Michigan.

Well, it was a step forward. He could totally understand Sara's wanting to be protective and sure of what they were doing here. This was a kid's life, and stuff like this could mess with a kid's head in a way that could scar them forever. He didn't want that.

Back at the table, the guys shuffled to let him back in and he picked up his drink and drained it.

"What was that?" Sam asked with a smirk. "New woman in your life?"

Drew gave a mirthless laugh. "You could say that." He lowered his head into his hand, elbow on the table. "Fuck."

The atmosphere went from friendly ribbing to leaden. "What's going on, Selly?"

"I need another drink."

"Uh . . . you've had about a dozen."

Drew raised his gaze to Sam and lifted the middle finger of the hand his head was resting on.

"Just watching out for you, buddy."

"That wasn't Christy, was it?" Gersh demanded.

"No. Haven't heard from Christy in months."

"She still seeing Cos?" Sam asked quietly.

"Far as I know."

"Fuck that."

Drew shrugged. "At least he's not my teammate anymore." The one good thing about his forced retirement.

"So who *was* that then?" Johnny prompted, signaling the waitress. She rushed right over, no doubt aware she was waiting on a table of pro athletes. All except one.

"Well, guys, this is a funny story."

. . .

He arrived at Sara's home Tuesday afternoon, his stomach cramped with nerves and his jaw aching from clenching his teeth. He walked up to the house, a two-story Victorian-style on a nice tree-lined street not unlike his own, set close to its neighbors. He climbed the steps and crossed a small veranda to ring the doorbell.

It was a great house, neatly painted and well maintained, although the veranda could use sweeping, and the windows needed washing.

The door opened and a woman stood there regarding him with a bitchy expression. "Drew?"

"Yes."

She held out a hand in a forthright manner. "I'm Peyton Watt. Sara's sister." He shook her hand, her grip firm. "Nice to meet you, Peyton."

"Come in."

He followed her in. She didn't look like her sister other than the blond hair and blue eyes. Her hair was longer than Sara's, just touching her shoulders in messy waves, and it wasn't one shade of blond, it was about a hundred, from buttery pale to honey to butterscotch. She'd be pretty if she wasn't wearing such a consti-pated expression.

His gaze tracked down her body as she led the way into the living room, taking in slender curves, a fantastic ass, and long legs in skinny jeans. Fuck. He should *not* be checking out her ass. He gave himself a mental smack on the back of the head.

Sara was in a reclining chair near the bay window and she used the lever to bring the back of the chair upright. "Hi, Drew."

He blinked at her as he walked across a patterned carpet toward her. The blond hair was gone; she wore a scarf wrapped around her head. Dammit, she'd been wearing a wig that day she'd approached him. His heart bumped in his chest.

The scarf on her head emphasized the thinness of her face, and the soft blanket tucked around her didn't hide her slight frame.

She lifted her hand free of it to gesture at the couch. "Have a seat. Would you like some coffee?"

"Sure. That would be great."

"What do you take in your coffee?" Peyton asked.

"Just black."

"Sara, you want anything?" Peyton looked at her sister and her expression softened. Drew watched, struck by the caring he saw on her face. The clear sapphire- blue of her eyes, the high cheekbones, and the sweet curve of her lips made it hard to look away from her.

Sara pursed her lips. "Could you make me one of those caramel lattes?"

"You bet. Be right back." And Peyton hurried through the adjacent dining room and around the corner, presumably into the kitchen.

Drew smiled at Sara as he sat on the couch.

She gave him a crooked smile back. "This is really weird, isn't it?"

CHAPTER 4

Peyton made two beverages in the Keurig, focusing on the task to distract herself. She was still freaked out about the news Sara had laid on her the other day after Drew had called. After all these years, it was insane that she happened to find out who the father of her child was.

Peyton's stomach had been churning with worry ever since. They knew nothing about this guy. Okay, Sara wasn't stupid and had done some investigation before she'd even contacted him, but still . . . they were bringing him into their lives, into Chloe's life, and the enormity of that scared the hell out of her.

Then she'd opened the door to see this big, gorgeous man standing on the veranda, and her stomach had swooped. Tall and broad with beard stubble and amazing hazel eyes, dark hair falling across his forehead, he was an intense physical presence, radiating energy. And when he spoke, his voice was deep, with an unusual husky quality that made her tingle.

This was extremely unsettling, since her *sister* had slept with this guy.

She drew a deep breath as she waited for the second beverage to brew, hands gripping the edge of the counter.

Okay, never mind that he was extremely attractive. They had much more important things to worry about, like whether he would treat Chloe right. They didn't even know how much of a relationship he wanted with her, only that he was agreeable to meeting her. And he was here.

The coffee finished brewing with a final hiss, and she carried the mugs into the living room.

"My sister's staying with me right now," Sara was saying to Drew. "She's not from here?"

"No, she lives in New York. I hate disrupting her life like this." Sara sighed. Peyton paused then forged onward.

Sara looked up at her as she handed her a mug. "Thanks, sis."

Peyton smiled and handed Drew his black coffee. "I'll let you two talk."

"You can stay, Peyton," Sara said.

Peyton hesitated. Did she want to be part of this conversation? It really was bizarre, since Sara and Drew didn't even know each other, and yet they'd created a child together. "I'll just get myself some tea."

"I'm sorry to hear you're not feeling well," Drew said to Sara as she left.

Peyton hated coffee, but the Keurig brewed tea, too, so she made herself a cup and then rejoined Sara and Drew.

"You're not married?" Drew asked Sara.

"Oh. No." She shook her head. "Wow, we really know nothing about each other, do we?"

"Nope." He gave her a wry smile.

"I uh, know about your divorce," Sara said.

They knew Drew wasn't married and that there were no wife and kids who'd be freaked out about his newfound daughter. His divorce from his gorgeous, sexy, blond wife had been big news on various sports blogs.

"My wife was cheating on me with one of my teammates."

Peyton's stomach tightened with sympathy.

"I'm sorry," Sara said.

"It sucked, but was probably for the best. After I retired, it was pretty obvious Christy didn't want me around. Things weren't great. A lot of it was my fault." He made a face.

An attractive, self-deprecating face.

A guy who looked like him should think he was the shit. And maybe he did, but he also had an attractive humble quality about him. Damn him.

"Tell me what's happened to you since college," Drew said.

"Well, I finished my degree, thanks to my parents and Peyton." She shot Peyton a glance and Peyton smiled. "It was hard, being a single mom, but I had a lot of support from family and friends. I got my law degree and practiced for a year at a law firm. The long hours got to me, though, so I moved to a job at First Insurance. It was better for work–life balance. They had great benefits, in-house day care, flexible hours. My parents still helped, and Peyton did, too, until she got a big promotion that took her to New York."

"That's awesome," Drew said quietly. He sipped his coffee. "I'm glad you had that much support."

Sara nodded. "I couldn't have done it without them." She paused. "I don't blame you, Drew. Not at all. You had no idea."

"I know." He nodded. "But thanks."

"What about you? I know you're an NHL hockey star."

"Was," he corrected shortly.

Peyton could see that was a sore spot for him. He wasn't happy that he wasn't playing hockey anymore. They knew about his injury and that he'd had to retire; it was everywhere in sports news on the internet, and research had turned that all up.

"Tell me about your family," Sara said quietly. "Will they be upset learning you have a daughter you never knew about?"

Drew appeared to contemplate that. "I have a big family," he said slowly. "Two brothers, one sister, lots of nieces and nephews. My parents love being grandparents." He paused, clearly thinking about a lot of stuff. "I think they'd be happy to know Chloe."

"So you'll tell them about her?" Peyton asked quietly then sipped her tea.

"I already have. When I got the DNA results."

Sara nodded. "Okay, that's great, but I just want to make sure we're careful of Chloe. She has no idea she has a big family, and that could overwhelm her."

"Does your family live here in Chicago?" Peyton asked.

"No. I'm from Canada. Grew up in a small city in Ontario. My folks are still there. My sister and one brother are in Toronto, and the other brother's in Vancouver."

Peyton nodded. "Do you plan to move back there?"

A notch appeared between his eyebrows. "I don't think so. I've lived here for eleven years. This is home now." He paused. "What family do you have?"

Sara looked at Peyton, who huffed a sigh and smiled into her cup. "We don't have much family," she answered. "Our parents died a few years ago. We have one aunt who lives in Los Angeles, a few cousins spread out around the country. Our grandparents are gone." She tipped her head back to look at the ceiling. "We're all we have left. Us and Chloe."

Drew's jaw tightened and he nodded. "I'm sorry."

"We're close," Peyton continued. "We always have been." "Peyton has helped me out so much," Sara said.

"You never married?" Drew asked quietly.

"No." She looked down. "There was a guy once . . . turned out he didn't want to be a dad to someone else's child." She lifted a thin shoulder.

"Good riddance to him," Peyton said. She'd hated that asshole for hurting her sister.

"Yeah," Drew agreed.

Sara leaned head back into the chair and closed her eyes. "Damn. I'm tired." Peyton jumped up. "Do you want to go upstairs?"

"No. Not now. I'm just tired from talking so much."

Shit.

"We need to move your bedroom downstairs," Peyton said. She'd suggested that the day after she'd arrived and had no idea why Sara was so resistant to the idea. They could turn the den into her bedroom and there was a bathroom close by on the main floor. Going up and down stairs was becoming a strain for her.

Sara sighed. "I guess we do."

"What can I do?" Drew stood, looking uncomfortable but determined.

"It's okay," Sara said. "We can manage. I'll just lie back and close my eyes for a few minutes. I'm sorry." She adjusted the position of the recliner so she was nearly flat.

"God, don't apologize."

"You two can talk."

Drew's chest lifted and fell. "Okay." He sat back down.

Silence filled the room. Drew looked at Peyton. "Tell me about Chloe," he said quietly.

Peyton nodded. "Well, she's almost twelve, as you know. She's just started seventh grade. She's an amazing girl." She smiled. "I might be biased, but seriously, she's very bright. Very mature for her age. She's a talented dancer."

"Dancer."

"Yes. She takes ballet and jazz dance lessons and she's on a competitive dance team. She also enjoys sports." She paused and eyed the man on the couch. "Um. I guess she gets that from you."

"She sure doesn't get it from me," Sara murmured dryly without opening her eyes.

Peyton smiled. "Yeah, Sara was more of an academic than an athlete."

"How about you?"

Peyton met Drew's eyes. He was asking about her? This wasn't about her. She gave a light laugh. "I wasn't as smart as Sara but I could run faster."

"Phhht." The noise came from Sara.

Peyton grinned. "What are you disputing? That you can run as fast as I can?"

"No. That's for sure. But you're just as smart as me."

"I ran track in high school," Peyton told Drew. "But I wasn't a straight-A student like Sara. Anyway, Chloe is a little crusader. She takes up causes at school and sinks her teeth into them. Right now she's on an anti-bullying mission because of something that happened to a kid in her class. She's pretty determined. It can be a good quality, but drove us crazy when she was little. She'd get an idea of something she wanted to do and there was *no* talking her out of it. There may have been the odd temper tantrum."

Drew smiled.

"She's pretty brave in some ways, but in other ways we've thought she's a little reckless."

"Ha." Drew rubbed his chin. "That's what my parents say about me." "Oh, yeah?"

He smiled ruefully. "Competitive and reckless are a dangerous combination. I was always trying to climb the highest tree, do the biggest jump on the ski hill, skate the fastest. Never worried about getting hurt, just had to be the best. Damn near killed my parents, though."

Peyton could see that. A man who was one of the best in his sport had to have a lot of drive on top of a lot of talent.

A sense of unreality descended on Peyton. All of Chloe's life they'd never known who her father was, where she got some of the traits they saw developing in her that were different from Sara or the rest of the Watt family. Even physical traits like her dark hair and athletic ability. Now they could have all those answers, put the pieces together for her. It was like finding the missing puzzle pieces to who Chloe was, although they'd never felt as if she wasn't a complete person. Because she was. A beautiful, bright, and dynamic young woman.

Peyton bent her head for a moment, emotion swelling in her chest. She'd been skeptical and nervous about inviting this man into their lives, but Sara was insistent that if she had this chance for Chloe to know her father they had to take it. Maybe it was going to be okay.

She lifted her head and met Drew's eyes, reading the nervous uncertainty in them. He came across as confident and fearless, but beneath the surface he was as freaked out about this as she and Sara were.

She still didn't know if that meant he was a terrible person who didn't want a child and would hurt Chloe, or if it meant he cared enough that he'd make a good dad. They'd find out, though, soon enough, and if he did anything, any freaking little thing to hurt her . . .

That wasn't real life, though. They couldn't insulate Chloe from being hurt. Sara's illness was proof of that. Chloe was going to lose her mom at a young, vulnerable age, and that fucking sucked.

"Excuse me." Peyton jumped up, trying to keep her voice steady. "I'm just going to get some more tea."

She rushed out of the room with her mug. In the kitchen she grabbed hold of the counter and stood with her eyes closed, her chest aching, heart pounding. Most of the time she kept her shit together, but every once in a while it just swamped her, the agony and hopelessness and helplessness.

She kicked the cupboard door with her bare foot then winced. "Are you okay?"

The low, rasping voice that spoke behind her made her jump.

She closed her eyes and breathed in through her nose. Nodding, she turned to face him, her hands going back to the edge of the counter. "I'm okay. Sometimes it just . . . gets to me. I try to hold it together in front of Sara, but . . . I'm sorry."

"Don't apologize." He took one step closer, his eyes fastened on her face. "It's understandable."

"Sara . . . ?"

"I think she dozed off."

39

She let out a short breath. "Okay. Damn." She lifted her chin. "This has to suck for you. It should be wonderful and amazing to meet the daughter you never knew you had, but here you are dragged into our family crap." Her lips trembled and she pressed them together.

"Well," he said, hands in the back pockets of his jeans. "I'm not sure if 'wonderful and amazing' is how I'd describe finding out I have a nearly twelve-year-old daughter I never knew about."

She looked at him sharply. "You don't have to be here."

"That's not what I meant. I'm just saying, I'm still in shock about this and I have no idea how to deal with it. But being sucked into your family crap actually puts my own problems in perspective. I feel like a selfish asshole being worried about what the hell I'm supposed to do about having a daughter. Christ." He rubbed the back of his neck and looked away.

"Oh." Peyton swallowed.

"My life is shit right now," he said. "Just being honest. And I'm competitive, but I think I can honestly say your shit is worse than my shit."

She stared at him, and then amusement bubbled in her chest and came out in a short laugh. "Yay. I win." She dropped her chin and shook her head then looked back at him. "I'm competitive, too."

His smile and the twinkle in his eye tugged at something inside her, a shared understanding. A shared sense of humor, no matter how bleak things were. That was important.

"Chloe has a sense of humor," she said softly.

"Glad to hear it." He rolled his eyes. "I haven't had enough of a sense of humor lately."

"You've been through some shitty things."

"Yeah." He acknowledged it, but didn't elaborate.

"What are you doing now that your hockey career is done?"

His jaw tightened. "Haven't quite figured that out yet."

"Ah. Well, I'm sure there are tons of opportunities for a guy like you."

"Tons."

His clipped tone made her pause and she studied him.

"Yeah, I'm basically unemployed," he said. "Might as well be honest about that up front."

"Oh." Peyton hadn't been thinking that. She tucked her hair behind her ear. "Well, we did run a credit report on you."

Drew huffed out a laugh. "Yeah, Sara told me about the background checks. Can't say I blame her."

"I'm glad you understand."

"Can you tell me more about Chloe?"

"Sure. Would you like more coffee?"

"I'm good, thanks."

"Well, just so you know, she's not perfect. Lately she's developed a bit of a tween attitude. There have been instances of eye-rolling and hints that she thinks her mom is an idiot. I haven't been the recipient yet because I'm just the aunt. We're close, but not close enough for her to disrespect me."

"Yet she'll disrespect her mom."

"Sure." Peyton shrugged. "That's what kids are like. It means she's absolutely secure in her love from her mom. She knows Sara will love her no matter how mouthy or bratty she gets." Peyton smiled. "I, on the other hand, could actually leave."

"Huh." Drew rubbed his face. "My knowledge about kids could be written down on a postage stamp."

"I'm no expert, either, Lord knows. But I was around enough when Chloe was small that I learned a few things."

"Do you like kids?"

An odd question. "I like some kids. Same as I like some adults."

His slow grin revealed a dimple in one cheek. "Smart answer."

"It's true. How can you say you like kids carte blanche? I've met some pretty snotty, badly behaved kids." She paused. "But I like Chloe. Which is nice, because I love her, because she's my niece, so it's really extra special that I actually *like* her."

"Yeah, I guess so." His forehead creased. "D'you think there are parents who *don't* like their kids?"

She pondered that. "I don't know. I guess it's possible. But we could have a big debate about nature versus nurture. I tend to believe that from the time they're babies, you're nurturing them into the people you want them to be. If you don't want a kid who's selfish, raise her with generosity. If you don't want a kid who's vain, raise her with humility."

Not that she'd ever have kids of her own. She'd ruled that out of her life years ago.

He leaned against the counter. "You don't think someone can be born selfish?"

She grinned. "Like I said, this is an ancient debate in psychology. I don't think it's an all or nothing question. Instead of asking if it's one or the other—nature versus nurture—I prefer to ask *how much* influence each has."

"A reasonable approach," he murmured. The he frowned. "Can I ask a really personal question?"

"Um, I guess."

"Sara's cancer . . . how much of it is genetic?"

Peyton gave him a sad smile. "There are genetic predispositions to melanoma, but she's the only one in our family who's ever had it, so they're fairly sure it's just by chance that she got it."

"Oh." His chest lifted and fell. "That's good. I mean, not for Sara . . . obviously."

His discomfort softened her heart. "She's been amazing through this—so strong. She fought this with everything she had." Her throat constricted and she swallowed. "She seems to have accepted that the battle is over."

"Have you?"

Peyton pressed her lips together. "I'm not sure, honestly. I think there will always be a kernel of hope inside me that some kind of miracle will happen."

"What can I do? I may be unemployed but I have money. We could have her seen by the best doctors . . ."

She shook her head. "She has been. She has excellent health coverage and she's a smart woman. She's always made sure to ask questions and keep asking them until she has answers." She paused. "And she doesn't want money from you, just so you know. She *has* money. Our parents left us very comfortable, and she has . . . *had* a great job."

Drew ran a hand through his hair and clasped the back of his neck as his gaze went to the ceiling, his lips pressed together. "Yeah," he said. "I know."

CHAPTER 5

Peyton gave him a long look, eyebrows elevated. "You know what?"

"I know she has money. You're not the only one who had a background check done."

She gave a slow blink, her sapphire eyes big and round.

Drew held out his hands, palms facing her. "Hey, you can't be upset about that."

Peyton rubbed the end of her small nose with her fingertips. "No, I guess I can't," she said slowly.

"Look, I've had more than one friend who's ended up in a situation not unlike this. One of my teammates was being extorted for money by a woman who claimed he was the father of her child. The paternity test proved it wasn't true. Another guy I know ended up married to a woman because she got pregnant on purpose to trap him. That didn't end well. It happens all the time."

"That's pretty cynical."

"It's realistic," he said shortly. "It's why I was skeptical when Sara first approached me. I didn't even remember her. It's why I expected that she wanted something. It's why I insisted on a DNA test, and when it turned out I am Chloe's father, I'll be honest—I still expected that Sara wanted something. I wanted to know as much as I could about her and her situation."

"I understand that," Peyton said slowly. "I guess I hadn't thought about this from your perspective. So all those questions you were asking . . . you already knew the answers."

"Some of them," he admitted. "And since we're being honest here, I'll also tell you that I've consulted a lawyer."

She blinked. "What for?"

"Just checking some things out. One of my friends told me about someone he knew who found out he had a five-year-old son. The mother sued him for child support for the past five years."

Her mouth dropped open. "For a child he didn't even know about?"

"Yep. Apparently laws differ from state to state, but here in Illinois she wouldn't likely win that."

Peyton's face now wore that pinched expression she'd worn when she answered the door.

"You look pissed," he said bluntly.

She drew in a long breath and sighed. "You're right. I have no right to be pissed. I'm a very pragmatic person. But I hate the thought that someone thinks Sara would do something like that. She's fiercely independent and determined. Even if she was financially destitute I doubt she'd try to get anything from you."

"I'm getting that," he agreed dryly. "Look, this is a weird situation. I know there are a lot of emotions involved, and a child meeting the father she never knew should be all sweet and joyful. But the reality is, I don't feel sweet and joyful about it."

"How do you feel?"

He had to think about that. "I'm honestly not sure," he finally said. "Things haven't exactly been going well for me lately, and I really didn't need another huge complication in my life."

"I'm sorry that you see Chloe as a complication."

She didn't say it in a bitchy, snippy tone. She said it calmly and sincerely.

"I'm sorry, too," he acknowledged. "And the last thing I want is for *Chloe* to feel like I see her as a complication. So this is tough. But I also have to admit I'm curious and also pretty fucking terrified, which is something I'm not used to feeling."

She studied him, looked away for a long moment, then back at him. "Thank you for being honest."

He lifted his chin.

"I better check on Sara." She pushed away from the counter and walked past him into the dining room.

He followed along behind. Jesus. This was so fucked up.

"Hey, sis." Peyton bent over Sara in the recliner. "You awake?"

"Yeah. Sorry, I fell asleep."

"That's okay. Drew and I were chatting in the kitchen."

"I should be going," he said quietly. "I'm sure this is tiring for you."

"Wait," Sara said. "There are a few more things we need to discuss."

He took his seat on the couch again and leaned forward. "Like what?"

"I want you to know what I've told Chloe about you."

"Oh."

"I mean, before we knew who you were. I told her the truth about us—that I met you at a party, we had sex one time, and she was the result."

"Jesus." He scrubbed a hand over his face.

"She knows how babies are made. I've told her that having sex with someone you don't know is not a good idea because there can be serious consequences . . . like a child. A child who grows up without a father. But I've tried to make up for that mistake every day of Chloe's life and I don't regret having her. I wanted her to know that. So I told her that I'm sure her father is a good man, and if he'd had any idea she existed he wouldn't have stayed away."

Drew's chest tightened.

"I haven't told her about you yet," she continued. "I wanted to meet you today and make sure this was the right thing to do." She paused, as if struggling for breath. "I've always wished I could protect her from everything . . . kids who didn't want to play with her in the playground, or mean girls who excluded her from birthday parties, or someday, a boy who will break her heart. I've always wished I could make her life easy for her. But that's not how it works. So we're going to take this risk. I can't stop you from hurting her if things don't work out."

For once in his life, *he* was the risk. Funny.

"Thank you for coming," Sara said. "I'll tell Chloe now about you."

Drew bent his head. "What if she doesn't want to meet me?"

"She will. I'm sure she will. She's always wished she had a dad." She paused. "When would be good for you to meet her?"

"I passed muster?" He quirked an eyebrow at Sara. She smiled faintly.

"That wasn't what this was about."

"Sure it was."

"Okay, maybe partly. I did want to know you a bit better before she meets you. And for you to know us a bit better."

Peyton made a sound, and Drew glanced at her, knowing she was thinking about the investigation he had done. "Already told Peyton this, but I did my own background checking."

Sara smiled. "Good."

Drew shook his head, unable to stop the grin that twitched his mouth. "Okay, so . . . this weekend? Saturday?"

"Sure."

"Want me to come here again?"

"Yes, if you don't mind. I'm not getting out much these days."

"Okay. See you then." He glanced at Peyton. "Will you still be here?"

"Yes."

He headed to the door and Peyton walked with him. In the small foyer she said to him quietly, "I don't think I'll be able to go back to New York for a while."

Sadness slid through him. "Is it that bad?"

"We have a meeting with the social worker from the hospice at St. Luke's Hospital tomorrow. Sara wants to stay at home as long as she can. I came to help, but if she wants to stay here until the end, she's going to need more care than I can give her."

"Fuck."

"Yeah. Anyway, I'll be here. Here's my card with my cell number on it. You can call me, too, if you need to."

"Thanks." He tucked the card in his pocket. "Do you have my address?"

"Yes." She smiled wryly. "But not your phone number."

She entered it into her phone as he recited it. "Okay. See you Saturday." In his car, he sat for a while. He wasn't even sure how long.

His brain was a snarled mass of thoughts and feelings, impossible to untangle and separate.

Selfish. He was selfish.

If he had to find out he had a daughter, why couldn't it have just been straightforward? He'd rather deal with a bitch mother who wanted nothing to do with him than this. The mother of his child was fucking *dying*. He didn't even know her and it had him twisted up in knots.

And her sister . . . Peyton. Walking into the kitchen, seeing her holding on to the counter, her shoulders up around her ears, her body vibrating with emotion . . . the obvious love and misery she felt at what was happening. It was fucking heartbreaking.

How the hell was he going to deal with Chloe going through the same thing?

At that moment he changed his mind. About the whole goddamn thing. He didn't want to meet a young girl who was going to make him feel even more of this crap and then destroy him when her mother died.

Christ. *Christ.*

He leaned his head on the steering wheel, his eyes burning. "I can't do this," he muttered. *"I cannot do this."*

Yeah, he'd known stuff about Sara. He'd been on the phone to a private investigator his lawyer had recommended, quick as a striped lizard on hot asphalt. Money talked, and he'd had info in days.

You know what was fucking weird? He'd met Sara and Peyton's father. More than once.

Jim Watt had been the CEO of LCC Technologies, not the wealthiest man in Chicago, but up there. He'd been on the board of directors of a number of charities including Paterson House, the nonprofit organization for kids that Drew had worked with since he'd moved to Chicago. They'd met at a few fund-raising events. He was a nice guy . . . personable and smart. What a bizarre small world.

Jim and Caren Watt had died in a boating accident on Lake Michigan a few years ago. It had been in the news, and Drew had been saddened to hear it, but never in a million years had he connected the family with the girl he'd hooked up with one night in college.

He lifted his head. He had to get his shit together.

But first he needed a drink. Hey, it was almost happy hour. He headed for Jimmy's. Which wasn't that damn far from where he was.

All this time, he'd been living in the same neighborhood as Sara and Chloe. For Chrissakes, his head was so fucked up from this. He needed a little get-together with his good friend, Johnnie Walker.

"Hey, Drew." The owner of Jimmy's Kitchen and Bar called to him when he walked up to the bar. "What's crackin'?"

"Just my knee." He grinned. "I'll have a Rusty Nail, please. Make it a double."

"You got it." Jimmy grabbed the bottle of Johnnie Walker. "Plannin' to start any bar fights tonight?"

Drew grimaced and rubbed his chin. "I never *plan* to start them."

Jimmy sighed. "Two in the last three months, man." He slid the glass across the worn wooden bar. "What the fuck is up with that?"

Drew looked down at the drink. "He was an asshole and he was bothering that woman."

"Okay, Knight in Shining Armor. And what about the one before that?"

"Douche was cheating at pool."

"Uh-huh."

"Okay, okay, I get it. No more fights."

"Good. I don't want to have to ban you from the premises."

"You wouldn't do that."

Jimmy grinned. "Still haven't found a job, huh."

"Haven't been looking."

"Well, that'd be the reason, then. You think someone's just gonna hand you a job?"

"*You* offered me one."

Jimmy grinned, leaning on the bar. "Oh yeah, I did. Let me know when you're ready to start bartending."

Drew picked up the glass and gulped the drink. "You know, that might not be so bad." How hard could it be? "But bartending's for college kids. Not a real job."

"Hey." Jimmy looked affronted. "That's an insult."

"Jimmy, you own the place. You're a businessman, not a bartender."

"Still, bartending is an honorable profession. Don't be such a snob."

Drew lifted the glass to his lips. "Snob? Me? My wife cheated on me and I have no job. If I had a dog, it'd be dead. I'm a country music cliché, not a snob. A loser."

Jimmy snorted. "You're not a loser. Anyone can win when everything's going your way. It's the guy who gets through all the crap that's the real champ."

Drew grimaced, thinking of Sara. Things weren't exactly going her way, either. Same for Peyton.

Peyton was pretty amazing. She'd taken charge of the situation, caring for her sister and her niece, obviously confident, smart, and dynamic . . . yet the love and pain and vulnerability she'd displayed tugged at something deep inside him. Not to mention that gorgeous face and sweet ass.

Wait. Why was he thinking about Peyton? Jesus, what was *wrong* with him? The television on behind the bar was on a sports channel, and coverage turned to the Blackhawks training camp. He watched Brent Busby, the sports reporter who'd interviewed him so many times over the years, interview some of his former teammates. He'd had beers with Brent in bars on the road.

The players he was talking to were sweaty and happy, talking about how good it felt to be back on the ice and how nothing was locked up in terms of the roster. Drew drained his glass and clinked it down on the bar. "I'll have another one."

"What did you think of him?"

Peyton looked over at Sara, both of them stretched out on Sara's bed, binge- watching episodes of *Suits*. "Drew?"

"Yeah."

"I don't know. Does it matter?"

Sara rolled to her side. "Of course it matters. I value your opinion." "It's hard to know much about someone after meeting him once."

"Yeah, but you can definitely form an impression. And you're always so good at that."

Peyton swallowed a sigh. "Okay, I think he's a good guy. I was a little worried that being a pro athlete he'd be all swagger and cocky attitude. And there's a bit of that. But I think he's trying to do the right thing and he's really freaked out by this. Also, he seems kind of . . . " She paused.

"What?"

"I don't know. Sad. Lost."

"Huh. Yeah. That's what I thought. Maybe he's heartbroken because of his wife cheating on him."

"Well, that would definitely be a kick in the teeth."

"And having to retire."

"That, too."

"So I should go ahead and tell Chloe?"

Peyton nodded slowly. "Yeah."

"Would you tell her for me?"

"No."

"Didn't think so."

Peyton smiled. "You're a good mom. You can handle this."

"You know I want you to be her guardian, right?"

"I know."

They'd talked about this when Chloe was born. Sara, being a practical lawyer, had made a will that included who she wanted to be guardian in case anything happened to her, along with how she wanted funds to be held in trust and disbursed. Of course at that time, she hadn't had much, still in college, and she also hadn't anticipated needing those arrangements this early in her life.

"You're still okay with that?"

Peyton, too, rolled to her side so they were facing each other. "Of course I'm okay with that. I'm terrified, but I'm okay."

"Why are you terrified?"

"I'm an aunt, not a mother. I'll feed her junk food and let her stay up late and then she'll be sick the next morning and miss school and flunk out and never get into college."

Sara laughed so hard she fell onto her back and started gasping. "Sorry, sorry," Peyton said, regretting her joke.

Sara smiled up at the ceiling. "No, I'm sorry. For putting this on you."

"Jesus, I've told you before. Don't apologize. I love you. I love Chloe. I love her *so* much. I'll probably screw up a lot, but I want you to know I'll do my very, very best for her."

"I know you will. And remember what you told me when she was little and I was scared of screwing up? You may not know what you're doing, but as long as you do it out of love, it'll be okay."

Tears stung Peyton's eyes and she, too, stared at the ceiling. "I remember." She swallowed. "Thank you for trusting me to raise your daughter."

"Fuck. I'm going to cry."

"Don't do it. Don't you dare fucking cry."

"Maybe we don't cry enough, Pey. We both try to be so strong. We both hate needing someone. Maybe we should just have a good cry and get it over with."

Peyton sucked on her bottom lip and turned her head on the pillow. "I've cried a lot. It hasn't helped. And I'm afraid if I start now, I might n-never stop."

Their eyes met and Sara's face blurred through the tears. "I know," Sara whispered. "I've cried a lot, too."

Peyton's throat ached and pressure built behind her cheekbones. "This fucking sucks so bad."

"It does. I'm dying, Peyton."

Peyton's nose stung. "Do you want to talk about it?"

Sara nodded slowly. "Maybe." She paused. "I don't really have any regrets. Other than not wearing SPF 50."

Peyton huffed out a little laugh even though it wasn't really funny. "That's good."

"I know it was stupid to have sex with a guy I didn't even know, and it could have turned out so much worse. But I don't regret it because it gave me Chloe. I guess I regret not finding out more about Drew so I could have found him sooner."

"Things happen for a reason. Maybe this is the time he was meant to have a daughter. And maybe Chloe has learned a lot about being a strong, independent woman by being raised by a single mom."

"Yes. Maybe." She sighed. "I regret wasting time on Jeff when he didn't love Chloe—or me—enough to be a stepdad to her. And . . ." She paused. "I want you to forgive me for the time I said you had thunder thighs."

"I forgave you for that a long time ago. Just like you forgave me for ruining your Kate Spade dress when I borrowed it without asking."

"I *haven't* forgiven you for that. I loved that dress." Sara's teasing smile squeezed Peyton's heart. "But I have forgiven you for stealing my boyfriend in high school."

Ugh. Did she have to bring that up? It had been a painful strain between them for months. Sara had been eighteen, Peyton sixteen, when the asshole Sara had been dating had dumped her and the very next day asked Peyton out. She'd known it was wrong, which was why she'd lied about it and covered up the fact she was seeing Andrew for weeks before Sara found out. The guilt had eaten at her for a long, long time . . . Sara had been heart-broken and she'd made it worse. "I didn't steal him," she said quietly. "I told you that. I didn't do anything to encourage him."

"I know." Sara shook her head. "I'm teasing. That was a rough time for us, but we both got sucked in by his charm. Eventually we also both realized he wasn't worth it—a guy who would do that. We had our conflicts—what siblings don't? We fought when we were little and competed for Mom and Dad's attention. But you've always been there for me when it really matters. Always."

Peyton's throat burned. "You've been there for me, too."

Sara reached for Peyton's hand and they held on to each other.

"I wish it was me," Peyton whispered. "And you'd be here for Chloe."

"Oh, God." Sara's voice thickened. "Don't say that."

"It's true."

Sara's fingers tightened. "It makes me so sad I won't see her grow up. I won't meet her boyfriends. Please . . . make sure they're good enough for her. Make sure she knows how important she is and that she deserves someone who worships her."

"I will."

"I won't know her husband or her children."

The pain in Peyton's chest was like a jagged knife slicing her open. Tears leaked from her eyes. She didn't know what to say. Nothing was right. She couldn't solve this problem, something she was usually so good at. So she said, "I love you, Sara."

"I love you, too."

CHAPTER 6

Drew called Sara the next day, late in the afternoon. Sitting in his family room, two beers inside him to give him courage, he picked up his cell phone and called her number.

Peyton answered. "Hi, Drew."

She had a nice voice, low and soft.

"Hi." He paused. "Uh, how are you? And Sara?"

"We're okay."

"Did you meet with the social worker?"

"Yes. It was . . . " She stopped. "It was informative. They're going to start sending home-care workers here to care for her, but Sara may have changed her mind about dying at home. She's not sure she wants Chloe to be around that, now that we know more about it. So tomorrow I'm going to look at the facility at the hospital. It's apparently lovely. I've had a look online. It seems very homey." Her voice wobbled a little. "I want to check it out, though."

"Of course." He sucked air into his lungs. "Look, I've been giving this a lot of thought and I'm having a change of heart."

Silence. "What does that mean?" Her voice had gone terse.

"I've changed my mind. About meeting Chloe. It's a bad idea. For all of us. I have nothing to offer her, and she has a lot going on right now."

More silence.

"So I won't be coming on Saturday. Just wanted to let you know." He paused. "I'm sorry. Please tell Sara I'm sorry and I wish you all the best." Jesus Christ, that sounded terrible. Sara was dying. What the hell was "all the best"? He pressed the heel of his hand to his forehead. "I'm sorry. Goodbye."

He ended the call, tossed his cell phone onto the table with a clatter and buried his face in his hands.

Fuck, he was an asshole. The worst, worthless piece of shit on the planet.

But he was right. Chloe was better off not knowing him. He was an unemployed bum who was such a loser his wife cheated on him, who drank too much and started brawls in bars. Who was terrified of a little girl and too cowardly to meet her.

His teeth ground together, his chest burned, and his throat ached. His muscles tightened to the point of pain. He pushed up off the couch and trudged over to the fridge for another brew.

What the hell was he going to do?

He looked around his empty house as he chugged back the malt beverage, letting the fizz burn its way down his esophagus. He needed to do something. Make some goddamn decisions. But just the thought of it overwhelmed him. Paralyzed him.

For the past twenty-four years of his life, he'd played hockey. Hockey had been his life. For the past twenty-four years, his coaches had told him what to do. What to eat and drink, when to sleep, what he needed to work on or practice more. He'd listened to them, followed their advice, played hard.

He'd had an agent who'd also told him what to do. A lawyer and a financial adviser. A fitness director, athletic therapists, team doctors. There'd always been someone there for him.

Now he had nothing. No one telling him what to do. No routine. No friends in the dressing room giving him shit or making him laugh. For the first time in his life . . . .he had no one.

Feeling lower than a snake's belly in a wheel rut, he drained the beer, clinked the bottle down onto the marble counter along with the others and yanked open the fridge to get another. He carried that back over to the couch where he threw himself down and grabbed the remote for the TV.

Not that he even wanted to watch TV, but the fucking silence in this house was making him nuts.

He tried to ignore the bleak, helpless feeling that tightened his chest as he surfed through a gazillion channels. The hopeless feeling that nothing was ever going to be right again; a dark, creeping feeling of doom that clawed at his insides.

He should have had the first knee surgery sooner. Years ago when it started bothering him. They'd told him . . . warned him . . . he'd been an idiot, invincible and determined to keep going. When he'd finally had the first surgery, it had helped. But not for long. Two more surgeries and he'd finally had to accept that his knee was fucked and he was in too much pain to play. His game was suffering and he wasn't helping the team. That was the worst part . . . letting his team down.

Fuck.

He slumped down into the couch and drank more beer, watching a rerun of *Die Hard* for about the hundredth time.

The sharp peal of his doorbell startled him. His head jerked up. Shit. Who was at his door? It better not be someone trying to save his soul because the mood he was in he was pretty sure he was beyond redemption. Hey, maybe he'd strip down and answer the door naked. That would scare them away.

Genius idea. He stood and whipped his T-shirt over his head, shoved down the athletic shorts he wore with no underwear, and headed to the door, leaving his clothes crumpled on the rug. Seeing the look on their faces would be the highlight of his shitty week. It actually made him grin.

He yanked open his front door, ready for their shock . . . but his own mouth dropped open at seeing Peyton Watt standing there.

His grin faded.

Her eyes went huge.

Her gaze tracked down his naked body all the way to his toes then back up. She met his eyes. "What the hell are you doing?" Her head moved from side to side in disbelief.

"Fuck me." He closed his eyes.

"No, thank you." She strode in past him. "Clearly you were expecting someone else, if that's what you want. Sorry if I'm interrupting other plans."

He stepped aside and moved behind the door, poking his head around it. Christ. "I wasn't expecting anyone," he growled. "I thought you were some Jehovah's Witnesses here to tell me about salvation."

She whirled around and stared at him. "Seriously? You answered the door naked, thinking it was Jehovah's Witnesses?"

"Uh, yeah." He rubbed the back of his head. "Seemed like a good idea at the time."

She gaped at him then burst out laughing.

Drew's jaw went slack, watching her. She stood on his shiny bamboo floor, the sun turning her blond hair to a glowing halo. She wore skinny jeans, red Converse, a flowy red and navy top with short sleeves, and she held the handle of her big purse in both hands in front of her thighs. Her face lit up with mirth was so incredibly beautiful he could only stare in awe, and her laughter was captivating.

He found his lips twitching in response.

"Oh, my God." She dropped her head forward briefly. "Can you imagine?"

"Uh . . . "

She bit her bottom lip and looked back at him, eyes gleaming.

For some reason she wasn't freaked out by his nudity, and he found that fascinating. He wasn't freaked out by nudity, either, usually; he was used to walking around dressing rooms and showers naked all the damn time. However, he wasn't a jerk.

"I should get dressed," he said, not moving.

"Okay. Right." She straightened her shoulders and narrowed her eyes. "I came here to ream you out. I am so pissed at you right now. You need clothes on for this." She turned her back on him and strolled into his living room. "Although I have to admit, your body is totally worth looking at."

His face heated. He still didn't move.

"Go on," she said, facing away from him. "Go get your clothes wherever they are. I'll wait here. And I won't peek."

He rolled his eyes and moved out from behind the door, closing it. "Thanks," he said dryly. "Appreciate it."

He strode behind her, past the kitchen and around the corner to the family room. He scooped up his shorts and stepped into them. Jesus. He was drunker than he'd realized. What the fuck had he been thinking?

He nabbed his T-shirt and carried it to the living room where Peyton waited. She could probably handle his bare chest. "Okay," he said. "I'm decent."

"Oh yes, you are," she said appreciatively as she turned. She took in his chest as he pulled the shirt on over his head. "Very decent."

He'd heard his share of compliments from women. Yeah, he was in good shape. He hadn't been working out over the past few months and he'd been drinking too much booze and eating too much junk food, but it wasn't like he'd been doing nothing—he'd played a lot of rounds of golf and done a lot of water-skiing and biking at Dougie's lake home in Wisconsin. So he hadn't put on weight or gone all flabby. Although if he kept up the lack of work-outs and proper diet, that was no doubt where he was headed. Fat old guy with a beer belly and skinny legs.

Christ.

Anyway, he was used to admiration from women, and for some reason he *really* liked it from her, but her praise made him actually feel guilty for taking his body for granted. Just because he wasn't earning his living with it anymore didn't mean he shouldn't take care of it. He'd been abusing it lately.

"Come in," he said shortly. "I was just having a beer." He turned back to the kitchen.

"Or six." She eyed the empties on the counter. Her gaze lifted to his face. "Is this how you spend your time now?"

His gut burned. "Yeah," he said shortly. "It is, actually."

She sighed and set her purse onto the island then walked into the family room and dropped into one of the armchairs. "Is that why you think you shouldn't meet Chloe?"

He resumed his seat on the couch. "Partly."

"I came here to give you shit and tell you that you can't change your mind now. But I'm kind of having second thoughts, too." She glanced back at the empty beer bottles. "Drinking to excess in the afternoon and answering the door naked. Not exactly appropriate paternal behavior."

"Chloe's not here," he muttered. "Also, I'm not hurting anyone. It was just a stupid prank."

"It makes me question your judgment."

"My judgment is fine," he snapped.

"Really." She lifted an eyebrow. "You'll forgive me if I disagree."

"Look. I'm going through a rough time right now. I can't do this."

"Why not?"

How could he explain it to her? His life was such a black hole already. And he was getting into a situation that was going to end with death, and everyone was going to be brokenhearted, and that scared the shit out of him. How was he going to comfort Chloe when he was so messed up himself? How could he have a relation-ship with her when he couldn't maintain relationships with anyone else? His wife rejected him. His team was playing on without him.

After his long silence Peyton said, "Look, I don't know what your problem is, but you can't do that to Chloe now. Sara already told her about you. She's overjoyed. In shock, too, but she definitely wants to meet you. It will crush her if you change your mind." She paused and when she spoke again her voice wasn't as steady or confident. "Despite my doubts about you, I can't let you do that to her."

Drew looked at her and when their eyes met he saw the tears shining there. "You really love her, don't you?"

"Of course I do."

How would he feel if one of his siblings was dying? He tried to imagine it. Thinking about Dustin dying, leaving his wife, Megan, with their two kids . . . yeah, he loved his nieces and nephews . . . maybe he hadn't spent enough time with them over the years. Quick trips home at Christmas and in the summer when everyone got together. Every time he saw the kids they'd grown up more and more. "Life is short."

She gave him a strange look. "Yes. It is."

"Fuck." He scrubbed a hand over his face. "I'm an asshole."

"Right now I agree with you." She tipped her head to one side. "Are you okay, Drew?"

"Of course I'm okay."

Her chin lowered. "Huh."

She didn't believe him. And he didn't blame her. He was drunk at five o'clock on a Wednesday afternoon, taking his clothes off to answer the door, reneging on a promise he'd made to his daughter —the first promise he'd ever made her and he'd let her down. Already.

"I'm sorry," he said quietly. "I guess I got a little freaked out by everything."

"You're not the only one." She leaned her head back against the chair. "Believe me, you're not the only one."

"How are you doing this?" he asked. "How are you keeping your shit together? You seem pretty composed."

"Ha. I'm a mess."

"You don't look like a mess." *You look pretty damn gorgeous.* Yeah, that was appropriate. *Not.*

"My boss is pissed at me for being away from work right now. I'm doing some work remotely, talking to clients, working on strategies for a new client. I'm getting stuff done, but it's not good enough for him."

"What do you do?"

She smiled. "You don't know?"

"I didn't investigate you. Just Sara."

"Ah. Right. I work for Sentinel. We're an online reputation management company. I'm a Director of Customer Success, and I work with a number of corporate clients."

"Reputation management? Is that what it sounds like?"

"Yes. Our customers range from individuals to Fortune 500 companies. We're kind of part PR gurus, part tech experts. Our services are designed to help people build and maintain a positive image online. We hunt down defamatory and unflattering web content and drive it off the first pages of web searches and replace it with positive information. Our company does even more than that, by helping our clients build relationships with their clients, monitoring online activity, and training them to be able to respond to negative comments and build positive content."

"Sounds cool."

"I love it. I moved to New York to take this job with Sentinel, one of the biggest reputation management companies. It hasn't gone quite like I expected, but I love my job and I'm getting great experience. Anyway, I'm here because Sara and Chloe need me, and I'm trying to help out. Meanwhile, I'm up till midnight answering emails and trying to keep my boss from having a myocardial infarction and stop our clients from panicking or deserting us. And my sister is dying." She rolled her lips inward briefly and closed her eyes. "You know all those stages of grief?"

"Yeah."

"They don't happen linearly. I thought I was past the denial stage, but I keep going back there. I keep thinking this isn't really happening. She isn't really going to die. It's just not possible. She's a young, healthy woman with so much life ahead of her." Her voice broke. "It's just not possible."

Drew's heart constricted.

"I'm trying to be strong and not fall apart for Sara's sake. But it's fucking killing me."

"Jesus," he muttered.

"Chloe's stressed, too. She knows what's happening. Her mom is dying. She has to be terrified. I need to be there for her, so she knows she won't be alone."

"Will you have her? After . . . ?"

"Yes. I'm her guardian. I see Chloe changing, losing some of her usual spirit. She loves to dance, and they got her signed up for all her usual classes, but she's talking about quitting. I know she wants to be with her mom."

"Understandable."

"Yes, totally. But after . . . we'll need to get her back into a routine."

"You live in a different city."

"I know." Her breasts rose and fell with her deep intake of air. He shouldn't be looking at her chest. But it was hard not to. "I haven't figured everything out yet."

"Moving to another city is a big change for someone whose mother just died."

"God, I know. I know." She shook her head abruptly and sat up straight. "Well. I didn't come here to cry on your shoulder. I came here to kick your ass."

"You almost got to kick my *bare* ass."

She bit her lip on a smile. "Yeah."

"Well, consider me ass-whooped."

"You'll meet Chloe?"

"Yeah." He shoved a hand through his hair, pushing it off his face. It fell back over his forehead immediately. "I will. If you can keep your shit together, I can, too."

"Well, you're the only one who knows this is just an act. I'm that close"—she held up thumb and forefinger nearly touching—"to losing it."

"It's a good act. And hey, I've done that whole 'fake it till you make it' thing. When I first got drafted into the NHL, every day I knew they'd made a huge mistake. I was playing with the big boys, the real deal, and I was terrified. I had to put on a lot of bluster and bravado so they didn't just run me over on the ice and leave me lying there bleeding."

She nodded.

"Sometimes faking it helps us feel like we're really doing it," he added. "We can convince ourselves."

"Yeah. That's true."

He knew how she felt. He was *that* close to losing his shit, too. In fact, if she hadn't shown up at his door, he wasn't sure . . .

"Do you have to get home?" he asked.

"Um. I guess so, yeah. Why?"

"Just wondered if maybe you wanted to get some dinner with me." He shrugged. "Just sitting here alone tonight."

She gazed at him, her expression not changing. He sensed her mind working. "Never mind," he said. "Stupid idea. I just . . . "

"Let me call home," she said softly. "I'll order a pizza for Chloe and Sara. There's a nurse with Sara right now."

She rose and walked over to her purse on the island. He listened to her talk to Chloe, telling her she'd be home in a while, and that she'd call and order pizza. Then she did that, using a credit card to pay for it. She was sweet with Chloe, briskly efficient with the pizza restaurant.

She probably felt sorry for him. He fucking hated pity. On the other hand, the idea of being alone filled him with dread. So he'd take her pity date. Not that it was a date, like a romantic date— just a . . . pity date.

Great. He was even pathetic.

CHAPTER 7

Peyton slipped her cell phone back into the pocket inside her purse. "Okay. Let's go."

Drew looked down at his T-shirt and shorts. "I should change."

"Okay, if you want." She shrugged. She assumed they weren't going anywhere fancy, so it didn't matter to her what he wore.

"Be right back."

He jogged upstairs.

She looked around the house. Really nice place. If it was an old house, it had been completely renovated. The kitchen wasn't super-huge, but generous, with dark wood cupboards and stainless-steel appliances including a gorgeous Subzero fridge. The empty beer bottles on the marble counter, cardboard pizza boxes stacked on the island, and dishes in the sink had her shaking her head.

She wandered over to the sliding doors and gazed out onto the deck with steps down to a patio and a large yard behind. Lots of room for a single guy. The deck was lovely but looked a little forlorn, the furniture bereft of cushions, no pots of flowers, and a barbecue under a plastic cover.

She turned back to the family room. While the living room

had looked pristine and a little sterile, albeit tastefully decorated in shades of cream, this room was lived in, with a pair of Nikes on the floor, a bunch of sports magazines and newspapers, and a book about exercise physiology.

Drew's footsteps thudded down the stairs and he reappeared, now wearing a pair of dark jeans and a white button-down shirt, whose cuffs he was turning back. It didn't appear he'd done anything with the longish hair that fell over his forehead or the days of beard stubble. "Okay," he said. "Ready."

Peyton picked up her purse. "I should probably drive."

He paused. "I'm not that drunk."

She lifted an eyebrow.

"Actually, there's a little place not far from here that I like . . . we can walk."

"Oh. Okay."

They strolled along the sidewalk beneath the leafy canopy provided by the big old trees, wrought iron-fenced rectangular beds of shrubs and flowers on one side; on the other, big old houses that she knew were worth millions of dollars each despite the unassuming ambience of the neighborhood. "I was surprised to see that you don't live very far from Sara."

"Yeah, I know. I was surprised, too." They walked on in silence for a moment. "Training camp started today."

She wasn't sure where that came from, but whatever. Then she realized . . . "This is the first one since you retired."

"Yeah. It was kinda getting to me."

"It must be hard, giving up something you love."

"Yep. I tried for the past few years to keep going, but in the end I was just making my knee worse."

"Is it painful?"

"Not all the time. I had a lot of rehab. Just doing certain things bothers it."

"I'm sorry."

"Hey, I'm not looking for pity. I've got enough of that for myself."

"Yes, I can I see you're riding the pity train. But the train has just arrived at the intersection of We All Have Problems and Suck It Up Buttercup."

He shot her a startled glance and then gave a choked laugh.

"Hey." She lifted one shoulder. "It's true. You said that the other day when we were talking in the kitchen. What happened since then?"

He scratched his chin. "I don't even know. I guess I just fell into a pity pit."

"It can be addicting, I know." She eyed him. "People use all kinds of coping mechanisms, and some aren't very healthy. Drugs, alcohol, self-pity. You can get yourself in trouble."

"I don't do drugs."

"Good to know," she said dryly.

"Okay, I get your point."

He directed her around the corner and they continued walking, this street busier with more traffic.

"Also, self-pity is not very attractive." Crap. Why did she say that? It made no difference to her how attractive he was. "In case you're having problems with the ladies," she added.

Which was doubtful, based on what she'd seen of him. Holy cannoli, the man was gorgeous, from the dark hair hanging over his forehead, his strong jaw with all that yummy stubble, wide, heavily muscled shoulders and chest, ripped abs and powerful thighs. Not to mention the package he'd had on display that she couldn't help but notice . . . whoa.

It had been a struggle to maintain her composure when he'd flung open the door to reveal him in all his naked glory, because all she'd wanted to do was stand and stare and possibly drool a little. She'd tingled in places she'd almost forgotten about.

"Yeah, that's not a problem," he confirmed with a hint of cocky attitude. Great. Not only was he a drunk, he was a womanizer.

He touched the small of her back as he came to a stop in front of a small restaurant and reached for the bright red door to open it for her. She walked into a long, narrow space with rough plaster walls and exposed wooden beams. A dark wood bar lined one wall.

Nope, it wasn't fancy, but nor was it a dive.

They were given an option of sitting on the patio, and Drew looked at her questioningly. "Sure," she said. "We won't have that many more patio days."

They were led out back to a charming, stone-paved area edged with shrubs, lots of hanging baskets overflowing with bright flowers, and Italian folk music drifting on the early evening breeze.

"This is really nice." She picked up her menu.

"Yeah, I like it. I come here a lot since it's so close and the food is great."

"I love little places like this that not many people know about."

"Yeah."

"Any suggestions of what to order?"

"Their pizza is fantastic. It's wood-fired. But their pastas are great, too, I like the pork ragu rigatoni."

"Major carbs."

"They have lots of salads."

"Mmm. They do. Tuscan kale Caesar salad sounds good."

"I'll get a pizza and you can try a piece."

She looked up at him and smiled. "Thanks. I'd like to try it."

"Would you like a glass of wine?" he asked.

"No, that's okay, I'm driving. But you go ahead."

"I'm okay. You were right. I drank a lot of beer today." He made a face.

"Are you an alcoholic?"

He choked and lowered his menu. "What?"

She held his gaze. "If you have a drinking problem, I need to know about it before you spend any time with Chloe."

"Christ." He frowned. "I drink, yeah, but it's not a problem."

She held his gaze.

He looked away. "Okay, I've been drinking a lot lately. But I'm not an alcoholic."

"I will never allow her to get into a car with someone who's been drinking."

"I would never do that," he said quietly. "I would never put her at risk in any way."

"Okay then, that's good." She paused. "I had to ask."

His thick eyebrows lowered over his eyes in an intense, brooding look that made her belly quiver. "I get that. I'm trying not to be insulted. I know you don't really know me at all."

The waitress appeared. Drew ordered appetizers of spiced olives and bread, and a pizza with fennel sausage, onions, and chili flakes. She requested the salad.

"So, let's get to know each other better," she said when the waitress stepped away. She tipped her head. "I know some basics about you . . . that you're Canadian. That you played your whole hockey career here in Chicago. That you were married for a couple of years but are now divorced, no other kids. Tell me something I don't know."

His gaze drifted away and across the patio. He said nothing.

She shifted in her chair and sank her teeth briefly into her bottom lip. Had she made him that uncomfortable?

"Okay, I'll tell you about me," she said. "I live in Chelsea, in Manhattan, in a tiny, expensive apartment. I don't have any really good friends in New York . . . some friends I go out with on weekends. My best friend from my childhood still lives here in Chicago and we're getting together this weekend."

"No husband or boyfriend?"

"No. I date, but it's mostly just for companionship. I'm a bit of a workaholic."

"Workaholic, huh."

"Yes. It's kind of funny. When Sara and I were kids, she was the overachiever who was always studying. I was kind of into boys and parties." She made a face. "But when she started her career, she changed . . . no, *she* didn't change. She just changed her priorities, I guess. She still wanted to succeed, obviously, but Chloe was the most important thing to her. She left a high-powered law firm to take a job as a corporate counsel."

Peyton hadn't totally understood Sara's change of heart when it came to her career. Although Peyton had liked to have fun in her teenage years, they'd both had firm plans for their future, including college degrees and successful careers. But Sara had a child, and Peyton didn't. Peyton never planned to have a family. She wasn't going to be one of those women who tried to balance work and life and had to compromise on both. She'd be there to give her all to her career.

"Yeah, she mentioned that."

"And I ended up the workaholic." She looked down and straightened the knife in front of her. "I hope I can put Chloe first."

"You will."

"I don't have time for a lot of hobbies," she continued so as not to get bogged down with emotion again. "But I run a few times a week, and I belong to a wine-tasting club that gets together once a month."

"Wine."

"Yes."

"You like red or white?"

"I like both."

"Thought maybe you were a teetotaler."

She grinned. "Did I sound all judgy about the booze?"

"Yeah."

"Sorry. I like my wine, believe me. But I'm a responsible drinker."

Drew grimaced. "Shot received."

She smiled at him. He wasn't stupid, anyway. "Okay, now you."

"Okay." He drew in a breath. "Outside of hockey and my hockey buddies, I don't have much going on. I used to work out a lot but I haven't been lately. I like golfing, so I've been doing that. I spent some time at home this summer with my parents. I do a kids hockey camp there every year, and my knee was good enough to be able to do that. I hung out with my friend Dougie and his wife and kids at their summer place. They have a boat and we did some skiing and fishing. Swimming. I...work with Paterson House." He paused. "Except I haven't done much recently."

"Tell me about Paterson House."

"It's a youth center that encourages kids to get involved with sports. Kids who wouldn't be able to afford it. I've done some fund-raising events for them and I used to go hang out and skate with the kids when I could."

Her heart softened in her chest as he talked about working with kids at Paterson House and his hockey camp. *This.* This was what she wanted to know about him, things that made him a good man, a man good enough to be Chloe's dad.

"You and your wife never had kids," she commented.

"Nope. We bought that house last year because I thought maybe we would, but . . . well, things didn't work out."

"I'm sorry."

"Hey, don't be sorry. It's probably for the best. Come to think of it, you and I might be kind of the same. I was pretty focused on hockey, hockey, hockey. If I wasn't playing, I was practicing or working out, and we were away on road trips a lot. Christy had to make her own life, and when I retired, I discovered it didn't include me."

"Well." She eyed him. "It does take two to make a relationship work. It doesn't sound like she was trying very hard, either."

The corners of his mouth lifted. "Thanks for that."

"Well, she cheated on you, right? That's not exactly trying to make a relationship work."

"You're right."

"Did you cheat on her?"

His jaw loosened. "Jesus. You don't pull any punches, do you? First you ask me if I'm an alcoholic, now am I a cheater."

She bit her lip. "I *have* been told I'm blunt. It just saves time, rather than beating around the bush."

"Right to the point," he murmured. "At least people know where they stand with you."

"There is that," she admitted. "I'm not one to be passive-aggressive."

"I'll consider that a positive."

She smiled across the table at him as the waitress reappeared with a bright- colored pottery bowl full of olives and a plate of bread. She set down a small bowl of golden olive oil, dark balsamic vinegar swirled in it.

"Do you like olives?" Drew asked, picking up his napkin.

"I love olives."

"Excellent. Help yourself. I got them to share. The bread, too."

She picked up an olive and popped it in her mouth, enjoying the salty tang with a little heat. "Yum. These are good." She paused. "They'd be really good with a nice glass of Sangiovese."

"Hey, I offered to spring for a glass of wine."

"You don't have to pay for dinner."

"Of course I'm paying for dinner. I invited you."

She wanted to argue, but bit her tongue. No sense making it into a bigger deal than it was. "Okay, so should I ask about your finances?"

He laughed, and his face was transformed from that dark and broody look into sexy charm. "Wouldn't surprise me if you did. Oh wait, wasn't that part of the credit check?"

"We don't actually know what's in your bank accounts," she said wryly, reaching for another olive. "But that doesn't really matter. Your character is more important than how much money you have."

He narrowed his eyes a little at her. "You sure about that?"

"Sara's already told you she doesn't want anything from you. The only reason she found you is because you're a little famous or something. If you'd been Drew Sellers, refuse collector, she might not have stumbled across you. But if she had, it wouldn't have mattered."

"Forgive me if I'm just a little skeptical of that. Remember, I know your background, too. You and Sara grew up in a pretty privileged environment."

She let his words sink in. "Well. That's true. But we're not snobs."

He lifted his chin then nodded. "Okay. Also . . . I'm not a little famous. I'm a *lot* famous."

She smirked at him. "I'd never heard of you. You can't be that famous."

"Not a hockey fan, huh?"

"Nope."

"Sad."

"Okay, you may be famous in some circles. Some kind of rough, sporty circles."

He laughed and the sound tugged at something deep down inside her. "Right."

"Are those your own teeth?"

He flashed them at her. They were perfect and white. "Yes. My mother made sure I always wore a mouth guard."

"Good for her."

Their meals arrived and they busied themselves with napkins and cutlery. The waitress refilled water glasses and Drew lifted a slice of pizza onto a small plate and passed it to her. She took a bite and her eyes widened as she chewed. "Oh, my God, that is so good."

"Right?"

Spicy sausage and a tangy tomato sauce, melty mozzarella all mingled in a delicious combination. "The crust is awesome," she said, trying not to moan.

"Maybe you should have ordered your own pizza," he teased.

"Maybe I should have. But the salad's really good, too. Great dressing."

"Now you know why it's one of my favorite places."

She definitely knew. And it said something about him because this wasn't an ultra-snobby expensive fine dining place, nor was it a fast food chain or a trendy "see and be seen" kind of place, all of which would have told her something different about him. She liked that it was unpretentious with quality food at affordable prices and a charming atmosphere.

He was unpretentious and charming and, she was pretty sure, a quality person, despite her earlier doubts. Sara was right that Peyton was often a quick and accurate judge of character, and the more she got to know Drew, the more she liked him. Despite a definite lapse in judgment by answering the door naked.

He'd made her laugh, though. And she *really* liked that.

Okay, it was good that she liked this man because he was going to be in Chloe's life. To what extent, she didn't know. But he was Chloe's father.

"So you *are* coming tomorrow?" she asked quietly between bites of salad.

"Yeah," he muttered, head dipping. "I'll be there. Sorry for being such a dick."

"I appreciate the apology. If not the language."

He glanced up.

She grinned. "Hey, I can take it. I work with a lot of men. But Chloe . . . you might want to tone down the F bombs and such."

"Ergh. I'll try."

"Though I'm pretty sure she's heard them." Peyton rolled her eyes. "Kids grow up so fast these days. Dear Lord, she talks about her friends having boyfriends."

"Shut up." Drew stared at her in horror. "*She* doesn't have a boyfriend, does she?"

"No." Peyton smiled. "But she's really pretty."

"I don't give a fuck. She's way too young for that."

"And she's starting to develop."

Drew's eyes widened and his mouth dropped open. "Christ." "Am I scaring you away?"

"Hell, yeah." He waved a hand. "Don't worry. I can control my F bombs, as you put it. Just . . . Jesus."

"And she's grown a whole lot taller since the last time I saw her, which wasn't that long ago."

Amusement at Drew's discomfort had her almost laughing out loud. It was so damn cute.

"You know what, Drew?"

"Uh, what?"

She leaned forward. "You're going to be okay."

He pressed his lips together then closed his eyes briefly, his shoulders tense. "Sure."

CHAPTER 8

Drew arrived at Sara's home on Saturday nervous as a rookie goalie on a Gretzky breakaway. He wiped his palms on his khaki pants as he waited on the veranda for someone to answer the door. The neighborhood was quiet, a man watering flowers across the street, a dog barking in the distance.

He was about to meet his daughter. It was fucking insane.

Peyton opened the door. "Hi, Drew."

"Hey."

She invited him in and he entered the house, cool, quiet, the air scented with something that smelled like raspberry lemonade. His gaze fell on the girl standing at the bottom of the stairs, leaning on the newel post.

She was beautiful. Long brown hair parted in the middle fell in waves past her shoulders. She gazed at him with a solemn expression, her dark eyes wide and clear. She was probably about five feet tall, slender, wearing jeans and a red T-shirt with the graphic #LikeAGirl on the front of it.

He'd seen her picture. He knew what she looked like. But this real-live girl standing in front of him with perfect creamy skin, shiny hair, and wise eyes that studied him as much as he studied her was heartbreakingly gorgeous. His heart banged against his sternum and his palms went even soggier.

"This is Chloe," Peyton said unnecessarily, seeming freakishly composed. "Chloe, this is Drew Sellers."

Chloe moved forward and Drew froze. Was he supposed to hug her?

But she extended a hand in a polite gesture and he took it. It felt so small in his. "Hi, Chloe."

"Hi."

Now she was closer he could see that her eyes weren't brown; they were hazel . . . like his, brown with flecks of green and gold.

"Are you really my dad?" she asked, her forehead creasing.

Christ. He shoved a hand into his hair. "Yeah. Weird, huh?"

Her lips quirked. "It is kind of weird. I Googled you."

Well, then. "Did you find anything you want to ask me about?"

"Well . . . my mom told me some stuff about you. So I already know you're divorced. And you don't have any other kids. But what about that time you got suspended because you hurt some guy?"

Drew narrowed his eyes and tipped his head. "You mean when I cross-checked Markham three years ago?"

"Yeah."

"Your Google skills are impressive, Chloe," Peyton commented. "Drew, come in. Can I get you coffee?"

"Sure." A beer would've been better but he was pretty sure Peyton wasn't going to be offering that. They moved into the living room where Sara was in the reclining chair again.

"Hi!" She greeted him with a tired smile. "You're here. Come sit."

He sat on the couch and Chloe took a chair across from him, tucking one leg under her, still studying him.

"Chloe was just grilling me about a bad play I made a few years ago," he told Sara.

KELLY JAMIESON

Sara turned wide eyes on her daughter. "What do you know about hockey?"

"Lots." She tossed her hair back. "Jason and Tyler play hockey."

Drew's eyebrows pinched together. They better not be "boyfriends." "That hit was supposed to be to his shoulder," he said. "He moved and I got his head. It was an accident, but the rules are the rules and I had to be penalized."

Chloe nodded. "Jason and Tyler think it's sick that I have a famous dad."

"That means . . ." Sara started to explain it to Drew.

"I get it." He smiled. "Does that give you some good cred?"

"Oh, yeah."

Drew shifted on the couch. So far, so good, but this was still awkward as hell. "So you just started seventh grade, right?"

"Yeah." She made a face.

"How's that going?"

"Good. I like school. Mostly."

"What don't you like?"

She tipped her head. "I don't like mean kids. I don't like Mr. Conridge."

"Math teacher," Sara supplied.

"I also don't really like math."

"No? I was good at math. What's your favorite class?"

"I like social studies."

"Huh. What are you learning about?"

"Major societies in history."

"Sounds fascinating." *Not really.*

Peyton walked in and handed him a cup of coffee. Black. She remembered. "Thanks." He smiled at her.

"Anything for you, Miss Chloe?" Peyton looked at her niece.

"I'll have a coffee."

"No, you won't."

"How old do I have to be to drink coffee?"

"Twenty-four."

Drew grinned at Peyton's response.

"As if." Chloe rolled her eyes. "I'll get myself some juice. Mom, do you need anything?" Chloe hopped off the chair.

"I'm good. Thanks, sweetie."

She disappeared with a hop and skip.

Drew rubbed his forehead then sipped his coffee. "She's beautiful," he said quietly.

Sara nodded. "Yes. She is."

He wasn't sure how he was supposed to feel about Chloe. He wasn't sure how he actually did feel . . . *terrified* would probably be the most accurate word.

He knew nothing about tween girls. About what they learned in school, how they dressed, what they were interested in. Maybe if he'd had a twelve-year-old son, he'd feel more at ease. They'd talk about sports and . . . and . . . okay maybe that wouldn't be much better.

Chloe shot back into the room with a burst of energy, holding a glass of orange juice. She set it on the table and bounced herself into the chair again.

"I hear you like to dance," Drew said, pouncing on an idea for conversation.

Her face closed up. "It's okay."

"Chloe." Sara spoke gently. "You love dancing."

"I don't want to go this year."

"Why not, sweetie?"

Chloe looked away. "It takes up too much time."

An uncomfortable tension materialized. Drew bent his head then said, "You want to be with your mom, right?"

Chloe bit her lip and met his eyes. And he saw the fear there. Then she looked away again. "I have a lot more homework this year, and I want to try out for jazz band."

Drew clenched his jaw. It wasn't his business. Which was fucking weird because she was his daughter, but he wasn't going to make the mistake of thinking that walking in here and meeting her for the first time gave him any rights whatsoever. He looked back and forth between Sara and Peyton, the atmosphere in the room heavy. "I think your mom wants you to do something you enjoy," he ventured.

"Are you worried about how you're going to get there, Chloe?" Peyton asked. "Because I'm here and I'll take you to dance classes."

"You're going back to New York," Chloe burst out. "But it doesn't matter because I *don't want to go.*" She leaped up and hurtled out of the room.

Drew watched her fly up the stairs then turned back to the two women. "Well, that went well," he muttered, rubbing the back of his neck.

"She's overwhelmed," Peyton said quietly.

"This is all a lot for her to process." Sara closed her eyes, her lips in a sad curve. "Let's not argue about it with her anymore. If she doesn't want to go, she doesn't have to go. I just don't want her spending all her time sitting here watching me die. I want her to have a normal routine."

Drew swallowed. "Could I go talk to her?"

Sara's eyes opened and met his. She nodded. "You can try. Good luck."

"I'll show you her room." Peyton rose to her feet. She climbed the stairs in front of him and walked to the second bedroom door on the left, which was closed. She gestured at it then turned and squeezed past him in the hall to go back downstairs.

Drew pulled in a breath through his nose, head tipped back, and knocked on the door.

"Go away."

He smiled. "It's me, Chloe. Can I come in?"

After a short pause, she said, "Okay."

He opened the door and entered the room, a generous bedroom with a twin bed against the far wall where Chloe sat cross-legged holding a cushion. The yellow walls were covered with multiple framed pictures and posters, the furniture all white.

The cover on the bed was a large floral print in bright yellow, red, blue, and green, and the rug on the hardwood floor had similar colors.

He looked around, nodding. For some reason he'd expected pink. "I like your room."

"Thanks."

Not very forthcoming. He approached the desk under the window and pulled the chair out to sit.

"This all sucks, doesn't it?" he said quietly.

She heaved a huge sigh. "Yeah."

"I don't have any great advice for you. I've never been in this situation. I can't even imagine what it's like."

"That's okay. I don't need advice."

"Of course you don't. You're twelve years old."

"Almost. My birthday is in two weeks."

"October what?"

"October fifth."

"Do you have big plans for a party?"

She bent her head. "No."

"I guess it's hard to think about a party when your mom's not feeling well."

"She said I could have a party. But she's not well enough for it."

"I'm sure Peyton would help."

"Yeah. I had this idea . . . there's this place that comes to the house with a whole bunch of video games."

"That would be cool."

"We'd still have to get food and a cake. I love birthday cake."

She looked so forlorn at the idea of not having a cake on her birthday. "I'm sure you'll have cake."

Chloe sighed.

"My sister Shawna loves birthday cake. It has to have multicolored sprinkles. Even though she's thirty-two."

One corner of Chloe's mouth lifted. "Oh. How many sisters do you have?"

"One sister. I also have two brothers."

"Whoa. That's a big family."

"Yeah, it was pretty crazy growing up."

"That would be kind of nice," she said wistfully, plucking at the cushion she held. "I always wanted a brother or sister." She paused. "And a dad."

"I'm sorry we never knew about each other."

"It used to make me mad, sometimes."

"At me?"

"At both of you. It made me mad that you didn't care enough about me to even find out who each other was. I know that doesn't really make sense because you had no idea I was going to be born, but that's how I felt."

"I get that." He nodded.

"Sometimes I didn't believe my mom when she said she had no way to find you. I figured you were a criminal or something and she didn't want me to know. Then sometimes I thought maybe you were like, the prime minister of Canada or something and that was why it had to be secret."

Drew couldn't help the laugh that burst out of him. "That would be quite a scandal."

"It happens." She shrugged.

"True enough. Well, I'm just me. This has been a shock for me, too." He looked across the room. "Do you want to talk about your mom?"

She hesitated. "I don't know."

"If you do, I'll listen. I'm not very good at talking about my feelings, but I can listen."

She smoothed a hand over the bright cotton duvet cover. "It makes me really mad." She huffed out a breath. "At the world. At God. At the doctors. At everyone, pretty much."

"Yeah." Hence the outburst earlier. He couldn't blame her. Not a bit. "I've been kind of mad at the world lately, too."

She eyed him. "Why?"

He leaned back in the chair. "I hurt my knee. They tried three surgeries to fix it and it didn't work. So I can't play hockey anymore. I love hockey. It's all I know how to do."

Her face softened.

"And my marriage ended."

"My friend Tyler's parents got divorced. They were fighting all the time, yelling and throwing things."

"Ugh."

"Yeah. Tyler hated it. When they finally told him they were splitting up, he was happy. Well, not *happy*. It's still kind of awful because they hate each other so much and when he's with his mom, his mom asks him questions about his dad and his new girlfriend and calls the girlfriend a skanky whore. Meanwhile, his dad says his mom is a lying, money-hungry bitch."

"Jesus." He clapped a hand over his mouth. "I mean, jeez."

"Is your divorce like that?"

"No." He shook his head. "We didn't even argue much. We had our lawyers work things out, signed some papers, and never talk to each other now."

"Well, that's still sad."

"Yeah, it is. So that's my life. Sad."

"And then you found out about me."

He smiled. "That's not sad."

She gazed back at him as if not sure to believe him. Then she nodded. "Sorry I had a little fit down there."

"We all have fits. Part of growing up is learning to keep them inside. Until we're alone or with someone we can trust and we can blow off steam. I'm probably not the best one to learn from, though, since I still blow up sometimes." *And start fights in bars.*

"Did you get in fights when you played hockey?" She leaned forward, eyes alert.

He smiled. "Sometimes. When you're passionate about something, sometimes you get carried away by emotion."

She tipped her head. "Is that why you and your wife didn't fight? You weren't passionate enough?"

He stared at Chloe. "Uh . . . yeah, that could be true." Christ.

Chloe nodded sagely. "I heard Grandma and Grandpa arguing once. I think it was because he'd made plans for them and didn't ask her and it was with some people she didn't like . . . they ended up *kissing*. And they were *old*." She wrinkled her nose. "Really old."

"That's another hard thing you've gone through. Losing your grandparents."

"Yeah." Her bottom lip pushed out. "I was really sad about that."

"Well, I can already see that you're a very strong young lady."

She gave him another doubtful look then dropped her gaze. "Thanks."

"So about the dancing . . . your mom says you don't have to go if you don't want to."

Chloe didn't look happy about that. "I feel guilty."

Drew's forehead tightened. "Why?"

"Because I *do* want to go. But I shouldn't." Her bottom lip quivered. "I should be here with Mom."

"Your mom wants you to be happy."

"How can I be happy when she's dying?" she cried.

Fuck, wrong thing to say. Wrong, wrong, wrong. "You can't." He held up a hand "You can't. I'm just saying, she wants you to have as normal a life as you can."

"Maybe I could go to one class. Like, just hip-hop."

He nodded and pursed his lips, not wanting to push things. "That sounds reasonable."

Chloe swiped her fingertips down the sides of her nose as if catching tears. "Yeah."

"Maybe sometime I could take you to class. Is there a way to watch? I'd like to see you dance."

She gave him that look again, a penetrating, wise look that was much older than her years. "Yes, you can watch. There are big windows in the dance studios. Lots of moms stay. My mom did, when she took me."

Was it smart to make plans with Chloe when he had no idea where things were going? He'd agreed to meet her but he'd tried not to think of much beyond that. Did he want a relationship with her? Did *she* want one with *him*? Both their worlds were in a state of chaos, which wasn't very conducive to forming bonds.

Or maybe it *was*. Maybe both of them experiencing all this upheaval in their lives could find common ground.

"Want to go back down and finish your orange juice?"

Her top lip lifted in a tiny sneer and she shrugged. "Sure."

He bit back a smile at the attitude and stood. She slid off the bed and tossed the cushion down.

He squinted at the Japanese anime posters on the wall as they walked out. There'd been a time in his life when he'd been into anime.

The faint sound of footsteps below them caught his attention. For some reason he had a feeling Peyton had stayed upstairs with them. Had she listened to their conversation?

"D'you like video games?" he asked Chloe as she bounced down the stairs in front of him.

"Yeah. I have an Xbox."

"Cool. Me, too."

"Xbox One?"

"Yeah."

He glimpsed Peyton taking a seat in the living room as they reached the bottom of the stairs. She turned toward them and smiled. "Hey."

Chloe went straight to her mom and slid into the recliner with her. With the two of them being so tiny, there was ample room for them. She laid her head on her mom's shoulder and the look on Sara's face made Drew's chest clench; her smile sweet and full of love.

"I'll go to hip-hop class, Mom," Chloe said. "It's my favorite."

"Okay." Sara stroked Chloe's long hair back from her face.

Drew glanced at Peyton. She had her fingertips pressed to her mouth. As if sensing his gaze on her she turned to him and their eyes met. "Thank you," she mouthed.

He lifted his chin.

"Can I show Drew my Xbox games?" Chloe asked her mom.

"Of course."

Chloe rolled out of the chair, careful of her mother. "My games are in the family room," she said. "This way."

She led the way through the dining room, past the counter that separated dining room from kitchen, down a narrow hall and into a bright room at the back of the house.

A big brown leather sectional on one wall faced white built-in bookshelves, an enormous television in the center. Chloe opened cupboard doors beneath the TV and pulled out gaming consoles.

"This is a great room for gaming," he commented. "Does your mom play with you?"

"Nah. She hates video games. So does Peyton."

"Well, then. What am I going to beat you at?" He rubbed his hands together.

Her laughter squeezed his heart. She pulled her long hair back into a tail behind her neck and released it. "You can't beat me at Dark Club."

"That's probably true since I've never heard of it." She wasn't playing Call of Duty or Minecraft. Which was probably a good thing. "Bring it, honey bun."

CHAPTER 9

"What were they talking about up there?" Sara quietly asked Peyton.

Peyton rolled her eyes and moved to sit closer to Sara. She only felt a little guilty about eavesdropping because she had to make sure Chloe was safe. "He was really good with her, Sara."

"Yeah?" She sucked briefly on her bottom lip. "That's good."

"I shouldn't have listened."

"No, you have to! We don't know him. Am I being paranoid and overprotective?"

"Of course not." She paused. "She was talking to him about her birthday. She wants to have a party."

"I know." She sighed. "I want her to have a party. I just have no clue what to do. Obviously, I don't think I'm up to elaborate decorations and food or even having a bunch of girls for a sleepover."

"She mentioned this place that brings video games to the house . . . I can check into it. And get a cake."

"Oh. That would be so good. Thank you, Pey."

"Of course. Want me to go check on them?" Sara bit a finger-nail. "Maybe just have a peek."

"Okay. I'll do that and then I'll bring a few more of your things down to the den." They'd started the process of moving Sara downstairs, which the hospice nurse had definitely supported.

She poked her head into the family room to see them engrossed in the screen. "You have to try to beat me to the start line in order to earn an extra rep," Chloe told Drew seriously, and he nodded equally as intently.

"How's it going?" Peyton asked.

"Good." Chloe waved a hand.

Drew looked up at her and winked.

Her lower belly did a flutter. Damn, that was a sexy wink.

She gave her head a shake. "I'll be up and down stairs bringing some more of your mom's things down."

Drew frowned and fixed his attention on her. "What things?"

"We're moving her bedroom to the den. It'll be easier on her than stairs."

"What things?" he asked again. "You need help?"

"Um, well . . . I can manage small stuff, but we're not sure about how to get the bed down. My friend Nik is coming shortly and she's going to help."

"You can't move a bed." He was probably right. "I'll help." He stood.

Chloe pouted.

Peyton motioned to him to sit. "I'll get everything off the bed and then I'll let you know when. You two play your game thingy."

One corner of his mouth quirked up. "Game thingy. Okay."

She headed upstairs to Sara's room. They weren't going to move all her clothes, obviously, just the few things she wore these days. She only needed her bed and nightstand moved; they could make do otherwise with what was there. Peyton packed up toiletries in Sara's bedroom and carried them to the downstairs bathroom.

The doorbell rang and she hurried to answer it, expecting Nik. She threw open the door and her best friend from high school stood on the veranda. "Hey!"

Nikeesha's smile flashed white in her dark brown face. She threw her arms around Peyton and they gave each other a big hug. "Hey, you."

"Come in."

Nikeesha entered the house that was like a second home to her after all the time she'd spent there as a teenager. "How are things?" she asked in a low voice, concern etching her forehead.

"Not great," Peyton whispered. She jerked her head. "Sara's in the living room. Come say hi."

Nik bit her lip and walked with her into the other room. "Look who's here," Peyton said to Sara.

Sara smiled. "Hi, Nik."

Nik crossed to Sara and bent to kiss her cheek. "Hi, gorgeous. How are you feeling today?"

"Tired, as usual lately."

Peyton's stomach cramped. Sara's condition seemed to be deteriorating rapidly, even in the few days she'd been there.

"Ah, I'm sorry, hon. What can I do?"

"You can help me move things down from the bedroom," Peyton said, striving for a cheerful tone. "But first come say hi to Chloe. And you can meet Drew."

Nik's big dark eyes widened. "Right. Drew. Gotta meet this dude." Peyton had filled her in on the situation on the phone the other day.

Chloe looked up as they entered the room and a smile beamed out. "Nik! Hi!"

"Hi, love bug. Watcha doin'?"

"Teaching Drew . . . my dad"—her voice faltered a little but she forged on— "how to play Dark Club."

Peyton watched Drew rise from the sectional and extend a hand to Nik. "Hi. I'm Drew Sellers."

"I can't believe this!" Nik said in an unfamiliar breathless voice.

Peyton frowned. "Uh, Drew, this is my friend, Nikeesha Harris."

"Pleased to meet you, Nikeesha."

"Drew Sellers!" Nik went on. "I am such a fan of yours!"

Peyton gave her friend a scrunched-face look. "What?"

Drew's lips curved with amusement. "You find that hard to believe?" he said to Peyton. "I did have a few fans."

"You had lots of fans!" Nik protested, her hand on her chest. "You still do!"

"Peyton never heard of me, so she thinks I'm nobody."

"I never said that." Peyton frowned at him. Oh, wait. He was teasing.

"My girl's not a hockey fan," Nik confirmed to him. "But I am."

"Since when?" Peyton demanded.

"You've been gone for years, Peybay. I've acquired a taste for hockey since you've been gone. Not to mention Lagavulin Scotch and hot yoga."

Drew grinned.

Peyton shook her head at her friend, smiling reluctantly.

"Let's play more," Chloe said, tugging Drew's arm.

"You ready to move the bed?" he asked Peyton.

"Give us ten minutes."

She linked her arm with Nik's and walked her out and up the stairs.

"He's gorgeous," Nik said, patting her chest over her heart. "I mean, I knew he was, but in person . . . sweet baby Jesus. That smile. Those eyes. Those muscles."

"Here, let me wipe the drool off your face." Nik laughed. "Did I tell you I saw him naked?"

Nik stopped and set a hand on the door frame, swaying, her mouth open. "Say what?"

Peyton grinned. "I went to his place to talk to him the other day and he answered the door buck naked."

"Lord, have mercy."

"Oh, yeah. Talk about drooling."

"Why does that never happen to me?" Nik pushed away from the door. "You see lots of naked men."

"Yeah, but they're usually unconscious." Nikeesha was an anesthesiologist. "True."

"I can't believe he's Chloe's father." Nik paused, her face going serious. "That's just crazy."

"Right? We had dinner last night."

Nik froze and gaped at her. "Naked times and then dinner. What is happening here?"

"Nothing's happening here." Peyton waved a hand. "I had to convince him not to change his mind about seeing Chloe. He was freaking out about it, I think." She frowned. "I'm a little worried about him."

"What? Why?"

Peyton sucked in her bottom lip. "He seems pretty down about having to retire. And about his divorce."

"He's divorced? I didn't know that!"

"What kind of hockey stalker are you?"

Nikeesha grinned. "I'm not that big a fan that I stalk their every move. Seriously, what happened?"

"His wife cheated on him. When I got to his place, he was drunk, all by himself."

"Oh." Nik pursed her full lips.

"He asked me to have dinner with him but I think it was because he was lonely."

"Oh, that poor, poor man. He needs companionship."

Peyton snorted. "I don't feel *that* sorry for him. Anyway, it was good, because I was a little worried about the drinking thing. But I made the mistake of telling Sara about it."

"Why is that a mistake?"

"Now she's worried that he's an alcoholic and he'll endanger Chloe's life."

"And you're *not* worried about that?"

Peyton paused. "Actually, I'm not."

"Hmm." Nik shook her head. "Okay, what are we moving here?"

"I'll empty the nightstand if you could strip the bed. We'll wash the bedding. I'll get clean sheets and we can make the bed again once we get it moved down there."

"She's not doing well, is she?" Nik pulled off the duvet.

"No. They gave her a couple of months and that was six weeks ago."

"Jesus."

"I know."

"Are you staying here until . . . ?"

"God. I don't know. I don't want to leave, but my boss is freaking out."

Nik nodded and balled up the sheets. "He's a jerk."

Peyton grinned. "Yeah, he is." Her smile faded. "I'm trying to take care of things as much as I can. There's a meeting I've postponed that can't be put off forever, and things I need to be in the office to do. My staff has questions and problems to solve." She sighed. "Maybe now we have hospice care coming in, I could go back . . . but I really don't want to leave her. Not now."

"Ugh." Nik picked up a pillow. "Are *you* okay?"

"Of course."

"Uh-huh."

"I have to be."

Nik shot her a warm look of sympathy. "I'll do anything," she said gently. "Just say what you need. Anytime."

"I know. Thank you."

They hadn't lived in the same city for a few years but they were still best friends, staying in touch online, having girls' weekends in New York, and lately Peyton's more frequent visits home to check in on Sara.

"We should do a night out," Nik said. "Get the old gang together. I'll make some calls."

"That would be fun."

Drew appeared in the bedroom door. "Ready?"

"You really don't need to do this," Peyton said.

"Girl, how else do you think we're going to get this bed down there?" Nik demanded. "Be sensible, not your usual stubborn self."

Drew grinned. "I like you," he said to Nik.

"Most people do," she said modestly.

Peyton pursed her lips and regarded them balefully. What the hell?

"I might need some help just to guide the mattress down the stairs." He pulled it off the bed and stood it on its side then lifted it and carried it out the door. Peyton stared.

"You bet." Nik tossed pillowcases onto the pile of bedding. She followed him out of the room. Peyton trailed along behind, biting her lip as Drew slid the mattress down the stairs.

"You're so strong," Nik said. Peyton rolled her eyes.

"Where's this going?" Drew asked.

"I'll show you the den." Peyton hurried down the stairs. "But we can leave it in the hall while we get the box spring down."

Drew nodded.

The bottom half of the bed was a little trickier, but between them all, mostly Drew, they got it down and set up again in the den. Drew lifted the mattress back on and helped Nik make the bed while Peyton arranged things in the nightstand and plugged in a lamp.

"There." She stood and surveyed the room. "All set." She tipped her head at Drew. "Thank you. Nik was right . . . we couldn't have done this without you."

"Hey. Glad to help. It's the least I can do. I guess I should get going, though. I'll go say goodbye to Chloe and Sara."

"You don't have to rush off." Peyton followed him.

"Actually, I want to have a word with Sara alone." They found Sara in the living room, Chloe apparently still playing her video game.

"You two talk," Peyton said. "We'll be in the kitchen." She grabbed Nik's hand and tugged her around the corner.

"I hope you have wine," Nik said.

"Oh, I do. And I definitely need a very large glass."

She filled in Nik on her visit to the hospice the other day as she got out glasses and opened the bottle of Chardonnay. "I don't know when it will happen. It'll be up to Sara to make that call, I guess. But she decided she doesn't want Chloe hanging around watching her when it gets near the end. She wants me to bring her for short visits, and she wants us there at the end if we can be."

"Your sister is amazing. She's got every detail looked after, doesn't she?"

"She does." Peyton peered down at the golden liquid in her glass. "I think it gives her a little bit of feeling in control when her life is really out of her control."

"I think I'd be too busy sobbing to worry about other people." Nik grimaced and sipped her wine. "Nice." She held up the glass.

"I guess we don't know how strong we actually are until we're faced with the toughest obstacles."

Nik nodded slowly. "That's probably true."

Drew appeared at the kitchen counter separating the room from the dining room. "Okay," he said. "I just talked to Sara. She's agreeable to me spending more time with Chloe."

Peyton nodded.

"So I'm going to say bye and fix a time to get together again."

"Okay. She'll be happy about that, I think."

Drew shrugged but looked pleased.

Peyton and Nik carried their glasses into the living room. Sara motioned Peyton over with an urgent gesture.

"What?" Peyton crouched beside the recliner. "Are you okay?"

"Yes, yes." She bit her lip. "I agreed he can see Chloe again. But I want you to be with them. Okay?"

Peyton regarded her sister. "Um, okay."

"Whenever she sees him. You're with them."

She'd do anything for her sister at this point, although she wasn't sure of the necessity of a chaperone or babysitter or body-guard or whatever role Sara had in mind for her. But if it set Sara's mind at ease about Chloe and Drew spending time together, of course she'd do it.

Chloe and Peyton accompanied Drew to the door as he left. He paused and turned to Chloe. "Can I give you a hug?"

Her lips pushed out and her small shoulders shook as she gave a short nod and moved closer. Drew crouched down and hugged her. Her arms went around his neck and squeezed. Then she jumped back and swiped her cheek. "See you next week."

"Yeah." Drew watched her as she bolted up the stairs. He turned to Peyton, a crease between his eyebrows. "Is she okay?"

Peyton sniffed, tears threatening. "Yes. She's good."

Drew rubbed his chest as if it was hurting. "Okay. Should I call you to arrange something?"

"Sure, that would be best."

They stood in the foyer. He gazed into her eyes. "I know you have doubts about me. Both you and Sara."

She said nothing.

"So I appreciate you letting me into her life." Her throat thickened. "She seems like a great kid. I don't really know how to be a dad to her, and it feels kind of late, but . . . maybe she and I can be friends."

"I think that would be very nice," she whispered.

He nodded, his face tight. "Okay. Thanks. Talk to you soon."

She closed the door behind him and paused, alone. The house felt suddenly emptier without his big, energetic presence. There was something about him . . . something compelling, something magnetic. No wonder Chloe seemed so taken with him.

She took a breath and straightened her shoulders to walk back into the living room where Nik and Sara were chatting. "Want me to check on Chloe?" she asked Sara.

"I think she's okay," Sara said. "Probably just overwhelmed. Give her a few minutes of alone time."

"Are *you* okay?" She sat and peered at Sara. "Are you happy with how that went?"

Sara smiled. "Yes."

"We got your things moved down," Peyton told her. "Thanks to Drew."

"That man has muscles on his muscles," Nik said. She glanced at Sara. "You don't even remember him from college?"

Sara covered her face. "Don't judge me. We'd been drinking. And it *was* a long time ago. It's kind of a blur."

"I remember watching him play," Nik said. "He was damn good. Big and tough. I remember once he blocked a shot and was out for the rest of the game—crazy! Who throws their body in front of a speeding hunk of frozen rubber like that?"

Peyton grinned. "I guess that was his job."

"True, but even so, that's a lot of dedication. Or stupidity." She tapped her bottom lip. "But I didn't get the impression he's stupid."

"No," Peyton agreed and gulped her wine. "I don't think he's stupid."

"Well, that's good to know," Sara said dryly. "Although I guess it's a little late to worry about Chloe's gene pool." She pushed the lever that straightened her chair. "I think I'd like to have a nap."

"Sure." Peyton set down her glass and helped Sara out of the chair. "Nice that you don't have to go up those stairs, right?"

"Yeah, yeah."

"I can fix things up a bit more in here," she said in the den, when Sara was lying down. "Just tell me what you want."

"Thank you, Peyton." Sara reached out and clasped her hand. "Again."

Peyton smiled down at her sister. "No need to thank me."

Back in the living room she sank down onto the couch. Nik had retrieved the bottle of wine from the kitchen and refilled both their glasses. "Well." She let out a long breath. "Sara wants me to go with Chloe whenever she sees Drew."

"Well, that's probably sensible, at first."

"I'm not sure what she's worried about."

"It's just that you don't know him yet. It will take time. Gradually she'll be more comfortable with it."

Peyton nodded. "Except, we don't know how much time she has left."

CHAPTER 10

What the hell was he going to do with a twelve-year-old girl?

Christ. He had no idea.

Drew looked around his home the next day.

Well, they could play video games. At least they had that.

He needed to clean the place up. Margaret, his cleaning lady, was coming tomorrow. That was good, but he could put away the golf clubs, tidy up all the newspapers and magazines that had piled up, and do some dishes. He could also go buy some real food.

He wasn't going to be cooking a meal for Chloe, but she might come over, and if she got hungry he wanted to offer her something to eat. Orange juice. That was all he knew she liked. But all kids liked junk food. Except that wasn't healthy. Ugh.

Sunday stretched out in front of him, long and lonely. It would be a day off for the guys; they rarely practiced on Sundays unless they had a game, which they didn't. He could call them and maybe set something up, see what was going on, find a sports bar where they could . . .

He put the brakes on that thought. He didn't need to drink every goddamn day. He set about doing the much needed tidying in the house, getting rid of pizza boxes and empty beer bottles, even cleaning out the fridge. There was some nasty shit in the back that he couldn't even remember putting there. That left the big appliance pretty much a barren wasteland of refrigeration.

Okay, a trip to the grocery store. He could do that.

Two hours later he was home with bags of food and the best intentions to actually cook himself a meal—once in a while, at least. He knew how to eat healthy. They'd been coached on good nutrition, and the team had always fed them well. Of course, that was a little different than doing it himself. Chicken breasts, vegetables, some fruit, boxes of pasta. Juice. And yeah, a bag of chips.

When that was put away, he leaned against the counter and surveyed the house. Once Margaret had done her stuff, the dust would be gone and the stainless-steel appliances all shiny.

Now what?

His head dropped forward. He sighed.

The gym. He could go work out. That would be a good thing to do. Yeah.

When he grabbed his gym bag, he recoiled at the musty stench emanating from it. Jesus. He hadn't worked out for a while. Apparently, he hadn't bothered washing his workout clothes after the last time, whenever that was.

He threw the dirty clothes into the washing machine and dug around in his big closet for another pair of shorts and T-shirt.

"Okay. Now I'm ready."

Fuck, he'd said that out loud. Now he was talking to himself.

Maybe he needed a roommate. Maybe one of the new kids on the team was looking for somewhere to live. He could help someone out that way. They'd have to pay rent, of course, but he could sort of mentor them . . .

Ah, what the hell was he thinking? *He* was the one who needed mentoring right now.

At the gym he set about his routine with determination. It felt good to use his muscles and expend some energy on something physical. Although it was pathetic that he couldn't do as many reps as he had been. Goddammit.

He couldn't stop his thoughts from turning to Chloe. Was it weird that he didn't love her? She was his daughter.

But he didn't even know her. It was like meeting someone else's twelve-year-old daughter. He *liked* her. He liked how she rolled her eyes at her mother and yet took care of her and wanted to spend time with her. He liked how smart she was, teaching him that video game as if she were the adult and he the kid, so well-spoken and thoughtful. He wanted to get to know her better.

He also liked Peyton.

He pumped his legs harder on the bike, challenging himself with some sprints. Peyton intrigued him. He had to admit to a physical attraction—she was beautiful; that was undeniable. But there was something about her that made him want to look at her all the time, and he loved it when she smiled. Not only beautiful, though, she was smart; and that night they'd had dinner he'd found himself fascinated by her, by her directness, her humor, and her obvious love of her sister and niece.

But there was no point in even thinking that because there was no way he could make a move on his daughter's aunt. Especially not now, with what they were going through. Probably not ever. Because that was just weird.

He rode the bike then did a bunch of push-ups and crunches. Sweating, he grabbed a bottle of Gatorade from the juice bar and chugged it back. He chatted with a couple of guys he didn't know but who recognized him, but escaped before they could ask him about his knee or what he was going to do now his hockey career was over.

He went home and thought about dinner. He hadn't used the barbecue out on the deck for a while. Why the hell not? He stepped out into the weak sunshine of a fall afternoon and yanked the cover off the barbecue then got out a couple of the chicken breasts he'd bought. He slathered barbecue sauce on them and let them cook while he microwaved a potato and mixed up a bag of salad he'd bought.

He ate it in the family room with the television to keep him company. The Rangers were playing the Bruins, so he watched the game. At first it made his gut ache, but he made himself keep watching. This was his life now. Watching, not doing. It sucked, but it was reality.

When his cell phone rang Monday evening and he saw Peyton's name on the screen he grabbed it to answer. He'd been thinking about when to call, what to suggest, so he was glad that she was calling.

"Yeah, we have a little problem here," she said after they'd greeted each other.

"What?" His gut clenched. "Sara?"

"No, she's okay. Well, not really. But it's Chloe."

"What's wrong?"

"She told a bunch of kids at school about you."

"Okaaaaay . . ."

"They didn't believe her."

He frowned. "What?"

"She told them her dad is a famous hockey star and they all laughed at her and said she was making it up."

"Fuck that!"

"Um, yeah, about the language thing . . ."

"Sorry. But seriously—fuck that."

She laughed softly. "I agree. She's pretty upset. The whole school is apparently talking about her like she's a nut job."

"Jesus Christ." He jumped up from where he sat on his couch. "I'll go to that fucking school tomorrow and shut their mean little mouths."

"Er . . ."

"I will. Of course I will. That's the only way they're going to believe her."

"Maybe we should talk to her teacher . . . "

Okay, she probably thought he was serious about being violent. "Sure. Whatever. I'll do that, too."

"Okay, hold up, cowboy. Let's not be rash here."

He sank back down onto the couch. "Yeah, I can be that way sometimes."

She paused. "Would you really go to the school?"

"Hell, yeah. They can't give Chloe a hard time. But I'd just talk to them." Another pause. "Sara will call the school in the morning. They'll tell us the best way to handle it."

"Okay. Sure." He rubbed his face. "Let me know. I can go anytime."

"Thank you, Drew."

"Can I talk to Chloe?"

"Of course. She's right here."

Chloe's smaller voice came on. "Hi, Drew."

"Hi, Chloe. You okay?"

"I'm okay." Her voice quivered. "It was a bad day."

"I heard that. Kids can be ass . . . uh, jerks."

"Yeah." She sighed. "I told my friends about you. My best friends believe me, but a bunch of other kids didn't. They started making fun of me and said I made it up."

"I'm coming to your school tomorrow."

"R-really?"

"Yeah. Your mom's going to call the school and we'll figure something out in the morning, but I'm going to come and make them choke on their laughter."

Maybe that wasn't quite the appropriate thing to say. But at least he didn't use the F word.

"I mean, I'll talk to kids and tell them it's true."

"Oh, my God. They're going to die!"

He lifted his chin. "Well, not sure about that. But we'll set them straight anyway. Nobody calls my girl a liar."

"Th-thank you."

"Anytime. Can you put your aunt back on?"

"Sure. Bye, Drew."

"Bye, beautiful."

"Hi, again." Peyton spoke.

"She okay?"

"She is now." After a pause she said in a low voice, "She came home crying her eyes out."

"Christ."

"I know. Sorry to bother you with this."

"It's not a bother. I was thinking of calling. When is Chloe's dance class?"

"Wednesday evening."

"Could I take her?"

"Um. Probably. I mean . . . okay."

"Is it a problem?"

"No, not at all. I'll check with Sara just to make sure. I was planning to take her."

"Okay, well, we can talk more about that tomorrow."

"Right. I'll call you as soon as we've talked to the school."

"Great. Thanks." He paused. "Thanks for calling me."

"Of course. Bye."

"Yeah, I have a Stanley Cup ring." He grinned at the kid who'd asked the question. "I have three of 'em, actually."

He sat in Mrs. Macauley's seventh grade homeroom classroom Tuesday afternoon.

"I don't wear them because they're huge," he continued.

"Which player has the hottest girlfriend?"

He blinked at the boy who'd asked the question. "Uh . . . "

Mrs. Macauley covered her eyes with one hand. Drew glanced at Peyton, standing at the back of the classroom next to the school principal, fingers to her mouth to hide her smile.

"All I know is, it's not me." Drew grinned.

Damn, he actually enjoyed being around kids. This reminded him how much he'd liked the work he'd done with Paterson House. He missed it.

"Do you think the NHL should ban fighting?"

Drew rolled his lips in as he thought about how to answer that. "No," he said. "But I don't condone fighting. And I don't think the enforcer role is needed anymore. But lots of players think that if there was no fighting there'd be more illegal stick work and hits from behind. I think it's more important to focus on those illegal hits to the head."

"How old were you when you started playing hockey?"

"I was six."

Once more he glanced at Peyton, aware of her in the room. Then he smiled at Chloe sitting beside him.

"Okay, let's say a big thank-you to Mr. Sellers for coming to talk to us today." Mrs. Macauley moved toward him.

The kids all yelled *"Thank you!"* and clapped and Drew smiled and gave a wave. He leaned down to Chloe. "I'll see you tomorrow. I'm going to take you to dance class."

She nodded, beaming at him. "Okay!"

They exchanged a quick hug, and then he and Peyton left, Mrs. Cardozo, the principal, walking them out.

"Sorry to have caused such a disturbance in the school," Drew said to her. "I guess Chloe didn't anticipate that kids wouldn't believe her when she told them she found out who her dad was."

"It's an unusual situation," Mrs. Cardozo said.

"Yeah, tell me about it," he muttered. "But it's a great thing."

"We're just so sorry for Chloe's situation with her mother," Mrs. Cardozo said softly.

"Yeah. Me, too."

They paused at the entrance to the school. "Thanks for letting me come and set things straight. Appreciate the interruption to classes for us."

"It was our pleasure. Chloe's obviously over the moon about finding you."

He bit his lip. "Yeah, no pressure at all."

She smiled. "Good luck with parenting a tween."

He and Peyton walked out to where he'd parked his car down the street. He'd picked her up at her place on the way there because Sara wanted her to be there, too. Also Sara apparently wanted her to be there when he took Chloe to her hip-hop class Wednesday evening. Whatever.

"You really impressed those kids," Peyton commented. "And you impressed me with how you handled yourself."

"Thanks, I guess." He glanced at her. "What did you expect? That I'd come in there and threaten to punch anyone who laughed at Chloe?"

She laughed. "No. I don't know what I expected."

"I've done stuff like that a million times. PR events and auto-graph signings, visits to hospitals and schools and nonprofit organizations. It's part of the deal."

It *was* part of the deal.

"I guess it is," she acknowledged. "Thank you."

He opened the passenger door of his Porsche for her and she slid in. When he was also in the car he said, "I feel bad that this caused problems for Chloe."

Peyton sank her teeth into her plump lower lip, drawing his attention to her mouth. Her lush, lickable mouth. He swallowed.

"Yeah, that wasn't fun when she came home crying. I know how awful that feels when you think people are making fun of you. But she's definitely been more moody lately, so things get to her more easily."

"Because of Sara?"

"Yeah, I think that's part of it, but it could also be hormones."

"Oh." That shut him up. Girl stuff.

"It all worked out."

He drove to the Watt home not far from the school.

"I went to that school," Peyton commented. "Sara and I both did. Some of the same teachers are still there."

"Wow. That's crazy."

"It kind of is. But it feels nice that Chloe goes there, too."

"It will suck for her to have to change schools."

Peyton's lips drooped. "Yeah."

He hesitated. "Do you have a plan for that?"

"Nope." She turned her face away to look out the side window.

"You seem like someone who likes to plan."

She huffed a laugh. "You figured that out about me, huh? Yeah, I like to plan. But for some reason, I can't bring myself to think about that. I know I need to, but . . . "

"You're still hoping it's not going to happen."

"Yes." Her voice was small. "Yes, there's still a part of me that doesn't believe this is really happening."

He reached out and slid her hand into his. "I get it."

Her hand felt good. Small. Delicate, but strong. Warm.

When she curled her fingers around his, his heart gave a bump. "Thanks," she said quietly. "Thanks for letting me have my false hope."

"Hope is never false," he said. "Hope is hope. There's *always* hope."

Her fingers squeezed his. She said nothing, though, because they both knew the reality.

Her phone chimed and she slowly pulled her hand from his to dig it out of her purse. She frowned as she read the screen.

"Problem? We're almost home."

She shook her head. "No. Well, yeah. It's my boss. Again." She rolled her eyes. "He's such a dick."

"Ugh."

"I can usually handle him, but right now his abrasive lack of empathy seems so fucking stupid in light of what I'm going through."

"Language," he murmured.

She shot him a startled look then smiled. "Sorry."

"Don't apologize. I'm pretty fond of the F word."

"So am I," she admitted. "I'm trying not to make it one of Chloe's favorites."

"So what's your dickhead boss bugging you about?"

"He's on me to get back to New York so we can reschedule a meeting I was supposed to have with a client last week. I've talked to them and I could bring him up to speed on the issues, but he's just being unreasonable. He's annoyed because I'm not jumping when he calls. He's a control freak."

"What if you flew back for a day to have the meeting?"

She rubbed her forehead. "I guess I could do that. I just hate leaving. Sara can't do much anymore and Chloe's not even twelve yet."

"I guess it would be weird if I stepped in?" He pulled up to the curb in front of Sara's home.

She turned to him. "Like...what? You'd come and get Chloe up in the morning and make her lunch and get her on the bus to school, spend the day with Sara and make them dinner? Maybe throw in a load of laundry?"

She was clearly being sarcastic. He frowned. "Yeah," he said shortly. "I can do that."

"Can you do it without a six-pack of beer?"

Heat flashed in his chest. "What the fuck does that mean?"

She closed her eyes and dropped her chin. "I'm sorry. That was bitchy."

"Yeah, it was. I know you don't think much of me, but hell."

"I'm sorry," she said again.

"What would be involved with staying with Sara all day?" Because he wasn't going to be up for doing anything that was very personal . . . and he had no clue what was involved in her care.

"You don't have to do that," she said. "You just found out you have a daughter, and it's understandable that you want to see her and get to know her, but our family problems don't need to become your problems. As you've pointed out, you have enough of your own."

He gazed at her, eyes narrowed. "Okay, yeah, I'm a selfish bastard who's been wallowing in self-pity. That doesn't mean I can't care about other people. Chloe is my family. That means you're my family."

"I'm not your family." She glowered at him. "We are not related in any way."

"True." And he was grateful to her for pointing that out because it made the lust that had heated his groin when looking at her mouth not so creepy. Even so, he couldn't act on it. "Fine. We're not family. But we've all been dumped into this mess together. We can at least be friends. And friends help each other out."

She stared at him and once again he couldn't help but notice her mouth . . . it was perfect . . . smooth and rosy, a full bottom lip and sweetly curved upper lip.

Her eyes flickered.

Then her lips firmed. "Right," she said briskly. "Friends."

CHAPTER 11

Peyton settled onto one of the benches facing the window of the dance studio where Chloe was currently waiting for class to start. Drew sat next to her and handed her a cardboard cup of tea he'd just picked up from the Starbucks across the street.

"Thanks."

His big presence and energy field made her skin tingle. His arm brushed hers and she resisted the urge to lean over and rub herself against him. God. What was wrong with her?

"You're welcome." He looked around the studio. "Nice place."

"It's a good studio. The owner is a friend of Sara's, actually. She danced professionally for a few years but she discovered she really loves teaching. Now she has a bunch of teachers working for her."

"Cool."

"This is only the third class this year, so we won't see them do much, I think." They watched Chloe talking and laughing with a couple of other girls, hanging on to the barre that lined the wall. Then everyone moved into a row and the music of Nicki Minaj was audible from inside the studio.

Drew frowned. "Those moves look awfully grown-up."

Peyton smiled and sipped her coffee. "Uh-oh. Protective dad alert."

"I'm just saying . . . they're kids."

She nudged him with her elbow. "It's just dancing. Come on, watch her. She's good."

After a moment he said, "She is."

They watched in silence for a while. Then Drew said, "Did you talk to your boss?"

"Yes, I did." She hesitated. "I've scheduled the client meeting for Monday morning. While I'm there, I'll meet with my team and also with some of the other departments that work on my projects and get as much done as I can that day. I can fly to New York Sunday night and be back Monday night, late." She caught her bottom lip between her teeth briefly. "If you're still willing to help, that would be awesome."

"Of course I will. Just tell me what I need to do."

"I'm going to talk to the hospice worker about coming that day to help Sara. But if you could make Chloe's breakfast and get her off to school, that would be great. I can write down times and stuff. I'll make her lunch. She gets home from school around four. It's okay if you're not there but could you help her get something ready for dinner and see if Sara will eat?"

"Sure."

"Then make sure she does her homework."

"Do you want me to stay until you get back?"

"Um, sure."

"Okay. It's all good."

"Thank you. You really don't mind?"

He turned and leveled a steady gaze on her. "Peyton. I don't mind." She held his gaze and nodded. They turned back to watching Chloe.

"How did you get into reputation management?"

She smiled. "My degree is in Public Relations. I developed an interest in reputation management and got hired by a small firm here in Chicago. I took an entry-level position there and my plan was to get some experience and hopefully move up or move to a bigger firm that hires more high-profile clients."

"What do you love about it?"

"I love the tech parts of it—searching out things and finding ways to either minimize them or emphasize them, depending on the client's goals. And I love solving problems for my clients, whether it's an individual who posted something stupid on Facebook and now it's come back to haunt him, or a company whose reputation has been tarnished because of something they did. I'm good at solving problems."

"I can see that."

She flashed him a quick smile. "I worked my way up at that company, and then I got headhunted by Sentinel and they convinced me to move to New York."

"Sounds like you had your whole life planned out and now you're doing exactly what you wanted."

"You say that like it's a bad thing."

He didn't answer right away. "No, not at all. Guess I'm just a little envious."

She bit her lip. Right. He'd lost the job he loved.

"You must be good at what you do," he said.

"I am."

She caught his smile out of the corner of her eye, but kept her gaze on Chloe. "Do you like living in New York?"

"Not as much as Chicago. I love Chicago. They're both big cities, but there's just something . . . I don't know. Big cities always have their problems. Part of it might be that I don't know as many people there. But I have a couple of friends at work and people I've met through the wine club."

"And all the men you date."

She grinned and slid a sideways glance at him. "That's thanks to Matchmaker dot com."

"Get out. Seriously? You use a dating website?"

"Sure. Why not?" She lifted a shoulder. "I'm not into picking up guys in bars and I don't have a lot of time. It's a reputable site, with lots of professionals on there. It's a good way to meet people."

"Huh." He frowned.

"Have you been dating? Since your divorce?"

"Well, I don't know if you'd call it dating."

"So *you* don't have an issue with picking up women in bars."

He snorted. "I guess not."

She decided she didn't really want to talk about that. "Chicago's the only city you've lived in since you started playing hockey?"

"Yeah. They drafted me in my freshman year of college. I played a year for their farm team, then I got called up and I've been here ever since."

"Do you like it? Or do you wish you'd been drafted by Los Angeles? Or Hawaii?"

He laughed. "There is no hockey team in Hawaii."

"Not much ice there, I guess."

"Just what goes in the piña coladas. But yeah, I like it here. It was an adjustment for me, coming from Thunder Bay, Ontario. Like you said, Chicago's a big city. But I've kind of gotten used to everything that's here—great restaurants and night life, Lake Michigan and the beach. The White Sox."

"You're a baseball fan?"

"Sure. I played baseball, too, when I was a kid. Much to my dad's dismay. He was a football player."

"You're just a star athlete, aren't you?"

He grinned and bumped her shoulder with his. "You can probably outrun me, though, now I have a bum knee."

Something warm expanded in her chest and she took a quick sip of her tea. "She really does love to dance," Drew said quietly. "Look at her face."

Chloe was immersed in the movements, smiling but focused, her body in tune with the music.

"Yeah," Peyton agreed. "I know why Sara wanted her to keep going to classes. To keep things kind of normal and do something she loves."

"Sara's a good mom."

"Yes, she is. The best. Okay, she might be a little overprotective at times, but that's understandable since she's raising Chloe on her own. And . . . " She sighed. "She may have sacrificed her career ambitions and her own social life because of Chloe. She had a few relationships over the years, but she always felt guilty leaving Chloe and so she never really tried very hard to find someone."

"No Matchmaker dot com for her."

Peyton smiled. "No."

"Does she regret that?"

"Funny you should ask. We talked the other day, and she said she doesn't."

"I'm glad she doesn't." Drew looked down. "Because it would be terrible to be dying and have regrets."

"I guess that's something we should all think about. Life can be short." Silence surrounded them, besides the other parents chatting and the music coming from the studio. She looked at Drew's hand resting on his thigh. His very muscular thigh. She remembered yesterday when he'd driven her home and had held her hand. It had felt so good. Big and strong and reassuring.

Her fingers twitched with the desire to reach out and hold his hand again. To feel that muscled thigh. Heat slid down through her body and she licked her lips.

Oh, God. She was so attracted to this man. The more she got to know him, the more he captivated her. What a disaster.

She stared through the window, not really seeing the dance class happening now, just trying to mentally smack herself in the face for feeling this way about Drew, about Chloe's father. Jesus. What kind of person was she?

She guzzled down her cooling tea and tried to slow her thudding heart.

It had been a long time since she'd had these kinds of feelings. She'd pretty much given up on finding someone she could have a relationship with. She'd been optimistic when she'd joined the dating site, thinking that eventually the law of averages would win out and if she went on enough dates surely she'd meet someone who would make her laugh and tingle and want to be with him.

She'd met a few nice guys, but in the end, she had more fun at work than she did with them, so nothing lasting had ever worked out. So she'd accepted that was the way it was meant to be for her.

Meeting someone now was the height of bad timing, with what else was going on with her life, not to mention the man that was giving her those tingly feelings was

Drew . . . her niece's father. Even though Sara and Drew had never had a relationship, it still seemed like exceedingly poor judgment to have those feelings for him. How could there ever be anything between them?

She needed to ignore the tingles and concentrate on the things she needed to focus on—her sister, Chloe, and her career. And probably in that order, right now, to her boss's frustration.

They emerged from the dance studio to find it pouring rain.

"Oh, no. I don't have an umbrella." Peyton stared at the wet pavement in dismay. Chloe danced out onto the sidewalk, turning her face up to the rain and doing a pirouette.

Peyton and Drew exchanged glances.

"Chloe! You're going to get wet!" Peyton called. "Let's just wait a few minutes until this passes."

"So what if I get wet?" She did a grand jeté, landing gracefully. "I'm not afraid of getting wet."

Peyton glanced at the sky, hoping there was no lightning. Drew smiled. "She's having fun."

She was. And maybe dancing in the rain was what you had to

do sometimes.

Thursday night Peyton tried to push aside her guilt as she went out with friends. Nik had arranged everything, and she didn't have the heart to tell her friend she didn't feel like going out. But things were settled with Sara, Chloe's homework was done, and the hospice worker was there so there really wasn't any reason not to go.

Nik picked her up and they met the group at Au Bar, an upscale Gold Coast bar and restaurant with black-and white-checkered floors and lots of wood and brass. Her friends all greeted her with hugs: Victoria, with whom she'd gone to high school, and her fiancée Katerina; Hannah and Aidan whom Peyton had met in college; and Jax, whom she'd worked with at Campbell and Partners when she started her career. Jax was a techy geek expert who'd developed an amazing integrated platform that gave real-time access to all social insights like demographics, geolocation, influence, in-depth sentiment, and topic categorization. Aidan was an attorney with a high-powered law firm in the city, Victoria now taught second grade, and Hannah was on her sixth job since college, now working in marketing.

"So sorry to hear about Sara," Victoria said, catching Peyton's hand and squeezing it. "It's just awful."

"It is." She gave them a brief update about her sister, though she didn't want to dwell on that all night. "But I want to hear about you guys. What's new?"

Jax was bored at Campbell and Partners. He'd started there about a year before she had and they'd bonded over a shared sense of humor and work ethic. Despite having lunches and happy hour drinks together for the years they'd worked at the same place, she'd never been attracted to Jax as more than a friend. They could talk for hours about work and she'd even given him woman advice a time or two.

Aidan was stressed and near burnout at his law firm. "Thought I wanted to work for one of the biggest firms in the city," he said, looking down at his drink. "And everyone said there'd be pressure working in that kind of environment. Idiot that I was, I figured I could deal with pressure. Hell, I like pressure. I always did my best work under pressure in college. But it's fucking getting to me."

He, Hannah and Peyton had met in their freshman year of college in psychology class. Peyton had been attracted to him at first, with his clean-cut good looks and athletic body, but he'd had a long-term girlfriend then, so she'd abandoned any thoughts of being more than friends with him. And they *had* become good friends. She hated seeing him look so miserable.

"The client is everything," he continued. "I get paid to resolve conflict, usually between two acrimonious and irrational sides. These conflicts are never happy things. I only get involved after things have gone horribly wrong."

"Sounds like my job." Peyton smiled.

"But you get some satisfaction out of making things *better*. Most of the time I'm just making things even worse . . . protracted, expensive law suits just drag things out and make people even more miserable."

Victoria was full of wedding plans and Hannah was thinking of quitting her latest job and going back to school. Peyton had lost track of how many jobs Hannah'd held. She'd graduated with a marketing degree and had never seemed to find something she loved enough to stick with.

"What's wrong with this job?" Aidan asked teasingly. "Not enough time off?"

She frowned at him. "That's not it. I can work hard, if it's something I care about. It's just so . . . pointless." She sighed. "I work for a company that makes boxes."

Peyton grinned. "They're a huge company."

"Lots of opportunity for advancement," Aidan added. "Wasn't that why you took the job there?"

"Yes. And the pay is good. But . . . " Hannah shook her head. "It doesn't feel like I'm doing much to make the world a better place."

"Ah." Peyton nodded. "You need something more connected with your values."

"Yes." Hannah glumly stirred her cocktail. "I just haven't found that place yet."

They ordered cocktails and a bunch of plates to share— sliders and shrimpcocktails and a meat and cheese platter. Conversation flowed, laughter relaxed everyone, and Peyton was glad she'd made herself come out. Keeping friendships took work and it was easy to let things slide in the business of life and especially being so consumed with Sara, but it was important to have those connections. To have a little fun, even though life was crap.

Kind of like dancing in the rain.

Drew dragged himself out of bed early Monday morning. He was actually a morning person, but his routine recently had been going out drinking, picking up women, and staying out late. With no reason to get up in the morning, he'd taken to sleeping in however long he wanted before getting up and trying to fill his day.

Today he had a reason to get up. He had to get over to the Watt household and make sure Chloe was up and ready for school.

A fast shower, a stop at Starbucks for a venti Americano, and a short drive later, he was there. Peyton had given him a key yesterday when he'd come by for some last- minute instructions and he used it to let himself in to the quiet house. That now-familiar scent of raspberry lemonade greeted him.

He passed by the den and peeked in the open door. Sara was sleeping in the dark room. The hospice worker would be here soon to give Sara her morning meds, get her showered and dressed, and hopefully some breakfast in her.

He jogged up the stairs and knocked on Chloe's door. "Yo, Chloe, you up?"

The door opened immediately. She wore a pair of shorts and matching tank top, white with a blue duck pattern. Her long hair would have made a comfortable home for a family of sparrows. She scowled. "No, I'm still in bed."

"Smart-ass."

She rolled her eyes. "I'm just getting dressed."

"Okay. I'll make your breakfast."

He headed back down. Peyton had showed him around the kitchen. Chloe apparently liked instant oatmeal with blueberries on top and orange juice. He microwaved the cereal and poured her juice while sipping his coffee. Just as she arrived to climb onto a stool at the counter, the doorbell rang.

He greeted the hospice worker, a pleasant woman named Isabelle, who knew her way to Sara's room.

"Peyton made your lunch last night," Drew told Chloe, who was now dressed in leggings and a zipped-up hoodie, her hair brushed out smooth.

"Yeah, she told me. You know, I'm old enough to look after myself. You didn't need to come over."

"Dammit, you mean I got up early for nothing?" Oops with the swear but Chloe just smiled. "I don't mind. Gives me a chance to see you again. I'll be here when you get home from school."

"What do you do all day?" she asked, spooning up oatmeal.

"Not much," he admitted. "Go online and see what's happening in the hockey world. Go to the gym and work out. Tomorrow I'm golfing with some guys. Unless it rains."

She nodded. "What time does Auntie P get home?"

"Around nine."

"So I'll see her tonight."

"Your bedtime is nine."

"I can read until nine-thirty, though," she said. "I think I should be able to stay up until ten. All my friends do."

Drew gulped some coffee. He had no clue if that was true. But somehow he had a feeling that pushing bedtime as late as possible was something all kids tried. Hell, pretty sure he'd done that himself. "Well, if she gets here before you're asleep, yeah, I'm sure she'll come say hi."

Chloe dawdled over her oatmeal and sipped her orange juice. Drew checked his watch. The last thing he wanted to happen while he was looking after her was missing the school bus and being late for school. "Better get moving."

"I have lots of time." She finished her cereal with the speed of a turtle in molasses and drained the last of the juice. She pushed the bowl and glass across the counter toward him and he grinned as he picked them up to put them in the dishwasher.

Chloe jumped off the stool. "I have to go say bye to Mom."

Drew wiped the counter while he waited for Chloe to return. When she emerged from her mom's room wearing a solemn expression, his chest hurt. He handed over her lunch. Her backpack sat on the living room floor, still open. She stuffed her lunch in along with a bunch of papers. "Okay, ready."

He'd been told to walk with her to the corner where the bus picked her up and they left the house in the fresh morning air, cooler now as autumn approached. It was the last day of September. The low sun beamed soft light through tree branches and between houses.

Chloe chatted about her friends and her day as if they'd always known each other. Then the school bus appeared at the end of the street and she had to sprint to catch it. Drew shook his head, remembering her dallying at home. She waved as she climbed on the bus and joined her friends, and Drew watched the big yellow vehicle drive away.

It was such a dad moment, he didn't move right away, standing on the sidewalk, his chest full of heat. Then he turned and walked back to the house.

Inside he checked in with Sara, now sitting up in bed. "Anything I can help out with here today?" he asked her.

She tipped her head to one side. In the time since they'd met again, she'd grown even frailer. Maybe he noticed it more than others because he didn't see her every day. "Drew? What are you doing here?"

He paused. He'd been here yesterday, had talked to her while Peyton explained the plan for her to fly back to New York. Sara didn't remember?

His heart bumped in his chest.

"I came to help get Chloe off to school while Peyton's away. Remember?" he asked gently.

Her forehead creased. "Oh. Oh, right." Confusion clouded her eyes. Damn. This wasn't good.

"She's on a lot of pain medication," Isabelle said quietly to him. "It can sometimes cause confusion."

"Is it Monday?" Sara asked.

"That's right." He smiled at her. *Shit, shit, shit.*

"Will you eat some of this yogurt?" Isabelle asked, approaching the bed with a container and a spoon. "It's strawberry, your favorite."

Sara regarded the yogurt without interest but took it from Isabelle. She scooped up one spoonful and ate it. Another bite followed but then she stopped.

Drew's gut clenched. Peyton had mentioned the lack of appetite, but seeing Sara eat so little and have no interest in more was awful. He tried not to let his feelings show on his face, though.

"Drew."

"Yeah?" He sat in the chair near the bed.

"Do you like Chloe?"

"Yeah," he said. "I do. I like her a lot."

"Do you . . . love her?"

He hesitated.

"Do you think you *could* love her?" Sara rephrased her question. "I know it's soon."

"Yes." This answer was definite. "I definitely think I could love her."

"Peyton will be her legal guardian," Sara said, though it was clearly an effort for her to talk. Fuck, she'd deteriorated even since that first Saturday he'd come by.

"I know."

"But if she wants a relationship with you . . . will you do that?"

"I will. I'll do whatever she wants, Sara."

"Thank you." Her smile was fleeting. She set the yogurt cup on the nightstand.

"Can you eat a little more?" he asked.

"No." She leaned back into the pillows. "It's okay, Drew. I just can't."

He nodded; his teeth sunk into his bottom lip. He glanced at Isabelle and she gave him a sad smile.

"I'll hang around a bit, if that's okay," he said. "Your grass needs cutting. Okay if I do that?"

"Sure. Thank you. That's nice of you."

It had been a while since he'd mowed a lawn; he paid a landscaping service to come and do it. But what the hell. He felt a strong need to make himself useful.

Isabelle followed him to the hall. "Is she in pain?" he asked quietly.

"No. Our focus is on keeping her comfortable."

"She needs to eat."

"I know it's difficult to watch someone refuse food and drink. The truth is, as her body shuts down, she'll be more comfortable without food to digest."

He stared at Isabelle. "We just let her starve?"

Her sympathetic expression didn't change. "She's dying, sir. As I said, our focus is on making her comfortable." She tipped her head. "Do you want to talk to the social worker? She's been here a few times to talk to Ms. Watt's sister and daughter."

Drew paused, emotions tangled inside him. "No. That's okay."

"We offer spiritual support as well as physical support to the patient," she continued. "You might find it helpful."

"I'm good. I'll just, ah, go mow the lawn."

She nodded and Drew strode blindly down the hall. This fucking sucked.

He stopped in the kitchen and gripped the counter with both hands. His head dropped forward.

It wasn't a goddamn surprise. Sara had been honest with him that day in the coffee shop. She was dying.

A heaviness in his chest and limbs weighed him down. Once more he had that sensation of being overwhelmed, like it was all too much. How the hell was he supposed to handle this?

How were any of them?

Peyton and Chloe's strength amazed him. How were they coping? How could Peyton bear to watch her sister decline like that? How could Chloe handle watching her mother die? She wasn't even twelve years old, for fuck's sake. He slammed a cupboard door shut, curled his hands into fists, and fought to control his breathing, his heart thudding wildly. *Fucking fuck this bullshit.*

Sara's landline rang. Drew pulled in a deep breath, lifted his chin and picked up the phone to peer at the call display. Chloe's school. He'd better answer it. He exhaled roughly.

"Could I speak to Ms. Watt, please?" the man on the other end asked.

"I'm sorry she's not well. Can I help you? I'm Drew Sellers . . . " He paused. "Chloe's father."

"This is Ed Lowell. I'm the vice principal at John Adams School."

"Yes, hi."

"We need someone to come pick up Chloe."

CHAPTER 12

Drew's heart lurched. "Why? Is she okay?"

"She's fine. However, she's dressed inappropriately for school. Her attire doesn't meet our dress code and therefore she has to go home to change."

Drew frowned. "What? Inappropriate?" He'd walked out with Chloe and she was dressed fine, from what he could recall. "How can that be?"

"Are you able to pick her up?"

"Well, yes, I can come, but—"

"We can discuss it more then."

Drew scowled as he ended the call and set the phone on the counter. What the fuck?

How could he have screwed up so badly on the first day he'd ever looked after her? What the hell was their dress code? Jesus.

He strode back to Sara's room to let her and Isabelle know what was happening. Sadly, Sara just seemed confused by what he told her. "I'll handle it, Sara." He gave her a reassuring smile. "Everything's fine."

He jumped into his car and drove to the school where he'd just been last week. He found Chloe in the office sitting on a chair, wearing a fierce scowl but also looking like she might cry.

"Hey, Chloe." He crouched in front of her. "What's going on?"

"As I mentioned on the phone, her attire doesn't meet our dress code." Drew looked over his shoulder at the man who'd spoken. "You must be Mr. Lowell. Where's Mrs. Cardozo?" They'd met the principal the last time they'd been there and she'd been awesome, aware of Chloe's home situation and understanding of the situation with the other kids, willing to let him speak to them.

"She's at a conference this week."

"I see." Drew rose and looked down his nose at the other man. "I don't understand what the problem is."

"We have a dress code here at John Adams."

"Sure," Drew said shortly.

"The students are all aware of the dress code and sign off on it at the beginning of the school year. One of the rules is that girls may not wear shirts that are low-cut in the front, back, or sides, or clothing that is excessively tight."

Drew lifted an eyebrow as he took in Chloe's baggy hoodie. "Chloe, show your father your top."

Her lips set in a tight line, she opened her hoodie to reveal a camisole top that hugged her torso. She turned to show Drew her back, and the top had a deep scoop. "She's also wearing leggings," Mr. Lowell said. "The tight top and tight leggings are not appropriate."

"It was hot in the classroom," Chloe said tersely. "I took off my hoodie because I was hot."

"And one of the boys in the class made a comment about her body," Mr. Lowell added, frowning.

Drew shook his head slowly. "Are you fu—" He stopped, ground his teeth briefly then continued. "Are you kidding me?"

"This is far from a joke, Mr. Sellers. We take our dress code seriously. There are reasons for it. We need to maintain order in the classroom and prevent distractions. Girls wearing skimpy clothing distract boys during class. We don't want anyone harmed by sexual violence or jealousy from other girls."

Drew's eyes nearly popped out of his head and rolled across the linoleum. Heat erupted in his gut and spread through his chest. He stared at the vice principal. The only words that came to mind were profanities, and he had to bite them back while he figured out what the fuck to say to this asshat.

"Where's the boy?" he eventually demanded through gritted teeth.

"Excuse me?"

"The boy. The boy who commented. Who is he and why isn't he in here, too?" Mr. Lowell looked confused.

"Are you telling me that a boy made an inappropriate comment about my daughter and he's not being reprimanded for it?"

"Uh . . . "

Drew got into Mr. Lowell's space, not even hesitating to use his size in an intimidating way. "I am not leaving here until that happens. I don't care if Chloe came to school wearing a bikini. He can't say things to her and not be told it's wrong." He pulled in a deep breath. "No matter what she's wearing, she is not responsible for someone else's actions. I want that boy's parents in here, and I want them in here *now*, so they can have a discussion with their son about how to control his impulses when he's around girls." He bit back another curse. "No matter what they're wearing."

Mr. Lowell stared at him. "I can't do that."

Drew sat in the chair next to Chloe and folded his arms across his chest. "Sure you can. I'll wait. I have all goddamn day." He glared at Mr. Lowell. "Furthermore, you pulled Chloe out of class, took her away from her studies and publicly shamed her because of how she's dressed. And you seriously don't see anything wrong with that?"

"Ah . . ."

"There is no way girls should be told that the way they're dressed is responsible for boys' bad behavior. We are doing something about this right now."

Chloe's hand slipped into his and squeezed it. He looked down at her, and the gratitude and admiration in her eyes pulled at his heart. He smiled reassuringly at her and squeezed her hand back. "It's okay, Chloe."

"I'll, uh, be right back." Mr. Lowell disappeared into an office.

The school secretary behind the counter stared at Drew then grinned. "You're on fire," she said. "Good for you."

Drew gave her a tight smile back. "Thanks. But this is bull . . . er, ridiculous."

"They announce the dress code every day," Chloe said to him quietly. "I know about it, but . . . I'm sorry. I messed up."

"No." He gentled the frown that still tightened his face. "It's not your fault, honey. We're going to fix this."

Her little mouth tightened and her chin quivered and then she nodded. "Thank you."

Peyton paid the taxi driver and then climbed out of the car with her purse and the briefcase that held her laptop. The light above the front door was on, illuminating the veranda. She recognized Drew's car parked in front.

The door was unlocked and she frowned at that, but maybe it was different for a man than for three women. She walked in and saw Drew on the couch in the living room watching the television. He stood at seeing her. "Hi."

There was something about him being in their home, waiting for her, greeting her, that affected her. He filled the space with his usual energy and bold presence.

"Hi." She dropped her purse and briefcase onto the table.

"Long day?"

"Yeah." She crossed to an armchair and sank into it, toeing off her shoes. "Long and weird."

"You look so different." His gaze wandered over her and she looked down at the blue pencil skirt and matching jacket she wore. "All professional."

"I *am* a professional," she murmured.

He smiled. "Things go okay at work?"

"Yeah. I was the Energizer Bunny of reputation management today." She grimaced. "Amazing how much you can accomplish when you have to. It was just weird, staying at my apartment last night then going straight to the airport from work." She paused. "How's Sara?"

His face tightened and he looked down at his big hands clasped in front of him. "She's okay. It seemed . . . she was confused a few times today."

"Oh." Peyton's eyes widened then closed. "I've been noticing that. They said it's all the pain medication."

"Yeah. Uh, Chloe's probably still awake." He took a deep breath. "There was a little incident at her school today."

"Oh, no." She leaned forward. "What happened?"

"They called me to pick her up because she was in violation of their dress code."

Peyton's forehead creased. "Really? What on earth was she wearing?"

"It wasn't that bad. I went to the school and dealt with it."

"Is she in trouble?"

"No. But she wants to see you when you get home."

"Okay." She stood right away. "Is *she* okay?"

"Yeah." He smiled. "She's good. Amazing. Awesome. We talked about it more over dinner. Then I helped her with her math homework. She showed me a Social Studies assignment she got an A on. She blew my mind."

Peyton's heart warmed. "Yeah. I'll go talk to her." She paused. "Are you leaving?"

"We should probably talk more about what happened . . . after you see Chloe."

"Okay." She ran upstairs in her bare feet and poked her head into Chloe's room.

"Hey, sweetie. I'm back."

Chloe was in bed reading. She smiled and set down the book. "Hi."

Peyton advanced into the room and sat on the side of the bed. "Drew tells me there was some kind of dress code situation at school today."

"Yeah." Chloe's face scrunched up.

"What happened?"

Her jaw dropped as Chloe related what had happened. "And Drew made Mr. Lowell call Scott's parents and they came to the school, too, and Drew told them the same things he told Mr. Lowell."

"Dear God," Peyton breathed. "How did that go?"

"They were mad at first, but then he told them if the sight of a girl in a camisole top and leggings was too much for their son to handle, they have a big problem. And they agreed with him."

"Really." Peyton shook her head.

"It was all kinds of embarrassing, but then after school I was talking to my friends and they all feel the same . . . the stupid rules are way stricter for girls than they are for boys and it makes us all feel like we're being pressured. We're *not* a distraction to the boys."

Peyton nodded, her mind whirling.

"And Drew told them that, too, and said that it was perpetuating rape culture to bring boys up to think that what a girl wears is responsible for their actions."

"Holy shit." Peyton covered her mouth.

Chloe laughed. "I know, right?"

"Rape culture? Dear God, what do you know about rape culture?" And what the hell did *Drew* know about rape culture?

"Auntie P. I'm nearly twelve." She rolled her eyes.

Peyton took a long breath in and let it out. "Okay. Well. You're all right now?"

"It was embarrassing, being pulled out of class like that. That never happens to the boys. But I'm okay. I think my friends and I are going to do something about this."

Peyton smiled. Another one of Chloe's crusades. She leaned down and kissed Chloe's forehead. "I think that sounds awesome."

"Drew stood up for me," Chloe said quietly. She peered up at Peyton through her eyelashes. "I really like him, Auntie P."

Peyton's heart turned over in her chest. "I'm glad you do."

"I liked having him here," Chloe continued. "He's good at math."

"Well, that's good."

"He also played World of Wizards with me."

"After your homework was done, I hope." She arched a brow.

"Yeah. And he even made us dinner . . . spaghetti. It was good."

"Great."

"Mom wouldn't eat any, though." She paused. "She's hardly eating anything."

"I know." She reached out to smooth Chloe's hair. "Remember, they told us that would happen."

"I know. It just . . . " Chloe's eyelids drooped. "I wish she would eat."

"I know. C'mere." She pulled her niece into a hug and they held on to each other for a long moment. "I'm here, sweetie. I'm here for you."

"I know."

It wasn't going to get easier. Peyton blinked back tears before she pulled away. "Time for lights out. Past time, actually." She glanced at Chloe's clock. "I'll go check on your mom."

"She was asleep when I came up to bed. I checked on her."

Peyton nodded and stood. "Night, sweetie."

She headed back downstairs and did poke her head into Sara's room. A night-light cast a soft glow, enough for her to see Sara's small face, eyes closed. Peyton touched her cheek gently then left the room.

It was like Sara was becoming the child in the family.

She bit hard on her lip as she returned to the living room and Drew. "All okay?" he asked.

This time she sat on the couch with him. "Yes." She blew out a breath. "I can't believe what you did."

She stared at him as he met her eyes. He shrugged. "It had to be done. No way was someone getting away with treating my daughter like that."

Her chest filled with a hot softness. "I don't even know what to say. I can't believe you did that, but . . . I'm so, so glad you did."

"I hoped you and Sara wouldn't be upset about it." He rubbed his face. "It caused a bit of a scene at the school. And Mr. Lowell's not too happy with me."

She couldn't take her eyes off him, something inside her going warm and gooey. "It's important. Thank you. Chloe said you helped with her homework, too."

"Yeah."

"She was a little upset about Sara not eating."

"So was I," he muttered.

"Did you tell her that?"

"No. No! It was after she went to school." He shoved a hand into his hair, pushing it off his face. As usual it fell back over his forehead immediately. "I cut the grass."

"Oh. Thank you." She'd noticed on the weekend it needed it, but hadn't had a chance to do it.

"I did a few other little things . . . fixed the leaky tap in the bathroom down here. Nailed down a loose board on the back steps."

"You're quite the handyman."

He smiled ruefully. "Not really. But I can figure out a few things."

"Thank you. Really. For being here today."

"Anytime. How was your boss? Did he expect you to stay?"

"Yeah. He said all the right things . . . it's fine, take care of your family, blah blah blah. But he was annoyed, I could tell."

"Asshole."

"Yeah. But he can't argue much when I got things moving for our new client and took care of a bunch of other things. Let's just hope there aren't any fires that pop up in the next while." She smiled. "I actually feel good about what I accomplished."

"Want to talk about it?"

She did. She really did. Having someone to share things with at the end of the day, both the successes and the crappy failures, was not something she'd ever really had. Guys she'd dated got a glazed-over expression if she talked too much about her work. "Well." She shifted on the couch, hiking her skirt up a bit so she could tuck one leg under her. Drew's gaze dropped briefly to her bare legs then darted back up to her face. "So this client we're working with—a big company, I won't tell you the name—has a major reputation image because the salaries and bonuses of their upper management recently were made public . . . and this is a company that received a major government bailout. Public outrage is growing and they've mismanaged it."

"Is your job always to help out companies that have screwed up?"

"Not always. Companies make mistakes. Sometimes they're avoidable, sometimes they're not. It's not my job to tell them how to run their company, just to help them deal with the repercussions. One of my current clients is dealing with a big smear campaign that we suspect was started by a competitor. And then there are clients we just work with to help them develop their brand and online reputation and we monitor it for them to make sure they're meeting their goals. That was what I started out doing, but I found I really enjoy the crisis management challenges." She paused. "I like fixing things."

"This is fascinating."

She eyed him. "Really?"

"Yeah. I had no idea such a job even existed. It's pretty cool." His eyes moved over her face. "You really do love your work, don't you?"

"I do."

"I miss that." He looked down at his hands. "I miss that excitement about getting up every day looking forward to getting to the rink, hanging out with the guys, practicing. And the games. Most of all the games."

Peyton bit her lip. "I know it's not my business, but it would probably be good for you to find something else to focus on."

"Well, yeah. But what? I don't have any education, other than a couple years of college. I don't have a clue what I could do. I'm no good at anything else. My buddy Dougie went into investment banking, but Christ, that would bore me to tears."

"Maybe go back to school?"

"At thirty years old?" He shook his head. "School was never my thing anyway."

"You're a very smart man."

He gave a huffed laugh. "Thanks. I did okay in school, but sitting in a classroom drove me crazy."

She nodded. "Maybe something connected with hockey still?"

He sighed. "Yeah, I've thought about options. Coaching. Scouting. Broadcasting. Nobody's beating down my door offering me jobs."

She tipped her head to one side. "Have you approached anyone about a job?"

"No."

"That might be a start."

"I just . . . " He stopped. "Never mind. Don't worry about me. I'll figure things out."

She nodded. "I know you will. I just wanted to . . . well, you helped me out and let me talk. I can do the same for you. If you want to talk or throw around ideas. I don't know anything about hockey but sometimes it helps to have someone to bounce things off."

"Yeah. That's true." He paused. "If you need to go back to New York again, let me know. I'm here."

She nodded slowly. It had been just her and Sara and Chloe for the past few years since their parents had died. Sure, they had friends—Nik helped any way she could, and Sara had friends who'd been coming by, but as Sara's condition worsened, some people felt uncomfortable seeing her. Having Drew there offering to help—no, not just offering, actually stepping up and *doing* things, huge, important things—felt so comforting.

She met his eyes in the dim room, the television now muted but flickering light.

Heat rose around them, a humming awareness. His gaze moved over her face, lingering on her mouth. She stared at him, an achy fullness growing low in her belly. Her skin prickled and her mouth went dry.

Once more she had to give herself a mental smack. She couldn't be feeling these things about this man.

Somehow she knew he was feeling them, too.

How annoying, that this physical attraction was flaring up like this between them. They didn't even know each other, so that was all it could be. She still had her doubts about him and whether he could be trusted to be a good father to Chloe. He drank a lot. He partied a lot. He had no job. He also swore a lot. But she had to mentally roll her eyes at herself for that one because a parent who cussed wasn't the worst thing in the world. Lord knows she had a dirty mouth a lot of the time, too; she was just better at hiding it.

And yet, after today, there was no denying that he was a good guy. A very good guy. Her heart swelled up with a rush of emotion.

She swallowed.

The silence had stretched on and she shook her head. "Okay," she finally answered him. "I'll keep that in mind."

He stood. "I better go. I'm sure you're tired."

She stood, too, and only inches separated them. She felt a magnetic pull to him and had to force herself to step back. "Thanks again for today."

"No problem."

She hesitated. "Are you coming to her birthday party this weekend?"

"Can I? She asked me if I'd come but I thought I should check with you."

She was his daughter. It was her birthday. It made Peyton's heart stab that he had to ask like that. His courtesy touched her. And how on earth could they say no after what he'd done for her today? "Of course."

"And I thought maybe I could come get her Sunday to do something special." She followed him to the door. "Sure."

"Okay. G'night, Peyton." He opened the door and stepped out onto the veranda.

"Good night." She closed the door but watched him jog down the steps and the sidewalk to his car.

It would probably be better if she didn't spend any more time with Drew. But Sara wanted her to be there when he saw Chloe. She'd promised Sara that. And this wasn't the time to do something that would upset Sara.

She'd just have to be stronger. She could resist the attraction she felt to him. She could do it.

CHAPTER 13

Something weird had happened to Drew. The paralysis he'd been feeling lately had changed into energy. He felt keyed up, but not sure what to do about it. He rejected hanging out at Jimmy's in favor of workouts at the gym. But he did agree to meet up with Dougie for a happy hour drink down near his office after a workout.

In the gym, he let his mind wander freely while he worked his body. He thought about a lot of stuff. He thought about Chloe and how she'd bounced back after being pulled out of class and humiliated. The discussion they'd had over spaghetti and how her friends felt annoyed by all the talk about dress code and how it was aimed mainly at the girls, and that the school's reaction to Chloe's appearance was more distracting than her appearance itself, and the unfairness of it. She and her friends wanted to do something to try to change that, and he'd cautiously suggested that they take a measured approach—do some research and present some facts to the school administration.

He also thought a lot about Peyton and the way she'd looked at him that night after she'd heard about what had happened at

Chloe's school. Her eyes had been brimming with gratitude and admiration, along with a look that was almost . . . surprise.

She apparently hadn't expected that of him.

That annoyed him unreasonably. In fairness, they really didn't know each other well, although they'd been pulled together into a situation that required a lot of personal sharing.

What really annoyed him, though—he kind of thought she was right to be surprised.

He'd felt like such a loser lately. He'd lost his wife, his job . . . his whole identity. He didn't even know who he was anymore. And he'd been down on himself—angry, irritable, hopeless. He knew he had to do something, but he just didn't know what or where to start. He'd felt as useful as a Zamboni in a puddle.

Now . . . he wanted to be better. He wanted to be worthy of Peyton's admiration. And Chloe's. Was it weird to think that they brought out something good in him? Something he hadn't even known he had?

Of *course* he'd stood up for Chloe. It didn't seem very heroic to him, but the look on Chloe's face had been almost worshipful, and Peyton . . . her wonder and awe had also been mixed with something more . . .

He'd felt that awareness sparking through his veins, that tug of attraction. There'd been goddamn electricity arcing around them.

He pedaled harder on the stationary bike and wiped sweat from his forehead. Yeah. She'd looked so fucking sexy in that snug little suit; the silky blouse beneath it opened in a V that revealed shadowy cleavage. He'd watched her run upstairs, the tight skirt hugging her ass in a way that made his depraved hands itch to touch. Squeeze. Fondle. He wanted to run his hands down those sleek bare legs, yank that ass back against his groin and grind into her.

It was getting that way every time he saw her, whether she was dressed in jeans, yoga pants and T-shirt, or a business suit.

On top of that, when she'd talked about her work and her face had lit up and been all animated, he'd been fucking mesmerized. Not only intelligent, she was vibrant and confident, too. She knew exactly what she was talking about and he could totally see her getting shit done.

That was a surprising turn-on.

Maybe that was what was making him feel different. He'd admitted he envied her for having that. He wanted that for himself again. He just didn't know how to get it.

He wanted to be better. He wanted to be worthy of the way she'd looked at him. In the shower after his workout, he closed his eyes. Thinking like that about

Peyton was unacceptable. He needed to wash that out of his mind just like he was scrubbing the sweat off his body.

Chloe on the other hand . . . being worthy of the look he'd seen on her face, too . . . *that* was something he could strive for.

He changed back into the dark jeans and striped button-down shirt he'd worn to the gym then drove to the bar Dougie had suggested on West Wacker. It was upscale and full of men and women in expensive suits, big windows overlooking the river. They sat at a small high top and Drew ordered a Rusty Nail. He'd just have one.

"So what's new?" Dougie asked. "How are things going with your daughter?" Drew updated him briefly on Sara's status then told him about Chloe and Peyton.

After a while he caught the expression on Dougie's face and stopped talking. "What? Why are you looking at me like that?"

"You're crazy about her."

Drew's face heated. "There's nothing between us. There can't be."

Dougie's forehead creased. "Dude. I was talking about Chloe."

"Oh."

Dougie laughed. "Hell, that was telling."

Drew scowled. "I meant it. Nothing. Chloe on the other hand . . . yeah. Wow. I think I *am* crazy about her."

"She's your daughter. It would be weird if you weren't."

"I don't know. Would it? Can that parental bonding thing happen with a twelve- year-old? It's not like I ever got to hold her or feed her or rock her to sleep when she was a baby."

"I don't know, man. That's an interesting question. But I don't know if it matters. What matters is how you feel now."

"You're a dad. You'd do anything to protect your kids, right?"

"Hell, yeah."

"I never got that before. I didn't know it would be so . . . "

"What?"

"I don't know . . . fierce."

"Yeah." Dougie nodded. "Fierce is a good word." Drew felt a little embarrassed talking like this. "Any decisions about finding a job?"

Drew scrunched his face and turned the old-fashioned glass in his hands. "Nope."

"Hey, you remember Jack Shipton?"

"Yeah." He was a former player for the LA Kings originally from Chicago. He'd retired a number of years back.

"I ran into him the other day at a luncheon where he was speaking. He has this business going . . . wait, I have his card." He pulled out his wallet and poked around in it then handed over a matte-black business card.

Drew studied it. Dynamo Sports Consulting. "What is it?" he asked.

"They work with retired athletes. Not sure exactly what they do, but he said they help guys transition from playing to other things."

"Huh."

"You don't sound enthused."

Drew shrugged. "I just don't know what's involved."

"It sounded like it would be good for you. They figure out a plan and do some branding or something . . . take the card. Give him a call. Or check out their website at least."

Dew tucked the card in his shirt pocket. "Okay, I'll see." He should be able to figure this out by himself, for Chrissakes.

He and Dougie talked more about Dougie's kids and then about hockey, of course, and the start of the season in about ten days.

"Well, better get home," Dougie eventually said, signaling for the check. "I'll get it," Drew said.

"I got it." Dougie insisted on buying.

"You going to Red's party next weekend on his yacht? He said he invited you." One of his former teammates was hosting a "start of the season" party. Drew had been surprised to be invited and not sure if he should go.

"Yeah! We got an overnight babysitter. Lisa's pretty excited about it."

"Great. Probably see you then."

There were eight kids at the birthday party, including Chloe— three boys and four other girls. Drew eyed the boys suspiciously when they arrived, but they were just kids, goofing around, having fun playing all these video games in the big tricked-out RV parked in front of the house. Drew was actually a little envious because wow, they had a lot of cool games. With four forty-six-inch high-def TVs, customized built-in vibration motors that were synched to the on-screen action, and stereo surround sound, whoa, this was so freakin' awesome.

What the hell. He wanted to play, too. So he joined the kids.

He'd helped Peyton shop yesterday for food after she'd agonized over what they should serve the kids. They'd picked up mega junk food—hot dogs, and salads, and of course the required cake, a two-layer white cake with thick frosting and bright-colored sprinkles.

"Are you playing, Mr. Sellers?" Jason asked, eyes wide.

"Are you kidding? You think I'm going to miss out on this sweet party on wheels?" Jason grinned and another dude—Tyler? —gave him a fist bump.

Drew got into the multiplayer game happening. His competitive nature surfaced and he became determined to kick tweenage butt.

They gave him some stiff competition, but at one point he scored major points. He thrust his fist into the air and yelled like he'd just scored the winning goal in game seven of the Stanley Cup final. Luckily the kids just thought it was cool that an adult was playing with them.

Eventually he bowed out and left them to their gaming. He loved seeing Chloe with her friends, laughing and teasing and having fun. They all seemed like good kids. Even the boys.

He joined Peyton in the kitchen where she was getting the wieners ready to grill. "Want me to cook those?" he offered.

"I can do it."

"Grilling is manly work."

She snorted, but a smile played on her mouth as she sliced hot dog buns. "Okay, if you feel a need to demonstrate your masculinity, be my guest."

"Chloe's having fun." Drew slid the wieners onto a big plate.

"That's good. This was a good idea—no noise or fuss in the house to disturb Sara."

"Until they all come in to eat."

"It'll be fine. Sara's having a good day. She wants to come sit out here when they're eating dinner."

"That'd be great." Without being asked, he opened the fridge and pulled out mustard, ketchup, and relish and set the bottles on the island. The dining table had already been set with colorful paper plates, cups, and plastic cutlery. "Is this hard for her?"

"Yeah." Peyton kept her gaze on the buns. "She knows this will be the last birthday she'll have with Chloe. She's with it enough today to realize that and it's making her sad."

"Fuck," he muttered, shaking his head. "Yeah."

Soon everyone was gathered around the big dining table,

digging into the food. The kids were wound up from the games, talking loudly and bouncing around. Sara sat smiling at them, though. Today she had on the blond wig that she'd been wearing the day she'd approached him in the coffee shop. Her skin was thin and dry and her body frail, but her smile made her look pretty.

A weird affection filled him. Nothing sexual, despite the fact that he'd slept with her once. It almost felt like that had been a different person. But he liked Sara and admired the job she'd done raising Chloe. He also admired her strength in dealing with this horrible illness.

Drew ate his hot dog standing in the kitchen at the island that overlooked the dining room, watching the party, watching Peyton bustle around looking after people, including Sara. Including him, when she poured more lemonade into his cup.

She was a kickass woman, but she was also caring and affectionate.

"Tyler, you need a haircut," she teased the boy. "Or maybe just a tattoo to go with it."

He grinned at her. "I asked my parents if I could get a tattoo and they said no."

"I can't imagine why." She gave him an innocent look. "What kind of tattoo do you want?"

"A hockey stick." He glanced at Drew. "You have any tattoos, Mr. Sellers?"

Drew met Peyton's eyes. Had she noticed his tattoos that day? Her cheeks grew pink. "I sure do," he answered. "One for each Stanley Cup win. And a maple leaf from when I was in the Olympics."

"Cool!"

As he moved across the kitchen to throw his paper plate in the trash, he overheard Tyler say to Chloe, "I still can't believe he's your dad."

Drew paused. There was a little ego stroke, considering how

down about himself he'd been feeling lately. But it mostly felt good that Chloe was happy.

Chloe had requested that her friends not bring gifts but instead donate to an anti-bullying group. After the cake had been demolished, parents started arriving to pick children up. Drew hung back, but the kids kept calling him to meet their moms or dads, and he smiled and shook hands with them, hearing more than once that they were a fan of his.

"Thanks," he said once again. "Means a lot."

Finally the house was blessedly quiet. Sara was in the den with the hospice nurse there to administer her evening medications and get her to bed. Chloe helped clean up the kitchen, talking about the party and how much fun it had been, then disappeared up to her room to probably chat with the same kids she'd spent the afternoon with.

Alone with Peyton, Drew hung a dish towel on the rack inside the cupboard door. "One successful party accomplished."

"Thank God." She slumped against the counter. "And now I get my wine."

He grinned. "That's your reward?"

"Yes. Yes, it is." She reached for a wineglass.

Drew opened the fridge and spotted the bottle of Sauvignon Blanc. He lifted it out and held it up. "This?"

"Yes."

"Corkscrew?"

"Top drawer right behind you."

He opened the wine and then moved toward her to fill her glass.

She reached for another glass and looked at him with raised eyebrows. He smiled. "Sure."

So he poured two glasses and they carried them into the living room and sat on the couch.

Peyton leaned her head back against the cushions, set her feet

DANCING IN THE RAIN

on the coffee table, and let out a long sigh. "Thank you for all your help. The kids love you."

"Yeah, they do."

She chuckled and nudged his knee with her foot. "So modest."

"Hey, it's been a while since I felt the love like that. Let me have this."

She eyed him. "Is it addicting?"

"What?"

"Being a star. Having all those fans adulating all over you."

He thought about that. "I think it can be addicting. Life-changing. Sometimes I hated the feeling of having my privacy violated, but for me, fame was never the goal. I loved playing. Being good at what I did meant that I got a lot of attention, and yeah there were times people were asking for autographs or interrupting a private dinner. But it's the fans who support us and keep the game going."

"But don't you get used to all the money? All the public adoration. The preferential treatment?"

"It's nice," he acknowledged. "And yeah, it's nice to get that positive reinforcement. But it's dangerous to think that's what makes your life worth living. Because it goes away . . . eventually." He looked down at his wine. "As I well know."

"But that's not what you miss the most."

"No. I guess I can't lie and say it's not a part of it, but I miss the guys. I miss the routine. I miss knowing what my day is going to be like. I miss the game."

She reached out and laid her hand on his thigh just above his knee, over his jeans, and gave him a gentle squeeze. "I'm sorry."

"For what?"

"Just sorry that happened to you. Sorry that you can't play anymore." "Yeah. Me, too."

He turned his head and looked at her. In the soft lamplight of the room, her blond hair glowed. So beautiful . . . she was so beautiful. Longing to touch her, to taste her, blazed through his chest.

145

Her blue eyes darkened. His gaze dropped to her mouth and her lips parted.

Heat and desire pulsed between them. "Peyton." He lifted his free hand and cupped her face, so gently, his thumb brushing near the corner of that mouth that looked like the first step to heaven.

She gazed back at him.

"I watched you all day. I can't stop thinking about you." Long eyelashes lowered and rose again.

He shifted closer and touched his mouth to her cheek. Her eyes closed and he felt the quivering of her body. He brushed his lips over her ear, down the side of her neck, and her skin was so soft and she smelled so damn good, luscious, like exotic flowers and dark vanilla and sex. It rushed to his head like a drug.

She made a soft sound in her throat and the hand on his thigh tightened. "Drew . . . "

His name was a breath on her lips.

He kissed her cheek again and she tilted her head, just enough to give him more access. When he grazed his teeth over her jaw, she shivered.

Vaguely, he knew this shouldn't be happening. But she wasn't stopping him . . . she was moving into him, her hand sliding higher up his thigh . . . and he used the hand cupping her jaw to turn her face to him. Their mouths hovered a whisper apart. Their eyes met and held, slow, intoxicating torture as he waited . . . and when those ridiculous eyelashes fluttered downward, he touched his mouth to hers.

She opened for him and he kissed her, slow, gentle, deep. When he pulled back to look at her once more, his breath stalled in his chest. So beautiful.

He took her wineglass from her and set both glasses on the coffee table. One hand returned to her face, the other glided into her hair and he took her mouth again. This time they both opened eagerly and he slid his tongue into her mouth. She was sweet, so goddamn sweet—the taste of her, the feel of her, the scent of her, all now filling his head with reckless lust. Hot need jolted straight to his groin.

She kissed him back, her tongue sliding on his. He tilted his head to go deeper, a groan rumbling up from his chest. Her other hand landed on his chest, fingers flexing against his shirt, igniting more fire inside him. He shifted on the couch to get closer to her, licking inside her mouth, nipping at her lips.

He slipped his hand downward, rubbing the side of her neck. The pulse at her throat fluttered under his thumb. His fingers dipped under the loose neckline of her T-shirt then under her bra strap to cup her small, round shoulder. When he dragged his hand back, his fingertips grazed over the top swell of her breast.

Her moan lit up every nerve ending in his body and he leaned in more, pressing her back into the couch cushions with his upper body. Her hand slid higher still on his thigh, inches from his aching dick. Now her other hand found skin, slipping inside the opening of his shirt, caressing his collarbone and shoulder. Hot need slammed into his balls.

"Sweet fucking hell," he muttered. "I want to taste every inch of you." He swallowed her gasp and kissed her again.

Her fingers curled over his shoulder and pulled him closer as they strained to get nearer to each other, their bodies generating enough heat to start a bonfire. Another frantic little noise in her throat made his dick jump.

A noise behind them slowly registered in the depths of his brain and with equal shock they jerked away from each other. Their eyes met in a second of shared dismay and he threw himself back into the cushions of the couch and away from her.

It was the hospice nurse leaving.

"Good night, Peyton," the woman said as she passed the living room on her way to the front door. "Your sister is sleeping."

Peyton leaped to her feet, tugging on her T-shirt then smoothing her hair. "Ah, thank you, Kishi."

She followed her to the door, disappearing for a moment.

Drew leaned his head back, eyes closed, his entire body throbbing with need, heat centered at his groin. He didn't hear Peyton come back until she said quietly, "That shouldn't have happened."

He kept his eyes closed, fighting the lust that still pulsed inside him. She was right. He *knew* she was right. But goddammit, that hadn't felt wrong. It had felt amazingly, heart-stoppingly perfect.

But this was a fucking messed up situation with so many complications and shitty threads tangled up with the beautiful ones. They didn't need to add more to that.

He sucked in a long breath and let it out then lifted his head and opened his eyes. "I'm sorry."

She shook her head, hands twisting together in front of her. "You don't need to apologize. We were both participating in that."

"Damn, Peyton." He surged to his feet and stalked toward her. He stared at her, and he recognized the frustration and disappointment he saw on her face. "Dammit."

"I know," she whispered, holding his gaze. "I know."

They stood like that, so close but not touching, surrounded by a web of longing and loss, desire and regret. The air around them vibrated with the tug of all those emotions, the tension between them.

"We can't do that," she whispered, sadness filling her eyes. "We just can't."

"I know." Fuck it, he did know. His hands clenched and unclenched. "I better go." She drew her bottom lip between her teeth and nodded, eyebrows sloped downward.

"I'll see you tomorrow." He was taking Chloe out tomorrow for their own birthday celebration.

She nodded and stepped aside so he could leave the room.

She drifted behind him as he walked to the front door and it took all his strength not to sweep her up into his arms and hold her and carry her out with him. He wanted to take her home, to have her in his bed, to explore every inch of that sexy body and equally sexy mind, to make her feel so good. The things he wanted to do to her were shockingly, dick-raisingly explicit.

But it couldn't happen. "Night."

"Good night, Drew."

He stepped out into the cool darkness, the air scented with crisp autumn. The breeze stroked over his hot skin as he strode to his car and climbed in. When he glanced back at the door, Peyton still stood there silhouetted in the light from inside the house. He pressed his lips together, started his car and pulled away.

Frustration turned to anger and he smacked a palm against the steering wheel. He shouldn't have let himself get so carried away. What kind of asshole was he? Yeah, they were clearly both attracted to each other, but they were on the same goddamn page —*they could not go there.*

It couldn't happen again.

CHAPTER 14

Drew had racked his brain trying to think of what to do with Chloe on Sunday for their birthday outing. He was getting a better sense of what she enjoyed, but he wanted to do something fun. Possibly the zoo? She'd probably been there a million times. Navy Pier? Maybe.

Then he'd tripped over the perfect idea, literally, as he nearly crashed into two teenagers in-line skating down the sidewalk in front of his place. Yeah! Skating. He hadn't used his for a while but it would feel great to skate. And he could teach Chloe. Assuming she didn't already know.

He arrived at the Watt home around eleven. He rang the doorbell, despite having a key, because that seemed politer. Chloe answered the door, her long hair in a messy bun on top of her head. Her smile seemed genuine but forced. "Hi, Drew."

"Hi."

"We were just sitting with Mom for a while." She started back toward the bedroom.

Drew followed. He stepped into Sara's bedroom, ready to greet her with a big smile. He was glad she'd been doing better yesterday.

But Sara was half-asleep, and didn't even seem to know he was there. He turned concerned eyes on Peyton, sitting in the chair beside the bed. Their eyes met with a clash of sparks. Heat swept through his body, remembering their erotic kisses last night.

He swallowed.

"She's not having such a good day today," she said quietly. "What have you got planned for you and Chloe?"

"Well, first lunch. Then we have a shopping stop to make, and then we're going to Lincoln Park."

"To the zoo?" Chloe asked.

"Nope. Do you own a pair of in-line skates?" She blinked.

"No."

"Okay then. That's what we're shopping for and then we're going skating."

"I don't know how to do that."

"I'm gonna teach you."

"Oh." She made a face. "Cool."

"Uh, does the shopping trip include a helmet?" Peyton asked.

Drew grinned. "Yes. And knee and elbow pads."

She nodded.

"How about you?" he asked her. "Do you have Rollerblades?" She'd made it clear that she'd be accompanying them on any outings until Sara was comfortable enough for him and Chloe to be alone together.

"God, no." She grimaced. "But that doesn't matter, because I'm not going with you today."

He went still. "No?"

"No." She looked away. "It's fine, though. I talked to Sara about it last night." Fuck, she was pissed at him about last night. Now things were going to be awkward and she was going to avoid him. Great.

He turned to Chloe, sitting on the bed, watching her mom, a somber expression on her face. Drew's heart ached for her. "Do you want to stay with your mom today?"

Chloe glanced at him then at Peyton.

"Go," Peyton said gently. "I'll be here. Spend time with Drew."

"Okay." Chloe slid off the bed.

"What time should I have her home? Five o'clock okay?"

Despite his happiness at seeing Chloe again, he felt an unreasonable dig of disappointment that Peyton wouldn't be joining them. Even though they both agreed there could be nothing between them, he'd been anticipating spending the afternoon with her, even buying her skates and teaching her to use them.

But Chloe was his number one priority. They'd spent time alone together before, playing video games, doing homework, eating dinner, but always with someone else in the house. Even so, they'd had some good talks and he was looking forward to a whole afternoon of getting to know her better and having fun.

"Is there somewhere you'd like to have lunch?" he asked her once they were in his car and seat-belted in.

She clasped her hands together in front of her and thought about that. "How about Red Lobster?"

"Sure."

"I *love* shrimp," she told him.

"Well then, you will have shrimp."

It was a bit of a drive, which they spent talking about school and her friends. She told him about the research she'd been doing into dress codes at school. "There was a Supreme Court case in 1965," she told him. "It decided that schools were allowed to use guidelines about discipline and students' rights. But you know what that case was about?"

"I have no idea," he murmured, mind blown.

"The kids wanted to wear black armbands to protest the Vietnam War. So it was really more about free speech and politics than how they dressed. So I think that telling kids they can't wear certain clothes is different than that."

"Did you talk to your mom about this?"

"Yes! She was a lot of help."

"Well, of course she was. She's a lawyer." He paused. "You think you might want to be a lawyer when you grow up?"

"Maybe. I'm kind of interested in civil rights."

Christ Jesus. This kid was smarter than he was. "So . . . in that 1965 case . . . the school didn't want them to wear black armbands because it was distracting?"

"Yes!"

"And how is that different than other clothing being distracting?" She frowned at him.

"Just playing devil's advocate," he said. "If you're going to use that as a basis to convince your school to change, they'll probably ask that question."

"Yeah. I guess." She pursed her lips. "I guess the difference is that the black armbands were a political statement and it could be distracting to people who disagreed, and maybe arguments could have started about that. But other clothing, like what I wore the other day, they say is distracting because it makes boys notice us for *other* reasons."

Pride burned in his chest. "Right."

"And like you said, boys need to learn how to behave appropriately no matter how a girl is dressed."

"Smart cookie." She grinned.

They ate lunch and had no shortage of topics of conversation. Then Chloe startled him by asking, "Do you really not remember my mom?"

He took his time figuring out a response to that. "I do remember her," he said. "But we didn't spend much time together, so I don't remember a lot."

"What do you remember?" She gazed at him with big, beseeching eyes.

He tipped his head back. "I remember that she was really pretty. Long blond hair, blue eyes, and a sweet smile. I remember she made me laugh." The night had honestly been forgettable . . . one more hookup in a string of them for him. But he wasn't going to tell Chloe that. "But we created something beautiful and lasting, even though at the time we had no idea." He smiled at her.

Something beautiful and lasting out of such an unremarkable night. It was both sad and lovely.

She nodded and looked down at the giant platter of shrimp in front of her.

"Do you think if you knew about me sooner . . . if you and Mom met up again before this . . . that you would have gotten married?"

Drew felt like the air had been sucked out of his lungs. "There's no way to answer that, Chloe," he said quietly. "But I want to be honest with you. So, no, probably not." Was that answer too harsh? Was she going to be hurt? But he didn't want her growing up thinking that kind of "what-if." They had too many "what-ifs" and "if-onlys" already.

"Things happen for a reason," he continued. "Even if we don't know what the reasons are at the time. Sometimes it takes a long time for us to see why something happened."

"Like Mom dying?"

His face tightened. "Yeah, even that. Things that are the hardest probably take the longest for us to figure out."

"Like you not being able to play hockey?"

He sat back in the chair. "Well. Yeah." He huffed. "That is taking me a while to figure out."

She just nodded again. "Do you wish you were still playing?"

"Hell, yeah." It was the one thing he knew how to do, and do well.

After lunch they went to a nearby sporting goods store. Drew walked in and when a sales clerk approached them, he said, "We need a pair of in-line skates for this kiddo." He set his hand on top of her head. "And all the accessories."

"Sure. Right this way."

Chloe tried on a few styles and wobbled around the store. They settled on a pair that felt comfortable and added a helmet, a bag to carry them in, and all the extra safety equipment she needed.

"Thank you, Drew," Chloe said at the checkout, eyes wide at the money he'd spent.

"You're welcome." He didn't mind dropping cash on someone who appreciated it. Nice to know she wasn't spoiled.

Soon they were on Lakefront Trail. The afternoon wind off the lake was chilly, but they'd both brought jackets. Chloe caught on pretty quickly but held on to him as they slowly skated along the path. In-line skates were different than ice skates but it still felt good to be moving.

"Show me how fast you can go," Chloe said to him.

With a grin, he left her at a run, getting up speed. Luckily there weren't many people around because he wanted to go *fast*. Wind rushed past his face as he skated. When he came to a low, flat rock he stepped up onto it, skated across it and came back down on the path. Slowing, he turned and skated back toward Chloe. As he neared her he did a hop straight up in the air, landing cleanly. Pain stabbed from his knee up his thigh.

Fuck, that hurt!

Goddammit, maybe his daredevil days were over. He came to a sharp stop near Chloe.

She laughed with delight and clapped. "That was amazing!"

He grabbed her hands and skated backward, tugging her along. "Come on. I'll teach you how to skate over that rock."

"No way!" She tried to pull her hands away but she was laughing.

"Kidding. Maybe someday."

"I'll never be that good."

He released her and she wobbled a bit but kept going. A lightness filled him, an expansive pleasure as he watched his daughter skating—her beautiful smile beaming, her cheeks flushed, eyes dancing. He wasn't sure what this feeling was, but he thought it might be . . . love.

. . .

Peyton regarded her sister with dismay after Chloe and Drew had left. After such a good day yesterday, Sara wasn't doing well today —confused and weak, refusing to eat anything at all. Peyton fought back tears as she sat next to her bed, holding her hand. The television was on, the volume low as neither of them were really watching, only background noise for Sara's sometimes labored breathing. The rattling, gurgling noises alarmed Peyton and she checked her watch. The hospice nurse should be here soon. She hated this helpless, scared feeling, the near panic tightening her chest.

She gave Sara a small piece of ice to suck on and smoothed lip balm over her dry lips. Then she moved to turn off the TV and start some music playing. Maybe that would be better for Sara.

"Where's Daddy?" Sara asked at one point. "Why isn't he here?"

Peyton's heart constricted and she smiled and stroked her sister's arm reassuringly. "It's okay, sis. He's okay."

When Sara started pulling at the sheet and comforter, Peyton held her hands and talked to her reassuringly, reminding her how happy Chloe had been yesterday with her friends.

When the hospice nurse arrived, Peyton shared her concerns.

"Moving her onto her side can sometimes help with breathing," the nurse said.

"But those noises don't cause her discomfort. I think we may need to change her medications to a patch if we can't get her to swallow the pills, though."

Peyton nodded and helped adjust Sara's position.

"And we may need to insert a catheter. If she's not getting enough fluids, we don't want any blockages."

Peyton sucked her trembling lower lip. "Is it time to move her to the hospice facility?"

"That's up to you. But yes, it may be."

"She wanted to make that decision herself, but I'm not sure she's lucid enough. Dammit, she had such a good day yesterday!"

"It can happen. Maybe she overdid it a bit when she was feeling energetic. We'll see what she's like tomorrow. But you may have to make that call for her."

She nodded again. "She didn't want Chloe to see her like this." Her throat ached and she struggled to control her emotions.

She found herself listening for the sound of a car or the door of the house opening as the time neared five o'clock. She so hoped everything had gone well today. Sara had still been hesitant about letting Chloe go out alone with Drew, but Peyton had convinced her that it would be fine.

And it wasn't because she didn't want to go with them. Yes, it would probably be smart to spend as little time with Drew as possible, given the potent attraction to him she felt and how things had exploded between them last night. But she genuinely believed that Chloe was safe with Drew. "He's not going to kidnap her," she'd said with a cheeky grin, earning a reluctant smile from Sara.

The sound of a car door closing out front had her head turning toward the window. Yep, Drew's Porsche.

She went to the door to let them in, Chloe laden with a bunch of equipment, her face glowing. Drew, too, looked wind-blown and happy.

"Here she is, delivered safe and sound, no broken bones," he said.

"You should see Drew skate," Chloe said. "He's amazing. And we had Red Lobster for lunch. I had three kinds of shrimp."

Peyton smiled at Chloe. "Awesome."

"You should see *Chloe* skate," Drew said. "She did great for her first time."

"I'm not as crazy as you," she said. "He was *jumping*. In *skates*."

Peyton turned to Drew, a strange stiffness in her body. "Thank you again."

"Please. Don't thank me." He paused, his smile fading. "I should thank you for letting her come. It was . . . " He bent his head and rubbed the back of his neck. "Good. It was good."

"I'm going to see Mom," Chloe said and disappeared.

"You could have come," he said in a low voice. "What happened last night . . . it won't happen again."

She wrapped her arms around herself. "I didn't stay home because of that. I talked to Sara last night and convinced her it would be fine for Chloe to go with you."

He gazed back at her, his jaw tight, his eyes stormy. His throat worked as he swallowed, and he gave a short nod. "Thank you. It means a lot to me." He paused. "Is Sara doing any better?"

"No." She related what she and the nurse had discussed. "I'm going to have to make the call . . . we're going to see how she is tomorrow. The nurse said maybe she just overdid it yesterday."

"I think . . . " Drew paused. "I think she made a huge effort yesterday for Chloe. Because it was her birthday and she wanted her to be happy. And like you said, she knows this is the last birthday she'll see."

She gazed at him. "You could be right," she said slowly. Her nose prickled with tears and she scrunched her face up briefly.

At the sound of footsteps hurrying down the hall, they turned to see Chloe, but she ignored them, swung herself around the newel post and ran up the stairs.

Drew's gaze swung back to Peyton. "Is she crying?"

Peyton, too, had glimpsed the tears. "Oh, God." She covered her mouth with her hands.

The ligaments in Drew's neck corded and his hands curled into fists. "Fuck. Should I go talk to her?"

"Let's give her some time." She sighed. "Come in. Would you like a drink?"

"Hell, yeah."

"I have wine or Scotch." At his raised eyebrow as he followed her to the kitchen, she said, "I bought the Scotch for Nik when she came over the other day."

One corner of his mouth lifted. "Right. Lagavulin. She has good taste. I'll have some of that."

She poured him a healthy shot and a glass of red wine for herself. "So your day was good? She didn't give you much attitude?" She leaned against the counter and sipped her wine.

"I'm waiting for that. That'll mean she trusts me, right?"

She smiled. "Right."

Silence expanded around them. "How's your job going?" Drew asked.

She closed her eyes. "Not great. I've been doing what I can, but other people are starting to have to step in for me with some of my clients. If Sara goes into hospice tomorrow, I'll call my boss and tell him I need to take a leave of absence. He's not going to be happy about that."

"For Chrissakes, your sister is dying. He has to understand that."

"He's not exactly the compassionate type. I do understand. I've been gone for a month now and there's a business to run. Clients are stressed because of their own problems and just want them fixed. I may need to make one more trip to New York to take care of a few things."

"I can help," he said. "Whatever you need."

She nodded. "Thanks." It did feel reassuring to have him there, saying that. The load of Sara's illness and her care, responsibility for Chloe, weighed heavy on her. She was strong enough to handle it and she didn't need anyone else. But having someone to share it with felt amazing. A lessening of the burden.

Which made her want to fling herself into Drew's strong arms, bury her face against him and let him hold her. Her throat thickened as she fought back that impulse and she choked down another sip of wine.

Was it weak to feel that way? To want someone to share the

burden? But being strong was getting so, so hard. It was exhausting.

"Maybe I should come with you to New York," he muttered. "And smack some sense into that boss of yours."

She blinked at him. Warmth spread through her at that kind of support. Even though it was ridiculous. She gave a shaky smile. "I can handle him."

"I'm sure you can."

They watched each other for a long, heated moment. Then Peyton bent her head, letting her hair fall over her face.

"I'll go make sure Chloe's okay." Drew tossed back the rest of the Scotch and strode out.

She listened to his footsteps on the stairs, remembering that first day he'd come and how she'd eavesdropped outside Chloe's room. She was curious how he would deal with her tears, and her fears, but surprisingly . . . she trusted him to do that.

CHAPTER 15

Drew read the text message from Peyton Monday afternoon after he finished his workout and sighed deeply. They had moved Sara to the hospice.

He swiped sweat off his forehead with a towel and stared at the phone in his hand, remembering how upset Chloe had been last night after seeing her mom. She'd tried to be brave and not let them know that she was so distressed, tried to hide the fact that she'd been crying when he went up to her room, but it was obvious.

He felt so fucking helpless.

He hadn't known what to say to her. He had no words. They'd all known this was coming, but as Sara's health deteriorated it became more real. And more painful. So he'd just put his arms around her and hugged her and said, "I'm sorry. I'm so sorry."

He'd hated leaving her like that, too. The only thing that helped was knowing Peyton was there for her. Peyton's love for Chloe was undeniable.

He also hated leaving Peyton. Because she was hurting too. And unlike Chloe, he couldn't hold her and comfort her when he didn't know what to say.

Fuck.

He'd worked out some of his frustrations in the gym, banging weights around. Now he wanted to smash something else. The urge to go get drunk and start a good bar brawl tightened between his shoulder blades. But no. That wasn't the way to handle this.

The way to handle this was to be there for Chloe and Peyton. And Sara. He texted Peyton back and asked what he could do.

Could you go to the house and be there when Chloe gets home from school?

Of course. Should I bring her there to you?

I don't know. I don't know what to do.

He sensed the despair in her message and hit the link to call her. "Hey."

"Hi. You okay?"

"Not really. This is hard."

"I know. But you're looking after Sara, making sure she's cared for and comfortable."

"Yes. They're wonderful here, and it's a lovely place."

"Does she know what's going on?"

"I think so." She paused. "I'm so scared, Drew."

"I know. I'll head over to the house now. Should I ask Chloe if she wants to see her mom?"

"Yes . . . that's a good idea. I don't want her to be upset, but she probably wants to be with her."

Dread tightened his gut, but he could handle this.

"I'll let you know. Call or text if you need anything else."

"Thank you."

Later that afternoon Chloe walked in the front door of her house and dropped her heavy backpack onto the foyer floor. Her eyes widened when she saw him. "Hi! What are you doing here?"

"Peyton's with your mom. They've moved her to the hospice."

She nodded, her eyes shadowing. "She told me last night they might do that today."

"Do you want to go see her?"

Chloe's lower lip trembled, but she raised her chin. "Yeah."

He nodded. "I'll take you. Just have to text Peyton and find out the address." Chloe traipsed into the kitchen and opened the fridge. He watched her stand and stare into it, her small shoulders slumped.

He and Peyton exchanged brief messages while Chloe poured herself a glass of juice and drank it listlessly. "Okay, we're set."

In the car Chloe looked out the side window and said, "I don't want to go to school anymore."

Drew pursed his lips. "No?"

"No. I should be with mom."

"I understand that." Should he try to talk her out of that idea? Or wait for Peyton to do it? Or hell, maybe it was better if she *wasn't* going to school this week. She was probably distracted. How was she supposed to focus on schoolwork? Her mom was dying and schoolwork didn't seem like a huge priority right then. On the other hand, maybe it was better for her to have a somewhat normal routine. "We can talk to your aunt about it."

He vaguely felt like he was passing the buck, but his position here was weird and he didn't want to overstep his boundaries.

The hospice ward of St. Luke's Hospital was lovely . . . for a hospital. A family room with hardwood floors, sunshine-yellow walls, furnished with couches and chairs and a fully equipped kitchen had an upscale home feeling. The rooms were all private and they found Sara's room easily. A nurse was there writing on a chart and Peyton sat next to the bed. Sara appeared to be sleeping. This room, too, was nice, although the attractive decor didn't hide the hospital bed or equipment.

"Hi!" Peyton smiled and held out a hand to Chloe. She caught his eyes briefly and he nodded, hanging back near the door. Chloe hurried over and Peyton slid an arm around her waist.

"Is she sleeping?" Chloe asked in a low voice.

Sara's eyes fluttered. "Chloe?"

"I'm here, Mom." Chloe reached out to grip her mom's hand.

"My sweet girl. How are you?"

"I'm good." Chloe's voice choked.

Drew caught Peyton's eye again. "I'll wait out there." He jerked his head toward the family room they'd passed.

She nodded. "Thank you."

Drew wandered down the hall, wrinkling his nose. It smelled like a hospital. Guess there was no way around that. He sat himself in an armchair and let out a breath as he surveyed the room, smiling at a woman who sat on the floor with a toddler playing with some blocks, and an older man and woman on a couch across from him.

He fucking hated feeling this way, angry and sad because people he cared about were hurting. But going back to the way his life had been before they'd come into it . . .back to feeling nothing but emptiness . . . would he rather do that?

Despite the agony of what was happening, he felt he had a place here. In whatever small ways, he was helping, even though he wished he could do more, wished he could make it all better and take all their pain away. And having a place here felt better than having no place at all.

Life was short.

It hit him like a body check from a two hundred and sixty pound defenseman, knocking the breath right out of him.

Life was short, and it was precious and important. And he'd been fucking wasting his.

Moping around, feeling sorry for himself, paralyzed, drinking away his feelings of hopelessness and worthlessness. Jesus. He dropped his head, his hands loosely clasped between his knees. He needed to get his shit together.

But how?

He reached for his wallet and pulled out the business card

Dougie had given him a while back. He studied it and then reached for his cell phone to call the number. He stood and walked out into the hall to find a bit of privacy. When he got voice mail he almost hung up, but forced himself to leave a message. "Hi. This is Drew Sellers, calling for Jack Shipton. Dougie North gave me your name and said I should give you a call. As you may know, I retired from the Blackhawks last season and . . . and I'm trying to figure out a new plan. Dougie said you might be able to help." He left his cell number and ended the call.

It was a step.

He returned to the family room and passed some time scrolling through social media on his phone. It was full of talk and news about the hockey season that was starting that week. The Blackhawks' first game was Thursday night. That feeling of missing out returned, the ache of regret in his belly. But he had to admit to a dash of excitement in there, too. The start of a new season was full of hope and optimism, the coming together of a new team, the veterans who'd been around and the newer players, all of them with the same goal—to win.

He still loved the game.

Depriving himself of hockey was maybe only adding to his misery. Maybe his happiness could still be found there. Somewhere.

There were also messages from his family because it was Thanksgiving back home, and they—not his brother in Vancouver, but the rest of the family—were together celebrating.

Chloe and Peyton walked into the family room and he stood. "Sara's asleep again," Peyton said. "We're going to go home. I can take Chloe. Sorry, you could've gone, I guess."

"It's okay." He studied Chloe. Her small chin was firm even though her eyes were sad. What a kid. "C'mere, kiddo." He pulled her into his arms for a hug, and she squeezed him tight with her little arms. He loved that.

"We're going to get some dinner," Peyton said.

"Come with us," Chloe invited, her head tipped back.

Drew met Peyton's eyes over Chloe's head. Tension arced between them. "Sure," Peyton said casually. "We're just going for tacos."

"Okay." It would actually be good to talk about the plan for the rest of the week. Maybe they'd have a chance to talk without Chloe for a few minutes about the school issue.

They met at Tacqueria El Jojoto in their neighborhood, a simple place with red tile floors, wood paneling and bright red booths. They ordered at the counter and found a table in the busy restaurant.

Chloe's sadness radiated off her in waves of pain and Drew ached for her. When the basket of chips and pico de gallo arrived, she picked up a chip and munched desultorily.

Peyton filled them both in on some information about the hospice. "We can visit her anytime. Twenty-four-seven, and we can even stay overnight if we want to. They have accommodations for families. They've changed her pain medication to a patch so she doesn't have to take pills anymore and they'll monitor that closely to make sure she's not suffering. Tomorrow I'll take more of her personal things so she feels at home." Chloe brought up school again. Peyton bit her lip. "I think you should go to school, sweetie," she said quietly. "We don't know how long it will be. But we can visit your mom every day. I'll go see her during the day and take you back in the evenings."

"I can take her in the evenings," Drew said. "You don't need to exhaust yourself going back and forth, and you need time to take care of other things. Would that be okay, Chloe?"

"Yes." Her red eyes looked like she was going to cry. "But I want to be with Mom."

Peyton now looked like she was going to cry, too. "When it's closer to the end, you can be with her as much as you want. I promise."

Drew read the conflict on her face, though, because he knew

that Sara had said she didn't want Chloe to see her near the end when things were bad.

"What else can I do?" Drew looked at Peyton. "What about your job?"

She grimaced. "Yeah, not sure what to do about that. I'll call Gord tomorrow. Maybe I can hang on a bit longer working remotely."

They ate their tacos, Drew's carne asada, Chloe's pollo, and Peyton's chile rellenos. The food here was awesome, but none of them were really enjoying it tonight.

Drew's cell phone rang and he made a face as he reached for it. The call display showed Jack Shipton. Ah, hell. This wasn't a good time for that conversation. So he muted it and let it go to voice mail.

Outside the restaurant it had grown dark. The crisp evening air smelled like autumn and Drew gave Chloe another hug goodbye on the street. "We'll talk tomorrow," he said to Peyton and she nodded. They both hesitated and once again Drew found himself reluctant to leave both Chloe and Peyton, and he sensed Peyton felt the same. They were drawn together into this turmoil.

"Okay," she agreed and with a brief smile she and Chloe turned away.

At home Drew listened to the voice mail from Jack stating he was happy to hear from him and how great it would be to talk about his rebranding. He saved the message, but didn't call him back. He'd do that tomorrow.

"I know this has been challenging," Peyton said to her boss the next day. She'd gotten a miserable Chloe off to school, shed a few tears herself in private then dried her face and squared her shoulders to deal with all the shit that had to be dealt with. "And I appreciate the support. My sister's now in the end stage of life. I wish I knew exactly how long this is going to go on, but we don't." Her voice wobbled a bit and she fought for control. "I'm doing the best I can to keep up and keep our clients happy."

"Well, they're not happy," Gord snapped. "We need you back here in New York, Peyton. Bev and John have taken over some of your accounts and they're busting their asses. If we can't count on you being here, maybe you need to rethink whether you still want to work here."

Stunned, Peyton stared blindly across the sunny kitchen. "Of course I want to work there," she said automatically. "But I can't leave right now. My niece just turned twelve, my sister is in the hospital now. I can't just leave her alone here."

She could stay with her father.

Peyton closed her eyes. She had no idea if that was even an option. Drew was a single man who'd been living a life of parties, women, and golf games. Sure he wanted to spend time with Chloe, but would he want her living with him full-time, being responsible for everything? Would Sara be okay with that? Her will stated that *she* was to be Chloe's guardian. Of course, that decision had been made long before Drew came into their lives. But Sara had reminded Peyton of that not long ago. She was the one Sara trusted to care for her daughter.

And did Peyton want that? She trusted Drew, but Chloe's life was in enough turmoil without handing her off to a man who was a near stranger, to live in a house she didn't know. Even if it was temporary. No. She couldn't leave Chloe.

"I can fly back again," she offered. "Spend another day or maybe two. But I really think it won't be long before my sister passes away and then I'll be back permanently."

"Okay. We have an important meeting Thursday. Be here then."

"Okay. I'll see what I can do."

She was going to have to call Drew and ask for help again. He'd been wonderful, stepping up, and he'd even offered to do this if she had to go back to New York, but it was still hard for her to ask for help. But this was for Chloe and Sara, and so she would do it.

She found his number and called him. "So I just talked to my boss. They want me back there this week."

"Damn."

"I know." She sighed and kicked her feet on the stool where she sat at the counter. "Apparently my job is at risk if I don't go."

"Ah, shit. I'm sorry, Peyton. I'm sure leaving right now is the last thing you want to do."

"Yep."

"You want me to stay there with Chloe?"

"Could you? It will probably be Wednesday and Thursday night this time."

"Of course. And I'll come by tonight and pick her up to go see Sara."

"Thanks. I'm headed there myself right away."

"We'll get through this," Drew murmured. "Stay strong."

She closed her eyes, his words sinking in and spreading warmth through her body. "Thank you."

The rest of the week, life was crazy—an evening flight to New York, airing out her stale apartment, back-to-back-to-back client meetings, staff updates, planning sessions, and risk assessments. Every discussion with Gord was filled with tension. It felt like he disagreed with everything she said and by the time she left the office late Thursday she had a mothereffing headache. She stayed in touch with Drew and Chloe and the hospice about how Sara was doing. Then she flew back to Chicago Friday evening. She went straight to the hospital from the airport having texted Drew and found out he and Chloe were there.

She walked into Sara's room, met with the scent of the raspberry-lemon candles Sara loved. She'd brought them earlier in the week, hoping that the scent would comfort Sara and be less hospital-like, and Drew and Chloe had lit one. The lamp on the table was the only light in the room, and Chloe was lying on the bed next to Sara, her arm around her. Drew sat in an armchair in the far corner.

The doctor had added a highly concentrated liquid morphine to supplement the fentanyl patch Sara wore, as well as some other medications to counteract the side effects of the pain meds, which made her drowsy. Periods of lucidity were fewer and further between due to the pain, lack of food, and the medication.

But at that moment Sara looked at her and smiled. "Hey. You're back."

She was aware enough to know Peyton had been gone. Peyton hurried over to the bed and bent to kiss her sister's forehead. Her skin was cool and dry. "I'm back."

"Chloe's been telling me more about her mission to change the school's dress code."

Peyton's lungs expanded with relief and happiness at seeing Sara like this. There might not be many more times like this. "She's an amazing girl."

Chloe smiled at Peyton, too. "Ashley's having a sleepover tomorrow night and I'm invited." Her eyebrows sloped down. "Do you think I should go?"

"Of course you should go," Sara said. "It'll be fun."

Peyton nodded her agreement. "We can visit in the afternoon."

"Okay."

Drew rose to his feet and strolled over. "I guess I'll be off."

She turned to him. "I'll walk out with you."

"I still have some things at your place," he said. "I can pick them up tomorrow."

"Sure." They walked down the hall together toward the elevators.

"Thank you so much for everything."

"Of course. Anytime. How were things in New York?"

"Ugh. Crazy." She shook her head. "I put out some fires and got some under control. Bought myself a little more time. Everything went okay with Chloe?"

"Yeah. Though I don't think she was being honest with me with she said you let her stay up until ten on school nights."

"Ha! No, she was not." She shook her head. "She's not above taking advantage of this situation to get what she wants, the little rascal. She's played a few sympathy cards to get things."

"It's hard to say no to her," Drew agreed, smiling. "It's probably hard to say no to her at the best of times."

"That is true."

They paused in front of the elevator, facing each other. "Chloe missed you," he said quietly. "And I did, too."

She pulled her bottom lip in between her teeth as she regarded him, her heart picking up speed. "Yeah. I missed you, too."

Before they could say or do anything else, she turned and hurried back to Sara's room.

CHAPTER 16

Drew texted Peyton before going over to her place late Saturday afternoon, to make sure it was okay if he dropped by to pick up his things. He'd left his clothes and a small toiletry bag there; nothing he'd needed last night.

She opened the door with a tired smile, looking gorgeous as always in a pair of jeans and a long-sleeved T-shirt, thick gray socks on her feet and her blond hair pulled up in a high ponytail that made her look about eighteen. "Hi. Come in."

Music played from some speakers somewhere, something smooth and mellow. He didn't recognize the song or the artist, but he liked it.

"Chloe's already gone to her friend's place," she said, leading him into the living room. "We went to visit Sara and then I dropped her off there."

"Sleepover. Guess that's a fun girl thing."

"Yeah." She turned to face him. "I was just cleaning the toilets." She grimaced. "So glamorous."

He grinned. "Has to be done."

"Why do I have a feeling you don't clean toilets?"

"Nope. Never. Okay, I might have cleaned a toilet once in college."

"Spoiled."

"Yep. I admit it." He held her gaze, and that familiar tension stretched between them. "You okay?"

She blinked. "Yeah. Why? Do I look that bad?" She touched her hair.

"You don't look bad. You look beautiful. Just tired."

She nodded. "Guess that's not a surprise."

"Anything I can do? Other than clean a toilet."

She laughed, and he loved the sound. "I wouldn't ask you to do that. Don't worry, I'm pretty much done. Was just going to pour a glass of wine and think about what to do for dinner since it's just me." She paused. "Would you like to join me?"

"I, uh, already have plans for tonight."

Her eyes shuttered but she smiled. "Of course you do." She moved to the kitchen. "I won't keep you. Your things are in the spare bedroom upstairs."

"Hey."

She paused and turned, one eyebrow lifted.

"My plans aren't anything huge . . . I'm invited to a party an old teammate is having. They said bring a date . . . why don't you come with me?"

She gazed back at him. "A date?"

He lifted one shoulder. "Just casual."

She tilted her head. "I don't know. I'm not exactly in a partying mood."

"I get that. Which is maybe just the reason to go to a party. We could both use a little distraction. A little fun. Why not? You're home alone . . . Sara's being cared for and you're only a phone call away if they need you. Chloe's at a sleepover."

She appeared to think about it, a faint notch appearing between her eyebrows. "I guess I really don't have a good reason to say no. Except . . . " Her eyes met his and held. And he knew what she was thinking.

He held up his hands. "We're friends. Right?"

She swallowed and nodded. "Right."

"Also, there's the fact that I was just cleaning toilets." She looked down at herself.

"Hey, there's lots of time. Go have a shower and change. Have a glass of wine.

I'll get my things and play World of Wizards for a while."

"You sure?"

"Yeah. Come on. Help me out here. I'm kind of dreading hanging out with my former teammates."

She still hesitated then nodded. "Okay."

He followed her into the kitchen where she handed him a bottle of red wine to open. He knew where the corkscrew was now and opened it easily then poured some into the two glasses she set on the counter.

She swirled, sniffed, and sipped the wine. "How is it?" he asked with a grin.

"Very nice. Um, what kind of party is this? You said casual, but what should I wear?"

"I'm going like this." He looked down at his jeans and dark button-down shirt. "Just bring a warm jacket."

"Oh. Okay. I'll be back in a bit."

"Sure."

She disappeared upstairs with her wine and like he'd said, he headed to the family room at the back of the house where Chloe's games were. The music kept the house from seeming too empty, which could be depressing as hell . . . knowing that Sara was gone and would never come back.

Forty minutes later Peyton reappeared. Her hair was down, in its usual stylishly messy waves, and she'd put on makeup . . . her eyes were shadowy and her lips shiny. She wore a different pair of jeans, dark skinny ones, with a thin black turtleneck top that was tight and showed off her curves. "Half my wardrobe is still in New York," she said, glancing down. "I hope this is okay."

"You look amazing."

She caught his eye and apparently saw the heated admiration there as her cheeks got pink and she dropped her gaze. Her uncertainty was at odds with her usual confident, take-charge attitude. Was it because of him? Because they were sort of going on a date? Except it was just as friends. It was clear to both of them that there could be nothing more than that between them.

Dammit.

He checked the time. "Still lots of time. Want another glass of wine?"

"Sure. But . . ."

"I won't have one," he said. "I'm driving."

She went and refilled her glass then came back and sat beside him on the couch while he played.

"I don't understand this at all," she said, nodding at the TV screen.

"Well, first I have to—"

"Don't." She held up a hand. "I don't even want to try. If I get into it I'll have to kick your ass."

"As if that could happen."

She smiled. "Also, I have no room in my life for this."

He shot her a wry smile. "Wish I could say the same."

He still hadn't called back Jack Shipton, figuring it was the weekend and he'd be more likely to connect with him Monday morning. But he was going to do it.

They were ready to leave when he paused and said, "I'm invited to stay overnight at the party. I don't know if you'll want to do that . . . but if you might, it would be a good idea to bring along anything you'd need."

"Overnight?" She frowned at him.

"Yeah." He shrugged. "They have lots of room and they thought it made more sense for people to stay over and not have to worry about drinking and driving."

"That's very responsible." She narrowed her eyes. "This isn't going to be some kind of kinky orgy, is it?"

He burst out laughing. "No. Red's married, my buddy Dougie is married, lots of the other guests are all married."

"You know that doesn't necessarily mean anything. Lots of married couples swap partners and do kinky stuff."

"How do you know this?" he asked, amused.

"Never mind. Okay. I'll pack a change of underwear and a couple of toiletries."

"Perfect."

Whatever she packed fit in her big purse.

He drove down to Monroe Harbor, lights in the buildings around them starting to come on with the setting sun.

"Um, where are we going?" Peyton asked, looking around.

"My buddy Red has a yacht here. That's where the party is."

"You're kidding me."

"Nope." He slid her a look as he turned into a parking lot. "It would be better in the summer, but he was waiting for some of the guys to get back in town for the season to have a get-together."

She bit her lip. "I can't do this."

"What? Why?" Then he remembered. "Oh, shit." His gut tightened. Her parents had been killed in a boating accident.

He found a spot and parked then turned to her. "I'm sorry, Peyton."

"You know?"

"Yeah." He reached for her hands. "You're afraid to go on a boat?"

"Well . . . I haven't been on one since."

"It'll be safe," he assured her. "Red's got a great captain and we're just going to cruise around a little . . . not far. Then he's going to dock in the harbor."

"I don't know," she whispered. Her fingers trembled in his hands and he gave them a squeeze.

"Shit. I don't want to make you do something if you're terrified."

"No. We're here." She swallowed. "It's okay."

"Are you sure?"

"Yes." She still looked nervous.

"I'll be right with you."

Her quick nod was jerky.

They walked through the docks and found Red's big white yacht. Drew had been on it before a few times, a couple of hot parties in the summer with lots of girls in bikinis, but this one would be tamer.

They were welcomed aboard by Red and his wife.

"This is Joe Berenson," Drew introduced Peyton. "We all call him Red. And this is his wife, Jessica."

"Why do you call him Red?" she whispered to him moments later. "His hair's not red."

"Red Baron. Berenson." He grinned. "Sorry. Hockey players have this weird habit of making up names for guys."

"Yours is Selly."

"Right." He smiled and reached for her hand again. It was icy cold. "Come on, let's get a drink and meet some of the others here." Maybe a drink would help relax her.

He felt like shit. This was supposed to be distraction from her problems, not something that made her even more tense and anxious. He hadn't even thought about the fact that the party was on a boat. He'd got that she didn't want to be alone in the house when she'd asked him to stay for dinner, and it had seemed like a good idea to invite her to the party.

The yacht was spacious with a big salon and beautiful bar. People were gathered there, moving around the long dining table that was covered with platters of appetizers and finger foods. Drew greeted some of the guys he knew and made introductions, then they approached the bar and got Peyton set up with a nice glass of wine and him with a beer.

"Doing okay, babe?" he murmured to her after a while.

She nodded and shot him a smile. "I'm okay. You're right. It's fine."

He studied her face. "I'm an idiot. I never even thought about what happened with your parents."

"It was a freak accident," she said. "I know it's very safe. I just . . . haven't done it."

"Well, now you're back in the saddle. So to speak."

"Mmm-hmm." She took a deep breath. "I didn't expect this."

"You're doing fine."

She sipped more wine.

They mingled with some of the guys he knew and he found he was more concerned about Peyton, making sure she wasn't nervous and that she met everyone and was included in the conversation, than he was about people feeling sorry for him. There wasn't a lot of hockey talk, and some of the people there weren't even hockey players; one of the guests, Jim Flannigan, was a radio broadcaster, and there were a couple of businessmen. Peyton had no trouble making small talk with people and he realized she'd probably grown up doing that, with her well-to-do family.

When he introduced her to Dougie, he got a holy-shit look from his friend. Dougie shook hands with her. "Well, I'm very pleased to meet you," he said to her. "Been hearing quite a bit about you."

Peyton shot him a look, too, but smiled at Dougie. "I never know what to say when someone says that."

He laughed, but his smile gentled. "I'm very sorry about your sister. This must be a difficult time for you."

"Yes. Yes, it is. Thank you."

Once everyone was on board, the engine rumbled to life and the yacht slowly moved out of the harbor and onto the lake. A few people went up onto the deck. He looked at Peyton. "Want to go up and see the view? The city's really gorgeous at night."

She squared her shoulders and gave him a tight smile. "Yes. I do."

"Attagirl." Her upbringing may have been pampered but there was no shortage of courage in the Watt family from what he'd seen of the three Watt women.

Up on deck the wind chilled their faces as they leaned against the railing and admired the glittering skyline, the reflection of the lights shimmering on the dark water.

"It is beautiful," she murmured. "Thank you for this."

"You're welcome. I'm glad you're here. You're actually distracting me from feeling sorry for myself."

"Is it hard being around your teammates when you can't play?"

"Yeah. It is, actually. But tonight's been okay. I think the guys are jealous of me having a hot chick on my arm instead of feeling sorry for me."

She laughed. "Hot chick. Right."

"You are."

She rolled her eyes. "Also, this isn't a date. We're friends."

"Right." But once again their eyes met and heat flowed between them. Peyton pulled her cell phone out of her jeans pocket to check it.

He eyed her curiously, hoisting an eyebrow when she looked up then tucked the phone away.

She shrugged. "Just checking. It feels weird to be doing something like this. I've been so immersed in family stuff for the last month. Over a month now."

"There's nothing wrong with taking an evening off for a little relaxation. You've been working your ass off, looking after everyone else, including your job." He wished he could do more to make things easier for her. Except he had a feeling things were only going to get harder.

"You're right. I know you're right. Having fun just doesn't seem like a huge priority right now."

"I know." He covered her hand on the railing. "But you're not letting anyone down by being here."

She smiled at him. "Thanks." She turned her gaze back to the dazzling skyline. "Can I ask you something?"

"Uh . . . maybe?"

"About Chloe."

"Ah."

"Do you love her?"

His chest constricted. "Sara already asked me that."

"Did she?"

"Yeah. But then she changed it to ask if I thought I *could* love her, as if she knew it was too soon for me to know that."

"And what did you say?"

"I said yes. And the truth is . . . " He pulled in fresh lake air through his nose. "I do love her."

She nodded. "That's good."

"It's fucking terrifying."

She shifted her weight against the railing to face him, her expression curious. "Why?"

"I don't know how to be a dad. I'm probably the worst dad in the world." She snorted. "Yeah, not even close, you ass."

He rubbed his face. "Okay, yeah. But still . . . it's a huge responsibility." Yeah, he loved talking about his biggest fears. *Not.* "I don't want to let her down. I don't want to fail her."

She studied him over the rim of her glass as she sipped her wine. "You don't like failing."

He swallowed. "Who does?"

"Nobody. But holding yourself back from her, and from a relationship with her because you're afraid of failing her, is probably . . . failing her."

His belly muscles went rigid and his chest burned. "I'm not holding back."

"No?"

Was he? He didn't even know. Maybe he was. His throat thickened and he cleared it. "I won't."

She nodded. "Love *is* terrifying. I love her, too."

"I know. She's lucky to have you."

Somehow Drew knew that the love of this woman was an amazing thing . . . that even though she didn't have a lot of people in her life to love—her sister, her niece, her best friend Nik—she had a lot of love. Somehow he knew that whatever she did in her life, she did it with everything she had, and that included love. Somehow he knew it was fierce and intense and loyal.

He rubbed at the heat behind his sternum and glanced at her empty glass. "You need more wine. Let's go back down."

"I need more of those shrimp," she said, following him down the circular staircase. "They're amazing."

They joined in a discussion about the upcoming beer festival that a few of the guys were pretty passionate about, and Jessica told everyone about the architectural open house coming up where you could tour amazing buildings.

"That sounds fascinating," Peyton told her.

"You should come! I'm a greeter at the Edson Building. I volunteer every year." Peyton smiled and made some noncommittal response, and Drew knew what she was thinking.

"It would be so nice to do normal things," she said to him when they had a moment alone. "Like go to a beer festival."

"It'll happen." He stroked hair off her face. "This is a tough time, but one day life will be sort of normal again."

She nodded.

Later, Jessica showed them the stateroom that would be theirs that night. Somehow Drew remembered that at least one of the staterooms had twin beds, but it now seemed that they all had double beds, except for one that slept four with a double and two bunk beds, which was apparently already occupied. He caught Peyton's eye and the look she gave him and shrugged.

"This boat is amazing," Peyton said. "It's huge. You'd never think from the outside it has all these bedrooms. And bathrooms."

"Heads," Jessica corrected with a smile. "Yes, it's nice that each stateroom has its own en-suite head."

They ate a delicious dinner, drank wine and mingled with people. He left Peyton on her own for a while, though he kept an eye on her from across the salon as she talked to Jessica and Jim's wife, Molly, and Dougie's wife, Lisa.

After cruising up and down along the shore of Lake Michigan, the boat docked again at the harbor. A few people left and the party became smaller and more intimate.

Dougie sat on a couch next to Drew. "So. What's with you and Peyton?"

"Nothing."

"That's what you said before. I'm not buying it. Not after seeing you with her." Drew shrugged, but his chest grew hot inside. "Nothing can happen. We're in the middle of a big family mess. Her sister's dying. She's looking after her and her niece. I'm trying to figure out how the hell to be a father to a kid I didn't even know I had until a couple of months ago."

"Why'd you bring her, then?"

Drew sighed and studied the patterned carpet. "She was going to be home alone tonight for the first time since her sister went into hospice. I thought a night out might distract her from all the shit that's going on."

"Uh-huh." Dougie tipped his drink to his lips. "Okay. And you're both staying all night?"

"Yeah. It made sense, rather than having to drive home late." "Uh-huh."

"Why do you sound like you don't believe a word I'm saying, asshole?"

Dougie smirked. "Because I don't. But whatever. Did you call Jack Shipton?"

"Yeah. I did."

"Hey, great." Dougie sounded surprised.

"Haven't actually talked to him yet," Drew admitted. "I'll try again Monday."

Dougie nodded. "So how *are* things with Chloe?"

Drew filled him in on the recent birthday party and in-line skating, and Chloe's struggles to deal with her mom's situation. Despite his chirping, Dougie was a good friend. He set a hand on Drew's shoulder and squeezed. "What a fucked up mess."

"Yeah."

"I've been riding your ass about doing something with your life. But you've got a lot on your plate. You know if there's anything Lisa and I can do, we're there. Maybe bring Chloe over for dinner someday and she can meet the kids."

Drew nodded. Dougie and Lisa had three kids ranging from four to ten. "Thanks, man."

He looked up to see Peyton watching him and Dougie. She smiled.

The party began to wind down as some of the other couples who were staying overnight made their way to their staterooms and Peyton made her way over to him. "Okay if I say good-night now, too?" she murmured. "I'm a bit tired."

"Of course." He paused. "I'll, uh, stay and have one more drink with Dougie while you get ready for bed."

She tipped her head to one side. "Such a gentleman."

"That's me. Don't seem so surprised."

"You do surprise me, Drew," she said quietly. "Thanks."

She disappeared and Drew turned to Dougie, regarding him with a cocked eyebrow. "Nothin' there, huh?"

"Shut the fuck up and get me another beer."

He needed the distraction now as he imagined Peyton getting ready for bed— undressing, putting on some kind of pajamas . . . what? What was she wearing? Christ, he had to share a bed with her and it was going to fucking kill him to not touch her.

CHAPTER 17

Peyton closed herself into the small but luxurious stateroom and stood still, looking around. The boat rocked gently. She'd never been seasick, so she wasn't worried about that, but the motion reminded her that they were on water. On a boat.

What could happen? Other than the engine blowing up and catching fire and the boat going down before everyone could get off.

Her chest tightened and she forced herself to take some deep breaths as she grabbed her purse and used the head. She washed her face and changed into the leggings and long-sleeved tee she'd brought to sleep in—not exactly pajamas, but she'd had no idea what the sleeping arrangement was going to be. Somehow she'd thought maybe she'd share a room with another female guest, but no . . . she was sharing a room (and a bed) with Drew.

She licked her lips nervously as she pulled back a puffy duvet and slipped into the double bed. It wasn't even a big bed . . . and Drew was a big guy. She left the wall- mounted lamp on for him when he came to bed and snuggled into the covers to try to sleep.

The sheets were soft and clean-smelling, the pillow perfect, but despite being tired, her eyes refused to stay closed, hyper-aware of the movement of the boat and every little noise.

She'd enjoyed the evening, meeting new people, and seeing Drew with his friends. They all obviously liked and respected him, despite the good-natured insults. Seeing him with his friend Dougie just at the end of the evening had made her heart tilt in her chest—the serious conversation they'd apparently been having, heads close together, then Dougie's hand on Drew's shoulder in a kind of male reassurance.

She liked that he had people in his life who cared for him, even though he maybe didn't turn to them as much as he should. Which was probably typical of many men. He didn't want to admit weakness. She knew he'd been struggling, but he'd also been struggling to hide that.

The door to the stateroom opened and her head lifted off the pillow. Drew. "Hi," she said quietly.

"Still awake?"

"Yeah." She sighed and rolled to her back.

"Are you okay with this?" he asked, unbuttoning his shirt. "I can go sleep on a couch in the salon."

She considered that for a moment, but the truth was, she wanted someone with her. "No. It'll be cold there. And weird. And . . ."

"And what?" He took off the shirt and she couldn't help but look at his amazing chest and abs.

"I'm a little nervous."

He made a rough noise then muttered, "Shit. Be right back."

He used the head and returned moments later, now wearing only a snug black pair of boxer briefs. When he pulled back the covers and climbed into bed with her, she stilled in a moment of delicious, buzzing anticipation.

"C'mere," he said in a low voice, reaching for her.

She rolled into him, all that warm skin and hard muscle, but since she was covered from head to toe it wasn't quite the erotic experience she anticipated. Nonetheless, he wrapped his arms around her and God, it felt good. So good.

"It's okay," he said, rubbing up and down her back. "Jesus, woman, what are you wearing? A ski suit?"

She choked out a laugh. "No!"

She felt his smile. "You couldn't be more covered up."

"I wanted to be warm, and I didn't know where I'd be sleeping."

"Even so, you're shivering."

"I know."

"Let me warm you up, Peyton." His hands roamed over her, spreading heat through her clothes. Heat that turned to tingles and a faint ache low in her belly. "I'm sorry. Just want you to feel good. Just for a while."

"I'm okay." She snuggled in, loving the heat of his body. The strength. The safety, even though some of her trembling was now due to excitement.

Time slowed and stretched out, Drew's touch over her back and hips and hair and the gentle rocking of the boat mesmerizing. Her lips were so close to the soft skin of his throat. She breathed in his scent, clean and spicy male, filling her head with it until she was a little dizzy, and her mouth longed to taste him. She knew she shouldn't, but at that moment it didn't seem to matter what else was happening in their crazy fucked up lives; all that mattered was right now, this moment, this man . . . and she touched her mouth to his skin.

She felt the faint rumble in his chest. Felt the tension in his muscles, his hands going still before resuming their sultry strokes. Felt the hardening of his cock against her hip.

"Peyton."

"Mmm." She kissed him again and he tasted so lovely.

His hand slid up into her hair and tugged it, sending pinpoints of sensation sliding from her scalp down her spine. In the low light, their eyes met, a nexus of heat and desire and wordless questions. Her lips parted and she saw his gaze drop there, felt his breathing change.

"Peyton," he whispered again.

He slid his hand around the back of her neck and drew her to him, their mouths nearly meeting, their gazes connected in a scorching lock. He waited. She didn't pull away. And he closed the breath of distance between them to kiss her.

She melted against him, a soft groan rising in her throat, opening to him in both surrender and conquest. She wanted to touch him, too, and slid a hand over his upper chest then his shoulder, the bones strong and hard, the muscles there firm.

They kissed for long, endless moments, his tongue sliding deep into her mouth, hers touching his bottom lip. Their bodies shifted, moving together in a flow of sexual heat, coming together in a perfect fit of arms and hips and legs.

That ache in her low belly intensified into a burning coil of need. Her breasts swelled and her nipples throbbed. She caressed the back of his neck, rubbed her fingers through his hair and kissed him back over and over until she was rocking her hips into him.

"Christ, baby," he panted against her jaw. His teeth scraped there and she shivered. "Peyton." He kissed her again, his tongue sweeping inside her mouth and she needed more.

"Yes," she whispered, hand gliding down his back over satiny skin. She let her fingertips learn every rise and dip of muscle and ribs, kept going until she encountered the elastic of the boxer briefs, and lower still to curve her hand around his magnificent ass.

"Fuck," he muttered, his body jolting.

"That's what I want," she whispered, squeezing his taut flesh.

"Oh, Christ, me, too." He pressed a hard, fast kiss to her mouth. "Wanna make sure, though, baby . . . "

"I just want this." She licked his stubbled jaw. "Right now. Right here. Just us. Please."

"Yeah." He reached for the hem of her top and eased it up higher. She sat and lifted her arms so he could pull it off over her head. Her nipples hardened even more at the brush of the cool air over them, her skin tingling everywhere with needy expectancy.

Please, please touch me, her body begged.

And he obliged, running big hands up over her ribs, slowly cupping her breasts. Her nerve endings electrified, all her breath left her lungs on a sharp exhale, and she struggled to draw air back in. Sensation sizzled through her veins.

"Peyton. Christ, Peyton, you're beautiful."

She felt beautiful, his hands worshipping her curves.

"Can't believe I'm touching you like this," he murmured and he tugged her back down to lie next to him while he caressed and fondled. He pinched her nipples between his fingers, shooting ecstasy straight to her core, rubbed his rough cheek over one breast then captured the nipple in his mouth. He sucked it with gentle pulls, his hand slipping down to lie flat on her belly above the waistband of her leggings.

This was crazy and irresponsible and soul-searing, getting hot and naked with Drew. But there was no way she could stop now as she floated helplessly on a tidal wave of lust. She arched her back into his touch, offering her breasts to him, her nipples for him to suck, and oh, *God*, the flood of liquid heat between her legs was immense. Her hips lifted and it was lovely when his hand slid lower, over the Lycra and cotton, to cup her pussy.

She gave a soft cry as he touched her there, holding her in a firm embrace, his hand between her thighs as he tugged at a nipple with his teeth. Pleasure seared through her from her breast to her clit.

"Wet," he murmured against her skin. He licked around her aching nipple. "You feel so wet, Peyton."

"I am wet," she moaned. "I can feel it. Touch me more . . . please."

"Oh, yeah." His hand rubbed in firm strokes that had pleasure twisting up so fast and hard she nearly came.

"Oh! Oh!" She covered her mouth with her hand, vaguely aware there were other people sleeping nearby.

"Let's see how wet you are, baby." His hand withdrew then pushed beneath her leggings and panties. "Too many clothes. Oh . . . yeah." He found her bare flesh, the hot slickness there. Her heart raced and her body tightened. Her first instinct was to slam her thighs shut against the jolting touch, but it felt good . . . so good . . . she relaxed and opened to him. "Need these off you."

He moved on the bed, a substantial shadow as he shifted to tug her leggings and panties down her legs. Her skin burned everywhere.

"Wanna make you feel good, Peyton." He shifted back down beside her, one arm sliding beneath her head, his other hand returning between her legs. "Wanna pet this soft little pussy. Christ, you're so soft." He stroked and patted her over her outer lips. "Where's that little bud . . . there it is." His long middle finger dipped between the folds and stroked up over her clit. She jerked against him and moaned. "You're small, baby . . . kept this hidden. Now I found it I can make you feel good."

He circled wet fingertips over the bundle of nerves and she felt it swell. That pinching need deep inside her became nearly painful. His lips tugged at her nipples again as he played, and her mind spun in a glow of light, blissing out at the sensations converging in her core, twisting up hot and high.

The temperature in the room seemed to have gone up several degrees. She was no longer cold, instead burning up from the inside out, shivering not because of coolness but because of erotic need. She watched the flex of his muscles as he moved beside her, let her eyes flutter closed when he shifted back up to claim her mouth in another long, drugging kiss.

More. She needed more. She reached for him, found his erection, and a long groan rose to his lips as she curved her fingers around him. Yes. Yes. Satisfaction swelled inside her, knowing he wanted this, too, he wanted . . . her.

"You have . . . something?" she managed to mumble, because she needed him inside her and please, please, please let him know what she meant, let him having something . . .

"Yeah." He laid a string of soft kiss over her cheek and jaw then rolled away from her and off the bed. She watched him shuck his snug underwear, her breath stalling in her chest as she viewed his cock, a thrilling sight—bold, aggressively long and thick, and beautiful. Her inner muscles squeezed in anticipation of him filling her with that luscious length and girth. He reached for his jeans and with quick motions had opened a condom and applied it.

His big hands stroking the thin latex down his shaft as he returned to the bed had more wet warmth surging between her legs. God. So beautiful.

The light of the wall lamp gilded his body into highlights and shadows, sculpting his muscles as he rejoined her on the bed. She drank in the sight of him even as her body ached for more of his touch.

He knelt between her thighs and coasted his hands up from her hips over her ribs and her breasts. "Look at you," he said hoarsely. "Gorgeous."

Her tongue swiped over her bottom lip as she gazed back at him. He was gorgeous, too, his dark hair falling across his forehead, his eyes hot, his mouth so firm and beautiful.

His hands found her thighs and opened her wider to him. Eager and aching, she reached for his cock and directed the head to her entrance. His breathing went ragged and his face contracted.

His hand covered hers and he pressed into her, the bulging crown wedged in her opening. They both went still, bodies pulsing. He swallowed and she regarded him with avid eyes as he slowly moved, pushing into her with fiery pressure. The tightness eased, pleasure flowing through her in waves of sweetness, then he filled her. His hands moved to her thighs and gripped her there, and his hips began a rhythm of slide and thrust, slow and sure. Her eyes fell closed on a wave of pleasure. Dear God. Bliss swelled inside her, almost unbearably huge.

"So deep . . . " He was filling her with those hard thrusts, winding up that hot coil of tension, taking her up, taking her higher. "Oh, God, Drew . . . so deep."

He stretched out over her, slowing his movements, kissing her mouth, resting his nose alongside hers, staring into her eyes as he rocked against her. Every motion stroked sensitive nerve endings inside her, flames licking over her. He was everywhere, inside her, his hands on her body, his mouth on hers. With every stroke and plunge, she sank deeper into it, her fingers tightening on his shoulders.

"Drew." His name was a breath on her lips, and she turned her mouth to him to kiss him again. Their lips met and clung as her orgasm built. She felt it rising inside her and she strove to meet that bright, piercing bliss that went on and on, intense and powerful and moving. She wrapped her arms and legs around him; squeezed him with every muscle she had.

"God," she gasped. "Drew, oh, my God."

"Good, baby?" He lifted his head and looked into her eyes and the rest of the world disappeared at the look there . . . a claiming, an ownership that thrilled her to her core even though she didn't understand it. He thrust into her again, her body still throbbing, and it was so sweet and hot she felt herself falling.

She couldn't even speak to tell him it was good, so good; just lost herself in the sensation of surging waves pulling her down into warm, shivering ecstasy. She was sinking, or maybe floating, holding on as tight as she could.

This man . . . Drew . . . his scent filled her head; he filled her body and gave her pleasure beyond anything she'd ever known. But he also filled a space in her life . . . and in her heart.

He opened his mouth on the side of her neck, sucked her skin in so gently, his breathing harsh and fast in her ear as he came, too, the strength and heat of his body covering hers, and she never wanted this to end.

CHAPTER 18

The call from the hospice came Monday morning.

Chloe had refused to go to school that morning. Sunday's visit with Sara had been difficult, and rather than force Chloe to go, Peyton let her stay home with the plan of visiting Sara that afternoon. But it was only ten o'clock when the head nurse called to tell them they should come right away.

She set the phone down on the kitchen counter, her body vibrating with fear and grief. Her heart galloped and her hands trembled as she set them to her mouth. She had to tell Chloe and she had no fucking clue what to say.

It was almost as if Chloe had known it was the end, and maybe she had sensed it with some mother-daughter connection. Last night the conversation between Chloe and her mom—well, really it had just been Chloe talking; Sara had been somewhat awake but uncommunicative—had brought tears to Peyton's eyes. "You're the best mom," she'd said, lying on the bed beside Sara. "I loved it when we had popcorn and movie nights. I loved it when you took me shopping and we both tried on crazy outfits. And even when I was mad at you because you wouldn't let me go to that concert without any parents, inside I was secretly glad because I was really kind of scared to go, and it meant you loved me."

God, how had a twelve-year-old gotten so wise?

"I'm going to be okay, Mom, because I learned from you. I know it was hard being a single mom, but you never complained. And I'll never forget everything you did for me."

A smile had ghosted over Sara's lips, and she'd managed to whisper, "I love you, Chloe."

"Love you, too."

They arrived back at the hospice to find Sara asleep . . . or unconscious. She didn't rouse when they spoke to her or touched her.

"Hearing is the last sense to go," the nurse told them quietly. "So you can keep talking to her."

Was it too late? Yesterday it had almost been like Chloe had known to say goodbye, like she'd given Sara permission to go. So Peyton held her sister's hand and told her, "You know I'll look after Chloe with everything I have. She has me, and now she has Drew . . . who also loves her. I asked him, Sara . . . and he told me you asked him, too . . . and he loves her. So she has love. And she was right yesterday—she *will* be fine. Not as fine as if you were there, because losing your mother always leaves a hole in your life, but you will always be with her, we know that. Like Mom is always here with us . . . right? And I'll be fine, too, because I've learned so much from you . . . I've learned the meaning of strength . . . " Her voice started to quaver and she paused. "I've learned courage from you. And I've learned grace from you. I love you, big sis."

Sara's fingers twitched in hers, and Peyton chose to believe that was a sign that

Sara had heard her. She wiped the tears that streamed down her face and sat quietly.

"Peyton." She turned at the low, deep voice and saw Drew

standing there with Chloe. Had he heard all that? Well, it wasn't anything he didn't already know.

Saturday night she'd slept with this man, shared her body with him, and it felt like she'd also shared her soul. He'd been there for her, easing her fears and not just about being on a boat on the lake, but all the fears that crowded her head every day, all day, the fears she shared with him . . . that she was going to fail. She wasn't going to be able to do this and she was going to fail Sara, and fail Chloe. And she was terrified.

For a while in his arms that night, he'd chased out the fear, and a swelling gratitude mixed with longing rose inside her as she stared at his somber face. She wanted to get up and throw herself into those strong arms.

"Chloe called me," he said softly. "I didn't know if I should come, but . . . "

Peyton nodded and wiped more tears. She smiled at her niece. "If Chloe wants you here, then of course you should come." She started to say something about saying goodbye to Sara, but remembered that Sara could possibly still hear them, and they shouldn't talk about her . . . they should talk *to* her. "Drew is here, Sara," she said. "He's here for Chloe, like I said."

She turned to Drew. "Do you want to say goodbye? We can step out of the room for a minute."

His face tightened and his throat worked, but he nodded. "Yes."

Peyton rose from the chair and set her hands on Chloe's little shoulders. "Let's give them a minute."

They stepped out into the hall. Chloe turned into Peyton and sobbed, "Auntie P. What are we going to do?"

Peyton hugged her niece, wishing she had the answer. More tears filled her eyes. "We're going to be okay."

Drew came out only a moment later, the look of panic on his face replaced with peace. "Thank you," he said to Peyton. He rubbed Chloe's back.

"Do you want to be with her, Chloe?" Peyton asked.

This was a tough decision for anyone, never mind a child. It was one thing they hadn't discussed. Finally, Chloe said, "Yes."

Peyton nodded and they returned to the room. She glanced at Drew over her shoulder. "Will you stay?"

He nodded.

Chloe climbed onto the bed as she often did and lay down beside her mom. Peyton sat and held Sara's hand. And they were with her.

"She's gone," the nurse said softly a while later.

Peyton nodded, the pressure behind her eyes and cheekbones so intense, her eyes so full of tears, the room was a blur. Her heart felt crushed in her chest. Chloe's face was wet and red, her lips trembling as she gave her mom a last kiss on the cheek. "Bye, Mommy."

Peyton almost lost it then, but held on to her control by her fingernails. "Stay as long as you want," the nurse said. "As long as you need."

Peyton carefully laid Sara's hand on the bed and turned her attention to Chloe, rounding the bed to stroke her hair and hold her shoulders. "I don't want to go," Chloe sobbed. "I don't want to go!"

Peyton sucked in a shaky breath.

"Maybe she's not really dead," Chloe said, desperation in her voice. "Maybe she's just sleeping. How do they know? Maybe it's not true. We can't leave her!" Oh, God. Pain knifed through Peyton's chest.

The door opened and Drew appeared. He took in what was happening, his eyebrows sloped down in a sad slant, his mouth tight.

Peyton met his eyes and nodded. He joined her and she stepped aside. "Chloe." He touched Chloe's shoulder.

"She might not be dead," Chloe sobbed.

Drew hesitated then reached out and picked her up. He turned her into his arms, cradling her head into his shoulder and she cried in racking, heartrending sobs as he carried her out of the room.

Peyton closed her eyes and tipped her head back, then took a last look at her sister. "Bye, Sara," she whispered. "Never forgotten."

CHAPTER 19

"I hate leaving you two."

Peyton bit her lip as she handed Aunt Laura a cup of coffee.

Her dad's sister had come from California for the funeral. Now that was done, she was flying back to San Francisco tomorrow.

"I wish I was closer to you." Aunt Laura picked up the mug. With her trim figure and hair in a stylish cut and most likely expertly colored, she didn't look the fifty-nine years old she was. "California is so far. Since your mom and dad passed, I've wished I could do more for you. Especially since Sara got sick."

"It's okay, Aunt Laura." Peyton tried to smile reassuringly. "We're grown women now."

"I know. And you're amazing. Your parents were so proud of both of you. Your job in New York—working with all those high-profile businesses. And Sara being a lawyer . . . and such a great mom." She sighed. "This is so unfair."

"It is." Peyton swallowed. She'd been struggling to keep her emotions under control all week, since Sara had passed away. Being so busy had helped.

The last week had been a blur, preparing Sara's funeral. She'd left detailed instructions of what she wanted with her usual practical planning. Peyton still wasn't sure how Sara had had the strength to do the things she had. Planning your own funeral had to rank right up there as one of the most horrible things in life to deal with.

There'd been a lot to do to carry out Sara's wishes. Having something to focus on kept her busy, and to her surprise, Drew had been there to help. She wasn't sure why that surprised her, other than this wasn't exactly a fun time and he really didn't have to be there. But he was. He'd stepped up to do so much, often without even being asked, and his broad shoulders had been dampened by tears more than once, between her and Chloe.

She'd been dealing with Aunt Laura and other family who'd come from out of town and friends who wanted to help. People she didn't even know—coworkers of Sara's, parents of Chloe's friends, old friends of her parents—stopped by with food and cards and flowers. They had so much food in the fridge Peyton wouldn't have to cook a meal for the next year. But the thoughtfulness touched her.

She'd also had to meet with Sara's attorney about probating her will. There were still a million things to be done with credit cards, bank accounts, investments and life insurance.

"What a difficult age for Chloe to lose her mom," Aunt Laura said. "Thank God she has you."

Peyton nodded. "I think I'm lucky I have her, too."

Aunt Laura's eyes crinkled up as she smiled. "You two will be okay."

"Yes. We will. It'll take some time, but we'll get through this."

"Please let me know if you need anything. Anything at all. I know you two girls are all grown up and independent, but please don't hesitate to ask if there's anything you need help with." Aunt Laura gave a short laugh. "I don't even know what that would be. But if you want to come to California for a visit to get away from things, I'd be happy to have you. Or I'd be happy to have Chloe if she wants to come."

Aunt Laura had a busy career herself, managing a hotel that was part of a large chain. She'd never married and had no children. She worked long hours but she apparently had an active social life with a new boyfriend and lots of other friends and activities she was involved with. Sara and Peyton had visited her many times during summer vacations when they'd gotten older. Aunt Laura wasn't exactly nurturing, but when they'd become teenagers, they'd been fascinated with her glamorous life as an independent career woman in a big city.

"I think Chloe might love that," Peyton said softly. "She might need a little time, but I know Sara and I both enjoyed the vacations we spent with you."

"She seems quite fond of her father."

"Yes." Peyton smiled. "It was weird timing, but having Drew has been a huge help to her. To both of us, actually."

Aunt Laura gave her a shrewd look that made Peyton wish she hadn't added that last part. "He's quite a man."

Peyton shook her head, her smile going crooked. "I don't know what that means."

"He's . . . very masculine. Strong. Intense. Protective."

Peyton swallowed. "I guess." No, she didn't guess. Aunt Laura was exactly right. Drew was all those things and more.

"I can see how much he loves Chloe, even though he's known her such a short time."

"Yes. He does. And I'm so happy about that. It's such a wonderful thing for her." "So yes . . . bad timing. But still a good thing that he's in her life."

"I agree."

"So your plan is to take Chloe back to New York with you?"

"That's the plan." A rock materialized in her stomach. She forced a smile.

"And where is Drew in that plan?"

Peyton dropped her gaze. "I don't know. There are a lot of things I haven't figured out yet. Don't worry. I'm not going to rush things."

"I know you'll do what's best. For all of you. It's a difficult situation."

Peyton sighed. "So difficult." She lifted her chin and straightened her shoulders. "We'll get through it, though."

"I know you will. You're strong. Strong enough to get through this. And smart. Just be smart enough to know when you need help . . . and be brave enough to ask for it."

Peyton stared at her aunt. Asking for help had always felt like a weakness to her. To her and to Sara. But when Sara had needed help, Peyton had made sure she was there for her, whether she'd asked or not. And she'd never, ever seen Sara as weak.

Her throat thick, she swallowed and nodded. "Thank you, Aunt Laura. I will."

The next day she and Chloe drove Aunt Laura to the airport then returned to an empty house. Things had been so busy they'd barely had time to register that Sara was gone. And she wasn't coming back.

It seemed to hit them both like a brick wall as they wandered through the house. Now that all the activity had subsided and everyone had left, the feeling of empty desolation slammed into them. The utter bleakness and devastation.

Peyton's stomach churned and she closed her eyes, standing in the middle of the living room. "Auntie P?"

Chloe's quavery voice unlocked her squeezed-together eyes. She regarded her niece, who looked like everything she felt— miserable and frightened and alone. She held out her arms and Chloe rushed into them.

She squeezed Chloe tight, pressing her face to her shoulder, her eyes burning and her nose stinging. "You're not alone," she whispered.

Chloe nodded, and Peyton felt her cotton sweater dampen

with tears as Chloe wept. Scalding liquid slid down her own cheeks. She fought to control her breathing, her lungs wanting to sob and gasp, but she had to hold it together. For Chloe.

Or maybe she didn't. Maybe Chloe was strong enough to know that she was hurting, too, with a wrenching, throbbing ache that went right to her marrow.

Sara was never coming back.

God, it was almost unbearable. Too excruciating to even think. And yet . . . it was real.

She'd lost her sister. Chloe had lost her mother.

A huge bubble of anguish swelled in her chest and a sob escaped her lips. "Chloe," she choked out. "Oh, Chloe. I'm so sorry. I'm sorry."

Chloe wept, too, in painful, racking sobs.

"We have each other," Peyton blubbered, beyond being able to control her emotions. "We have each other. Always. I know it hurts." She squeezed Chloe tighter. "I know it hurts so much. But we have each other."

Chloe sobbed more, her weeping tearing at Peyton's heart, shredding it even more. She wanted to scream and rail and shake her fists with helpless anger. This should not have happened to this beautiful girl. This should not have happened to her amazing sister.

This should not have happened.

"I don't want to go to school," Chloe said a week later, folding her arms across her chest and frowning.

It was Sunday night, nearly two weeks after Sara had passed away. Chloe had been away from school that full two weeks, and Peyton was trying to convince her she needed to go back.

"I know it's hard, honey, but you need to do this."

"I just don't want to go. School is stupid."

"You like school."

"Not anymore. Everything is stupid."

Peyton couldn't disagree with that. She'd had a stupid conversation with her stupid boss on Friday where he'd insisted she be back at work next week. She sighed. "I'm sorry, Chloe. I know how you feel. But we have to get back to regular life."

"People are going to be all weird. And I don't know what to say to them."

"What do you mean, weird?"

"Like, all uncomfortable. Even my best friends were weird when they came to the funeral. They don't know what to say, either."

"It's hard for people to know what to say," Peyton agreed. "I don't know, either." She blew out a breath. "But I think your classmates might surprise you."

She'd spoken to the school principal, of course, to let them know of Sara's passing and that Chloe wouldn't be at school for a while, but Mrs. Cardozo had said that Chloe's homeroom teacher would speak to the students and prepare them for Chloe's return. And she'd spoken to her Friday and told her Chloe would be back Monday.

"Fine, I'll go." With attitude, Chloe stomped upstairs to get ready for bed.

It was time to get back to a regular routine, especially Chloe, who needed that. Peyton, however, wasn't exactly sure what normal was going to look like now.

Her career and her life were in New York. Her boss was pressuring her to get back. Others had taken over a number of her clients, the ones who'd needed more immediate attention, but she still had accounts she needed to deal with. She'd been away nearly seven weeks and although there was a lot she could do working remotely, she needed face time with her staff and clients and, unhappily, Gord.

But how was she supposed to do that? She was Chloe's legal guardian. Was she supposed to pack her up and move her to a strange city, to a strange school where she knew no one, right after she'd just lost her mother?

She moved around the quiet kitchen, putting a few last dishes in the dishwasher then turning it on, wiping the counter, rinsing out the sponge.

She'd have to sell the house, which would be a huge undertaking, with all the furniture and Sara's possessions. They'd gone through this once already, after their parents had been killed. Now she had to do it again, Lord help her. Much as she liked to plan, she hadn't been willing to go there in her mind until now.

Maybe sitting down and actually coming up with a plan for all the things she needed to handle would be a good idea.

Tomorrow.

She'd do it tomorrow.

Exhausted, she turned out the lights and climbed the stairs to her room. The emotion of it all was draining, and she was done in every night, yet she hadn't been sleeping well.

She missed Drew.

They hadn't slept together again, obviously with everything that had occurred, but he'd been around so much she was starting to count on his being there. Which was a very bad thing. There was no point in coming to rely on someone who wasn't going to always be around.

As she changed into the long T-shirt she wore to bed, she acknowledged another thing that bothered her about moving Chloe to New York—taking her away from Drew. He'd only just come into her life and she was getting to know him, getting closer to him. And he . . . he loved her.

She slid into bed and shut off the light, then lay there staring at the ceiling.

She had to be practical about this, though. She was Chloe's guardian. Decisions about these things were up to her and needed to be made with practical considerations. She had a career that was important to her, an apartment, friends . . . well, not close friends, but still . . . she had a life.

But she'd seen the sacrifices Sara had made for her daughter.

Was she being selfish, thinking about herself and not what was best for Chloe?

This. This was what she'd been terrified of. That when it came right down to it, she wasn't going to be good enough. That she couldn't take care of Chloe the way she needed to. She was going to screw it all up.

Her eyes burned, but no tears came.

In the back of her mind, she recognized that grief and exhaustion were influencing her emotions and her thought processes. She just needed time.

CHAPTER 20

Monday morning Drew roamed around his house, restless and feeling at loose ends. The last few weeks had been so busy, and now . . . now that things were settling down, he was back to his lonely, worthless life.

Fuck.

Okay, he couldn't slide back into that black tar pit he'd been in. He just couldn't. He needed to fucking do something.

Hockey season had started. Since the first game of the season, a couple of days before Red's party on his yacht, he'd barely been aware of it. He'd mindlessly watched a couple of periods a few evenings when he'd gotten home, beat from running around meeting with the funeral director, ordering flowers and looking after Chloe while Peyton did a million other things.

The first thing he had to do was call Jack Shipton. It had been over two weeks since he'd first contacted him. They'd played a bit of phone tag, but then Sara had passed away and things had gotten crazy.

He hadn't been procrastinating on it. Really.

He sighed as he made the call, but once again ended up leaving a voice mail. "Hey, sorry that I disappeared," he said. "My, uh, daughter's mother passed away and things have been a bit busy. But I still would like that chance to connect."

My daughter's mother? That was fucking weird, but how else was he supposed to describe Sara? My baby mama? The girl I slept with once in college and never saw again but had a child with? My... He paused. My lover's sister?

Yeah, there was no denying that he'd only spent one night with Peyton, and yet their relationship was so much more than he'd had with the mother of his child. That night on Red's yacht was burned into his memory. They'd both known it shouldn't have happened, but it had and it had been fucking amazing. He'd wanted her for so long, tried to keep his distance even though the sparks burned whenever he got too close to her. He knew she felt the same.

Had he taken advantage of that situation by not speaking up and making sure Red's wife put them in separate rooms? Maybe. He couldn't be sorry about that, though.

Too many things had been in the way of their being together since, and he wasn't sure what that meant. There were still all the reasons it wasn't a good idea for them to be together—Sara, Chloe, Peyton's job, and his lack of a job.

For some reason that just made him feel like he had to get his shit together. Because that night with Peyton had been *good*, and not just that night, all the time they spent together made him feel like maybe he had some reason for being here; maybe, just maybe, he wasn't a complete asshole loser.

He drove to the arena, entered through the player entrance and chatted with Kamon, the security guard there, then sat in the stands with some of the media people, drinking a big cup of coffee while he watched the practice. He grinned at some of the antics, nodded when Gersh made a nice shot on net, frowned at Johnny who was pissing around, not paying attention. Then he got watching one of the young guys, Dave Acker. He watched him shooting the puck at Booker in the net, Booker easily making save after save. Acker was hitting it harder and harder and still not getting it past Booker.

Drew pursed his lips, watching the young player. *Hang on to the puck. Change the angle.* He mentally coached the kid. Apparently his telepathic skills weren't very powerful because Acker didn't do what he willed him to. Drew shook his head.

It didn't hurt as much as it had, watching these guys on the ice without him. He hung out and talked to a few of the guys and the trainers. It felt so normal, and yet he still had that sense of not really belonging anymore. The guys were great—laughing and trash-talking him. But it wasn't the same.

When he left the arena as he had so many times as a player, he paused. When he'd been playing, he'd spent plenty of afternoons at Paterson House, working with kids. Why couldn't he do that?

So after grabbing some lunch, he drove to Paterson House.

"Hey, Drew!" Hal strode toward him, hand extended. "Long time no see!"

"I know, I know. My bad."

"Heard you retired last year."

"Yeah." The words weren't quite as much a punch in the jaw as they had been. "My knee just couldn't handle it anymore."

"That sucks man. What are you up to these days?"

"Not much, actually. Had some personal stuff going on but I'm trying to get back on track now. Thought I'd stop by and say hi to the kids and see what's going on."

"They'll be thrilled."

Drew doubted that, but to his surprise, even a washed-up NHL player was still exciting to these kids who loved the game and idolized players, but whose family couldn't afford to pay for hockey fees and expensive equipment.

He was also surprised at how much fun he had, joking around with the boys, some of whom he knew from last year, some he was meeting for the first time.

"Next time I'll bring my skates," he promised them as he left later that afternoon. "Be ready."

"When are you coming again?" Brendan asked.

"Uh, not sure." Jesus, it wasn't as if he had a full schedule. "How about tomorrow?"

"Yeah!"

He left the center with a warm softness in his chest that actually felt kind of good. He was just starting his car when his phone beeped. He pulled it out. Jack Shipton.

"Hey, Jack," he answered. "Finally we connect."

"Yeah, I was wondering what was going on. Sorry to hear about your . . . loss."

"It's a weird situation," he said, shoving a hand into his hair. "Anyway, the funeral was last week and I finally had a chance to get back to you."

"Why don't we meet? You want to come to my office? Or maybe have lunch one day?"

"Lunch sounds good." Casual. Less intimidating.

They arranged a time and place to meet and Drew dropped his phone on the passenger seat. He still wasn't sure what this was going to do for him, but it was at least somewhere to start.

Then he picked up his phone again to make a call. Peyton answered.

"Hey," he said. "It's me."

"Hi. How are you?"

"Good. You?"

"I'm okay. Today was weird."

"Why?"

"Chloe went back to school."

"Yeah, that's why I was calling. So she did go? She didn't seem enthused about the idea."

"No, she wasn't. We had a little discussion about it last night. But she went."

"She okay?"

"I guess so. She's pretty . . . quiet."

"Can I talk to her?"

"Of course."

"Wait. In a minute. What are you two doing for dinner?"

"I have five hundred casseroles in the freezer."

He laughed. They'd joked about all the food that kept arriving at the house. "Want to join us?" she asked.

He'd been about to offer to bring food over, which was ridiculous, but felt helpful and was an excuse to see them. So he said, "Sure. Thanks. I'm just leaving Paterson House, so I can be there in half an hour or so."

"Okay."

"I'll talk to Chloe when I get there."

"Tell me why today was weird."

He and Peyton were alone in the kitchen after dinner. She'd heated up a beef stew that was actually pretty damn good, and put together a fresh salad.

He'd talked to Chloe about school, although her answers to his questions were one word. He tried to coax a couple of smiles out of her, but clearly she was hurting. After dinner Peyton went upstairs with her and got her going on all the homework she had to catch up on after being away a couple of weeks, while he started cleaning up. She'd just rejoined him.

As usual it was hard to keep his hands off her. Awareness made his skin itch and his groin tighten. He couldn't stop watching her as she moved from the counter to the dishwasher, taking in the curve of her ass in a pair of tight black yoga pants. Her pert breasts lifted the thin hoodie she wore on top.

"I was here all alone," she admitted. "It was good, in a way. I got a lot of work done. I was on the phone most of the afternoon, and I accomplished quite a bit. And I even went for a run for the first time in weeks. It just felt funny . . . you know, with Sara not here."

"I know."

"How about you?"

"Went and watched a practice. Then I stopped by Paterson House. I used to do that a lot."

"That's good."

"It was. I'd forgotten how much I enjoyed hanging out with those kids."

"Do you skate with them?"

"Yeah. I guess it's sort of coaching, but sometimes we hang out after and talk about other things. Some of those kids don't have much in their lives."

"My boss is bugging me again about getting back to New York." She closed the door of the dishwasher.

His gut clenched. "Yeah?"

"Yeah. There's really no reason not to now."

No reason? Was she fucking kidding? There were a *ton* of reasons. He gripped the dish towel in two fists, his jaw tight. "What are you going to do?"

"I don't know. I tried to make a plan today, but . . . " She gave a dry laugh. "My decision-making skills seem to have deserted me."

He didn't know what to say.

This wasn't a surprise. He'd always known her life was in New York. But somehow the idea of packing up her and Chloe and moving to another city had seemed . . . ridiculous. Like it couldn't really happen.

And yet, he had no say in it.

"What I *did* decide is that now is not a good time to make big decisions," she continued. "Everyone says that when you're grieving you shouldn't make major life changes. I can't wait forever, but I do know that this isn't a good time to uproot Chloe."

"I agree." He paused. "You know I'm here to help. Like when you made those trips to New York . . . I can look after her while you're gone."

She eyed him. "That could work."

Relief relaxed the knot in his gut a little.

Then she grimaced. "It's not ideal, but hopefully it will keep my boss off my back long enough that I can prepare Chloe."

He nodded. "I'll go check on the homework situation."

He found Chloe talking on the phone. He regarded her with raised eyebrows. She frowned at him.

"Done with your homework?" he mouthed, knowing she couldn't possibly be.

"I have to go," she said into the phone. "Yeah. See you tomorrow." Pissed-off tween attitude radiated off her in waves as she set down the phone. "What?"

"I came to see if you need any help."

She rolled her eyes. "No, because I'm *never* going to get caught up." She heaved a dramatic sigh. "I might as well just quit seventh grade and try again next year."

He laughed. "Yeah, right. You're not even two months into the school year. You have lots of time to get caught up."

They reviewed what she had to do. Yeah, there was a lot but she was a smart kid.

"If you work until eight-thirty, we can play World of Wizards for half an hour."

She shrugged, but her eyes sparked. "I guess so."

He jogged back downstairs and found Peyton in the living room, sitting on the couch, staring into space.

"What needs to be done here?" he asked quietly, sitting next to her. "Do you want to put the den back the way it was?"

She rolled her head toward him on the couch cushions and gave him a tired smile. "That doesn't need to be done right away. Makes me tired just thinking about it." She rubbed her neck. "I need to make an appointment for a massage. If I don't go regularly, I get killer headaches."

"I give pretty good massages."

She eyed him with eyebrows arched.

"Sit here." He pointed to the floor in front of him.

She slid off the couch and positioned herself between his thighs. He set his hands on her shoulders and began kneading the muscles there. "Jesus. You *are* tight."

She made a soft sound of pleasure that went straight to his dick. "Feel good?"

"Oh, yeah."

"I've learned a thing or two from all the massages I've had from trainers. One thing is that all these muscles are connected." He worked over her scalenes, dug his thumbs into her traps and then used his fingertips on her pecs.

"Jesus Christ, that hurts!"

"Want me to stop?"

"No . . . ."

He smiled. "You're tight everywhere." He kept working, finding knots and pressing on them to release them. "This would be even better with some massage oil. And you naked."

She huffed out a laugh. "Shush."

He bent down and brushed his lips over her neck. "I'm serious."

Her muscles all tightened up again. "This might not have been a good idea."

"Don't worry, I'm not about to do you right here on the couch with Chloe upstairs." He paused. "But I have missed you."

"Drew." She let out a soft sigh. "We can't . . . "

"Yeah, I keep telling myself that."

His touching her body, though, even through her thin shirt, had that awareness between them sizzling up again. He saw her peaked nipples as he massaged her shoulders, felt the change in her breathing when he slipped his fingers beneath the neckline of her shirt to dig into her pecs again . . . so close to those sweet, lush tits.

Then he set his hands on top of her shoulders and gave a squeeze. "There. I promised Chloe a half hour of video games."

"What? When she has homework?"

"I told her if she worked until eight-thirty, we could play for half an hour."

"A bribe."

"I'd rather call it an incentive. Or maybe a reward."

She looked at him over her shoulder with a pursed-lip smile then pushed to stand, straightening her T-shirt. "Okay, fine."

CHAPTER 21

"When are we moving to New York?"

Peyton's head snapped around to look at Chloe, sitting at the kitchen counter, swinging her legs, playing with her bowl of cereal. "What?"

"Moving to New York. When?"

"I don't know."

"So we *are* moving."

Peyton didn't answer. But when she looked up she caught Chloe rubbing the heel of her hand under her eye. Shit.

"That's where I live, Chloe."

"I know, I know!" Chloe jumped off the stool. "I'm done."

She started toward the stairs, but Peyton called out, "Chloe."

"What?"

Peyton gave her a long look. "If you're done, take your bowl to the garbage and empty it and put it in the dishwasher."

With tight lips and a wobbling chin, Chloe did as she'd told her then disappeared up to her room.

Peyton sighed. Chloe was going through a rough time. But even so, she couldn't get away with being a total brat.

"I don't need you to walk me to the bus," Chloe announced

KELLY JAMIESON

when she returned with her backpack. "I'm old enough to walk by myself."

Peyton kept her face neutral. This was probably true. It wasn't far. It was a safe neighborhood. Sara had kept walking with her probably more out of habit than necessity. Her insides tightened up, though, thinking about it. No matter how safe the neighborhood, terrible things could happen in the blink of an eye. If anything happened to Chloe . . .

"Humor me," she said. "Let me walk you one last time."

Chloe rolled her eyes and sighed. "Fine."

Peyton grabbed her jacket and followed Chloe out. Halfway there, she stopped on the sidewalk and said, "Okay. You go on."

Chloe gave her a curious look then a shrug. "See you later, Auntie P."

Peyton returned home, the house once again strangely empty. Today she was having lunch with her friend Jax. They'd been good friends when they worked together, and at Sara's funeral they'd talked about getting together to talk shop one day.

Drew greeted Jack Shipton with a firm handshake in the restaurant where they'd agreed to meet for lunch. He hadn't seen Jack in years. "Good to see you, man."

"You, too."

They took their seats and made some small talk as they looked over the menu. Drew ordered a coffee and the Cuban sandwich and Jack said, "That sounds good. I'll have the same."

The server took their menus away with a smile.

"So," Jack said. "Dougie North mentioned you might be calling me. Said he gave you my card."

"Yeah." Drew's insides were twisted up like pretzels, but he tried to appear casual, leaning back in the seat of the booth. "I had some other personal stuff going on the last few weeks, so it took a

216

while for me to get back to you. I'm honestly not sure what you can do for me, though."

"Let me tell you a bit more about my business," Jack said. "I started this consulting company a few years ago, after my own retirement. I had a hard time after I left hockey, and I knew some other guys did, too. Retiring from a pro sports career is a whole different thing than retirement for most people, especially when it's a choice that's forced on you because of injury."

"Yeah." Drew grimaced. "That's me."

Jack nodded. "When I retired it was my choice, but even though I was ready it was still a hard decision. For athletes, much of our identity is wrapped up in our sport. We usually dedicate so much of our life to our sport, starting at a young age, which means we don't usually acquire interests in other things. Some guys who go to college and get a degree in something are smart, but not everyone thinks about their future when they're a teenager and healthy."

"Me again," Drew said dryly.

Jack smiled. "I don't think other people really get it. How devastating it is when you lose your whole identity. I mean, lots of people struggle when they retire. It's hard when you no longer have a purpose in your life, when you're not contributing anymore. But for athletes who've devoted their whole lives to their sport, it's even harder."

Drew nodded slowly. "Wish I'd talked to you about this sooner," he said jokingly.

But not really joking. This guy got how he felt. He wasn't a complete weirdo.

"You probably felt like you didn't accomplish everything you wanted to in hockey, right?" Jack asked.

"Yeah."

"Which leads to a feeling of loss and disillusionment when we can't play anymore."

"Yep."

"So, do you have any ideas of what you're interested in doing?"

"Not a goddamn clue. I'm beginning to think there's nothing I can do."

Jack nodded. "I get it. Sometimes we have blinders on and can't see that the same skills that made us successful hockey players can also make us successful in other careers."

Drew gave him a skeptical look.

"That's where our counseling comes in."

"Counseling?" Drew wasn't sure he liked the sound of that. "Are you talking about a shrink?"

Jack laughed. "We have a sport psychologist who works with us. Also a woman who's a career counselor. We work as a team, trying to find out what your interests and abilities are."

Drew sucked in a breath and let it out. "I don't know about this."

"Look, we've seen that guys who retire because they *have* to, not because they *want* to, are a lot more resistant to the idea and more resistant to help. They sit around waiting for someone to come knocking on their door. You've probably already realized that isn't going to happen. You're going to have to put yourself out there, and that's not easy. We can help."

The server arrived with their lunches.

"I'm sure when you were playing you were put in lots of situations where you had to adapt. I got put on the penalty kill even though I wasn't the best defender. Guys get put on the power play even though they aren't high scorers. It's probably happened to you and you've made it work or you wouldn't have had the success you did. That's an important skill in life and in any workplace. So are things like teamwork, work ethic, and accountability."

Drew picked up his thick sandwich. "Yeah."

"I get it," Jack continued. "You've been doing one thing your whole life. Deep down inside you're terrified that you don't know how to do anything other than play hockey."

Drew's insides tightened even more and he wasn't sure he wanted that sandwich after all.

"I was there," Jack said. "And I can tell you from experience that's not the case. Look at Dougie. We helped him figure out what he was interested in, the training he needed to get, and some job search skills."

"Fuck," Drew muttered. "The last thing I want to do is sit in a goddamn office all day."

"No one's saying you do. There are all kinds of options. What's one thing you're really good at?"

"Scoring goals."

Jack narrowed his eyes thoughtfully as he chewed his sandwich. "Okay. That's something to talk about. What else? What's something outside of hockey that you really enjoy?"

"Golf. Hey, I'll become a pro golfer." Jack laughed.

"I went to Paterson House the other day," Drew said more seriously. "It's still hockey . . . but it was a lot of fun working with the kids. I run a hockey camp for kids every summer back home. I'd forgotten how much I enjoyed that."

Drew looked away, chewing his sandwich. And his gaze fell on Peyton walking into the restaurant. His heart gave a bump in his chest at seeing her, a surge of pleasure then confusion about why she was there.

She looked amazing, as always . . . blond hair gleaming in those tousled waves, dressed in a figure-hugging sweater dress and high-heeled boots. She beamed a smile . . . but not at him. He watched her cross the dining room and throw her arms around another man.

Peyton had agreed to meet Jax at The Village Yard, an upscale restaurant on South Michigan near the office tower that still housed Campbell and Partners. They'd gone there for lunch a number of times when they worked together and it had also been a nice place to take clients. He was already seated when she arrived and he waved at her across the dining room. She was glad she'd dressed up a little, with all these business people there having lunch.

Jax stood and opened his arms for a hug. "Hi, Peyton."

"Hey, you." She hugged him back. Jax was an attractive guy, a little over six feet tall, lean and fit. He wore his brown hair a bit long and shaggy, and his dark-framed glasses gave him a hipster look. She knew he was super-smart and funny, but even though she liked him a lot she'd never been attracted to him in any way.

She slid into the chair opposite him at the small square table covered with a white cloth, undoing her coat then draping it over the back of the chair. "Thanks for suggesting this place. I miss it."

"I'm sure there's no shortage of great restaurants in New York."

"No, of course not. But I miss Chicago."

"Do you?" He tipped his head.

"I do." She sighed. "Not sure how much longer I'll be here." She picked up her menu. "Hmmm. Hard to resist the fish and chips here." They were made with a Guinness batter. "Though I should have a salad."

"You look like you've lost weight." He frowned.

"Why, thank you."

"You didn't need to lose weight."

She grimaced. "I know. I haven't been trying. Just . . . stressed. You know."

He nodded sympathetically. The server came and he ordered the soft shell crab, and Peyton gave in to the temptation of delicious greasy fish and French fries.

Once their menus had been removed, she folded her hands on the table and glanced around.

Then she froze as she made eye contact with Drew across the room. He was staring at her with an intense scowl.

She blinked and lifted her hand in a wave, a smile breaking out on her face, although the scowl took her aback.

"Someone you know?"

"Yes . . . Drew. Chloe's dad."

"Oh, yeah. I saw him at the funeral. Cool dude." He glanced around briefly, too.

"I should go say hi. Excuse me for a minute?"

"Of course."

She rose and crossed over to the booth where Drew sat with another man, a little older than him. "Hi!" she greeted him. "I didn't expect to run into you here."

"Yeah, me, either." Dressed in a pair of black dress pants and a striped shirt, his usually unruly hair neatly brushed back, Drew rose and so did his companion. "Peyton, this is Jack Shipton. Jack, Peyton Watt."

"Good to meet you." Jack shook her hand.

"Sorry if I'm interrupting," she said with a smile. "Just wanted to say hi."

"Not a problem. Just a business lunch," Drew said vaguely, his face still tight. He sent a sharp glance across the restaurant toward Jax. "You?"

She studied Drew. with raised eyebrows. "I'm having lunch with a friend."

Tension emanated from his taut body and his thinned lips, so she didn't elaborate any further.

"I should get back to him. Enjoy your lunch."

She returned to the table where Jax sat. "Yeesh," she muttered, reaching for her water glass.

"What's up? He didn't look very friendly."

She waved a hand. "No idea. So. What's new at Campbell?"

He sighed. "Nothing. That's the problem."

They talked shop for a while, Jax sharing his frustration about dealing with the same old clients, same old problems, and management that wasn't interested in exploring new technologies or taking on different kinds of clients.

"We were a good team," he said. "You're good at dealing with the PR stuff. I'm good at the technology."

"We *were* a good team." She smiled. "But I left for the same reasons you're unhappy about."

"And yet you're not completely happy at Sentinel, either, are you?"

She wrinkled her nose. "Not completely. I have great clients. And a great team. The micro-management from my boss gets to me, though. I've learned a lot from him but our personalities just don't mesh."

"Well, that's business, I guess. Too bad we can't like all our coworkers." She laughed. "Yeah."

"It would be great to be able to pick everyone you want to work with. I'd pick you and . . . and Aidan. And Hannah."

"Hannah?" Her eyes widened. "The girl who can't hold a job longer than a year?" He shrugged. "She has a lot of good skills. She just needs to find her way."

"And Aidan? He's a lawyer."

"He'd be great at reputation management. Knowing the law is a definite asset. Hey, we have lawyers working for us."

"True." She tapped her fingers on the table. "That would be your dream team, huh?"

He grinned. "It would."

Their food arrived and they continued to talk technical stuff like tools for social media listening, SEO optimization and online branding.

Peyton tried to keep from looking over at Drew, but he was like a magnet to her eyes. And every time she glanced his way, he was watching her, still with that intense look on his face.

He'd said it was a business lunch, but what kind of business did he have? He still didn't have a job, although he didn't seem to be hurting for money. Maybe this was a job interview of some sort? And damn, she'd interrupted it.

She focused back on what Jax was saying about problems training a client to use the dashboard he'd developed.

The server approached them about dessert, which they both

declined, and he left the check. Jax pulled out his cell phone. "Ugh," he said, checking messages. "I'd better get back to the office."

Peyton reached for the check, but Jax snatched it up first. "No way," he said. "Lunch is on me."

"Aw, thank you."

"It was really good to see you again, Pey."

"You, too."

She glanced over at Drew one last time as they left the restaurant, and again he was staring at her as Jax set his hand on the small of the back to guide her through the tables.

They hugged again on the sidewalk. "Keep in touch," Jax said. "If you decide to stay in Chicago you could probably have your job at Campbell back."

"Well, you didn't do a very good job on selling me on that," she said with a wry smile. "Telling me how unhappy you are there."

"Right." He grimaced. "But it would be a job. You know. If you really needed something."

She smiled and nodded, and his words stayed with her as she walked to where she'd parked her car. How much did she miss Chicago? How much would she sacrifice to stay there for Chloe's sake? The thought of going back to Campbell was mildly depressing. Been there, done that, moved past it to bigger and better things.

She kept thinking about that even at home as she got to work on her actual job. Since Drew had offered to help again, she arranged to go to New York at the end of the week, this time figuring she could be away two days now. She asked Aaron to book flights and set up client meetings, as well as a meeting to sit down with Gord and touch base.

The doorbell rang shortly after two and she frowned as she dragged herself away from her computer to answer it.

Drew.

"Hi," she said, answering the door with raised eyebrows.

"Hi." His eyes were hard, his mouth a straight line, and his nostrils flared as he stepped into the house. He shut the door behind him with something just short of a slam.

She blinked and him and touched her throat. "What are you doing here?"

"Who was that you were having lunch with?"

"I told you . . . a friend. Jax Morland."

"You got all dressed up and went downtown to have lunch with a friend . . . who you hugged."

"Uh . . . yeah." She tilted her head. "Are you . . . are you *jealous?*"

His eyes narrowed. "Fuck, yeah."

She gave a soft snort of laughter. "Well, at least you're honest."

"Fuck." He rubbed the back of his neck. "I fucking hated seeing you with him. Hugging him. Laughing with him."

Her pulse quickened and her breathing turned shallow. "Drew . . ."

"What?" He reached for her and yanked her up against him. He still wore his leather jacket.

"You shouldn't be jealous."

"No. I shouldn't be. But fuck, Peyton, I was. Burning, pissed-off, punch- someone's-lights-out jealous."

She smoothed a hand over his hair. Her thoughts tangled up with emotions, a feeling of pleasure that he cared along with dismay, knowing he shouldn't care like that, and neither should she. And yet . . .

His head bent and her eyes fluttered closed as his mouth claimed hers. She melted into him, her hands around his neck, her belly tightening with lust.

His mouth still on hers he tried to wrestle his jacket off. They broke apart briefly, and she grabbed a sleeve and pulled, too. The jacket dropped to the floor and he hauled her up against him once more, his hands going to her ass, lifting her.

Automatically she wrapped her legs around him. With her

pussy pressed against his groin, she felt the growing hardness behind the fly of his pants.

His mouth slid over her jaw, nipped at her earlobe, sucked on her throat. Her head fell back and he spun them around and started walking.

"Where are we going?" She held on tighter. "Your bed."

CHAPTER 22

"We don't have much time." Peyton gripped his shoulders. "I know."

His strength impressive, he carried her up the stairs and into her room. With no direct sunlight, the bedroom was lit but not bright. Next to the bed he released her and her feet found the floor. His hands went to the hem of the T-shirt she'd changed into when she got home and drew it up and over her head. She reached for the buttons on his shirt.

In moments they'd stripped each other naked and he tumbled her onto the bed, coming down with her.

He shoved his hands into her hair and held her head as he kissed her, fiercely, greedily. She opened for him and his tongue slid inside, confident and strong. Her hands grasped his shoulders as his kisses turned her insides to liquid heat.

He kissed her jaw, her neck, her collarbone. Shifting down the bed, he cupped her breasts. "Look at these beauties," he said hoarsely before taking a nipple into his mouth.

She gave a soft cry as a stream of pleasure ran from nipple to pussy. He plumped her breasts up for his ravaging mouth, suckling and licking at sensitive flesh. Her head tossed on the pillow and an unbearable ache in her pelvis had her hips lifting.

He moved lower still, kissing his way down her belly, then his big hands were on her thighs, parting them. She whimpered, more heat surging there, and he kissed her leg, the patch of curls on her mound and her other leg. "Mine," he growled. "This pussy is mine."

"You're such a caveman." She cupped her own breasts and squeezed. "Lick me."

"Oh, hell, yeah." He dropped kisses all over her pussy lips, one arm sliding beneath a thigh to grip her where thigh met hip, his other hand pressing the other leg to keep her wide open for him. She lifted her head to look down at him, his dark head between her thighs so erotic, she shivered.

His mouth teased her with gentle kisses and nibbles. She threw one arm above her head and arched her back, her nipples throbbing. Then he kissed her deeper, his tongue probing, licking over inner tissues, circling her clit. When he closed his lips over the nub, she gave a low wail and tossed both arms over her head, her chin lifting, eyes closing. She lost herself in it, in the sensation of his mouth there, sucking on her, making her clit swell, heat coiling inside her. Her stomach muscles contracted hard. She turned her face into her arm, her heart racing, her body on fire.

He drew back and she whimpered, but he was pausing to insert two fingers into her vagina. "That feels good," she gasped. "Yes . . . do that."

He was watching his fingers as he fucked her with them, his expression blistering and intent, and God, that was so hot. The hand beneath her leg curled around to press flat on her lower belly where she ached. He curved the fingers inside her and found a sensitive spot and her body undulated on the bed, hips and spine lifting and rolling. When he bent his head and licked over her clit again, she reached for his head and tangled her fingers in his hair.

He groaned. "Oh, yeah, babe."

She caressed his head, gripped and tugged his hair again, her body starting to shake as that tension inside twisted tighter. Her whimpers became higher pitched and faster.

"Yeah, fuck yeah, you taste so good." He licked again. "So goddamn good."

His fingers kept fucking her, stroking over that spot, and he closed his lips over her clit and sucked. She let out a small scream as pleasure ripped through her, her back arching right off the bed. He drew it out, on and on, her clit burning as she shuddered over and over.

He gave one last gentle swipe of his tongue over it and crawled up over her. She reached for him and he kissed her again, long and lush, tasting faintly spicy. He took his weight on his arms and she lifted her legs to his hips as they kissed.

"Fuck, need a condom," he growled.

"Drawer beside the bed. Hurry."

He reached over and yanked the drawer, but in his haste he pulled too hard and the whole drawer fell out, crashing to the floor, spreading all her crap. "Shit!"

"It's okay." A smile tugged at her lips. He rolled to the side and reached down to snag one of the small packets, rolled it on with lightning speed, and was back between her legs. His knees spread wide and planted into the mattress, he watched her face as he directed the head of his cock to her opening.

She bit down on her bottom lip, watching him, too. He was so beautiful, sleek and muscled. She was still throbbing when he entered her, thrusting in with barely controlled impatience and lust. Her body closed around him and a ripple of pleasure ran through her. "I-I think I just came again."

"Christ." Seated inside her now, he leaned down to kiss her again, one hand going to grip her calf. She slipped her hand around the back of his neck as his tongue filled her mouth, and she moaned.

His hips rolled against her, his cock sliding in and out with blissful pleasure, and he lifted his head to gaze into her eyes. It was so intimate and erotic, heat flashed through her veins and she could only gaze back at him helplessly as yet another orgasm built inside her.

"Love that," he gasped. "Love making you come like that . . . with my mouth. With my cock."

"Yes . . . ." Another wail slipped past her lips as more pleasure washed down through her, not as intense as the first one but no less delicious.

"It's fast," he groaned against her lips. He buried his face in the side of her neck. "Too fast . . . but holy shit, there it is . . . yeah."

He pounded into her in jolting pumps once, twice, three times . . . then he went still with a shout muffled in her hair. She squeezed him as he pulsed inside her in release.

They collapsed together in a sweaty heap, him rolling to the side but taking her with him. Their hands stroked over each other and they shared small kisses. He moved slowly inside her in a last few strokes, still hard.

"Wow," he muttered moments later. "That was spectacular." "Although short."

He gave a lazy grin and his hand landed on her butt in a small tap. "I thought I proved my amazing endurance that night on Red's boat."

"Okay, yes, you did. Today I'm impressed with your efficiency and time- management skills."

"Thank you. Good to know I have some skills."

"Oh, you definitely do." She snuggled in with drowsy delight. "Who was that you were having lunch with?"

"Ugh. He's got some kind of counseling business that helps athletes figure out what they want to do with their lives after hockey."

She jerked her head back to stare at him. "Oh, Drew. That's so good."

He scowled. "What's good about it?"

She blinked. "Don't you want to find a new career? I thought . .
."

"What?"

"Well, I don't know what your money situation is, but even if
you don't need to work, I think it's important to have something in
your life . . . some reason for getting up every morning. A feeling
that you're making a contribution. Accomplishing something."

"Fuck." He closed his eyes.

Concern tightened her chest. "You do want that, right?"

"Of course I do. I just don't know . . . I haven't figured out what
it is yet."

"Well, that's what this Jack guy can help you with . . . right?"

"I guess. I feel like such a fucking loser."

"No. God, no." She touched his face with her fingertips. "This
has really been getting to you, hasn't it?"

He didn't respond. Probably saw it as a sign of weakness, the
big tough hockey dude. "I know I may not have had the best
impression of you when we first met," she said softly. "But I've
gotten to know you, Drew Sellers. I never knew you when you
were a hockey player, but the man I've come to know is a good
man . . . strong, loyal, intense, and committed. Fearless."

His jaw tightened. Then he let out a long breath. "It's been
better lately. I have been feeling like I have a reason to get up in
the morning. That I am contributing. Because of Chloe. And . . .
you."

Her heart swelled. "I've kind of been feeling that way about
you . . . I mean, I had plenty of reasons to get up in the mornings . .
. but sometimes I just didn't want to face the day lately. You've
made it easier."

He opened his eyes and they blazed at her. The heated connection stretched out. "Good," he finally said in a hoarse whisper.

Peyton glanced at the clock beside her bed. "Holy shit! We
have to get up and get dressed."

They both scrambled out of bed. So much for afterglow. He disappeared into the bathroom to get rid of the condom while she yanked on her yoga pants and T-shirt.

They made it to the kitchen when Chloe walked in the front door. Her eyes lit up at seeing Drew, but then she shuttered them with tweenage disinterest, apparently not surprised to see him there. "Oh, hey, Drew."

Peyton exchanged an amused glance with him.

Chloe opened the fridge and peered inside. "Do you think you could buy some Coke, Auntie P?"

"No."

Chloe shot her a frown over her shoulder. "Why not?"

"Because your mom didn't want you drinking pop. It's liquid death."

"Oh, my God, it is not. Everyone drinks it."

Peyton just smiled. "Right. Everyone in the world. Have a glass of milk."

Chloe sighed and pulled out the milk carton. "Can I have a snack?"

"How about some crackers and cheese?"

"*I'd* like some crackers and cheese," Drew said, rubbing his flat abdomen.

Peyton moved to the cupboard and pulled out a box of crackers, still smiling. "All righty then."

After they'd all munched and Chloe had minimally updated them on her day, she went up to her room.

"She'll talk more later." Peyton wrapped up the block of cheese. "It usually comes out when nobody's interrogating her."

Drew laughed. "Okay, I better go. I'm coming back tomorrow, though." She tipped her head to one side as she opened the fridge. "Yeah? Why?"

"I noticed that your headboard on your bed is loose. I better fix that for you."

She bit her lip, eyeing him up through her eyelashes. "Thank you. I'd appreciate that."

"I even brought lunch."

Peyton looked up from her computer, sitting on the couch in the living room with her feet in thick pink socks on the table the next day. "Hi. And yay. I'm starving." She swung her feet to the floor and set her laptop aside. "What'd you bring?"

He held up a bag. "Your favorite spinach salad from Greens."

"Why do I smell fries?" She sniffed.

"Because I got a club sandwich and fries."

She bounced over to him and plucked the bag out of his hand. "You're going to share the fries, right?"

"Do I have a choice?"

She laughed. "Nope."

She led him to the kitchen and they sat at the counter on stools and ate. And he totally let her steal his fries.

"What are you working on?" he asked her.

"A search engine optimization makeover for a client. And research for another client—they're a food service company and they want to expand into Europe, but their competitors over there are putting a lot of commentary about them online that's not flattering."

"Huh."

"We'll fix it," she said confidently. She took another fry. "Have you told your family about Chloe?"

Drew blinked, his sandwich halfway to his mouth. "Yeah," he said slowly. "I called my mom and dad when I got the results of the paternity test."

"How did they react to that?"

"They were shocked, of course. It wasn't exactly something I was proud to tell them. But we've talked and emailed a bunch of times since then. Now they can't wait to meet her."

"Really?"

"They're talking about coming here for American Thanksgiving."

She grinned. "That's so weird."

"What is?"

"How you called it American Thanksgiving. It's just Thanksgiving."

He smiled back at her. "Nope. It's American Thanksgiving. Our Thanksgiving is in October." His smile faded. "It was actually the day Sara went into hospice."

"Oh. Were you celebrating that day?"

"Nah. It's just me, and it's not a holiday here. Anyway, they may fly down to meet her." He paused. "That would be okay, right?"

"Of course." She forked up some spinach and chewed, her forehead creased. "Maybe we should prepare her for that."

"Yeah. I can talk to her about it."

"What's your family like?"

"They're great." He looked down at his food. "All four of us kids played hockey, so my parents were pretty busy."

"Whoa. No kidding."

"Even my sister Shawna played."

"Did any of the others play professionally?"

"Nope. I think Dustin could have. He went to Boston University, too, and he got drafted in the seventh round. But he decided chances of him making it in the NHL were pretty slim, so he just finished his degree. He's an engineer."

"And your other brother?"

"Trent. He stopped playing hockey when he went to university in Vancouver. He's an accountant. Shawna played a bit in high school, but then she got more interested in boys."

"That happens. And they all know about Chloe, as well?"

"Yeah. Also super-curious to meet her. Not sure when that'll happen. They all have busy lives." He told her about his nieces and nephews, and she talked about when she and Sara were kids, and the high expectations their parents had placed on both of them.

"But they loved us," she said. "And when Sara got pregnant they were totally supportive of whatever she wanted to do."

"That's great."

"Do you think you're more like your mom or your dad?"

"Ha. That's easy. I'm so much like my dad it's scary."

"Really?" She rested her elbow on the counter and set her chin on her hand, seemingly engrossed.

"Oh, yeah. He was an athlete, too, except he played football. He actually played in the CFL. Canadian Football League," he added. "It killed him that none of his boys wanted to play football, and yet he drove us to all those practices and early-morning games."

"High expectations also?"

Drew considered that. "Yeah. I guess so. I mean, I didn't feel pressure . . . but I did want to show him that all the time and energy he put into my hockey was worth it."

"You put pressure on yourself," she said shrewdly.

"I guess anybody who has a goal they want more than anything does that."

She smiled. "True."

After they ate he went down to the basement to grab a wrench. He knew where the tools were since he'd used them a few times to do small repairs.

"You're seriously going to fix my bed?"

"Hell, yeah. That's why I'm here." He paused at the bottom of the stairs. "But we *will* have to check it out after and make sure I've done a satisfactory job."

CHAPTER 23

Peyton went to New York Thursday and Friday. Drew stayed at the Watt home Thursday night because it was Halloween. Chloe was now "too old" to go trick-or-treating, but wanted to stay home and hand out candy to neighborhood kids, so Drew helped do that.

"What are you wearing?" she demanded when he came downstairs from the room he'd taken as his.

He grinned. He'd donned a hockey jersey and helmet and carried a stick. He'd also put black around his eye to create a huge shiner and blacked out his two front teeth. "It's my costume. I'm a hockey player."

Despite Chloe's mild scorn, he'd been a hit with the kids that came to the door. He even took a selfie and sent it to Peyton.

In the morning he got Chloe off to school then headed home. They'd agreed he'd pick Chloe up after school and she could spend the night at his place since it was Friday and Peyton couldn't get a flight back until Saturday morning.

So for the first time ever, Chloe was having a sleepover at his place.

This wasn't freaking him out at all. Oh, no. He'd made a rush trip to IKEA and spent a whole day putting together bedroom furniture for one of the empty rooms then making the bed with the new sheets and comforter he'd bought. He knew from her bedroom decor she liked bright colors so he'd gone with that. He'd gone grocery shopping to stock up on the things he now knew she liked. In the end they'd ordered pizza and were watching a movie—Hunger Games, chosen by Chloe and which he hoped like hell was appropriate.

"Did you hear there's a *World of Wizards* movie coming out?" she asked him.

"No, I didn't. That's cool."

"I know! I can't wait to see it. I think it starts next week."

"We should go."

"Can we pause the movie? I need a bathroom break."

"Sure." He picked up the remote and hit the button. Another piece of pizza would be good.

He returned to the family room couch and relaxed, chomping down the thick crust double cheese pizza and washing it down with a glass of iced tea. He finished the piece, considered one more . . . nah. He was full.

He tapped his fingers on the couch, bounced his knee. Waiting . . .

Jesus, what the hell was taking so long? Did she fall in the toilet and drown? He frowned and pushed up off the couch. Down the hall he paused outside the main floor powder room. He heard nothing. He knocked gently. "Hey, you in there?"

"Yes."

"Are you feeling okay?"

"Um . . ."

His heart punched against his sternum. "What's wrong? Are you sick?" It couldn't be the pizza already . . . and *he* felt fine.

"No."

"Chloe. What's wrong?"

After a short silence the doorknob turned and she cracked the door open. Her cheeks were pink and her eyes looked a little red and puffy. Aw, fuck. She was crying? Jesus. Was it about her mom? That probably wasn't unexpected. But why was she locked in the bathroom?

She sniffed and looked up at him. "Um . . . I have a problem."

"What is it, kiddo?"

"I, uh, started my period." She dropped her gaze.

He froze in place. "Oh."

Christ! What the hell did he know about girl stuff like this? "Do you . . . feel okay?"

"I'm not sure." She rubbed her belly. "This has never happened before."

"You mean . . . " Fuck! He was messing this up. "This is your first?"

"Yes." She nodded miserably. "And I don't have . . . anything."

His eyes popped wide. *He* sure as shit didn't have anything.

She bit her lip, eyes teary. "I think maybe I need to go to the store. Or go home."

"You want to go home?" He frowned.

"I have some things there. My mom bought them for me a while ago, so I'd be ready . . . but . . . "

"Right. Okay. But there's a drugstore just a couple of blocks away. We can pop over there."

Fuck, fuck, fuck. Why did this happen tonight of all nights? Why couldn't it have happened when Peyton was here? She was probably an expert at feminine hygiene products and knowing what to do and what to say. Also it figured that Sara had planned ahead enough to buy her daughter napkins or whatever it was she used.

He hesitated. "You're okay for a little while?" She nodded, her cheeks even pinker.

"Okay, let's go."

"Sorry about this," Chloe said on the way there.

"Hey, no need to apologize. I guess I'm supposed to make some kind of moving speech about how you're a woman now, huh?"

"Please don't."

He grinned.

She found the feminine products aisle with the confidence of a twenty-year-old, but her self-assurance diminished in the face of rows and rows of different packages. Tampons—unscented, super-absorbent . . . sport? Who knew. Pads—ultra-long, ultra-thin, wings, no wings, heavy flow, leak guard. He winced.

Chloe bit her lip as she studied the shelves. She picked up a package then put it back. Drew glanced around. Maybe some kindhearted female shopper would give her advice. But there was nobody else around.

"You, ah, probably want pads," he mumbled. "If this is your first time." He had no idea, but he suspected tampons might be tricky and there was no way in goddamn hell he could be any help with that whatsoever.

"Yes," she agreed. "Um, can I buy two kinds?"

"Buy ten," he said. "Whatever you need." He fidgeted with his car keys. "Do you want to phone Peyton?"

She rolled her eyes. "I can do this." She selected two packages and started toward the checkout at the front of the store.

"Do you need anything for pain?" he asked. "You know . . . cramps? We can get some Midol." He'd heard girls talk about that. "Or I have other painkillers at home."

She hesitated. "I don't need anything right now, but I guess we could get something just in case."

Chloe's cheeks went fiery as the teenage boy rang the items through, but she maintained an air of nonchalance as Drew paid for them. She picked up the bag, her head high, and sailed out of the store.

Back home she disappeared upstairs to the bathroom there and returned moments later. "We can start the movie again," she said regally, curling up on the other end of the couch.

He was totally distracted, though, a weird pinching sensation in his chest. Pride filled him at how she'd handled this. His little girl had her period. She was becoming a woman. He'd only just found her, and he'd missed so much.

Wow, being a dad was making him all sappy. And he didn't even care.

Peyton arrived at Drew's house Saturday morning to pick up Chloe on her way home from the airport. He eyed her hungrily as she walked in. Fuck, he'd missed her.

He'd told her about getting help with his life, with trying to figure out what to do with it. She'd been supportive of that. He found himself wanting to be the man she described . . . strong, loyal . . . fearless.

Ha. That was fucking funny. Fearless.

Yeah, he'd been a risk-taker in his life. A daredevil who skated fast, hit hard, took chances. He wasn't afraid of much. But the one thing he was terrified of . . . was failure.

And with Peyton in his arms, in her bed, looking at him with that soft expression, he'd been even more terrified. What he'd said had been true . . . with Chloe—and Peyton—in his life, he'd started to feel like he had some purpose. Helping them get through the ordeal they'd just been through, and were still going through. Getting to know Chloe and being a dad to her. Getting to know Peyton and being . . . something to her.

He'd been so fucking jealous, seeing her with that guy, hugging him and laughing with him. That kind of scared him, too.

The risk was huge. The hugest risk he'd ever taken, and the more involved he got in their lives, the bigger it was. This time he was fucking terrified.

So when Chloe ran upstairs to get her things, even though he wanted to pull Peyton into his arms and give her a long, hard kiss, he kept his arms crossed, leaning against the counter casually.

"How did things go?" she asked.

"Fuck." He rubbed his face. "Good. I guess."

Her eyes widened. "What happened?"

"She got her period. For the first time."

She stared at him. "Oh, wow."

"Yeah. I was completely unprepared for that."

He told her the story and about their run to the drugstore. "I should go talk to her. Make sure she's okay. This is a big deal." She bit her lip. "It's something she needs her mother for."

He squeezed his eyes shut. "Yeah. I knew I fucked it up."

"No." She moved toward him and patted his chest. He wanted to back away from her because if she touched him he wasn't sure he'd be able to resist putting his hands all over her, but he was against the counter and couldn't move. He curled his hands into fists to avoid temptation. "No, I'm sure you didn't. I think you handled it just fine."

"She's probably scarred for life."

Peyton's lips twitched. "Let's hope not. Be right back." She ran up the wide staircase to find Chloe.

Drew paced around his kitchen. What was she saying to her? Probably that perfect sappy speech about her being a woman now, the things he hadn't known to say.

She came back long moments later. When she caught his expression, she said gently, "She's fine."

He nodded. "Okay, good." He blew out a long breath. "How did things go in New York?"

"Good. Mostly. You know."

"The boss wants you back."

"Yeah. And he's right. I really need to get back there. I asked him to give me a month to get things organized and transition Chloe."

His heart clenched. "A month."

She tucked some hair behind her ear. "Yeah. That's still going to be hard, but at least I've given him a time frame that we can work with, so I think that satisfied him. On the flight back I started a spreadsheet of all the things I'll have to get done."

He nodded, not sure he could speak.

Chloe bounded down the stairs with her backpack. "Are we going now?"

"Sure." Peyton smiled. "Want to say thanks to Drew for helping out?"

Chloe stopped short of an eye roll but made a face. Nonetheless, she barreled over to him for a big hug. "Thanks, Drew. When are we going to see *World of Wizards?*"

He caught Peyton's eyebrow lift and managed to choke out some words. "I'm not sure. Need to check the schedule."

Chloe said to Peyton, "We talked about it last night. It's going to be so good!" The house felt suddenly vacant after the girls had left.

His life felt vacant. One month.

Drew's somewhat cool greeting when she arrived at his place had taken Peyton aback.

Later that day she sat in the living room with her laptop while Chloe was out with friends at the mall. She had work to do and a spreadsheet of things that needed attention before she and Chloe could move to New York, but her thoughts kept drifting to Drew.

She'd missed him while she'd been gone, especially at night in her empty, lonely apartment, and her empty, lonely bed. She couldn't stop thinking about how he'd touched her, tasted her, turned her on until she was shivering and aching. All the orgasms he'd so generously given her and how much she'd loved making him feel good, too.

She'd also been thinking about his confession that he was seeking some help to figure things out. That was so good. She wanted so much for him to be happy and successful.

But . . . why?

Obviously she cared about him. But she couldn't *care* about him . . . not like *that*. It should feel awkward between them, with what had happened between him and Sara—her sister—and their resulting child. And at first she'd resisted the attraction to him because of Sara. But again, this wasn't sleeping with her sister's boyfriend. They were adults, different people, and the truth was . . . being with Drew felt right.

But she was going back to New York, taking Chloe with her. She had a career that meant everything to her. Well, almost everything, now she had Chloe. She also now had a commitment to return to New York at the beginning of December. So whatever it was that felt "right" was coming to an end. And maybe Drew was thinking along those lines, too, recognizing that their time was limited and it was probably better to not get into things too deeply.

Very wise. Yes.

She needed to focus on Chloe and being there for her. The poor sweetheart had gotten her very first period and had felt alone and embarrassed at having to tell Drew. Sure, he was her father, but they still didn't know each other that well, and . . . well, it was the kind of thing a girl needed her mother for.

Peyton's throat clogged up thinking about that.

She needed to focus. There was much to do . . . sorting out a school for Chloe in New York, packing, getting rid of things they didn't need, figuring out what to do about the house. Selling it didn't feel right . . . maybe she could rent it to someone?

She opened up her spreadsheet with a sigh.

Drew was on the ice Monday with a group of teenage boys at Paterson House. They were having a scrimmage, and his eyes kept going to one of the bigger boys, a kid who was pretty good. He had a way of finding the puck and he was a great skater, taking it to the net . . . yet his shots hardly ever went in. And it wasn't that the young goalie was that stellar.

Drew sensed the kid's frustration. To him it was crystal clear what was going on. "Hey, Bryson," he called to the kid. "You want to stay after and work on a few things?"

Bryson glided toward him on his skates. "Like what?"

"Like scoring goals."

Bryson frowned. "I was trying."

"I know you were. You were trying hard. I might be able to help you with that."

Bryson lifted a shoulder. "Okay."

"Roofing the puck worked back when you were like, ten, and the goalies were smaller," Drew told him. "Now you have to get out of that habit. But the first thing you have to learn is to hang on to the puck longer."

"Huh?"

"I was watching you. I know it's instinct to get rid of it as fast as you can, shoot it as fast as you can."

"The goalie will be watching me. He'll know where I'm going to shoot if I take too long."

Drew grinned. "That is probably true. But if you have a great shot, and you shoot at the right place, he still won't be able to stop it."

They worked on it for a while and he could tell that Bryson was excited about what he showed him. And Drew himself left the hockey arena feeling pretty damn good. A sense of accomplishment filled him and damn, that was sweet.

He wished he could have videotaped Bryson and then played it back to show him exactly what he was talking about. Maybe he'd try that. Next time he'd bring his iPad.

He'd been thinking about some of the things he'd talked to Jack Shipton about. They'd met a few times since their first lunch that day. He was supposed to think about things he was good at, and things he enjoyed. Well, he could add this to the list . . . helping kids. Teaching.

Coaching was something he'd considered as a possible career goal. He'd talked to Jack and Melody, the counselor, about it. He knew he couldn't step into a role as a head coach of an NHL team, and honestly, he wasn't sure if he wanted to coach a team at any level.

He thought about watching the practice that day, when Acker had been shooting pucks at the net and missing or hitting the goalie straight on. He thought about how he'd itched to get down there and give the guy some tips. Acker had a coach—several coaches, in fact—and yet it seemed so obvious to Drew what he needed, he couldn't believe that coaching staff hadn't addressed it.

Who the hell was he to tell another NHL player what he was doing wrong? Was he being an arrogant idiot to think he was that good that he could make a difference? Sure, he'd just had some success teaching a kid, but adults—professionals, no less— was a whole different thing.

He'd been a pretty damn good goal scorer, though. It still made his gut ache that he'd never broken goal-scoring records or won the awards everyone had expected him to. The last few seasons his points had been lower because of his fucking knee and being out for surgeries, but when he'd played his best...he'd been one of the best.

Yeah. He had. And Jack had reminded him of that, too. He needed to regain his confidence, remember that he had a lot to offer. He just had to figure out exactly what that was and who he was going to offer it to.

CHAPTER 24

Over the next week Drew worked hard on figuring things out. Taking control of his life.

He and Peyton spent afternoons together when they could, making sure her headboard was repaired satisfactorily (and they thoroughly tested it), but also talking about all kinds of things. They were both busy, though—Peyton trying to manage her clients and their crises and take care of all the things on her moving spreadsheet, which he fucking hated hearing about, and him spending long hours working on his plan, laying out a step-by-step process for scoring goals, recording Bryson and another hockey player on his iPad, showing them what he was talking about, teaching them his strategies. After another session on the ice, Bryson had scored three goals in his next game. Drew was eager to try his process out with someone else.

"It's coaching, but it's very specific and technical," he said to Jack and Melody in a meeting at their office one day. "I don't know if the Blackhawks would be interested in it."

"It is pretty niche," Jack agreed. "But I actually think you have something here."

"You don't know if they're interested unless you ask them," Melody pointed out.

Drew grimaced. "True." Everyone had told him people weren't going to come knocking on his door and he got that. He was going to have to man up and get out there.

But that was a good thing. He'd be taking control.

"You need a plan," Jack said. "Let's get to work."

So he dropped by the United Center and sought out Step. He agreed to sit down with him and watch his video and have a look at his step-by-step plan for scoring goals.

Step called in Coach Gregson to watch and listen, too. They asked a bunch of questions and seemed interested.

"You know you're still a valued member of the club," Step said, clapping a hand on his shoulder as they walked out of his office. "This team has a long history of moving former players into the front office or hockey operations. We want to work with you."

So he left that meeting feeling pretty good.

Drew had asked if he could pick Chloe up Thursday after school and take her out to the *World of Wizards* movie that was opening that day. Peyton knew Chloe'd been excited about this movie for months, so she'd agreed. She had no interest in seeing it, so it was great that Drew would take her.

When Drew arrived home with Chloe at five o'clock, she was surprised to see them that early.

"Did you not get in?" she asked, thinking maybe there'd been big lineups for the opening.

"We went to the early show." Chloe unwrapped a scarf from around her neck. Peyton frowned. "Early show? How early?"

"One-thirty."

Her eyebrows flew up. "One-thirty! What about school?"

Chloe slid Drew a sly glance. "Drew said I could skip school for the afternoon because this kind of movie doesn't come out very often. I've been waiting so long for it!"

Peyton gaped at Drew. "You took her out of school? To see a movie?"

He nodded, the corners of his mouth lifted in a small smile. "Yeah, and it was *great*. Wasn't it, kiddo?"

Chloe nodded enthusiastically. "It really was! Then we went to Red Lobster. I gotta go tell my friends about the movie. They were so jealous!"

Peyton crossed her arms and gave Drew a long look. "She's still not completely caught up from the time she missed when Sara died. What on earth were you thinking?"

His smile faded. "I was thinking it would be a fun treat for her."

"Fun! She had school! You can't take her out of school to go to a movie, for God's sake!"

"She missed a couple of classes," he said patiently. "I told them she'd be away. She got her homework assignments ahead of time, which she can do tonight. It's no big deal."

She continued to stare at him, her jaw slack. She shook her head. "I can't believe you did that."

His eyebrows pulled down over his nose. "It's not that big a deal, Peyton," he said firmly. "The world didn't end. She's not going to flunk seventh grade because of it."

Heat flashed through her veins. "Life isn't all fun and games. Much as you might like to think it is."

"What the fuck does that mean?"

"It means you can't just play hooky because you want to do something fun."

"Why not, if it's not hurting anything? Christ, it's not like I've pulled her out of school every day."

"That is *not* responsible parenting."

His jaw tightened and his eyes narrowed. She watched him pull in a long breath through his nose. "Duly noted," he ground out.

She pressed her lips together. "It's done. Just . . . would you ask me before you do something like that again? I'd appreciate a chance to discuss it."

"Don't worry. It won't happen again. Tell Chloe I'll see her this weekend." He spun around and strode out of the house.

Peyton set her hand on her chest where her heart was thudding. Well, shit.

Seriously, he couldn't do stuff like that.

She climbed the stairs and poked her head into Chloe's bedroom. She sat cross- legged on her bed with a book open.

"Hey," Peyton said. "So you had fun this afternoon."

Chloe nodded. "The movie was so good. We laughed a lot." She bit her lip and peered at Peyton. "Is it okay to have fun?"

Peyton went very still. "What do you mean is it okay to have fun? Drew shouldn't have taken you out of school, if that's what you mean."

"No. I mean . . . I still feel so sad about Mom. But I was laughing at the movie and I felt like maybe that was wrong, that I shouldn't be happy."

Peyton closed her eyes and walked over to sit on the end of the bed. "It's okay to have fun, honey. Of course it is."

"Are you mad at Drew?"

Peyton's lips tightened briefly, then she sighed. "I was surprised. I don't really approve of skipping school. But . . . it made you laugh." She managed a small smile and reached out to give Chloe's striped sock-clad foot a squeeze.

"Drew said he'd take us to a hockey game sometime."

"Oh."

"That would be fun."

Peyton swallowed. "Yes. I haven't been to a hockey game for a long time."

"I've *never* been to a hockey game."

"Well, that would be really cool, then. Are you doing homework?"

"Yeah."

"Okay. Call me if you need anything."

Downstairs she found her cell phone and called Drew's number. "Yeah?"

"You're pissed."

Silence vibrated in her ear.

"I called to apologize," she said. "I overreacted. I was taken by surprise and . . . and, well, I don't condone skipping school, but . . . you made Chloe happy."

After a beat, he said quietly, "Thanks for the apology. Open the door."

"What?"

"Open the door."

Frowning, she moved to the front door and peered out the window. She closed her eyes and dropped her forehead briefly against the door at seeing him on the veranda, leaning against the railing, ankles crossed, cell phone at his ear.

She opened the door but spoke into her phone. "She's doing her homework right now."

He pushed away from the railing. "Great."

"I'm sorry I was a bitch." Now he was only inches away from her, and her gaze fastened on his.

"You're not a bitch. We're all just doing the best we can." They both lowered their phones.

She nodded, heat flowing through her body at the intent expression on his face "That's true. Come in."

CHAPTER 25

Even though she'd apologized and they'd had a hot make-up make-out session on the couch, Drew was still rankled by the things Peyton had said when they'd argued. He didn't even want to admit how much it had ripped his guts apart at how she'd thought so little of him. He'd been so goddamn afraid of screwing up, of being a bad dad, and sure as shit, he'd gone and done it. He hadn't thought that all through, but it hadn't seemed such a heinous thing to skip school for one afternoon. And it had made Chloe so happy.

It had also bugged him that Peyton said she wanted him to ask permission before doing basically anything with Chloe. He was her father.

And he had no rights whatsoever.

It was killing him, thinking about Peyton taking her to New York.

Of course, it was killing him thinking about *Peyton* being back in New York, too. He just had no clue what to do about it.

Like the rest of his life. No fucking clue.

Just when he started to feel like he had a little control over things, that things were finally going his way, that he had people he cared about who maybe cared about him, too . . . they were going to be taken away from him.

That sucked.

But what could he do about it?

Feeling like he needed to do something, get back some smidgen of control, he made an appointment to see his lawyer.

"Biological parents do have a right to seek child visitation or child custody," Tyrell told him, sitting at a round table in his office. "Although the new laws no longer refer to it as 'custody.' Now we talk about shared parental responsibility and shared parental time."

"Huh."

"It makes it less adversarial," Tyrell said. "There's no winner or loser, as is often the outcome of custody battles. Under the new framework, parental responsibilities are broken into categories like education, health, religion, and extracurricular activities. The court can allocate the respective responsibilities either jointly or solely to the parents. In any case, the courts use the best interest of the child to decide cases involving unmarried fathers. Generally, unless there is evidence otherwise, the courts make the presumption that having both parents involved is beneficial to the child."

"That's good."

"For fathers who weren't married to the mother when the child was born, the first step is legally establishing paternity."

"Done." Drew explained that he'd done the DNA paternity test before meeting Chloe. Not that Sara had argued about it at all. She'd been completely in agreement.

"Then we pursue visitation or custody rights. But before we go to court, there's no reason you can't negotiate this yourself, with your daughter's guardian."

"Yeah, there is. She's taking Chloe to New York. That's where she lives."

KELLY JAMIESON

"Ah." Tyrell sat back in his chair. "I see. Well. So you want full responsibility for your daughter?"

Drew swallowed. "It seems to be the only way I would get to see her at all."

"Well, the court determines custody according to the 'best interest of the child' standard. Illinois law doesn't provide for allowing the children to decide which parent they want to live with, but the court might consider the child's wishes. I expect they'll assign a social worker to the case who will interview Chloe. It's generally preferred to not involve the children in court proceedings."

"Christ, yeah." Drew rubbed his face. He sure as hell didn't want Chloe involved in a legal battle. Even a social worker getting involved, interrogating her, probably interrogating *all* of them . . . *fuck*. His gut churned at what he was contemplating and he wasn't sure he had the balls to actually do this.

But what other choice did he have? Move to New York?

This thought gave him pause. He hadn't even considered that. His life was here, but how much of a life was it? He didn't have a career like Peyton did in New York, and Chloe's school and friends were here. He sighed. Maybe that was something to think more about.

"So it's a matter of deciding the child's best interests," Tyrell continued. "Not which parent is the best. They look at a number of factors, including possibly the wishes of the child, the relationship the child has with each parent, the child's adjustment to school community, home, mental and physical health, domestic violence history—"

"Jesus Christ," Drew interrupted. "There's none of that."

Tyrell smiled and nodded. "I'm just outlining all the things the courts look at. They also look at whether either parent is a sex offender."

"Christ," Drew muttered again.

It probably wasn't in his favor that he hadn't even been in the picture up until a few months ago, whereas Peyton had been around Chloe's entire life.

This all just sounded ugly and painful. But he loved Chloe.

"So Chloe's aunt is her legal guardian? Was this approved by the court?"

Drew made a face. "I don't know. I never asked that. I'm going to assume yes, since Sara was an attorney and she had made arrangements for everything else before she died."

"I'd suggest you find out more about that if you can. Some people name a guardian in their will, but that still has to be approved by the courts after the person dies."

Drew frowned. Well, he knew he was going to have to talk to Peyton about this at some point.

"I would strongly suggest trying to work out a parenting agreement with the legal guardian," Tyrell said. "It will be much less stressful on both you and the child, and it will certainly save you a lot of money in legal fees."

"I thought lawyers looked for ways to charge people as much money as possible."

Tyrell had been his lawyer for years and Drew trusted him enough to say that. Tyrell laughed. "Yeah, that's one of the required courses in law school—how to chase ambulances, pad your billable hours, and generate revenue for your firm."

Drew grinned crookedly. "Seriously, thanks for the advice."

"So I assume you don't want me to move forward with peti tioning the court for custody."

"Not right now. I'll be in touch. Thanks, man."

He left Tyrell's office with a head full of confused thoughts and mixed emotions. He'd taken another step in regaining control of his life. He'd made an appointment with his lawyer to find out more about what the legalities of his situation were and how he could possibly get legal custody of Chloe—at least shared custody.

He hadn't heard back from Step about his proposal when he picked up Chloe for her dance class on Wednesday. While waiting for her to come downstairs, he confessed to Peyton his worry about it.

"What's your plan B?" she asked. "If they don't want to do that."

"I've never been one for backup plans. Usually I get what I want first time."

The corners of her mouth lifted. "I know. You're spoiled."

He snorted.

"Seriously, Drew. It's great when things come easy. But when you have to work for them . . . it makes success even sweeter. You can do it. Come up with a plan C even, in case plan B doesn't work, either."

"Having a plan B or a plan C feels like I'm expecting to fail."

"And I know how much you like to fail."

"I fucking hate it."

"I know. But having a backup plan doesn't mean you're going to fail. It's just thinking ahead. Anticipating different outcomes and exploring solutions. Sometimes the outcome is because of something outside our control. Sometimes it's within our control. Doesn't it make sense to think about all those things, and then if it's something within your control you can deal with it? That helps ensure success, not failure."

"You're so goddamn smart." He couldn't stop the smile that tugged his lips.

"I know." She grinned. "So are you, though. I know you can do this."

Her unquestioning support and honest assessment bolstered his confidence.

He'd been envious of her plans and thought-out strategies for her life and for her clients. Well, he was learning that, too.

"You're right. I can."

His confidence in what he was doing had built. Peyton's words jacked up his determination. He was going to do this, whether it was with the Blackhawks or with someone else. So the next day he sat down and did a bunch of research into elite local prospects, and Friday met with a few kids from a Major Midget team of fifteen- to seventeen-year-old players in the Eastern Illinois Hockey League. Once more he pitched his ideas, offering to work with them pro bono for the chance to prove himself at a higher level. Who could say no to free? The parents knew him and his NHL career.

These kids were taking their hockey seriously, hoping to play Tier II hockey. The parents were excited to have their kids work with him, which was a bit of a comfort to his bruised ego. He was going to do initial assessments then set some goals for them that he would hopefully help them achieve.

It wasn't the end goal, but he was happy to be doing something he loved and believed in. And luckily he didn't need the money and he had the luxury of time to prove himself.

CHAPTER 26

Drew had a date.

He glanced at his watch as he left the rink where he was working with the midget players late Friday afternoon. He'd better hustle to get home and change.

That evening Chloe was going over to Ashley's place for a sleepover and he and Peyton had a date.

An actual date.

It wasn't their first . . . exactly. They'd had dinner together that day he'd opened his door to her naked. But that was different. They'd gone to Red's party on his yacht. They'd said they were just friends, but that hadn't been friendship they'd been feeling that night.

Tonight was the first time they'd planned to go out as a couple.

He had a feeling Peyton was as hesitant about it as he was. And yet how could they not? They snuck around while Chloe was at school, pretending there was nothing going on. When they had this chance to be together, out in the open, how could they not take it?

He'd debated in his mind for days what they should do. They

could do the expensive romantic dinner thing. That would be nice, but they'd shared many meals.

So he told her to dress warmly and when they got in his car, he headed toward the Loop. He parked near Daley Plaza.

"What are we doing?" Peyton asked as they left the car.

"We're going to the Christkindlmarket."

"Oh, my gosh! Really? I haven't been to it for years." She actually did a little skip that reminded him of Chloe.

"It's the first night."

The white lights in the trees, the lit-up booths of the vendors and the glittering skyscrapers rising around them created a magical feel. The big Christmas tree glowed with colored lights and ornaments. A few small snowflakes floated down from the sky, sparkling in the night air.

"It's so beautiful." Peyton gazed around with a wistful smile as they strolled into the plaza.

Christ. He hoped this wasn't going to make her sad. Big holidays like Thanksgiving and Christmas were probably hard after the death of a family member. But he could make that better. They weren't exactly a family, but they'd become . . . something. His parents were coming for Thanksgiving. Somehow he'd make it all okay for her and Chloe.

Well, nothing could make it okay. But he'd make it as good for them as he could. They checked out all the booths, looking at carvings and glass sculptures and

German steins. Peyton paused at a booth full of Christmas ornaments, her gaze moving over them. When Drew saw the look on her face, his heart dropped.

He gently turned her and pulled her into his arms. Their bulky jackets were between them but he felt her trembling. "I am *so* sorry," he said in a low voice. "I thought this would be fun, but it's making you sad."

"*I'm* sorry," she mumbled. "It's beautiful here. But thinking about Christmas without Sara is just . . . heartbreaking."

"I know. I know. I'm sorry." He rocked her for a moment until someone jostled them and then he drew her gently away from the booth. "Let's go somewhere else. Let's go have some Glühwein."

"That's a good idea."

They found the tent serving the hot spiced wine and sat for a bit, listening to the music from a German Oompah band in the chilly air. With her pink cheeks and sad smile, a big plaid scarf wrapped around her over her black jacket, and chunky knit mitts holding her cup in both hands, Drew's heart tripped as he regarded her across the picnic table.

So much for his fun date idea.

"Don't look like that," she said. "I'm fine. Some moments are hard."

"I know. Do you want something to eat?"

"Yeah. That would be good."

"I'll go get us food."

He purchased weißwürste, sauerkraut, and fried potatoes and returned. This time he sat next to her at the table as they shared the food and listened to the music.

"Yum. This is awesome."

"It is good."

Peyton's mood seemed to elevate, or maybe she was just trying hard, and after they'd eaten they wandered around more until the market closed.

"Now we need to warm up," Drew said as they buckled up back in his car.

"I hope you mean in bed."

He laughed. "Great idea. But I have one more stop planned before that." He drove to Logan Square and he led her into a bar he'd been to a few times. It had a great cocktail menu, but what appealed to him tonight was the big fireplace and huge antique sofas. They scored one near the fire and he slid his arm around her and snuggled her into him as they waited for their drinks.

"This is nice." She looked around at the old brick and dark wood interior.

"Yeah. I thought on a chilly night this would be a good place for a nightcap." He pressed a kiss to her hair. "And then after this, I'm going to take you home and fuck you senseless."

She shivered and set her hand on his thigh. "I can't wait."

As they sipped their drinks and talked in the dark bar, firelight gilding Peyton's hair and face, sultry jazz music playing in the background, heat and tension hummed between them. He couldn't stop touching her—her silky hair, her smooth cheek, her slender shoulder. He watched her talk, mesmerized by her lips.

Jesus. He was crazy about this woman.

"Let's go," he said abruptly as soon as they'd finished their drinks. He set his glass down sharply.

Her smile illuminated the room and his heart as they rose off the big couch and grabbed their jackets.

They went to her place. She'd left a couple of lights on and he turned them off as they headed straight upstairs to her room.

"Did I tell you how beautiful you look tonight?"

"No. No, you didn't."

"That was a serious oversight. You're always beautiful, though, Peyton." He reached for her hands and drew her closer, their bodies brushing together. She gazed at him wide-eyed.

He slid his hands up under her sweater, over her ribs, over silky skin, until his fingers grazed the undersides of her breasts. He bent his head and pressed his mouth to her neck and breathed in her soft fragrance, that lush vanilla and flowers scent. She shivered against him.

He pressed his mouth there in an openmouthed kiss, drew her flesh into his mouth in a gentle suckle. She gasped.

He pulled her sweater up and over her head then smoothed his palms over her shoulders.

She flattened her hands on his chest, let her head fall to the side as he kissed her neck, shoulder, dragged his tongue across her collarbone.

"You taste so good," he murmured. "And smell good. And feel good . . ."

"Mmm. Thank you." She threaded her fingers into his hair and held his head as he kissed her throat. "I think you smell good, too."

His lips paused over the pulse beating there, a quick, excited flutter. He sucked the flesh gently into his mouth and she gasped. He licked her throat, nipped at her jaw, drew his tongue across her soft bottom lip. A moan vibrated inside her throat. Her fingers scraped across his scalp, sending tingles showering down through his body like sparks. His hands cupped her breasts, her sheer lace bra a fragile barrier between them.

He wrapped his arms around her, kissed her deeply, felt her arms slide around his neck. He wanted to be closer to her, as close as they could be. His fingers went to the button of her jeans and the zipper, and he helped her wriggle out of the snug denim. Then with his hands beneath her ass in a tiny thong, he lifted her against him. She wound her legs around him, clutching his head as he carried her like that to the bed.

"Drew!" She gasped as he tossed her onto the bed and she bounced gently on the duvet. Her mouth was swollen, eyes sparkling, hair mussed.

"Christ, you're sexy." His fingers went to the button of his own jeans.

She rose onto her knees, watching him. "I want to undress you. I've never done that."

"Oh." He smiled. "Okay."

She scrambled off the bed, brushed her hands over his chest, lingering to rub over each nipple. Sharp sensations moved over his skin at her touch. Urgency rose in him, the need to take her immediately, to be inside her.

Then she undid his pants, lowered the zipper slowly, and gently pushed them to the floor. He stepped out of them, shoving his socks off, too, and her hand cupped him through the soft cotton of his boxer briefs. His erection throbbed and stretched the fabric. He gritted his teeth, closed his eyes as she went to her knees in front of him.

"Peyton."

"Mmm?" She laid her cheek against his hard cock, eyes closed. Fingers stroked, then she kissed him through the cotton.

"I can't take . . . much more . . . we have to make sure . . . "

She stroked him again, pressed her nose there and took in a big breath. Fuck!

Pressure gathered and built in his spine, his balls drew up tight.

He reached down and hauled her to her feet. He found her little thong underwear and with two fingers, yanked hard and ripped them on one side.

"Drew!" Her shocked gasp inflamed him even more, his blood surging hot and urgent through his veins and especially into his dick. So close, so close . . . he threw her down onto the bed, wishing he could be more gentle, take his time, but Christ, his orgasm was building higher and he was dangerously close to coming.

He quickly found a condom then came down over her roughly, pushing into her hot pussy. She was wet, thank Christ, and her cries of surprise, her hands clutching at him, urged him on.

He pushed into her once, twice, three times and then he exploded, heat and light surrounding him, her wet warmth hugging his cock. She lifted her legs, clenched his hips with her thighs, and he felt the sting of her fingernails on his ass as she pressed up to meet his orgasm.

"Peyton. Peyton." He poured himself into her in hard, hot jets, shuddering through a blinding climax. There wasn't even time to make her satisfied, and he always tried to make sure she came first. He grunted and gasped through his release, the vague thought flickering through his mind that he'd make it up to her later. But right now he was out of control, lost, buried balls-deep in her, shooting his seed into her—and he loved it.

Moments later, collapsed next to her on the bed, he opened his eyes to see her watching him. She smiled and stretched, "Wow. That was great."

He didn't move. "Sorry."

She stroked his hair. "You're apologizing? I just said it was great."

"You didn't come. I always make you come first."

"Mmm. That's true. But I can take care of it . . . . " She slid her hand down over her stomach and between her legs.

Drew's eyes flew open and he made a low, rough sound as he watched her.

She closed her eyes, rubbed in small circles and drew in a long breath, pushing her breasts up, still wearing her bra. Her thighs fell wider, and she breathed in tiny pants, small whimpers falling from her lips. Her eyes drifted closed and he watched her abs tighten as her hips lifted and she shuddered through an orgasm.

He swallowed. "Holy hell. That was hot."

They rolled languorously onto their sides and faced each other. Drew cupped the curve of her hip with his hand and she set her hand on his chest. She reached for his face, stroked his cheek and jaw with the backs of her fingers, brushed her fingertips across his mouth. His lips parted. She slipped her fingertips inside, stroked across his tongue.

Heat built inside him again. He stroked over her hip and thigh, up to her waist, then he kissed her. His mouth covered hers, moved over hers, pushed her mouth open to take her in. His tongue stroked, teeth nipped her bottom lip. She kissed him back, wrapping her arms around him and one leg, too. She moaned, arched against him. "Drew, oh, Drew."

He found the clasp of her bra and opened it then tossed the pretty lace aside. He moved over her to suck her nipples, plumping one breast up to his mouth, then the other, tasting her

DANCING IN THE RAIN

sweetness, loving the tightness of each nub against his tongue. She shivered and gasped. Goddamn he loved making her feel good.

His dick was hard again already. "Fuck," he muttered. "Hang on." He wanted to take a chance on using the same condom, but that was risky, so he made himself get rid of it and roll on a new one. Then he returned to her and reached for her again.

They rolled together across the wide bed, mouths fused, bodies joined. A groan rumbled from his throat. He fisted his hands in her hair, held her head for his long, drugging kisses. She rolled her hips against him until he shoved a hand between them to find his cock and pushed into her.

"Sweet, Peyton. So sweet."

His hands held her beneath her knees, pushed them to her chest as he drove into her. She met his thrusts with her own, her fingers twisted in the duvet. He released one knee and thumbed her swollen clit.

"Love making you come. Love making you feel good, baby."

She whimpered her response. His thumb moved on her clit and then her pussy squeezed him as she came, her body rippling, small noises of ecstasy escaping her. He groaned, held her pussy, pressed into her, and his eyes fell closed as he poured himself inside her in hot, thick pulses.

CHAPTER 27

"Is Drew your boyfriend?"

Peyton's head snapped around to stare at Chloe where she sat at the kitchen island late Saturday afternoon. "What?"

"You two went out last night together. And I saw you kissing him goodbye when he left earlier." Chloe made a face of distaste, but also looked upset.

Drew had still been there when Chloe had been dropped off by her friend's mom. They'd been out of bed, showered and dressed, and sitting in the kitchen, and hadn't thought Chloe would think anything of it. But when he'd left . . . they *had* shared a scorching-hot kiss. And dammit, how had they not known Chloe would see that?

"Oh."

"So is he your boyfriend now?"

"Oh, Chloe." She sighed and sat down on the stool beside her niece, facing her. "It's complicated."

Chloe's small face tightened.

"He's not my boyfriend." She felt like a knife was slicing open her heart as she said that. "We sort of like each other . . . . " She actually felt a little dizzy saying that, because hell, it was so much more than "sort of liking" him. "But . . . well, we're moving to New York, and . . . and he's staying here."

"I'm never going to see him again."

"No! That's not true. Of course you'll see him."

Chloe opened her mouth as if to question that then closed it. Her eyes got glossy and her chin quivered. "I'm losing everything! I lost my mom. Now I'm losing my dad. *And* all my friends."

"Oh, Chloe." That knife twisted with a painful rotation, stealing her breath. "Oh, Chloe, I know, I'm so sorry."

Chloe jumped off the stool and ran upstairs.

She couldn't do this. She couldn't do this to Chloe.

Chloe was right. She'd lost so much. Her little heart was breaking and that made

Peyton's heart hurt, too, so much.

After a few minutes she picked up her phone and called Nik. "I need advice."

"About what?"

"I'm sleeping with Drew."

After a beat of silence, Nik said, "I'm on my way over."

"Bring wine."

"Well, duh."

Peyton smiled.

Nik walked in holding a bottle of Zinfandel.

"Wow, you don't skimp," Peyton said, recognizing the label. "I think for this we only needed a cheap red. A very large bottle of cheap red."

Nik grinned. "Please. This is huge news. This deserves a big wine."

Peyton opened the wine and poured generously into two big glasses. She handed one to Nik and led the way into the living room where she sat cross-legged on the couch.

"Okay, spill," Nik said, sitting at the other end of the couch. "I don't know how this happened . . . ."

One of Nik's eyebrows flew up.

"Okay, I do know how it happened. The first time. He took me to a party on a friend's boat and we stayed overnight and shared a room. I was cold and nervous and . . . and well, he's pretty gorgeous."

"No argument there."

"But somehow it turned into us having sex a lot. And . . . Chloe saw us kissing this afternoon when he left. She wants to know what's going on."

"Oh, frak."

"Right?

"So . . . what *is* going on?" Nik sipped her wine. "Apart from a lot of secret sex."

"I don't know. Nothing. How can it? I'm moving back to New York."

Nik pursed her lips.

"When I reminded Chloe of that, she got upset. She thinks she'll never see Drew again."

"She's getting close to him," Nik murmured.

"Yes." Peyton sighed and looked down into the burgundy liquid. "I can't do this to her. Moving her to New York is going to be so disruptive to her. I've known that all along, but I just thought . . . I didn't have a choice. My job is there. The one I've worked so hard for. My apartment, my life."

"Your apartment isn't that great," Nik said. "No offense. And I know you have new friends there, but it's not like you can't keep in touch with them if you move. And it's not like you have a husband or even a boyfriend there you have to consider."

"True." Peyton sighed.

"But yeah, I know your job is important to you."

"It is."

"Is it your job that's important? Or your career?"

Peyton frowned. "What do you mean?"

"I think it's really your career that's important." She looked at Peyton over the rim of the glass as she sipped. "A job is a job. It

266

can be replaced. But it's your career that lasts. It's something you build over time."

"Which is why I moved to New York."

"Yes. But it's also why you could make another change. Why not? You hate your boss. Why not try something different?"

Peyton closed her eyes. "Oh, God. I don't know." She swallowed another mouthful of wine. "Jax said I could probably get my job at Campbell back. But that seems like a step backward."

Nik tipped her head to one side. "I get that. But building a career doesn't always go linearly. Sometimes you take a step backward . . . or even sideways, maybe . . . before you move forward again."

Peyton thought about Drew and his career. About the step backward he'd been forced to take. It hadn't been his choice; it had been forced on him.

"You think I should do it?" she asked her friend.

Nik smiled. "I can't tell you what to do. Chloe's only twelve. People move across the country all the time, or around the world, even. Kids survive. They adapt and make new friends. In ten years, this will be a faint memory."

"Or she'll be scarred forever. Sure, people move, but when her mom has just died? And she's just found the father she always wanted?"

"You're obviously miserable at the thought of hurting Chloe. Will your job make up for that? Will it make you that happy?"

Peyton closed her eyes and tipped her head back. The answer was clear. "No," she finally answered. "It won't."

"There you go. As for what to do if you stay here in Chicago . . . there are options. You don't have to go back to Campbell. What about starting your own consulting business?"

Peyton squinted. "Have you been talking to Jax?"

"No." Nik's forehead creased. "Why?"

"Because that day we had lunch, he was talking about putting together a dream team of reputation managers . . . him and me."

"Of course." Nik waved a hand.

Peyton smiled. "And Aidan and Hannah."

"Hannah. What does she know about reputation management?"

"Probably not much," Peyton admitted. "I questioned that, too, but her marketing background would probably help with clients who need online branding and marketing."

"Can you afford not to work while you start a business?"

"You know I can." One corner of Peyton's mouth kicked up. "I haven't touched the money I inherited when my parents died, and half of this house is still mine. Not that I want to sell."

"Call Jax. Right now."

Peyton laughed, but her insides were in knots. The possibilities were exciting. Running her own business . . . why not? She had experience, she had contacts . . . she could do this. But it was scary as hell. Quitting her job on the spur of the moment, the job she'd worked so hard at to succeed . . . her stomach rolled.

"Hey," Nik said softly. "I know you're not one to make snap decisions. You like to think things through. So think about it."

Peyton nodded. "Okay. I will."

"You don't have to cook for us." Drew crowded Peyton up against the counter in the kitchen and pressed his lips to her temple. It was the Tuesday before Thanksgiving and she'd just returned from another two-day trip to New York. "We can go out. We can make this Thanksgiving totally different for you. I know it's going to be hard here without Sara."

She nibbled her bottom lip then peered up at him through her eyelashes. He had a point, and truthfully she was kind of dreading the holiday. "Maybe we could do it at your house?"

He nodded quickly. "That's a great idea. We can all help cook."

His parents were arriving Wednesday night. She and Drew had already been through the whole discussion about whether

Peyton should join them for Thanksgiving dinner or not. She'd told Drew that Chloe could spend the weekend with them getting to know her grandparents and she would do something else, but he would have none of that, insisting that she had to be there. She felt like an outsider . . . Chloe was a part of that family, but she wasn't.

She also felt lonely, so when Drew insisted she be part of the festivities, she didn't argue with him. Then she'd offered to cook, but somehow Drew understood that this Thanksgiving had to be different or she and Chloe were going to totally lose it.

"We can go shopping," he continued. "Tomorrow morning. I'll pick you up and we can get a turkey and all the things we'll need."

Her heart bumped and she nodded. This felt so . . . family-like. So couple-like. It was weird, and yet it felt right. "Okay." She hesitated. "Um, I need to tell you something."

"What is it?"

"Chloe saw us kissing on Saturday. When you were leaving."

"Oh."

"She asked me if you were my boyfriend."

He stared at her blankly. "Uh, what did you say?"

"I said we like each other, but you're not my boyfriend." His eyebrows snapped together over his nose.

"So it's probably better if we don't, uh, you know, be too demonstrative in front of her."

He swallowed, his jaw clamped tight. "Sure. Right."

They spent the next morning driving from store to store, picking out a fresh turkey while making jokes about Drew's preference for breasts and thighs, loading up tons of produce, buying bottles of wine and making a last stop at a bakery to pick up pies. They argued over pumpkin versus apple, debated a compromise on a pecan pie and ended up buying all three.

"We don't need three pies!" She shook her head.

"Are you kidding me?" Drew muttered. "I can eat a whole pie myself."

She laughed and elbowed his ribs. "Good thing you've been working out."

She was both curious and nervous to meet Drew's parents. As she and Chloe waited for him to pick them up Thanksgiving morning, she asked Chloe, "Are you excited to meet your grandparents?"

"I guess so."

"That doesn't sound excited."

Chloe studied her polka-dotted socks. "What if they don't like me?"

"They'll love you, Chloe. How could they not? You're smart and beautiful with a huge heart."

"I don't even know them."

Peyton got it. "I know. But you will."

"I'm glad you're coming, too."

Peyton smiled. "We both miss your mom, but we're together and this is going to be fun."

She had no idea if that was true or not, but whatever.

Drew arrived with a big hug for Chloe and a private smile for Peyton that made her insides flutter. It felt like sneaking around, but Peyton knew it was for the best. Things didn't need to be more complicated than they already were.

At his place, he led them to the kitchen and family room, where his mom was already bustling around, preparing food. "Mom, this is Chloe. Chloe, my mom."

Peyton hung back as Mrs. Sellers gazed at Chloe, blinked and clasped her hands in front of her. "Chloe," she murmured. "Hi."

"Hi." Chloe shifted from one foot to the other. "Um, what should I call you?" Mrs. Sellers smiled and they were joined by another man, definitely an older version of Drew. "You can call me Janet," Mrs. Sellers said with a smile. "Someday if you want to, you can call me Grandma, but I know it's weird right now."

"And I'm Jim." Mr. Sellers stepped toward Chloe and extended a hand. "Happy to meet you, Chloe."

She shook his hand and gave him a nervous smile. "And this is Peyton," Drew said. "Chloe's aunt."

She shook hands with Janet and Jim.

"Well," Janet said. "I'm glad we're all here together. We can get to know each other a bit better. But first we have to get that turkey in the oven."

Peyton had never cooked a turkey by herself before. She and Sara had attempted it together after their parents had died, with one spectacular failure of raw turkey and another dried to a crisp. "I'm not very good at turkey," she said to Janet.

"Well, I've done it a few times," Janet said with an easy smile. "I'd love some help, though."

They moved into the kitchen where Janet already had the turkey sitting in the kitchen sink. "Did you have plans for stuffing it?" she asked. "I didn't want to take over."

"I was just going to make the basic bread stuffing my mom used to make."

"Perfect."

The day passed quickly. Jim and Drew argued over football, Jim shaking his head at the "American football" games on the television in between serving drinks and snacks and helping in the kitchen. Janet was so easy to talk to and lovely; by the time they sat down for dinner Peyton felt she'd known her all her life. Chloe was more at ease and was telling them all about her latest cause— shark finning.

"They cut off the fins of sharks," she explained earnestly. "And toss the body back in the water. But the shark can't swim without its fin and it sinks to the bottom of the ocean and suffocates. It's very cruel."

Peyton winced at the unfortunate dinner conversation, even though she was proud of Chloe.

"That *is* awful," Janet agreed.

"What the hell do people use shark fins for?" Jim asked.

Peyton bit her lip on a smile. Ah, well, Drew swore in front of Chloe and it hadn't seemed to corrupt her.

"Shark fin soup," Chloe said. "It's very popular in China. They also use it in some traditional Chinese medicines, and it's used in some cosmetics and pet foods. The shark fins can be worth thousands of dollars, so even though it's illegal, some fishermen still do it."

"That's terrible."

Chloe nodded. "There are thirty-nine species of sharks that are endangered."

"How do you know all about this?" Jim asked.

"I did a project on it at school. And I'm working on a fundraiser to raise awareness about products that contain shark fins so that people won't buy them, and so we can send money to Shark Heroes. It's an organization that works to protect sharks."

Peyton watched Jim and Janet exchange glances. For a moment she thought Janet was going to cry, but the older woman blinked a few times then smiled. "That's amazing, Chloe."

Chloe smiled and shrugged. "I like doing things like that."

Peyton sipped her wine, her own chest full of pride and love for her niece. She glanced at Drew and the look on his face seemed to reflect her own feelings, his eyes warm and admiring on his daughter. Then as if sensing her looking at him, he turned his gaze to her and they shared a connection of spirit, joined by their love for Chloe. And then the warmth in his eyes changed, sparking hotter, and her lower belly did a little flip.

She dropped her gaze to her plate. "This turkey is so good. Thank you for helping, Janet."

"Oh, my goodness, it's my pleasure. This is certainly a different holiday for us, but I have to say, it's . . . wonderful."

And Peyton agreed. She was still sad and missing Sara, but this *was* pretty wonderful.

CHAPTER 28

Peyton turned to Drew in her living room to set her hands on his chest, Chloe having gone up to get ready for bed after he'd driven them home. She rubbed through his sweater and damn, it felt good. "That was a lovely day. Your parents are great, and I could see they really liked Chloe, too."

"Yeah." He hesitated. He'd seen it, too. He wasn't sure if he'd fucked up epically by having them meet Chloe . . . because now not only was *he* going to be crushed when Chloe and Peyton moved to New York, his parents would be, too. And yet . . . as when he'd found out about Chloe's existence . . . how could they live their lives knowing about her but never meeting her? He sucked in a long breath and said, "I went to see a lawyer."

Peyton regarded him with a crease between her eyebrows. "Why?"

"About getting custody of Chloe."

She stepped back, her eyes widening. She stared at him. Time stretched out. His gut tightened.

"Are you serious?" she finally asked.

"Yeah." He rubbed the back of his neck. "I'm her father. Her biological father. I have some rights. I don't know all the laws, but

I did some research online. I talked to my lawyer about what I have to do."

She still stared at him and his insides twisted even more. "You want to take her away from me?"

His jaw tightened. "No. That's not what I want. But if you take her to New York, *you're* taking her away from me."

Her arms wrapped around herself as if she was freezing. "So you're basically blackmailing me into staying here."

"No! Jesus." He shoved a hand into his hair. This wasn't going well, but then, he hadn't expected it was going to be easy. "I just want to keep her in my life."

Her face blank, but her lips tight, she nodded slowly. "I understand." She stood. Her chin lifted. "You can leave now." She rushed to the door and flung it open. Cold air blasted in. "I'll see you in court."

"Peyton . . . come on. Don't." He moved toward her but she backed away, her eyes sparking.

"Don't touch me. Don't talk to me. Just get out."

His jaw locked. "Could we talk about this?"

"No! I'm not giving her up!" She fought to keep her voice low so Chloe wouldn't hear. "Sara made me her guardian. That was what she wanted!"

"That was before I was in the picture."

She glared at him. "She didn't change her mind after you came into the picture."

He swallowed. "I know, but . . . " *She hadn't had very long.* He couldn't bring himself to say the words. "She asked me if I would have a relationship with Chloe, if she wanted. So I think she wanted that, too."

Peyton's lips parted. "Please leave."

"Fuck." He cast one last miserable glance at her, her mouth set in a stubborn line, her eyes narrow, her posture stiff and unyielding. "Come on, Peyton. You're going to take her away from her home and her school and her friends . . . and me. Are you so fucking focused on your precious career that you can't see what you're doing?"

Her eyebrows pulled down and her hand went to her throat.

"You've got your whole life planned," he snapped. "So much that you can't adapt when something changes."

Her eyes widened and the flash of hurt in them made his heart stab.

"Well," she said in a tight voice. "You *didn't* have your whole life planned, and *you* weren't doing such a great job of adapting when *your* life changed."

He narrowed his eyes as he received the shot with another spasm of his heart. Then he turned and walked out the door.

It shut behind him with a bang and he stood on the veranda for a few seconds. Anger heated his blood and his hands curled into fists. Dammit. Why wouldn't she just fucking listen to him?

He had a right to have his daughter in his life. Yes, he knew that Sara had made Peyton Chloe's legal guardian, but it was true that there hadn't been time for her to change her mind about that after she'd found him. If she'd lived longer and he'd spent more time with her and with Chloe, she would have wanted him to be involved in Chloe's life.

Wouldn't she?

Peyton's direct hit about how he hadn't been adapting to life after hockey was like a knife in his gut, twisting. The doubts that had been eating away at him since he'd had to retire reared up again.

Fuck.

He bounded down the steps and stalked to his car. He wasn't giving up on this. He needed to do this. He needed to prove he could be a good father. He needed to prove that to himself.

When he got home, Dad was in the family room still watching football and complaining out loud about the American rules. Drew stomped into the kitchen and started slinging plates into the dishwasher. His mom turned and gave him a level look as she covered a container of leftovers. "Something wrong?"

"No." He slammed the dishwasher shut. "Hmm. You seem upset."

"I'm fine."

"Chloe's an amazing girl," Mom said quietly.

"I know." His response came out as a snarl and he sucked in a long breath and tried to relax.

"I can see how much you love her already."

He nodded, his throat tightening. His jaw clenched and then he said, "Peyton's taking her to New York to live."

Mom nodded. "Yes, I got that." Her eyes shadowed. "That upsets you."

"I don't want to lose her. I just found her."

"Are you talking about Chloe? Or Peyton?"

His head snapped up. "What?"

Mom smiled. "I saw the way you looked at Chloe. The fondness you have for her. But the way you looked at Peyton . . . the way she looked at you . . . I'm pretty good at sensing things and I'm not usually wrong. There's something between you."

It struck him like a fist to his chest . . . he didn't just love Chloe. He loved Peyton.

He closed his eyes. "I was talking about Chloe. But yeah . . . there's something between Peyton and me."

"What are you going to do about it?"

He ground his molars together. "I went to see a lawyer last week about trying to get shared custody of Chloe."

She blinked. "Oh. That's . . . not what I expected you to say."

"I just told Peyton that."

She tipped her head to one side. "I gather that didn't go well."

"Fuck, no."

Mom didn't even flinch at his language. He'd heard *her* drop the F bomb a time or two.

He slumped against the counter. "I don't know if I can really do that to them. It's gonna be ugly if I do. And hell, I don't even know if I'm good enough to be Chloe's dad."

Mom's eyes flew open. "What? What are you talking about?"

"Mom. I have no job. I don't know what I'm doing with my life."

"I thought you were working on something."

"I am, but . . . I don't know how successful that's going to be. I'm a washed-up, divorced hockey player. I want Chloe in my life, but . . . " He shrugged. "Peyton loves her, too. She's her guardian. She's great with her. Peyton has her whole life and career planned out and I don't know what the hell I'm doing. Chloe's probably better off with her."

Mom's face scrunched up and she rubbed her forehead. "It's not easy, is it?"

"Nope."

"But thinking you're not good enough to be her dad is ridiculous. First of all, you *are* her dad. Second, you love her. That's all it takes."

"No. It takes more than that."

She studied him with raised eyebrows.

Dammit, she did know stuff. He didn't know how she knew stuff but she did. "You're not a failure because you had to retire from hockey," she said. "And you're not a failure as a father if you make mistakes."

He shifted against the counter.

"You've failed before," she continued. He frowned.

"Many times. Learning to skate, how many times did you fall down? Too many to count. But you were determined. You got back up and kept going. You missed shots on net. You worked hard to be better. You didn't make your bantam team your first try. You tried again. For heaven's sake, Drew. Failure isn't falling down—it's falling down and refusing to get up."

Drew closed his eyes, remembering months back when he'd

been drinking and screwing around and fighting in bars . . . basically not getting back up. Yeah. That was failure.

This was the second woman to give him shit tonight. Jesus.

"Don't be afraid of failing as a father. You'll be missing out on so much joy if you don't even try."

He let her words run through his head. "I thought I was trying! By fighting for custody of her!"

She winced and tucked some hair behind her ear. "I think if you do that, you might win Chloe . . . but you'll lose Peyton."

He stared at her.

"I know you're competitive," she said. "But this kind of competition could be so destructive. In the end, nobody wins. Think about what you're doing. Think about what you really want. And don't be afraid of failing at *love*. Because you'll be missing out on so much joy if you don't even try."

Peyton stood in the foyer, trembling, her eyes closed.

What had just happened? Was he seriously going to try to take Chloe away from her?

She'd already been considering other options, but his words about having her life so planned out, being so focused on her career that she couldn't look out for Chloe, had felt like a punch in the heart.

She trudged into the living room and sank onto the couch, her head in her hands, trying to sort through her tangled thoughts.

She already knew she couldn't do that to Chloe. Her chest felt like it was full of hot coals as she thought about what she'd said to Drew . . . that Sara wouldn't have changed her mind. And that he hadn't been adapting to retirement very well.

She shouldn't have said that. It wasn't true. He'd been through hell, and he was working hard at it, picking himself up. But she'd been hurt, and protecting her heart had made her lash out.

And she knew that Sara wanted Chloe to know her dad, and

even though she hadn't had a lot of time, she'd accepted Drew and felt comfortable enough that she let him take Chloe on his own. But would she have actually shared custody with him, had she lived?

There was no way to know that. Sara loved her daughter fiercely, but Peyton knew that it was an unselfish love. That Sara wanted the best for Chloe no matter what. It was why she'd allowed Drew into their lives in the first place.

Drew was right. She was the selfish one.

She jumped to her feet and paced to the window. Snow tumbled down from the low clouds obscuring the sky, blanketing the ground in white, clumping on the shrubs.

He was also right about her being rigid. Not wanting to veer from her plan. Trying to protect her own life . . . her life in New York, her precious career, the plan she had for world domination. Ha.

She leaned her forehead against the icy glass of the window and closed her eyes again as pain nearly took out her knees. What really hurt? That Drew would actually do that . . . would actually try to take Chloe away from her.

She got that he wanted his daughter. But she thought he cared about her, too. Pain pulsed from her heart out to her fingertips and her throat squeezed. Jesus, love was fucking painful. She'd lost so many people she'd loved. First her parents then Sara. Was she going to lose Chloe and Drew, too?

Tears slipped from beneath her clamped-shut eyelids.

Her cell phone started ringing in her purse where she'd dropped it on the table in the foyer. She swiped at tears on her face with both hands and hesitated. Maybe it was Drew? Hope burst in her chest as she hurried over to get it.

It was her boss.

She frowned at the call on Thanksgiving evening but answered it. "Peyton speaking."

"Peyton. It's Gord."

"Hi, Gord. What's up?"

"We have a big problem."

Her forehead tightened and she wiped more tears. "What?"

"North Star Airlines just had a plane slide off the runway."

"Oh, no." She touched her fingertips to her mouth. North Star was a big client of theirs. Of hers. "Is anyone hurt?"

"Not on the plane, but it slid onto a highway and hit a car. A young girl was killed."

"Oh, my God." She closed her eyes.

"Yeah. This is a disaster and we need to get on it right away."

She bit her lip. Yes, North Star was her client. Yes, she had to help them with this. Her head dropped forward. Why now?

She pulled in a big breath and let it out. "Okay. I'll get a flight back first thing in the morning. I'll email you the details."

"Great."

She ended the call and bit her lip. Hell.

The way things had just ended with Drew . . . the last thing she wanted to do was call him and ask him to take Chloe. Forceful bands tightened around her chest.

She forced herself to take a few deep breaths, pacing back and forth across the living room.

She'd had her life all planned out . . . the career that was going to move her up in her field, the success she was going to have. She'd never planned to have a family.

That was going to be her secret of success . . . she wouldn't have to worry about work/life balance; she'd be there to give her all to her work and she'd rise up the ladder until . . . what?

She wasn't sure what her actual end goal was. CEO of Sentinel? Or another big company? Running the whole show herself? Was that what she wanted?

If it was, why not run her own show, like Nik had said?

She sank down onto the couch and stared blankly across the room.

Balancing work and family wasn't something that would hold

her back. It would make her life *fuller*. Because she loved Chloe and in the end . . . that mattered more than anything.

Oh, God.

But first she had to deal with this crisis. She hauled her weary ass up the stairs to talk to Chloe.

"Hey, kiddo." She knocked on Chloe's open door and stepped into her room. She was in bed, the lamp on beside her, reading. "Ready for bed?"

"Yes. Can I read for a while longer?"

Peyton didn't even know what time it was. Or if it was past Chloe's bedtime. "Sure. Uh . . . I just got a call from my boss. We have a bit of a crisis to deal with. I need to go to New York." She paused. "Do you want to come with me for a few days?"

Chloe blinked and her face took on a wary expression. "Just for a few days?"

"Yes." Peyton swallowed. "I have to deal with this emergency, but while I'm there . . . I'm going to give them my notice. I'm going to quit my job."

"Seriously?" Chloe gaped at Peyton.

Peyton nodded, smiling. "Seriously."

"You're going to move here?"

"Yes."

"What are you going to do?"

"I'm not sure right now." She smiled and patted Chloe's knee. "But I'll figure it out."

"I don't have to go to a different school?"

"Nope."

"I can keep working on my shark finning awareness project?"

"You sure can."

Chloe heaved a huge sigh then tossed her book down and lunged forward to fling her arms around Peyton's neck. "Thank you, Auntie P." She sobbed. "Thank you."

Peyton's heart squeezed. "I love you, kiddo. We're in this together, for always."

Unless Drew takes you away from me. "I can't wait to tell Dad."

Peyton blinked. When had she started calling Drew Dad? That was . . . nice. Her heart squeezed. "Uh, right." She bit her lip. Would this make any difference? Was there any possibility of shared parental time? Because she would fight him if he wanted full custody. Threatening something like that made her competitive nature stiffen her resolve. He may have said that to keep her from taking Chloe to New York . . . and in that regard he'd won, dammit. Even though she wasn't doing it for him.

Maybe. Not totally for him. She'd done it for Chloe and what was best for her, but there was no denying that her heart hurt for both Chloe and Drew when she thought about them not seeing each other. She knew how much he'd come to love Chloe already and she couldn't take that away from him.

Fuck, she loved him. And he was such a jerk.

"You can tell him when we get back," she said. "I'm going to try to book a flight for tomorrow morning. Luckily Monday is an admin day for your school, so we don't have to be back till Tuesday."

"I can miss school."

"No, you can't." She repressed a smile. "But I think I'll be able to deal with things over the next few days. You'll need to pack a bag for a few days."

"I'll do it right now!" Chloe jumped out of bed, eager for any excuse to delay bedtime.

CHAPTER 29

"The weather was terrible." Gord was updating her about the accident as she and Chloe traveled by taxi from JFK to the office. When she'd turned on her phone in the airport after they'd deplaned, she'd seen five missed calls and five text messages from Drew, and two voice mails— one from Drew sounding pissed and asking her to call him back, the other from Gord, also sounding pissed.

How fun.

She'd waited until they were in the taxi on their way to the office to call Gord. "It was really blustery here last night, windy and snowing," he continued. "The plane was landing at LaGuardia and at first it apparently seemed like they'd managed to safely land. The crew was all experienced and respected. But then they couldn't stop and skidded off the runway. They went through a fence and onto a roadway. There are twenty-five people with minor injuries, and like I said, the one fatality."

"They've never had a fatal accident before," Peyton said.

"Nope."

North Star airlines had been steadily growing to become one of the largest and most successful airlines in America. They'd built their reputation as a "fun" airline with personable staff who excelled at customer service, humorous advertising campaigns, and a casual corporate culture. They'd also won awards for quality, with their on-time record, baggage handling, and low numbers of customer complaints.

"Their CEO has already addressed the media this morning," Gord continued. "Of course they contacted us right away to help with further developments and communication."

"Of course." She'd read the news reports online and watched a video of the press conference. "That's what I'm here for."

At the office Michael Chan, CEO of North Star, was already there with several other executives from North Star and representatives from their communications department. She met Gord outside the boardroom.

"Uh . . . " His gaze fell on Chloe. "Who's this?"

"My niece, Chloe." Peyton set a hand on top of Chloe's head. "She's going to hang out in my office while we work."

Gord frowned. "You can't bring a kid to work."

"Don't be a dick, Gord," she said. "I brought her."

At first she wasn't sure if he'd actually heard her. His eyes widened and his mouth opened then snapped shut.

"I'll be there in just a few minutes." She led Chloe to her office and got her set up on the computer. She also had her book and her Nintendo and the homework Peyton had insisted she bring along. "You come get me if you need anything, okay?"

"I won't. I'll be fine. I won't interrupt your meeting. Your boss isn't very happy."

"I know. He hasn't been happy with me for a while." She grinned. "So it's good that I'm quitting."

Chloe smiled back at her and twirled around in the office chair. "I like your office. I want to work in an office like this."

"Well, maybe you will one day, when you're a big civil rights lawyer." She bent and kissed Chloe's forehead and returned to the boardroom.

They quickly brought her up to speed.

"Okay," Peyton said. "I applaud you for what you've done to help everyone immediately affected by the crash."

"Our staff is working overtime to handle the customer service line we set up and to contact people affected."

She nodded. "I absolutely recommend continued transparency. It will be important for you to be the face of the company, Michael. We don't want anyone to wonder who's in charge. You'll need to be the leader here. Not only will you have to communicate with the public and with the families of people impacted, but also with your staff, to maintain their morale. You'll need to keep them just as informed about everything." She looked at her notes. "I also recommend being very careful to not assign blame to anyone right now. Obviously the investigation will turn up more info, but definitely we don't want to blame the crew, nor do we want to blame the airport at this time."

Michael nodded, and the others at the boardroom table also made quick notes. "We'll need to use various communication channels to keep staff informed," she said. "Make sure to express your appreciation for the long hours and their dedication to dealing with your customers. Also make sure you assure the public that North Star will fully cooperate with regulators, and with the airport."

"Of course," Michael said. "I do want to make sure that we get to the cause of this."

"If you can go above and beyond the government investigation, you should do that," she advised. "I know your safety record is important to you. That will go a long way to reassuring key constituents . . . customers and investors, regulators, staff. Employees, suppliers and other stakeholders pay as much attention to a crisis as customers." She paused. "Obviously our goal is to keep the public response to this as positive as possible, under the circumstances. On top of that . . . " She looked at Michael. "We can look at this as an opportunity for North Star . . . a test of your core values and your promises to customers. Does North Star walk the talk? This is a chance for you to show the world that you do. If we handle this right, you can come out of this stronger."

"We need to rethink our upcoming ad campaigns in light of this," their VP of Communications said.

"Absolutely. While your image as the fun airline is gold, that won't be appropriate right away."

They discussed more strategy, Peyton laying out a plan for Michael's communication to the public over the short-term. "I'll meet with my team as soon as possible to work up a long-term plan, as well."

They'd be thrilled about being dragged into the office on a holiday weekend. After the folks from North Star had left, Peyton was also walking out of the boardroom when Gord called to her.

She turned to him.

"You're supposed to be back here full- time beginning of December."

She sucked in a breath. "Yeah, about that. I'm not going to be able to do it." He frowned. "You need more time? Because we can't do that. We've been flexible and generous with you, but we need you here, in the office, doing your job."

"I have been doing my job," she said. "Mostly. Under the circumstances, I think I did a lot. I'm sorry, Gord, but I'm resigning." She tried to keep her expression professional. "I apologize for dragging this out, but I didn't realize how hard it was going to be to uproot Chloe from her life in Chicago. I'll work on a strategy for dealing with this crisis over the next few days, but I won't be coming back to Sentinel." She straightened her shoulders. "I've enjoyed working here and I've learned so much from you. But family has to come first."

She believed that. She'd always believed that. She'd just never imagined herself quitting a job by saying those words.

He nodded, his mouth a grim line. "I understand. This is probably for the best." Chloe had kept herself busy and they took a taxi to her apartment. Friday night of the holiday weekend in New York was vibrant, the city buzzing and sparkling with Christmas anticipation and cheer.

"I haven't been here for a long time," Chloe said as they entered the apartment in the dark.

"I know." Sara and Chloe had visited her many times but not recently. She'd had Chloe on her own for visits in the summers, and Sara and Chloe had spent one Christmas there after their parents had died, but after Sara had not been feeling as well, it had been more important for Peyton to visit them in Chicago.

She flicked on lights and took off her coat. "I know my cupboards are bare," she said. "So we're going to have to order in. How about Thai food?" She had a favorite little place not far from there that delivered.

"Sure."

It had been a long day, starting with the early-morning flight, the work she'd done on the plane, and then the afternoon meeting. She looked around her apartment as Chloe carried her small bag into the spare bedroom. Bleh. This didn't even feel like home anymore.

She remembered the texts and the voice mail from Drew, which she hadn't replied to. After she ordered their food, she texted him back.

Sorry, got your voice mail. Chloe and I are in New York. Talk to you next week.

Drew slept like shit and woke up irritable and with a sore neck Friday morning.

He'd been flip-flopping in his bed all night, replaying that awful conversation he'd had with Peyton. He'd fucked up.

He admired her for how she had her life so organized. He

shouldn't have said what he did about her being too focused on her career to care about Chloe. He knew how much she loved her niece.

She'd struck back and hit his soft spots with that crack about how he hadn't been handling retirement very well, reminding him that Sara had had doubts about him.

But remembering the hurt look on her face had his stomach heaving. He couldn't take Chloe away from her. He couldn't put them all through some kind of custody battle. But he couldn't lose them, either. He didn't know what the answer was, but he had to fix this. He'd go over there and make her talk to him.

Mom and Dad were already up when he trudged downstairs. "Thank you, Mom," he said with heartfelt gratitude upon seeing the full coffeepot.

She handed him a mug and he filled it and took a gulp. "I'm going over to Peyton's," he told her.

She smiled. "Good idea."

"Maybe this afternoon we could all go to Navy Pier or something." Assuming Peyton forgave him for last night.

"That sounds fun," Mom said.

Dad shrugged. "Sure."

He quickly showered and changed from sweats into a pair of jeans and a sweater then headed over to the Watt home. On the veranda, he rang the bell, but nobody answered. He rang again.

With a frown he pulled out his keys and studied the one he had to the house. Yeah, he had to make sure they were okay. So he used his key to enter.

"Anyone home?"

The house was silent and clearly empty. He poked his head into a few rooms but nope, nobody there. They'd gone out somewhere, obviously. He felt a little weird being there uninvited, but maybe he could hang out until they got home. Maybe they'd just gone out for breakfast or something.

He made himself another coffee in the Keurig in the kitchen then turned on the TV in the living room to watch a sports show.

An hour later they still weren't home. He rinsed his mug and set it in the empty dishwasher. Okay, where the hell were they?

He pulled out his phone and called Peyton's cell phone. It went straight to voice mail. Was her phone off? That was weird.

Heaving a sigh, he left and drove home.

"They weren't there," he explained shortly to his parents. "And she's not answering her phone."

Mom's eyebrows knit and she sank her teeth into her bottom lip briefly. While he sprawled on the couch watching TV with Dad, he tried again a few times to call Peyton, again getting voice mail. So he sent her a text.

"Guess that's not going to work out for this afternoon," he told his parents, trying to be casual even though he wasn't sure whether to be more pissed or worried.

Instead they went Black Friday shopping, pretty much his idea of hell, but Mom was all excited about the deals even though the exchange rate sucked right now. All afternoon he was checking his phone, sending more text messages, trying not to be obvious that he was obsessed. He finally got a response from Peyton while they were having dinner in a restaurant just off Michigan. When he read it, his blood raced hot through his veins.

What. The. Fuck.

They were in New York? Had she seriously taken Chloe and run to New York because of what he'd said?

Jesus Christ.

He was so irate he couldn't even tell his parents. He was also so nauseated he could barely eat the prime rib he'd ordered. He set the phone down and tried to smile at what Mom was saying about Chloe and her shark finning project, while contemplating booking a flight to New York that fucking night.

But he had no idea where Peyton lived.

Monday morning he got the call from Step that they wanted

him to work with a few players using his new plan for increasing goal scoring.

Fuck, yeah!

He pumped a fist into the air as he talked to him in his kitchen. This was fucking fantastic! He'd have a real role, with real responsibilities, something he had to deliver on. He wouldn't just be hanging around the arena morosely, trying to be part of something he no longer contributed to.

Excitement sizzled through his veins as they arranged a meeting for the next day. When he ended the call, though, he sobered. He'd been giving serious thought to moving to New York, if that was what he had to do to be with Chloe and Peyton. How would he do that now? How could he lay this all out for the team and ask them to commit when he was going to pick up and leave?

His ass hit a stool and he slumped against the island. Shit. How fucked up was this timing?

"Before you call Drew, I need to talk to you about something."

"Okay." Chloe set the cordless phone back down on the kitchen counter.

It was Monday evening and they were home from their trip to New York. Peyton had cleared out her office at Sentinel. As she'd suspected, once she'd given her official notice that morning, they didn't want her dealing with clients. So she was done there and unemployed.

She and Chloe had started packing her things to move to Chicago. She'd have to make another trip back to deal with subletting her apartment and shipping everything, but she got quite a bit done.

Chloe was excited to tell Drew that they weren't moving to New York after all. But first . . .

"Would you want to live with Drew?" she asked Chloe quietly.

Chloe blinked. "I don't know."

She clearly hadn't thought about that. "I know Drew loves you and wants you to be part of his life. We need to talk about what that would look like. I mean, Drew and I need to talk about it, but if you absolutely don't want to live with him, I need to know that. And if you do, I need to know that, too. It could be a part-time thing."

Chloe nodded slowly, eyes wide and troubled.

"You don't have to decide right now," Peyton hastened to assure her. "This is something to think about and something for us to talk about."

As hurt as she was by what Drew had done by going to a lawyer and threatening to take Chloe away from her, she was going to have to get past that and have a civil discussion with him about what this meant.

She also had to find a job.

Setting that aside, though, she smiled at Chloe. "I just wanted to talk about that before you call him, because he might bring it up."

Chloe's chin quivered. "I don't know what to tell him."

"You don't have to tell him anything, sweetie." Peyton reached out and smoothed Chloe's hair. "If he says something about it, you can tell him you want to think about it. And after you talk to him, pass the phone to me."

"Did you have a fight with him?"

Peyton swallowed. "Why do you ask that?"

"I just . . . you said you liked each other, but every time I mention him, you get . . . tense."

Peyton tried to keep her face relaxed, a reassuring smile in place. "Everything's fine." She apparently hadn't done very well at keeping her anger at Drew hidden over the past few days.

Chloe called Drew's number. "Hi!" she said when he answered. "It's me, Chloe." Peyton listened to her niece telling Drew about the trip to New York. "And Auntie P quit her job," she said. "We're staying here in Chicago! Isn't that great?"

Peyton smiled, her chest full of warmth.

They talked for a few more minutes, apparently making arrangements for Drew to take her to dance class Wednesday night, and then Chloe said, "Auntie P wants to talk to you, too."

Peyton took the phone with trembling fingers. "Hi."

"Hey." His voice was unexpectedly gentle. "This is . . . a shock."

"Why?" Bitterness crept into her tone and she fought it back because Chloe was listening. "Isn't this what you wanted?"

"Peyton. I wanted to talk to you, to figure out a way—"

"Yes, we do need to talk. Perhaps next week one day we could meet for lunch?"

Again, the formality of her speech seemed to take him aback, and it took a moment for him to reply. "Okay," he agreed. "What day works for you?"

"Any day."

"Hang on. I'm kind of busy this week. Uh . . . lunch would be hard. I gather you want to do this when Chloe's not around?"

"Yes."

She heard a low noise of frustration. "I could stop by tomorrow morning."

"I'd rather meet up somewhere." If she let him in the house and they were alone, she was afraid of what might happen between them, because despite her anger and hurt, she still had a whole lot of other feelings for him and that could not happen.

"For fuck's sake."

She smiled at Chloe, trying not to wince. "It seems you're really busy. That's good."

"Yeah, it is. Okay, I'll figure something out for tomorrow. Where should we meet?" She named a restaurant on West Webster not far from both of them.

"Fine," he bit out. "See you then."

CHAPTER 30

"I know you've talked to a lawyer, but I'd rather not get lawyers involved if we don't have to. I'm hoping we can come to an agreement that's best for Chloe."

Drew narrowed his eyes at Peyton across the table in the busy, noisy restaurant. Nothing intimate or personal about this place.

He studied her, so beautiful and yet so brittle, he worried she might snap with a sudden movement. Her fingers kept moving, touching things, arranging cutlery, her hands rubbing together, her jaw tight and her eyes cool.

She'd taken the wind out of his stubborn sails with this news of quitting her job and moving to Chicago. When Chloe'd told him that last night, his knees had damn near given out. He'd been so pissed that Peyton had taken Chloe to New York, terrified that they were never coming back, relief had turned his bones to liquid. He was almost afraid to believe it was true, but apparently it was as Peyton had just confirmed. He'd also been relieved that he wasn't going to have to bail on the Hawks after gaining their support for trying out his ideas.

"Agreement about what?" he asked.

"Custody."

She was willing to share custody of Chloe? "It's not called that anymore. It's parental responsibilities."

"What?" Her forehead creased.

He shrugged. "Apparently these days parents don't share custody. They share parental responsibilities."

"Oh." She hesitated. "Is that what you want?"

"Of course. I thought I *had* been sharing responsibilities."

"Yes. You have." She swallowed. "Do you want more than that, though? Do you want her to live with you?" She was clearly fighting for control, but the words came out stiffly.

"Maybe."

Her face tightened even more. "All the time?"

He closed his eyes. He knew what he wanted. But how had things gotten so fucked up?

"I'm not trying to take her away from you, Peyton," he said quietly. Should he tell her that he'd already decided he couldn't go through with a custody battle? That he'd been trying to reach her so they could talk about things? Yeah, when he'd found out they'd gone to New York, his flare of anger had made him determined to take action, but again, he'd known he couldn't go through with it once he cooled down.

"That wasn't the impression I got the other night when you specifically said you'd consulted a lawyer about getting custody of her."

"I didn't handle that very well."

She gave a mirthless laugh. "No shit."

He swallowed a sigh. "I didn't expect you to quit your job."

She lifted one shoulder in a tiny movement. "Whatever."

Christ, she was killing him. "What are you going to do?"

"I don't know." The words came out clipped, between clenched teeth. "But don't worry. I can afford to support Chloe."

"Jesus, that's not what I'm worried about."

"Look, I asked Chloe to think about whether she wants to live with you. I think we should take her wishes into consideration."

"Of course." Maybe Chloe wouldn't want to live with him. They'd only met a few months ago. He would totally understand that if she didn't. Maybe one day she would. "I don't want to rush things. I'll continue taking her to dance class on Wednesday nights and . . . and taking her out on weekends." He looked down at his own hands, clasped on the table, and realized he was almost as tense as she was, his knuckles pale. "I'll take what I can get, Peyton."

"I think we should have something more structured than just a vague plan to 'take her out.'"

His teeth ground together. "Fine. You like plans. You draw something up. Then we'll talk again."

He lifted a hand to signal the server that they wanted the check, frustration expanding in his chest.

Peyton reached for her purse and he slashed a hand through the air. "Don't even fucking think about it. I've got this."

She opened her mouth as if to argue, with her usual stubborn competitiveness. He glared at her and she pressed her lips into a grim line. "Thank you."

He tossed cash on the table since he couldn't be bothered to wait to pay with a credit card and shoved his chair back. "I have to go. I have a meeting at two."

She nodded stiffly and rose. "Yeah, I have . . . " Her words trailed off. Then she straightened her shoulders. "I have a lot to do also."

He walked out of the restaurant nearly blind, ignoring everything around him, his chest on fire.

This wasn't what he wanted. Goddammit, she was stubborn.

Luckily his week was full with working with the midget players he'd talked to last week, getting on the ice with them and recording their shooting, then analyzing it and working with them on his strategies for scoring. He was still going in to

Paterson House because that felt good. And he was punishing himself in the gym, working out until sweat was stinging his eyes and his muscles felt like memory foam.

He took Chloe to her dance class on Wednesday, and picked her up after school on Friday to take her out for pizza.

"Auntie P asked if I want to live with you," Chloe said over a deep dish pie brimming with spicy tomato sauce and cheese. He caught the wariness in her eyes.

Drew held her gaze steadily. "Yeah. She told me that."

"Do you want that?"

"I would love that," he said. "But we're still getting to know each other. And you're settled in your house with Peyton. We don't have to decide anything right away. Maybe once in a while you could stay over, like you did when Peyton went to New York."

She nodded. "That would be cool." She dropped her gaze. "I feel bad because she quit her job for me."

Christ. He didn't know what to say. "I feel bad, too," he finally said in a low voice.

"I thought maybe if I lived with you, she could stay in New York. But . . . " Her voice quavered. "But I'd miss her. And anyway, she already quit her job."

His jaw dropped. He shook his head violently. "No, Chloe. She didn't want that. She would miss *you* too much."

"Yeah. I think she was upset when we talked about me living with you."

No shit. "I think we all just need time to get used to all these changes. It's been hard for everyone."

When he took her home, Peyton greeted him with cool reserve and handed him a piece of paper.

"What's this?"

"A schedule. You asked for it."

He stared at the table she'd created with Chloe's weekly schedule, his name by a few items. He resisted the impulse to crush it in his fist. His teeth hurt from clenching them. Then he nodded. "Fine."

He caught Chloe watching them, her mouth unsmiling, her eyes shadowed and darting back and forth between them.

He forced a smile. "I mean great. This is really helpful. Thanks, Peyton." He turned his smile on Chloe. "Gimme a hug, kiddo."

She moved into his arms and he held her little body close for a brief moment, his heart tilting. Then he released her. "Night. See you Sunday for the game."

The Blackhawks had an afternoon game he was going to take her to. "Night, Dad."

His heart contracted at the sound of that name on his daughter's lips. He felt like an imposter, like he didn't deserve to be called that. But he remembered his mom's words. *You just have to love her.* He could do that.

When she'd run upstairs, he and Peyton faced off again, the air around them heavy and electric.

"She knew something's wrong," he said roughly. "We have to do better around her."

Her eyes closed briefly. "Yes. You're right."

He didn't want to leave. He wanted to pull Peyton in for a hug, but not like Chloe's. A totally different kind of hug. He wanted to feel her curves against him, to wrap her up and tell her everything was fine. To tell her he was sorry he hurt her, that he was working hard to be a good enough dad for Chloe and a good enough man for her. But judging by her unyielding posture and her cool gaze, he wasn't there yet.

So he said nothing, took the schedule, and left.

"This is the dream team."

Peyton smiled at her friends gathered around the table in the restaurant where she'd invited them to meet for lunch—Aidan all clean-shaven and businesslike in his expensive suit and tie, Jax with his shaggy hair, hipster glasses, and black turtleneck, Hannah's red hair glowing against the moss-green sweater she wore. They'd all been surprised to see each other since Peyton hadn't told them the others would be there.

Jax grinned.

"What dream team?" Aidan frowned.

"You're not happy in your job, are you?" Peyton asked him.

He grimaced. "Fuck, no."

"Neither is Jax. *I'm* unemployed. Hannah, how's your job going?"

She shrugged. "It's okay."

"Jax and I had lunch back at the end of October and he was saying that if he could have a dream team of reputation managers, it would be us." She gestured in a circle to include all of them.

"I'm not a reputation manager," Aidan said slowly.

"But you'd be so good at it." She smiled. "And having someone who knows the law would be a huge asset."

"I don't do reputation management, either," Hannah said, her forehead grooved.

"But you know marketing. Think about it . . . with Jax's tech skills and the experience we have with both day-to-day reputation management and crisis management, a lawyer and a marketing specialist . . . it really is a dream team."

"What are you suggesting?" Aidan asked, interest sparking in his eyes.

"I think we should start our own reputation management company." They all stared at her.

A smile broke on Jax's face first. "I am so in."

Aidan sat back in his chair. "That's kind of crazy."

Peyton pouted.

"But also kind of genius." He tipped his head to one side.

"I don't have any money," Hannah said. "We need money to start a business."

Peyton nodded. "Yes. We'd need to do a business plan and figure out what our start-up costs would be. It might not be that much. We'd need office space, obviously office furniture and computers, access to programs and resources for social media monitoring and SEO evaluation, insurance, a budget for advertising . . . "

"And clients. We'd need clients." Aidan lifted an eyebrow.

"Well, yes." She looked at Hannah. "Depending on what it all looks like, you could stay at your job until we get up and running. Maybe you'd rather be an employee than a partner?"

Hannah pursed her lips. "I don't know. Let's talk about that when we know what kind of money we're looking at. I get bored easily. I don't want to invest a bunch of money into something that I'm going to bail on in a year. On the other hand, if it was my own business . . . and it was up to me to make it succeed . . . maybe I wouldn't be bored."

"I've got some money set aside," Aidan said.

"Me, too," Jax added.

"As do I," Peyton said. "I see this company as being high-end. With high-profile clients who are willing to pay top dollar for the best reputation management."

They started throwing out ideas, suggestions for where to locate, and possible clients they could contact. The excitement built among them until Peyton could feel it buzzing in her veins. The more they talked, the more everything seemed to come together.

"It's getting close to Christmas," Peyton said an hour later. "I say let's really get moving on this in the New Year."

"Man, I am pumped," Jax said. "This is what I need to feel excited about work again."

"Yeah," Aidan admitted. "Me, too."

"I'm kind of excited about it, too," Hannah said. "Even though I have a lot to learn."

"You've already had a couple of great ideas about increasing online visibility," Peyton said. She scrunched her face up with excitement. "This is going to be so good!"

They agreed to set up an online chat group where they could continue their planning and parted ways out on the sidewalk.

Peyton walked over to Michigan Avenue and strolled past the stores all decorated with Christmas greenery, decorations, and sparkling lights. Her excitement faded in the face of all the holiday cheer. Christmas was getting her down.

Their first Christmas without Sara. Drew had made Thanksgiving into something new and different. But now she was without him, too.

She and Drew hadn't talked much over the last couple of weeks since their lunch to discuss how they would share Chloe's time. They'd fallen into a routine with short exchanges when Drew picked her up or dropped her off. Despite the schedule she'd made, she'd tried to be flexible when Drew made plans outside the arrangement.

She missed him. She missed their afternoon sexathons, which had been as much about talking and sharing their lives and laughing together as it had been about the hot sex. She missed him hanging around for dinners together or playing video games with Chloe or helping her with her homework. He still did those things . . . but at his place. The emptiness of not having him in her life as much magnified the tough moments of loss she still felt about Sara.

She'd already done her Christmas shopping so there was no reason to go into the gift shop she passed by, but its window dressing pulled her in. She meandered around the store with its eclectic mix of gift items, picking up a cool phone case that Chloe would love for the smartphone Peyton had gotten her for Christmas. Then she wandered into the men's area.

She'd taken Chloe shopping for Drew's gifts. She'd picked out a couple of video games for Drew and a cool set of desk organizers that Chloe thought he needed because he spent so much time in his home office lately, working on his consulting business.

But then she saw a mug and she stopped and smiled. She picked it up and hesitated. Oh, what the hell. Call her crazy, but it was just something small.

She'd thought about taking Chloe to Jamaica or somewhere else hot for a Christmas that was completely different, but she'd been hesitant to do that because she was sure Drew would want to see Chloe over the holiday. She supposed they'd better talk about that, and what the plan was. Because she liked plans.

The hurt from their argument had faded. And she could now admit that Drew's words, painful as they'd been, had been true. And they'd helped her look inside herself and figure out what was really important.

Love.

Love was important. Love and family. Chloe, of course.

But she loved Drew, too. And the empty ache inside her grew stronger every day that passed. Did she have the guts to tell him that?

Drew sat with Jack and Melody in their offices later that week. "This is so great!" Melody said, beaming.

Drew grinned and nodded. "I know. I'm pretty pumped."

He'd gotten a call from Alec Gerdano, a Blackhawks prospect playing with their farm team, who was struggling with his goal scoring. He was anxious to improve his play so he had a better chance of getting called up should the need arise for a winger, and a better chance of staying on the roster if that happened. He'd heard about the work Drew was doing, not through the team but because Cameron, one of the midget players Drew was working with, was his cousin. Cameron's parents had been raving about him, and Alec had called to see if Drew was taking older clients.

He sure as hell was.

He was happy as hell to be working with the Hawks, but aware that his contract only ran until the end of this year. When he was no longer tied to them contractually, he wanted to make sure he had other things in his back pocket, specifically, clients who were willing to pay him to work with them one-on-one.

Look at him with a Plan B.

"This is exactly what I've been working toward," he said to Jack and Melody. "I know I can help him score more goals."

"The confidence looks good on you," Melody said with an approving smile.

"Thanks to both of you." He inflated his lungs and slowly let the air out. "I know it's just one client, but it feels like progress."

And again, his determination to succeed was bolstered. He was going to fucking nail this.

"It's huge," Jack agreed.

Drew's cell phone rang. He pulled it out to glance at the call display, not sure if he'd take it or not. He didn't recognize the number. He was tempted to ignore it, but something made him feel he should answer.

"Excuse me," he said to Jack and Melody. They both nodded and he swiped to answer the call. "Hello."

"Drew." He recognized Chloe's wobbly voice. "I, uh, need you to come get me." He frowned. "Right now? Where are you?"

"I'm at the mall. At Suzy's."

"Who is Suzy?"

"It's a store." For once, her tone held no OMG-you-are-so-clueless attitude. "I need you to come."

"How did you get to the mall?"

"Taylor's mom drove us here."

"Can't she drive you home?"

Silence. He glanced at Jack and Melody and mouthed, "Sorry."

"What's going on, Chloe?"

"She's coming, too, but I need you to come."

"Okay. Be there as quick as I can."

"Th-thank you."

He ended the call and said, "Sorry guys. Chloe needs me."

"Of course. We'll meet again."

His daughter needed him and that was all that mattered.

He drove to the mall and found a parking spot, no clue where this Suzy store was. Of course he entered through a door that was the opposite end of the mall from the store, which he located on a directory.

Suzy's was a very small, very crowded shop full of girly crap—jewelry, scarves, makeup, and all kinds of accessories, lots of Christmassy stuff. He looked around and didn't see Chloe. Christ, talk about a bull in a china shop. He eased his big frame between two big racks of earrings and spoke to the girl at the customer service desk. "Hi. I'm Drew Sellers. My daughter called me and said I had to pick her up here. You don't happen to know . . . "

"She's in the back," the girl said with a haughty look. "Come with me."

She led him through more pink and glitter to a small door, which she opened for him. He stepped into an area full of cardboard boxes holding yet more feminine trappings, and a small office. He spotted Chloe and another young girl sitting on chairs over against a wall. He headed straight there.

"Mr. Sellers?" A woman popped in front of him.

"That's me. What's going on?"

"Chloe Watt is your daughter?"

"Yes."

"I'm Rebecca Schinkel. Your daughter was caught shoplifting."

CHAPTER 31

Drew's head whipped around to stare at Chloe. Then he turned back to Ms. Schinkel. "What? Really?"

"Yes."

He pinned Chloe with a disbelieving stare. "Did you steal something, Chloe?"

"N-no."

Another woman rushed in at that moment. "Taylor! What is going on here?" Taylor's mom was apprised of the situation. "Impossible," she stated. "Taylor would never do that."

"We have video evidence of it, Mrs. Percy," Ms. Schinkel said. "Would you like to see it?"

Drew turned a sharp gaze onto Chloe. Guilt was all over her small features. She pressed her lips together, he guessed to stop them from trembling because she looked like she was about to cry.

"Are you going to have her arrested?" Mrs. Percy demanded.

"She's twelve," Ms. Schinkel said, frowning. "No. We called you so you're aware of this and can deal with your children." She spoke to both Taylor's mom and Drew.

Drew lifted his eyebrows. "I want to see the video."

"I'm not staying for this." Mrs. Percy reached for Taylor's hand and pulled her up. "I have never been so insulted in my life. We're leaving."

She dragged her daughter out the door and into the store. "The video," Drew grated out.

Ms. Schinkel clicked a mouse on the computer on a desk and he watched grainy images of Taylor and Chloe giggling over some cosmetics. They were talking and then Taylor glanced around and slipped something into her backpack. More talk and then Chloe did the same.

"That's enough," Drew said quietly. He looked back at Chloe. "Not only did you steal something, you lied about it."

Her bottom lip quivered.

"Did you give it back? Whatever it was you took?"

Chloe reached for her backpack and pulled out a flat container with small squares of what looked like lip gloss. She handed it to Ms. Schinkel.

He turned to Ms. Schinkel. "Thank you for contacting me about this. We'll definitely be dealing with it." She nodded. "Let's go, Chloe."

He let her lead the way through the store, ignoring the shake of her little shoulders even though it made his heart fucking bleed. But she was in deep, deep shit.

"This way." He stalked through the mall, dodging Christmas shoppers as Chloe nearly ran to keep up with him.

He opened the door for her and relieved her of her backpack, which he tossed into the backseat. Then he started the car. Snowflakes were starting to drift down from the overcast sky.

"I'll take you home," he said through gritted teeth.

"Are you going to tell Peyton?"

His head whipped around to stare at her. "Of course I'm going to tell Peyton." The tension in the car was thick as he drove to the Watt home. Drew unlocked the front door with his key and let them in. The beep of the door alerted Peyton, who appeared from the kitchen holding a dish towel. "Hey, you're . . . home." She caught sight of Drew. He was agitated from what had just happened, but even so he caught the reaction to him on her face that she quickly hid.

She didn't hate him.

"Yes, we are," Drew said grimly. "Chloe has something to tell you."

"You said *you* were going to tell her!" Chloe glared at him, arms stiff at her sides.

"I was wrong. You're going to tell her."

"Tell me what? What is going on?"

Chloe's eyes closed and her lips quivered again. Finally she said, "I got caught shoplifting."

"What!" Peyton's eyes damn near popped out of their sockets. "Shoplifting?" She turned wide eyes on Drew.

He nodded. "It appeared to be some lip gloss."

Peyton's eyebrows drew down. "I don't understand. Why would you do that, Chloe?"

Tears slipped down Chloe's cheeks but she said nothing.

Now Peyton looked like she was going to cry. "That is so not like you, Chloe. What's going on?"

Chloe sniffed.

"*And* she tried to lie about it," Drew added. "I asked her if she did it and she said no."

"Oh, no." Peyton shook her head. "How did you get involved?"

"Chloe called me."

"Why?" She looked at Chloe. "Why did you call Drew?"

"I thought he would stick up for me!" Chloe cried. "I should have known. *Nobody* sticks up for me!" Sobbing, she ran upstairs.

Drew and Peyton faced each other. Sparks made his skin tingle.

"Come in," she said quietly, leading the way to the living room. She sank into a chair, still clutching the dish towel.

Drew dropped his ass onto the couch facing her, elbows on his knees. "What happened?" she asked.

He related what had transpired. Holding her gaze, he added, "Unlike Taylor's mom, who refused to believe her precious girl could do something like that, I looked at the video. Fuck." He dropped his head forward. "I wanted to believe Chloe when she said she didn't do it. I wanted to say this was all bullshit, she'd never do that. But . . . "

"Oh, God. Drew."

"She's pissed at me."

"Yes."

"Fuck. I never wanted to let her down. I fucked up again."

"No." Her certain tone had his head lifting. His gaze met hers. "You did the right thing."

He stared at her, his eyes burning. "She's mad at me. And she's hurting."

"She is," she agreed. "We all are. I overreacted that day when you took her to that movie. She's overreacting now. But you did the right thing. She can't get away with stealing and lying, no matter how much she's hurting."

He stared at her, the pain in his chest spreading down into his gut, but then easing at her words. He nodded slowly. "I have no idea why she did that."

"I guess we'll have to ask her, but I don't know if she'll even understand. Maybe for the attention? The peer pressure? The risk-taking?"

"Christ." Drew closed his eyes. He knew only too well the adrenaline rush of taking risks. "That's my fault, too."

"Don't be ridiculous. It's not your fault at all."

"I'm surprised you're defending me."

Her eyes shadowed. "Why would that surprise you?"

"Because I thought you hate me."

She closed her eyes and shook her head, her face tightened

into lines of what looked like pain. "I don't hate you, Drew," she whispered.

Their eyes met and held. A weird bubble inflated in his chest, a sweetness but also a longing, for something more . . . something he couldn't have.

"I guess one or both of us has to go talk to her," Peyton said. He watched her lips move, and hunger to taste her rose inside him. "Maybe a little while for her to think about things is a good idea, though."

"Do we punish her?"

"Hmm. Good question." Then her eyes narrowed at him. "You don't believe in spanking, do you?"

"Christ, no!" His jaw slackened. "No one ever dares set a hand on that girl!"

She smiled. "Okay, good. I think she's supposed to experience the consequences of her actions." She frowned. "Getting caught is humiliating. Knowing that we're disappointed in her is a consequence."

"I know what to do." He nodded firmly, his jaw set. "I'm going to take her to a police station to talk to a cop."

"What?" She gaped at him.

"Just so they can tell her what would be the consequences of doing that if she was older—getting arrested, put in jail, charged . . . maybe having a criminal record. Maybe she should see what a jail cell looks like."

She blinked. "That's a great idea."

"I have them once in a while."

She smiled slowly. "This isn't exactly what you signed up for, is it?"

"What do you mean?"

"I mean . . . finding out you have a daughter, meeting her, having some kind of relationship with her . . . that's one thing. But the past few months have been hell . . . and now this."

He gazed into her eyes. Yeah, there'd been some tough

moments in the past few months. But there'd been a lot of amazing, joyous, soul-stirring moments, as well. He knew what she was talking about. He'd thought the same thing. Way back before he'd even met Chloe he'd panicked. He didn't have to meet her. He didn't have to do any of this. He could walk away from all these tough moments. Except . . . he couldn't.

"I love her," he said quietly. "There's no going back. And that means taking the bad with all the good. And there's lots of good."

Her eyes went shiny. "Oh."

He didn't just love Chloe. He loved Peyton, too.

They continued to stare at each other, and the tension in the air around them changed, became electric. Hot.

He needed to tell her. His life had been so empty without her. It had been empty before he'd met her, and she'd filled it with light and vitality and purpose. He'd struggled to find meaning, and he'd been terrified of being a failure. But like his mom had pointed out, being afraid of failing meant that you were missing out on all the fun, all the joy of living life fully. All the love.

Having Chloe in his life was amazing, and she, too, gave him a reason for being and gave him a love he'd never expected. His love for his daughter was fierce and powerful. He wanted to hold her when she cried, haul her over the coals when she did wrong, be proud of her successes and show her that he had faith in her when she failed. He wanted to be a man she could learn from and look up to.

But this woman . . . Peyton . . . he loved beyond anything. He wanted to be the kind of man she deserved, and her eyes shining at him with admiration for how he'd handled this, assuring him he'd done the right thing when he'd been worried he'd screwed up . . . made him feel like a king. She had faith in him. He needed her stability, her fearlessness, her willingness to tell him when he'd fucked up but also her faith in him to do good.

But he wanted to be there for her, too . . . she'd been through as much hell as he had, and even though she was the strongest woman he knew, he wanted to lighten her load. He wanted to take care of her, protect her, and share her burdens.

"Peyton."

Their eyes still locked on each other, he shifted forward on the edge of the couch, and at the same moment, they both opened their mouths and said, "I miss you."

He closed his eyes briefly, his lips lifting into a smile, then he opened them to see her smiling, too. "Come here."

"No, you come here."

They both burst out laughing.

"For fuck's sake, it's not a competition," he said. "We're both so goddamn stubborn and that's been our whole problem."

"You're right." With a small smile, she rose from the chair, tossing the towel down. He reached a hand out to her to take hers and draw her down to sit beside him.

"I'm sorry." He stroked her hair back with both hands then cupped her face with utmost gentleness. "I'm sorry I hurt you."

"You were right. I needed to figure out my priorities."

He shook his head. "I always knew Chloe was your priority."

She gazed back at him, her eyes shining. "Yes," she whispered. "But so are you." His chest filled with fizzing bubbles. Did she mean . . . ?

"I love you."

They both said it at the same time again. Drew choked on a laugh and leaned his forehead against hers. "Christ, Peyton. Let me do this."

Her eyelashes fluttered. "I wanted to tell you . . . I'd decided today I had to tell you."

"Yeah?"

She nodded, her beautiful face still framed by his hands.

He brushed his mouth over hers once, twice . . . the third time he lingered there in a tender kiss that made his heart pump faster, made his whole body burn.

"I just decided now," he admitted, and rubbed his nose alongside hers. She smiled. "Even though I was scared as hell, I had to tell you. I had to take the chance. I couldn't risk missing out on what we could have because I was too fucking stubborn to tell you how I feel. Too afraid to find out you don't feel the same."

"I love you so much. I'm so proud of you as a dad. And I'm so proud of you as a man, how you're taking charge of your life and moving forward."

"I wasn't very proud of myself. I'm still working on it."

"Drew." She clasped his wrists and stared deep into his eyes. "You went through hell. You lost everything that was important to you—your career. Your identity. Your wife. Anyone would have a hard time getting through that."

"You called me on my bullshit. What did you say about the corner of Sack Up and Shut Up Streets?"

She choked. "Um, it wasn't sack up, it was the corner of We All Have Problems and Suck It Up Buttercup."

"Yeah, that." He smiled. "Anyway, you made me realize I needed to get my head out of my ass. And then Sara . . . the day she went into hospice care, I remember just being slammed with it . . . that life is short. Way too short to sit around crying about what we've lost. You and Sara . . . and Chloe, too—you all made me ashamed. The way you handled adversity." He touched her cheek. "I'm proud of you, too. Of everything you are. The strongest person I know. The bravest. I'm even proud of your goddamn lists and spreadsheets and schedules."

A tear glistened at the corner of her eye. "Thank you for making me realize that I can't spend every minute of my life trying to get ahead."

He gave a soft snort. "Yeah, and thank you for making me realize that I do need to have some goals and purpose in my life. And my biggest, most important purpose is making the two girls I love happy. Looking after you and supporting you and maybe playing hooky once in a while to have fun."

The tear slipped down her cheek, followed by another one

from the other eye. He brushed them away with his thumbs. "Don't cry. Please don't cry. It guts me." She gave a tiny nod and a shaky smile.

He held her face and met her eyes again. "I would have moved to New York, Peyton. I came over here that day . . . the day you went to New York. I was going to tell you that. I didn't want a big battle. Like my mom told me, even though I like to win...we'd *all* lose."

More tears welled up.

"If that's what it would have taken for us to all be together, I was willing to do it. But fuck, you pissed me off with that move."

"I'm sorry. I was pissed, too. I was . . . hurt. That you would try to take Chloe away from me, when I love her so much. And when . . . " Her voice hiccupped. "When I cared about you so much. It really, really hurt."

"I'm sorry. I was a dick."

She huffed out a laugh. "You kind of were. But I wasn't so nice myself."

"Right after that, I found out that the Blackhawks want me to work with some of their players using my goal-scoring strategy."

Her eyes flew open wide. "No! Really?"

"Really. We've already started. And I have my first paying client outside the team."

She blinked at him then slowly smiled. "That's fantastic, Drew. I'm so proud of you."

"Yeah. Me, too."

"I knew it would happen."

Their gazes held as they shared a warm smile.

"Of course, that was the worst fucking timing," he continued. "I was afraid you'd taken Chloe to New York and I was going to have to follow you both there, just when they'd agreed to give me a shot. I didn't know how the hell I was going to bail on them. Christ." He leaned his forehead against hers. "When Chloe told me you were staying here . . . I wanted to drop to my knees I was so goddamned relieved."

He found her mouth with his and kissed her. Their lips clung and her breathing changed. Her arms slid around his neck and their bodies moved closer, her breasts against his chest, their thighs touching. He slid a hand up into her hair and tilted his head to deepen their kisses.

Finally they both drew back, panting a little. Her cheeks glowed and her long eyelashes fluttered.

"Should we go talk to Chloe?" he asked.

"I'm right here."

They both jerked their heads around to see Chloe standing in the entrance to the living room. She'd obviously been crying, her nose pink and her eyes puffy. But she almost looked like she was . . . smiling, her eyes alight.

Drew slanted Peyton a curious glance and her eyebrows pulled down. Well. Drew faced his daughter. "You saw us kissing?"

"Yes."

He nodded. "Good. Because you're going to see a lot of it."

She rolled her eyes. "Eew."

Peyton sucked her bottom lip in between her teeth as Drew met her dancing eyes. "Okay," Peyton said. "We'll try not to do it too much."

"Did you two make up?" Chloe asked. Drew sighed inwardly.

"You've both been so sad," Chloe said, twisting one ankle around the back of the other as she stood there. "I hated it."

He exchanged a pained glance with Peyton. Shit. "Come here." He held out a hand to Chloe and he and Peyton rearranged themselves beside each other on the couch.

Chloe stepped closer, took his hand and sat next to him.

His two girls, on either side of him. For a moment he couldn't speak, his chest so full of emotion. He swallowed. "Peyton and I made up," he confirmed quietly. "We had an argument a while ago."

"Over me."

His throat constricted. "No," he said firmly. "It wasn't over you. We were both being stubborn and I was being stupid."

"I was being kind of stupid, too," Peyton said, and Chloe's lips twitched.

"We both love you," he continued. "And we both wanted what was best for you. The problem was, we didn't want to admit what was best for *us*. So we're going to be together from now on. Are you okay with that?"

"Yes." The word came out of her in a rush. "Yes. I want you to be together." Her eyes glistened with tears again. "And I want to be with both of you."

"Oh, Chloe." He pulled her in for a hug, feeling Peyton trembling beside him.

"We do love you, Chloe," Peyton said, reaching out to rub Chloe's back. "So much. Forever."

"That's all I wanted," Chloe sobbed against Drew's neck. "I just wanted us to all be together."

"Is that why you stole that lip gloss, Chloe?" Peyton asked softly.

"Y-yes. I'm sorry! I'll never do it again."

"Damn right," Drew muttered, but his heart contracted sharply. He caught Peyton's eye and the expression of dismay on her face.

She touched her fingertips to her lips. "I'm sorry, Chloe. I'm so sorry."

Fuck. Their obstinacy had caused pain for Chloe. That could not happen. He could tell Peyton felt the same.

"I just wanted you to be together," Chloe sobbed again. "I know it was wrong. Then I was afraid I made things worse and you would both h-hate me."

"No," Peyton said quickly. "We could never hate you, Chloe. We don't like what you did and there will be consequences to your actions. But we will always love you."

"It's all okay now," Drew said. "It's all okay."

It wasn't *all* okay. He knew that. Chloe had lost her mother. She'd been through major upheaval in her life. But she had the same strength her mother and her aunt had, and they'd get through this. It would be okay. He'd spend the rest of his life making sure she was okay.

"I don't know if anyone's hungry," Peyton said, her voice a little quivery. "But it's past dinnertime."

Drew considered that. "I'm starving."

Chloe sat up straight and reached for the box of tissues on the table behind the couch. She mopped her tears and runny nose and nodded. "I'm hungry, too."

"I was getting things ready for dinner when you got home." Peyton stood. This all seemed mundane and anticlimactic after what had just occurred, but Drew stood, too, and followed the girls into the kitchen. He ached to hold Peyton, to be close to her; okay, yeah, he wanted to fuck her boneless. And he had so much more he needed to say to her, to make sure she knew how important to him she was.

But hopefully he had the rest of their lives to make sure she knew that.

CHAPTER 32

"Want you naked."

Peyton smiled as she pulled off her clothes in her bedroom.

Chloe was in bed and asleep. They'd warned her that Drew would be sleeping over. She probably didn't really want to know that, but he wanted to be open with her. He and Peyton were done sneaking around and having afternoon quickies. He was going to take his sweet time with her tonight, worshipping her body, showing her how much he loved her.

They moved to the bed, and he pulled back the duvet and laid her down gently, golden hair spread beneath her head, all smooth glowing skin, shiny eyes, and enchanting smile. He undid the buttons of his shirt, pulling it out of his jeans at the same time, eyes wandering over the slender curve of her arms, the shadows between her legs, the way her toes curled into the sheet. And she watched him, too, eyes moving over his shoulders and abs as he shed his shirt, heating as he stepped out of jeans, socks, and underwear. He lay down beside her, hand on her belly, elbow bent, his head propped on his hand. "I love you, Peyton."

Luminous blue eyes turned to him. "I love you, too."

His chest clenched with emotion and he pressed his face

between her breasts, breathed in her scent, then kissed the inside curve of each full breast. When he brushed his lips over her nipple, she drew in a sharp breath.

"Yeah," he whispered. "You like that. I know."

He took a nipple in his mouth and sucked, rubbing his tongue over it. She tasted so sweet and her whimpers told him how much she loved what he did to her. He moved to the other nipple, tasted it, too, played with it with his mouth while his fingers plucked at the other, tested the weight of her breast then squeezed it.

"That feels so good," she moaned, fingers sifting through his hair. Her body twitched and writhed against him. "So good."

He drew back to study her nipples after his attention, now red and stiff. A fist squeezed his throat and his heart banged crazily against his ribs.

He moved over her and she reached for his dick. He throbbed at the touch of her soft hands, soft yet firm, stroking him in long pulls that sent pleasure licking over his skin.

"Inside me," she said. "Please."

"Condom . . . "

"Do we need one?"

He paused and met her eyes. "You're safe with me, Peyton." He already knew she was on the pill from the times he'd used the bathroom and seen them in the vanity drawer.

"And you with me." Trust shone in those blue eyes.

She guided him into her. He felt her slickness, then her heat surrounded the head of his cock. He eased in farther, every muscle in his body taut with the effort not to pound into her as fast and deep as he could. Ownership and reverence and desperate need rushed through him as hot velvet squeezed him, and a low, rough sound tore from his throat. He held his weight on his elbows as she parted her legs wider, and he pushed into her. The air ripped out of his lungs.

"Peyton, oh, God."

"I know." Her hands clutched his ass, pulling him deeper. "Fuck me, Drew."

His groans mingled with her sighs as their bodies came together, perfect, simple, right. He pulsed inside her, going very still, his hands in her silky hair. Nose to nose, their gazes locked on each other in a connection that was so intimate; not just their bodies but their hearts and their souls and their lives. "Love you," he gasped. An overwhelming desire to protect and take care of her, to be with her forever, made his eyes sting.

Love was fucking scary. He'd thought he had it once before and it had been crushed. He'd found it again and almost lost it because of his stupid fears. Loving again was probably the biggest risk he'd ever taken because of the power it gave Peyton to utterly destroy him.

But at that moment he trusted her with that power. He saw the love in her eyes, the shadows of regret for how they'd nearly lost each other, and the absolute trust *she* had in him. And he was going to be worthy of that trust till his last breath.

His hands framed her face, and his gaze held hers. He saw a reflection of his own devotion, his own longing, his own hope, in her eyes, drawing him in. "I love you, Peyton."

Her hands stroked over his back and he felt the tenderness in her touch, heard her pleasure in her muffled whimpers, leaned in and felt her love in the brush of her breath against his mouth. "I love you, too, Drew."

They moved together in a rhythm already familiar, already perfect. Pleasure coiled deep inside him as her rocked into her sweet pussy. Right where he belonged.

Her body tightened beneath him and around him as she climaxed, squeezing him inside and out. She muffled her cry and he watched her face, humbled by her beauty, awed by the ecstasy he saw there because of him, gratified by her love. Pressure tightened the base of his spine, sliding into his balls, building to his own almost unbearable peak of pleasure. Her hands gripped his hips as he drove into her again . . . and again . . . and exploded. Lights flashed as his lids squeezed shut against the intensity of his orgasm, and when he poured himself into her in long, hard almost painful pulses.

Peyton's body still trembled from the shattering orgasm she'd just had, overwhelmed by not only the physical pleasure but also the deep bond she felt with Drew. It was almost too much, too intense, too good. It scared her a little and yet she wanted this more than anything else.

She kissed his shoulder, his face buried in the side of her neck, his breath warm on her skin.

"The good thing about those afternoon quickies was that we could be as noisy as we want," he mumbled.

Laughter bubbled up inside her. "It *was* kind of hard to be quiet," she agreed.

He shifted off her and they settled beneath the warmth of the duvet, curling into each other. He pressed his cheek against the top of her head and she felt his smile. "What do you want for Christmas?" he asked her long moments later.

She huffed. "I don't know. Okay, I do know. I just want us all together."

"I think I can arrange that."

"You were so thoughtful of us at Thanksgiving," she murmured, stroking his firm biceps. "That meant a lot to me. Christmas could be a little hard this year."

"I know."

"I thought of taking Chloe to Jamaica."

"We could totally do that."

"Really? Or would it be weird?"

"Why not be weird?"

"I don't know. Christmas is supposed to be snow and hot chocolate, a fire in the fireplace and Santa coming down the chimney."

"Hopefully not while the fire's burning." She swatted his shoulder.

"Chloe doesn't still believe in Santa, does she?" He lifted his head to peer at her. "I hope I didn't say something wrong."

"No, she doesn't believe in Santa." She smiled at his distress.

"Okay. Because I was gonna say, pretty sure Santa could find us on the beach in Jamaica."

She laughed. "I bet he could."

"We could go to Thunder Bay. But trust me, it's not nearly as exciting as Jamaica."

"Will any of your siblings be there?"

"In Jamaica?"

"No!"

He chuckled. "No siblings are going home for Christmas this year." Her forehead tightened.

"Does that mean your parents will be alone?"

"Yeah. But it happens."

"I don't like that." She pouted her bottom lip out. "Do you *want* to go to Thunder Bay?"

"Eh. It's a long trip. You can't fly direct from here. But I guess we could do it."

"Would your parents like to go to Jamaica?"

He paused. "I like how you think, sexy girl."

She grinned. "Maybe we should see what Chloe wants to do."

"Hell, no. Come on! We're the adults. We get to make the decisions. What's gotten into you, boss lady?"

His teasing lightened her heart after all the sorrow and hurt she'd felt lately. "Your point has merit."

"Right? I'm finally a grown-up. A dad. I get to decide these things." She lifted her eyebrows at him.

He smiled slowly. "Okay, *we* get to decide these things."

She smiled, too, getting that he was pushing her buttons. "We need to seriously talk about this. What's happening here. What this is going to be like."

"Yeah. We do." He kissed her cheek. "We will."

"Christmas is next week. It would cost a fortune to go away."

"Eh. Whatever."

"Do I have to remind you that we're both unemployed?"

"I guess money's another thing we need to discuss."

She gave him a crooked smile. "Yeah. I guess so."

"Among other things. So we both don't believe in spanking."

Her smile widened. "Are you talking about Chloe or me?"

"Oh, ho. I *really* like how you think, naughty girl."

She fluttered her eyelashes at him. "Seriously. Let's stay here for Christmas. But maybe we could do it at your place again?"

"You got it."

"You could invite your parents again, if they don't mind coming all that way."

"I think they'd love it. And my mom will be so proud of her baby boy."

"What?" She turned amused eyes on him.

"She knew there was something happening between us, and I'm pretty sure she was pissed as hell at me for messing things up."

"Really?"

"Yeah. She has this weird women's intuition or something. She senses things." He rolled his eyes and Peyton grinned. "I told her I'd talked to a lawyer about getting custody of Chloe and she . . . well, she didn't ream my ass out, but she basically told me if I fought that battle, we'd all lose. And she was right."

"I like your mom."

"She likes you." He brushed his lips over her hair. "So, yeah. We'll have Christmas at my place. You two can stay overnight and we'll open presents in the morning and make our own traditions."

Her heart squeezed so hard she couldn't breathe. "I like that."

CHAPTER 33

Chloe's scream made them all wince. "A phone! My own phone!"
She clasped it to her chest. "Seriously?"

Peyton nodded, smiling. "Yes."

They were gathered in Drew's living room Christmas morning
in front of the quickly purchased and decorated tree. The selec-
tion at the place he'd picked it up hadn't been great, so it wasn't
the prettiest tree . . . a little lopsided, with a couple of bare
branches. No matter.

Chloe and Peyton had gone through Christmas ornaments at
their place and brought over some of their favorites, some that
had been Peyton and Sara's parents'. One ornament was a red ball
with a picture of the scales of justice, and "lawyers never lose their
appeal."

"I gave that to Sara the Christmas after she passed the bar,"
Peyton had said with a sad smile as she hung it on the tree.

He'd make sure they hung it every year and remembered Sara.

Another one was a ballet dancer that had been given to Chloe
one year, which they also hung with care. And he'd gone out and
bought a few new ones, some of which they hadn't seen.

Peyton opened the small box and pulled out her ornament. "A

bottle of wine," she said approvingly, lifting the delicate glass by its ribbon. She smiled at Drew. "Thank you."

Chloe giggled when she pulled out a shark hanging from a red ribbon. "I love it."

"I didn't get you an ornament," Peyton said, handing Drew a small wrapped box. "And I feel like this is way too small of a gift. I actually bought it last week . . . before . . ."

"I have exactly what I want." He took the box and met her eyes in shared agreement. He bent his head and opened it to pull out a coffee mug, painted with the words "Best. Dad. Ever."

He stared at the mug, head down, throat thick. Then he sucked in air and looked up at her. "Best. Gift. Ever."

The warmth in her smile made his chest hurt.

They finished with the gifts. His parents spoiled Chloe with books and a Bluetooth speaker for her room and a couple of video games.

Instead of another turkey, they were cooking a prime rib roast for Christmas dinner. He approved of this as a new tradition.

The day passed with an afternoon walk in the snow, video games, and lots of laughter. When Mom said grace before dinner, they bowed their heads.

"For good food and those who prepare it, for good friends with whom to share it, we thank you, Lord. And let us remember those who are not here and thank you for the time we had with them. Amen."

Drew watched Peyton's lower lip tremble and Chloe's rapid blinking as they, too, said, "Amen."

He met his mom's eyes.

"And I don't mean Christy," Mom said.

Drew's eyes popped open wide, then he slid a glance sideways to Peyton. She bit her lip, now looking like she wanted to laugh.

"Jesus, Mom."

Unrepentant, she picked up a big bowl of salad. "It's true."

"They had no passion," Chloe said. "That was their problem."

Drew bugged his eyes out at his daughter then shook his head. "Okay, it's true." Not a problem he and Peyton had. He caught her knowing smirk as he handed her the platter of beef.

"Peyton, tell us more about this business you're starting," Dad invited her. She'd filled him in on the plans she and her friends were making. It sounded fantastic. He had total faith in her that she would succeed at this. The fact that they were both going through a similar process of trying to build a business connected them and they'd talked for hours, bouncing ideas off each other and problem-solving. Until her smart brain made him hot for her sexy body and he carried her up to bed.

Now Mom and Dad seemed equally impressed. Goddamn, he liked it that they liked her. Mom had been pretty irate when Christy had cheated on him with one of his teammates, but he knew the two of them had never exactly been friends, so her distress at his marriage ending was because he'd been hurt, not because she'd miss Christy. Funnily, it had never really bothered him that his mom didn't love his wife.

But he wanted her to love Peyton.

And why wouldn't she? Peyton was awesome. Okay, a little stubborn and rigid sometimes. They'd work on that. And he'd work on being a responsible parent. They'd work on bringing out the best in each other. They'd been through some tough times and he wasn't stupid enough to think that life was going to be all rainbows and flowers and glittering fucking unicorns from here on in, but that was okay because they'd be together.

EPILOGUE

April

"April showers bring May flowers."

Drew shook his head in disgust at the rain pouring down on them as they drove to Lincoln Park in the dusk. *Fuck!*

Luckily he had a big golf umbrella that would cover them but still, this definitely put a damper on his plans. Hah. Damp.

"There are already flowers, though," Peyton noted, gazing around with a smile. "Spring is so lovely."

The last four months had been a dizzying blur of ups and downs. There'd been moments of bliss and sadness—Chloe's outbursts of anger at the world as she continued to deal with the loss of her mother, as well as her successes. They'd argued over parenting decisions all while knowing they trusted each other completely to have Chloe's best interests at heart. They'd coasted into a routine where they spent more and more time together, and dividing up "parental responsibilities" wasn't an issue. They'd both worked their asses off to establish their new businesses, sharing successes and setbacks, celebrating and commiserating. Drew had finished the season with some real successes—NHL players whom he'd helped increase their scoring output, a half a dozen AHL clients, and more NHL, AHL, and college players he would be working with over the summer. He'd been so busy he could hardly keep up. Peyton and her partners had opened their doors and also had a growing client list that kept them busy.

He parked at the zoo parking lot and unfurled the umbrella to hold it over Peyton's head as she alighted from the car. "Are we going to the zoo?" she asked, peering around.

"No, just for a walk." He sighed. "Sorry about the weather."

"We can do it another time."

No, they couldn't. "Well, let's just make the best of this."

"Sure." She tucked her arm into his. "Oh, my God, it smells so good."

The air carried a rich, fresh scent of wet earth, greenery and spring flowers as they strolled along the paths toward the pond. Drew tried not to keep from running, anxiety and adrenaline and the goddamn rain making him want to sprint.

There were no other people around, since everyone else in Chicago was smarter than him and knew to go in out of the rain.

As they approached the bridge over the pond, Peyton said, "Do I hear music?"

"Hmm." He pretended to listen. "I don't hear anything."

They turned a corner, and then the music was audible, soft strains drifting among the raindrops.

Peyton slanted him a curious frown. They walked farther and Peyton's steps slowed as they neared the bridge and she saw the glow arising from the dozens of candles there. She stopped and turned her face to Drew. "What's going on?"

He smiled. "Come on. Let's go see."

He tugged her along onto the bridge. The lights of the downtown skyscrapers glimmered through the drizzle, the skies darker than usual because of the low clouds, the trees in the park mounds of shadow.

Candles glowed all around them as they walked onto the

bridge, arranged on the ground and on the big stone slabs at various levels. They were completely alone.

"How on earth are those candles burning?" Peyton peered down at them. "Oh, they're not real. But they're still beautiful."

Good thing they weren't real or this whole thing would be a washout. Again, ha. "Here." Drew paused in the middle of the bridge, the two of them surrounded by golden candlelight and the glittering skyline. "Hold the umbrella." He curled her fingers around the handle then released it to her. He reached for the flowers sitting on one of the flat rocks and handed them to her.

She blinked at them. "They're gorgeous." Blush-colored roses glowed in the deepening dusk, drops of water glinting on them like diamonds.

Dragging air into his lungs, he pulled the ring out of his pocket and went down on one knee.

Peyton's mouth dropped open as she clutched the umbrella in one hand, the flowers resting in her other arm. The knee of Drew's pants was immediately soaked, but what the hell.

"I love you, Peyton." He met her eyes. Rain dampened his hair and his face. "My life was empty. I was struggling to find a . purpose. Terrified of failing, but not realizing that the real failure is not even trying to get back up when you're down. You brought so much into my life, Peyton—courage, strength, light and love." He paused. "You are my purpose."

She smiled, her bottom lip quivering.

"I love you so much. I want to be the man you deserve and I'm working hard at it every day. I need you so much, but I want to be there for you too, in all ways— protecting you, sharing your burdens and sharing your triumphs. Peyton . . . will you marry me?"

"You're getting all wet." She drew in a shaky breath.

"I don't care." His hair was hanging in his eyes now, water dripping off it. He swiped it aside, his heart slamming against his ribs as he awaited her answer.

"Yes." She blinked rapidly, eyes glowing. Her smile was luminous. "Yes, I'll marry you. Get up here under this umbrella."

He reached for her left hand and slid the ring onto it. "There." Satisfaction deepened his voice at seeing his ring on her. Claiming her. "You're mine."

He rose to his feet and closed in against her, hands on her waist. The umbrella shook above them in her trembling hand as she lifted her left arm to stare at the ring. He took the flowers and set them aside.

"Oh." She blinked even more at the big solitaire sparkling on her finger. "It's so beautiful, Drew."

She tossed the umbrella aside with a low laugh and flung her arms around her neck. The rain beaded on her black coat and glistened on her golden hair. She turned her face up to him, so beautiful. "You're crazy."

"Crazy about you. Dance with me."

She set her hands on his shoulders, her eyes flickering between his face and the diamond on her finger.

"You're so beautiful, Peyton. You make me better. I love you."

"I love you, too. And you make me better, too, Drew."

"It wasn't supposed to rain. But sometimes life isn't about waiting for the storm to pass. You just need to dance in the rain. I learned that from Chloe." He lowered his head and kissed her, slow, tender, full of his love for her. "I'm not much good at romantic shit or poems. But . . . " He paused, waiting for the music to change. Perfect. "Listen to this song . . . it says what I feel."

She cocked her head and listened to Chicago's "You're the Inspiration."

They moved to the music as a silvery mist fell around them. He watched her face as she absorbed the lyrics . . . everything he felt for her. The meaning she brought to his life. Her eyes went wide and soft, and her lips parted as their gazes stayed locked on each other, nose to nose, bodies pressed damply together, dancing in the rain.

He found her mouth with his again. Kissed her. Again and again. Her hands slid into his damp hair and then he wrapped his arms around her and crushed her to him, overwhelmed by the emotions swelling inside him.

"I feel the same," she murmured when the song finished. "I love you." His chest swelled and heated, his heart pounding.

"How did you do this?" She waved a hand.

"I had a little help." He looked over her shoulder. Footsteps crunched on the path and Chloe and Nik appeared, each holding umbrellas. "Look who's here."

She turned in his arms and smiled. "Oh, my God." Chloe ran at them. "Did she say yes?"

Drew's eyes stung. "She did."

"Did you know about this?" Peyton demanded of her niece as they parted to both hug Chloe.

Chloe beamed. "I did. And Nik."

"So you're not really over at Ashley's."

"Nope. Er . . . I'm not in trouble for lying, am I?"

Peyton's throaty laugh grabbed his heart and squeezed. "Not this time." She looked at Nik. "You were in on this?"

"Yeah." Nik grinned. "Congratulations."

Peyton shook her head. "Thank you." She pulled in a breath. "Okay, you guys, we really need to get out of the rain."

"It's stopping," Chloe said, holding out a hand. And it was.

"How did you do this?" Peyton asked again.

Drew grinned. "I'd like to say I did it all myself, but like I said . . . I kinda suck at the romance stuff. I went to this company that arranges romantic proposals. But I picked the place and the music myself," he assured her. "And the flowers. And definitely the ring. They set this up a few minutes before we got here. They'll come and take it down."

"I'm gonna head out," Nik said. "You all enjoy your moment."

"Thank you, Nik," Drew said.

She winked at him. "Happy to help."

Peyton's chin dimpled and she moved in for a hug. "Love you, Nik."

"Love you, too. We'll talk tomorrow, okay?"

Peyton nodded, and Nik headed back off the bridge, leaving the three of them. Chloe bounded over to the railing to look at the skyline.

"I wanted romance," Drew murmured to Peyton, pulling her close. "But I wanted Chloe involved, too. I asked her permission first."

She smiled. "What would you have done if she said no?"

"I don't know," he admitted. "I guess I would have listened to her. I wouldn't want her to be unhappy, but . . . I wasn't going to change my mind about this."

Her face softened, but she bit her lip. "We're going to be kind of a weird family."

Chloe overheard that. "What's weird about it?" she asked with a frown.

"Well . . . I'm your aunt. But I'll also be your stepmother. And Drew's your dad, but he'll also be your uncle."

"Whoa. That is weird." Chloe tipped her head to one side. "But kind of cool, too. And whatever. Lots of people have weird families. Tyler's parents are divorced. Brittany has a stepfather and a stepmother, and they all get together all the time, for school things and holidays. Kaley has two dads. They're gay," she added in matter-of-fact explanation.

Peyton raised her eyebrows and met Drew's eyes. "Well. I guess that's true. There *are* many different kinds of family units these days."

"A family is the people you love," Drew said. "The people who are there for you when things are shitty. Er. Tough."

Chloe rolled her eyes.

"*And* when things are good. I want to be there for both of you. Always."

Life wasn't always easy. It took courage to make the best of what life handed you, to live a life that had meaning and purpose . . . and love. It took courage to put yourself out there and risk your heart. He'd found that courage with them—but then, it was easy when someone became more important to you than your own fears and self- doubts. More important than anything else in the world. Love was the biggest risk of all . . . but it was all that mattered.

§.

Thank you so much for reading Big Witch Energy! If you like standalone romances with heat, heart, and humor, check out Firecracker!

Arden Lennox's charmed life may be in pieces, but she'd sooner get her hoohaw bleached than move back in with her parents. She's no longer the prom-queen princess married to the football star. She's a broke, penniless widow, and it's time she stood on her own two feet.

An under-construction unit in a quaint Chicago brownstone is cheap (free), but it comes with an unexpected surprise. Tyler Ramirez, her brother's gawky high school best friend, is now a smoking hot firefighter who spends most of his spare time in her unit hammering, drilling, and screwing. Usually with his shirt off —a temptation she has no intention of indulging.

One-click FIRECRACKER now!

Read on for an excerpt!

EXCERPT FROM FIRECRACKER BY KELLY JAMIESON

Tyler rolled out of bed at the crack of noon on Sunday.

Hey, he'd just come off a twenty-four-hour shift. He'd only had a few hours' sleep due to not one but *three* drug overdoses they'd had to respond to…typical Saturday night. He'd crawled into bed when he got home at eight thirty to grab a few more z's.

He yawned and stretched as he walked naked to the bathroom to crank on the shower. After that and a pot of coffee, he'd be good to go.

Two full days off stretched ahead of him. A gorgeous summer Sunday, judging from the bright sunlight streaming in the bathroom window. He'd see what Jamie and Mila were up to; maybe they'd hit the beach or something.

After a shower and a rub of a towel to his hair, he started coffee then returned to the bedroom to pull on a pair of loose athletic shorts and a faded navy CHICAGO FIRE DEPARTMENT T-shirt. He looked at the mail that had arrived yesterday while he'd been at work. Nothing interesting.

He poured coffee into a travel mug and headed downstairs to find Jamie, but paused outside his apartment door. He needed to get bathroom measurements from Apartment Four so he could go to Home Depot and pick up some stuff. Maybe he should do that now.

He ducked back inside his apartment to grab a tape measure and a notepad. He shoved a pencil behind his ear. Juggling his coffee and the other things, he crossed the hall. But when he tried the knob, it was locked. Huh.

They hardly ever locked their doors in the building, since it was just the three friends, and the exterior doors were always locked. But he had a key, so he retrieved it then let himself into the apartment.

He'd helped Mila and Jamie unpack Arden's things a couple of days ago. They hadn't touched the really personal stuff, but unpacking her sheets and pillows had felt weird. Even weirder because it was *Arden's* sheets and pillows. The girl who'd starred in every single one of his teenage fantasies.

The apartment even smelled different now…must be because of her things being there…an exotic fruity floral scent. He strode purposefully to the bathroom and yanked open the door.

The female scream that split the silence nearly ripped his eardrums open.

"Jesus Christ!" The items he was carrying flew out of his startled hands, the tape measure and the mug clattering to the floor, the note pad skidding down the hall. As he staggered back, he caught a glimpse of naked woman.

Smooth, tanned skin. Long dark hair. The sweep of a hip and —sweet mother of God— the curve of a breast tipped with a dark nipple. And wide, horrified eyes as she grabbed a towel and held it in front of herself.

"Get out!" she shrieked then let out another piercing scream. "Aaaaah! Help! Jamie! Help!"

Jesus, fuck, it was Arden. Tyler held up his hands. "Hey! Hey! Calm down."

She made some frightened noises.

"It's me, Tyler! Remember...Tyler Ramirez? Jamie's friend?"

She gaped at him, the little blue towel she clutched not covering much. Now *he* wanted to whimper. She was fucking gorgeous.

Still.

"I am so sorry." He kept his eyes firmly on her face, smiling tentatively. "When did you get here?"

"Um." She looked like she was having a heart attack. Good thing he was a trained EMT. "Yesterday."

"Shit." He grimaced. "I could've sworn Jamie said you were arriving Monday."

"No." She swallowed. "Are you really Tyler?"

He frowned. She didn't even recognize him? "Yeah."

"Oh. Okay. Um...could we continue this conversation when I'm dressed?"

He smacked his forehead and turned around. "Yeah. Of course. Dumbass," he muttered under his breath. "I'll, uh, wait in the living room."

He picked up his things, rubbing at the hardwood floor he'd just refinished weeks ago, hoping like hell the travel mug hadn't scratched the new finish. Looked okay. Then he strode back to the living room where they'd arranged her furniture. He was going to fucking kill Jamie.

He set his things down on the granite counter and pressed the heels of his palms to his eyes. Christ, that vision was seared into his retinas for the rest of eternity. Naked Arden Lennox. Holy shit.

Okay, okay, calm down, dude.

He was over that high school crush. Way the fuck over it.

She was here and he was an idiot.

He'd been trying to imagine what it would be like to see Arden again. It had been, what—eleven years since he'd seen her? Nah, he'd seen her one year at Christmas when she'd been home…so maybe nine years ago? Whatever. So he'd had a crush on her. That was a long time ago. He'd been a kid then, and she'd married someone else. She was a widow now, mind you, but still. They were different people.

And he'd just embarrassed them both.

A few minutes later, Arden appeared, now dressed in a pair of cropped black leggings and a loose tank top. And yeah, she was still just as beautiful with those big brown eyes, creamy smooth skin, and sweetly curved lips.

"Well, that was a great reintroduction, wasn't it?" Tyler said with a grin. "I really am sorry. I had no idea you were already here. I came to get some measurements so I can get started on your bathroom next week."

She still seemed shaken and annoyed. "I guess there was a miscommunication about when I was arriving."

"Yeah. I'm going to murder your brother." He frowned. "I'm surprised he didn't come running to your rescue. That scream was loud enough that everyone in Lincoln Park probably heard it."

"He's not home," she admitted. "He and Mila went out to get breakfast a little while ago. They're going to bring back something for me, so I jumped in the shower."

"What? They're not bringing *me* anything?"

"Actually, I think they are, but they didn't want to wake you up."

"Oh. Okay." He paused. "So you screamed for him even though you knew he wasn't here."

She made a face and her lips twitched. "I figured a burglar wouldn't know that."

"Quick thinking. Luckily I'm not a burglar."

"How did you get in?"

"Through the door."

Her eyebrows rose. "You have a key?"

"Yeah. Uh…is that a problem?"

"I'd kind of like to know when someone's coming into my apartment."

"Interesting concept."

She frowned, and he couldn't stop his grin. Jamie and Mila wandered at will in and out of every other apartment, and he'd learned to lock the door if he really needed privacy.

"We hardly ever lock our doors inside, since the outside doors are always locked. But we all have keys to one another's apartments just in case. I'm in this unit all the time working on it. But I'll try not to get in your way."

She nibbled her bottom lip. "Jamie told me you're still working on this place. I knew that was part of the deal."

Right, right. Apparently she'd had to sell her house. Jamie'd told him that she'd discovered after her husband had died that he hadn't exactly been in good financial shape.

She moved past him to the kitchen and reached into a cupboard for a bright yellow mug. "Would you like some coffee?"

"Got some, thanks." He picked up the travel mug that had bounced off the floor minutes ago. Luckily the lid had stayed tight.

He watched her pour coffee into the mug. "You haven't changed at all," he blurted. Maybe she had a bit—that smile she'd beamed around seemed to have dimmed a little.

Her lips curved up reluctantly and she curled her hands around the mug. "Thank you. You sure have."

He rubbed his face. "You really didn't recognize me?"

"I think you were sixteen the last time I saw you. You weren't even shaving, probably, and you had braces." Her gaze swept over him, lingering on his chest and shoulders. "And you've…filled out."

The air in the apartment thickened, and Tyler's blood heated at her perusal of his anatomy.

Then she blinked and added, "You were a pretty scrawny kid."

Okay, maybe that *hadn't* been sexual interest and a flirtatious comment. And her reminder that she'd viewed him as a kid was even more deflating. "Huh. Yeah, I guess I was. I work out a lot now; we kind of have to stay in shape to do our job." He scratched the side of his neck.

"You're a firefighter, Jamie says."

"That's right."

"That's a hard job."

"Sometimes. Sometimes it's also boring as hell." One corner of his mouth cranked up. "But I work with a great group."

"I understand I have you to thank for getting my stuff unpacked." She waved a hand.

"Partially." He grimaced. "I helped. Mila's the one you should thank. She was all concerned about you feeling comfortable when you get here. I'm afraid Jamie and I were kind of clueless males."

"Well, it did help, so thank you." She sipped her coffee.

He wanted to say something about her husband, but fuck, this was awkward. He swallowed. "I'm sorry for your loss...of your husband. Jamie told me about it." He cleared his throat. "Of course."

Yeah, he was smooth. As smooth as Lake Michigan in a winter windstorm.

"Thank you. It's been a tough year." Her mouth tightened and her eyes flickered, but she kept her head high.

"I'm sure. But you made the right decision to come home. Family's important."

She blinked at him and nodded. "That's true."

"Jamie's been worried about you."

"Aw." She rolled her eyes and lifted her mug to her lips again. "Yeah, I know. Truthfully, *I've* been worried about myself." The corners of her mouth quirked up.

Her humor in the face of adversity made his chest warm.

"But I'm fine," she added. "So...you said you needed some measurements...?"

"Right." Christ. He was distracted watching her, kind of blown away by the fact that he was standing there with Arden Lennox. Er, Arden Hughes, now. "Yeah, I can do that." He set his cup down and grabbed his other things, then booked it into the bathroom.

Here that scent was even more evident...warm and feminine and sexy, the air still slightly steamy from her shower. He paused a moment to breathe it in. Damn. Letting out a long, slow breath, he checked out the room. Yeah, it would be good to get this done. He started measuring and jotting notes, ignoring the dripping pink puffy sponge, the bottles of shampoo...his gaze fell on the body wash. Bombshell. That was the scent. Jesus Christ.

He scrubbed a hand over his face and refocused on work.

The sound of thudding feet up the stairs reached his ears, then voices in Arden's apartment as Jamie and Mila returned. He heard Jamie shout, "Hey, Ty! You up?"

"He's here," Arden told her brother. "In the bathroom. Measuring something."

Seconds later, Jamie appeared in the bathroom door. "Dude. You want waffles?"

"Hell yeah." Tyler slid the pencil back behind his ear. "I was afraid you forgot about me."

Jamie grinned. "Nah."

Tyler followed the scent of bacon back to Arden's kitchen, where Mila was making herself at home per usual, pulling out plates while Arden opened the bags of food.

"From the Waffle Shack," Mila announced. "Best waffles in town. And bacon. We don't go there *every* Sunday, but..."

"We go there a lot," Tyler said.

Arden smiled, but seemed a little bemused by the people who'd invaded her kitchen as they all filled plates with food and moved to her small dining table.

"I don't have any napkins," Arden said apologetically.

"No worries! We got some." Mila pulled paper napkins out of a bag and handed them around.

"You don't want that butter, do you?" Mila asked Jamie, reaching for his plate.

Jamie pretended to stab her hand with his fork. "Yes, I do."

Tyler handed over a small container of whipped butter. "Here you go, butterball."

"I love butter," Mila confessed to Arden. "I probably shouldn't have it, but thank you, Tyler."

"You don't *look* like someone who likes butter," Arden said.

"She eats like a goddamn elephant," Jamie said. "And yet still looks like a stickman."

"Stickman! Seriously?" Mila scowled at Jamie.

Tyler ignored their insults. "Who wants to go to the beach today? I feel like some beach volleyball."

"Sure," Mila said. "It's a nice day. I'll need to shave my legs."

"Thanks for sharing that." Jamie shook his head and forked up more waffle. "Yeah, the beach sounds great."

"Arden?" Tyler looked at her, trying to make his expression friendly and casual. "You want to come?"

She stared back at him for a moment, and he wondered what was wrong. Did he have bacon in his teeth? She nodded slowly. "Okay." Then she gave her head a shake and looked down at her plate.

"Hey, let me text Olivia and book a cabana at the Beach Ball Café." Jamie pulled out his phone.

"You'll never get a cabana at this short notice," Mila said.

"Pfft." Jamie bent his head as he texted.

Tyler's own phone buzzed in his pocket, and he pulled it out. "Norton." He made a face. "Should I invite him?"

His cousin Norton was close to their age, a couple of years younger, and hung out with them sometimes. He was a good guy, but easiest to handle in small doses.

"Sure, invite him," Mila said easily. "Arden's going to have to meet him some time."

"I apologize in advance, Arden," he said as he tapped in a text message. "He has a good heart."

Arden laughed. "Ooookay."

"And I'll see what Garth is doing." Mila turned to Arden. "Garth's my boyfriend."

"Got a cabana," Jamie announced triumphantly a moment later.

"That's so cool!" Arden looked more animated than she had all morning.

"Norton will meet us there," Tyler added.

"Perfect. Let's clean up this mess and get going."

"It's okay—" Arden started.

"Hell no, we invaded your apartment and made the mess, so we'll help clean it up." Jamie began picking up dishes.

"Maybe next weekend I can make you all waffles," Arden said. "I make pretty good waffles, if I do say so myself."

"You can cook?" Mila and Jamie both said at the same time, staring at her as if she'd just announced she'd cured cancer.

"Yeah. I like cooking."

"Me too," Tyler said. "I cook for the guys at the station all the time."

"You don't cook for *us*," Jamie complained.

"You can *definitely* make us waffles next Sunday," Mila said to Arden.

"I'll drive to the beach," Jamie offered. "There's room for all of us in my Jeep, and since you have tomorrow off, Ty, that means you can drink."

"Hey, how was your date Friday night?" Tyler asked Jamie as he too carried dishes into the kitchen.

Jamie's lips thinned and his gaze slid away. "Uh. I had fun."

Mila started choking and leaned against the counter. Was she laughing?

341

"Do I need to Heimlich you?" Tyler asked her.

She waved her hands and shook her head. "I'm okay," she wheezed.

"What's so funny? And why are you looking so weird?" he said to Jamie.

"The date didn't turn out like he expected," Mila said.

"You met this chick on Spark, right?" Tyler said, naming a popular dating app. "You thought she was amazing."

Mila collapsed onto the counter in a fit of giggles.

"What?" Tyler demanded, grinning too.

Arden looked back and forth among the three of them, wide-eyed. "Oh we *have* to hear this. Come on, Jamie."

"Tell them, Jamie," Mila choked out.

"Okay, okay. This chick seemed really perfect on Spark—hot, fun, a little geeky. Sounded perfect. So we met for a drink on Friday…turns out she's a drag queen."

"You mean he," Mila corrected.

"Well, he's Honey Deville onstage, but he introduced himself as Danny when I met him."

Tyler and Arden burst out laughing at the same time.

"How did that even happen?" Tyler asked.

"It was totally my bad." Jamie waved a hand. "That's the embarrassing part. I've never used Spark before, and I didn't read the whole bio or swipe through all his pictures, so I just saw the Honey picture."

"But here's the best part." Mila waved a hand at Jamie to go on.

"He was a really nice guy," Jamie said. "So I stayed, and we had a few beers. It was a fun evening." He hitched one shoulder and shut the door of the dishwasher, looking around at them all earnestly.

Tyler laughed. "Are you seeing him again?"

"Not on a date. But we might hang out and play Call of Duty sometime."

"Oh, Jamie." Arden shook her head, an affectionate smile brightening her face.

Tyler looked at her across the small room. There it was—the smile. The one that had made his knees weak and his heart stutter. It lit up her eyes and transformed her face from girl next door to glamour queen.

And goddammit…it still made his heart stutter.

§

Firecracker is available at all major retailers!

To my sister, who is kicking cancer's butt. As Peyton did from Sara, I've learned the meaning of strength, courage, and grace from you. I love you.

ACKNOWLEDGMENTS

When my agent Emily Sylvan Kim and editor Sue Grimshaw told me they wanted me to write a "bigger book," a stand-alone romance, maybe about a retired hockey player . . . maybe an injured hockey player . . . who maybe has a child he didn't know about . . . I was all, I don't know . . . babies aren't very sexy and an injured hockey player is depressing and I'm not sure I want to write a secret baby story. And then I started thinking about Drew . . . and Drew was pretty damn interesting and charming. Okay, Drew was irresistible. So I had to write his story! And I started thinking about Chloe . . . only she wasn't a baby, she was older and there was a good reason she was a "secret" and she was pretty irresistible, too! And I started thinking about Chloe's mom and I realized that she wasn't the woman for Drew. It was her sister Peyton who was perfect for Drew, even though there was much to keep them apart. I wasn't sure if I could write the story I had in my head, because I knew it was going to make me cry . . . and it sure did. More than once. These characters grabbed my heart and tore it apart! Peyton and her sister were so brave, going through their crisis, and so was Chloe, and I love that Drew discovered his own strength through these three strong women who appeared in his life.

So thank you to Emily and Sue for putting this idea into my head and letting me run with it.

Thank you also to my Sweet Heat Reader Group—as I wrote this book, I was going through a difficult time personally, and you were there every day supporting me and making me laugh.

Thank you to the amazing, efficient Stacey Price, who takes a load off my shoulders and helps me keep going.

Thank you to my friend and fellow author PG Forte for shark finning! You never know when the most casual comment inspires something!

Thank you to friends and fellow authors Kinsey Holley and Jennifer Bernard for the advice about twelve-year-old girls—it's been a while for me!

As always to the amazing team at Loveswept, who put the beautiful cover on this book, polished the book up all shiny and put it out there in the world—thank you for all your support!

And most of all, thank you to my readers! I'm so happy to share my stories with you and I continue to be honored that you buy and read my books.

OTHER BOOKS BY KELLY JAMIESON

HELLER BROTHERS HOCKEY

BREAKAWAY

FACEOFF

ONE MAN ADVANTAGE

HAT TRICK

OFFSIDE

POWER SERIES

POWER STRUGGLE

TAMING TARA

POWER SHIFT

RULE OF THREE SERIES

RULE OF THREE

RHYTHM OF THREE

REWARD OF THREE

SAN AMARO SINGLES

WITH STRINGS ATTACHED

HOW TO LOVE

SLAMMED

WINDY CITY KINK

SWEET OBSESSION

ALL MESSED UP

PLAYING DIRTY

BREW CREW

LIMITED TIME OFFER

NO OBLIGATION REQUIRED

ACES HOCKEY

MAJOR MISCONDUCT

OFF LIMITS

ICING

TOP SHELF

BACK CHECK

SLAP SHOT

PLAYING HURT

BIG STICK

GAME ON

LAST SHOT

BODY SHOT

HOT SHOT

LONG SHOT

BAYARD HOCKEY

SHUT OUT

CROSS CHECK

WYNN HOCKEY

PLAY TO WIN

IN IT TO WIN IT

WIN BIG

FOR THE WIN

GAME CHANGER

ABOUT THE AUTHOR

Kelly Jamieson is a best-selling author of over fifty romance novels and novellas. Her writing has been described as "emotionally complex", "sweet and satisfying" and "blisteringly sexy." She likes coffee (black), wine (mostly white), shoes (high heels) and hockey!

Subscribe to her newsletter for updates about her new books and what's coming up, follow her on Twitter @KellyJamieson or on Facebook, visit her website at www.kellyjamieson.com or contact her at info@kellyjamieson.com.

Printed in Great Britain
by Amazon

63056522R10201